SHADOWS IN THE WATCHGATE

Mike Jefferies was born in Kent but spent his early years in Australia. He attended the Goldsmiths School of Arts and then taught art in schools and prisons. A keen rider, he was selected in 1980 to ride for Britain in the Belgian Three Day Event. He now lives in Norfolk with his wife and three stepchildren, working full time as an author and illustrator.

MIKE JEFFERIES

Shadows
in the Watchgate

Grafton

An Imprint of HarperCollins*Publishers*

Available by the same author

LOREMASTERS OF ELUNDIUM
The Road to Underfall
Palace of Kings
Shadowlight

THE HEIRS TO GNARLSMYRE
Glitterspike Hall
Hall of Whispers

Grafton
An Imprint of HarperCollins*Publishers*
77–85 Fulham Palace Road,
Hammersmith, London W6 8JB

A Grafton Original 1991

1   3   5   7   9   8   6   4   2

A catalogue record for this book is available from the British Library

ISBN 0 586 21512 3

Set in Garamond

Printed in Great Britain by
Hartnolls Ltd, Bodmin, Cornwall

*To my wife, Sheila, who stood with me
on the threshold of Goats Head Alley -
I dedicate this fantasy*

Acknowledgements and thanks to:

Charlie Skelton of the Norfolk Motor Company who gave me the afternoon of a lifetime in a Lotus Esprit Turbo.

The Sally B Foundation, Elly, Captain Sissons and Jimmy Jewel for the breathtaking trip in Sally B, the only B-17 still flying in England.

Graham Barton of Battle Orders for the information on the Navy Colt percussion revolver.

And lastly thanks to the crew of the Massingham Fire Engine. I am sure there are a thousand tiny mistakes but I know you'll never let me forget them.

Contents

Although this story took place in the city of Norwich, the names of the people and places have been changed to protect the innocent.

Prologue

Hidden in the January shadows of Shuttlecock Alley stood Daruma, the shop that dealt in books about magic. Behind its shuttered windows and crumbling façade lay the fountainhead of all dark and forbidden knowledge. The devil's window. Claustrophobic neighbouring buildings shrouded it from prying eyes and dabblers in evil. Inside, black secrets lay nearly buried beneath the weight of millions of innocent spells, remedies and chants that were stored there pressed between the bulging endpapers of the countless volumes, parchment broadsheets and unbound manuscripts that had been crammed and haphazardly piled into the mountainous racks and bookshelves that crowded the shop.

The gloomy, all-enveloping silence was suddenly broken. The outer door creaked and swung open. A bell jangled somewhere in the depths of the shop behind the towering walls of books and a tall, stooping figure with thinning white hair shook the light powdering of snow from his shoulders and stepped in across the threshold. His piercing glance took in the shrivelled squirrel's carcass that hung just inside the entrance, a guardian against evil, and noticed the shadowy forms of others browsing in the narrow corridors of books.

Ludo Strewth, the taxidermist, blinked at the melting snowflakes clinging to his eyelashes and widened his eyes against the gloom as he sniffed at the dry and musty atmosphere. He wet his lips with a thin smile of anticipation and moved quietly and almost unnoticed deeper into the shop.

The squirrel spun slowly on its wire, following him with its dead eyes as he began to search the overcrowded bookshelves for the Ledgers of the Dead. He knew they must be hidden somewhere there amongst so many secrets.

He was searching for information of a special burial. He thought he knew where criminals had been hanged in the vicinity of Norwich during the eighteenth and early nineteenth centuries, and he was looking for the record of their unmarked graves. For the first time he was dabbling in the black arts and knowingly touching fingertips with the devil.

He needed the body of a hanged man that had been untouched by the resurrectionists. He needed a body steeped in evil, shrunken and mummified by time, so that its severed right hand, embalmed and preserved in secret oils, could become the touchstone of his magic spell. He needed to have his own Hand of Glory.

He had stumbled on the thief's spell years ago. It was handwritten on a scrap of yellowing parchment he had found trapped between the pages of a book on embalming. At that time he had laughed at the idea of people using or believing in magic and had almost cast the scrap into the fire grate in his preparation room above his shop in Goats Head Alley. But as the years passed and his skills as a taxidermist began to decline, the idea of using magic to rekindle those talents, of harnessing a power to help preserve everything beautiful, mushroomed as a dark canker in his mind. It strangled his reason, and layer by layer it pushed his sanity into the shadows.

Let those who rest more deeply sleep,
Let those awake their vigils keep.

Ludo muttered the beginnings of the spell to himself as he traced his fingertips across the dusty spines of the books in the shelves in front of him. He suddenly froze and swallowed the words, for he sensed someone approaching. He glanced quickly to his left and saw a young man emerging from the depths of the bookshop, his thick-rimmed spectacles reflecting the winter light.

Dec Winner paused momentarily. There was something familiar about the tall stooping figure in the long overcoat who was browsing the aisle in front of him. He adjusted the heavy armful of books on fungal growths and poisons that he was carrying and smiled as he tried to recollect where he had seen the old man before. But he had no time to think or to pass a comment before the man froze him with a stare, hunched his shoulders and turned away, disappearing into another warren of narrow aisles.

Dec frowned. He must have been mistaken. He pulled his coat collar up as he moved towards the door, but paused again on the threshold, his hand upon the latch, and glanced back for a second, more careful, look. Then he remembered. He had seen the strange old man once, hurrying through the old part of Norwich, carrying two stuffed owls, one in each hand. Dec scanned the gloomy aisles but the tall figure had vanished from sight. He shrugged and turned back towards the door, pushing his way out into the worsening snowstorm, but the memory of that wild-eyed and piercing gaze lingered with him as he hurried away down Shuttlecock Alley.

Behind him in the shop the dead squirrel had slowly begun to turn.

*

'Perhaps there is something special that you are looking for?'

The soft voice of Theopus, the bookshop's custodian, and his light touch upon the taxidermist's arm made Ludo jump. He hadn't heard the silent approach and he spun around to see a small wizened figure in a brown dust coat at his elbow. Instinct warned him to mask the real purpose of his visit.

'I am researching eighteenth-century crime and punishment,' he stuttered, 'and . . . and . . . my thesis is almost complete; it only lacks a detailed graph to show where the majority of criminals were buried during that period. Of course, the graph would also reflect the difference between crime in the major cities and the rural communities. I have researched dozens of church records but since most gibbeted criminals were buried in unhallowed ground they haven't been of much help.'

Ludo paused and sucked in a shallow breath as he watched the bookseller digest his lies. 'A friend sent me here,' he continued, lightly waving his long thin fingers at the crowded walls of books. 'He said that you might have a copy of the Ledgers of the Dead for that period.'

The oppressive silence of the shop swallowed up the taxidermist's words.

'It's just numbers, numbers and places that I need. I promise I won't get in your way,' he offered helpfully, cracking his knuckles nervously one by one.

Theopus's eyes narrowed and he carefully searched every line and wrinkle on the taxidermist's anxious, smiling face. No one but the Grand Council was supposed to touch the Ledgers of the Dead, they shrouded so many secrets, so many dark deeds, and yet he hesitated to say no. The tall, stooping old man looked so harmless, and he had probably spent years working on his research.

'Yes, I do keep the Ledgers of the Dead,' he answered at length, 'and I will let you see them, but you can only copy numbers and places. The names of the dead that you see you must forget. They must be allowed to remain here in their last resting place.'

Ludo nodded eagerly, his eyes gleaming with triumph, and he followed closely on Theopus's heels as the custodian led him through the warren of narrow aisles towards the back of the shop. The shrivelled squirrel's carcass rotated on its copper wire and followed them with its dead eyes.

'These are the Ledgers of the Dead,' Theopus announced in a hushed whisper as he stopped on the threshold of a small inner library and swept his hand towards a row of dusty black leather-bound volumes in the centre of the far wall. Each mottled spine had the county of its origin engraved in thin silver funereal letters.

'You may lay them on the table,' Theopus muttered, indicating a small circular ebony table carved with magic symbols that stood in the centre of the room.

In the distance, a telephone began to ring. The persistent double tone cut through the silence and Theopus glanced in its direction and then looked hesitantly at the taxidermist. He hadn't intended to leave him alone for a moment. He hesitated on the threshold.

'You must promise to take only numbers. Places and numbers. No names.'

Ludo smiled and nodded as Theopus turned and hurried to answer the call, crying, 'I'll only be a moment.'

Ludo watched the wizened custodian disappear before he strode across the library and scanned the row of volumes. He pulled out the heavy tome for Norfolk. He wasn't at all sure what to expect and he let out an exclamation of surprise as he turned the yellowed linen pages to discover that they were crammed not only with countless names of the dead but beside them were tiny maps and steel engravings of where each and every one of them was buried. Quickly he found the section devoted to a small area around Norwich and ran his finger down the list of villages and hamlets, stopping as he reached the name of Gibbet Hill. He laughed softly. It was a wild and untouched place of briars and brambles. If there was a body there it would suit his purpose perfectly. He glanced at the spidery outlines of the map. There was a gallows in the shadow of an oak tree and beneath the tree a line of shallow graves. Underneath the map one name stood out in blackened letters.

Thomas Dunnich
Gibbet Hill
1776

Ludo licked his lips with delight; he had found exactly what he was looking for. But he also realized that there wasn't enough time to make a detailed copy before the bookseller returned. There was only one way he could keep the information. Gripping the top edge of the linen page close to the spine he tore it out with a single, brutal movement. The sound of the cloth ripping along its weave was louder to his ears than hail on an iron roof and it jarred his nerves with guilt. He swallowed and glanced anxiously towards the doorway, afraid that the bookseller would reappear, then stuffed the crumpled page into his pocket. He snapped shut the ledger and returned it to its place on the shelf.

Hurrying out of the inner library he made his way towards the outer door of the shop, reaching it just as the bookseller appeared in the doorway of his office. Ludo waved a frantic hand at him as he threw open the door and snow flurries swirled across the threshold to envelop him.

'There's something I have forgotten. I have to run,' he called out above the noise of the storm and then he slammed the door behind him and vanished into the blizzard.

Theopus ran to the doorway but the tall stooping figure had already disappeared. He looked up fearfully to the spinning squirrel. His guardian had warned him of the approach of evil.

'What nightmare have I unleashed?' he whispered, wringing his hands together as he stared out into the storm.

1

Gibbet Hill

Darkness smothered the summer countryside with its cloak of secrets and the church bells had long ago struck the midnight hour. Somewhere in the distance a dog barked, and night creatures rustled through the gloomy undergrowth. But nothing moved on Gibbet Hill in the silver moonlight or touched the gaunt black shadows cast by the solitary oak tree crowning the top of the hill. Below the oak, a ring of blackthorn and ancient cordwood guarded the summit of the hill, their seeds scattered long ago in the winter winds as the last criminal to be hanged there was cut down and anonymously buried in the shadow of the tall oak.

Beneath the thorn bushes a pheasant coughed in alarm and a nightjar arose, noisily flapping its wings, and flew across the summit to settle in the branches of the oak. Ludo Strewth began to force a slow passage through the ring of bushes. He cursed and muttered angrily under his breath as the leather snatch bag that hung from his shoulders snagged and caught on the sharp thorns, making the branches rustle and scrape in the moonlit darkness.

Anxiously he glanced over his shoulder as he broke free of the last clinging branch and searched the shadows, listening, straining his ears for the sound of following footsteps, of people wishing to spy on his secrets.

The night silence thickened all around him and he let a

breath of relief escape his lips. Hunching his shoulders against the chill night breeze he glanced up at the withered branches of the oak and rummaged in his pocket for the crumpled page he had torn from the Ledgers of the Dead. In the moonlight he could just make out the outlines of the illustration, which showed where the gallows had stood in the shadow of the oak and where a line of shallow graves had been dug for those poor unfortunates who had danced in the empty air on Gibbet Hill.

Ludo struck a match, and as he shielded it from the wind he studied the map. He didn't care about the identities of the dead or the nature of their crimes; to have been gibbeted was enough to make his magic work. He moved slowly around the base of the oak until the main fork in its branches matched the tiny steel engraving on the page.

'The graves must be just here,' he muttered, stepping slowly backwards, scanning the ground in front of him.

'Yes,' he cried, fighting to muffle the excitement in his voice as he made out a row of shallow depressions in the moonlight.

Unsnapping the catch on his snatch bag he withdrew an old trowel, speckled and pitted with rust, that gleamed blackly in the gloom, but he hesitated, worrying which grave belonged to Thomas Dunnich. A voice of evil from somewhere deep in the tangled roots of his insanity urged him to search for the grave of Dunnich before all others. It would be the last, the freshest, buried in the shadow of the oak tree. The voice laughed inside his head and promised him perfect beauty, everything he ever desired, if he chose the right corpse. Tonight he would exhume the corpse of Thomas Dunnich, the last criminal to be hanged on Gibbet Hill, according to the records. Another voice awoke inside his head. Like an old creaking door it chafed his nerves, urging him to sever the right hand of Thomas

Dunnich and make a Hand of Glory. It promised with goading whispers that the chants and spells would bring back to life every one of the rare and beautiful creatures that he had prepared and mounted in the secret rooms above his taxidermist's shop.

Slowly he searched the surfaces of the shallow graves. Some instinct told him. That must be the last one. The one set slightly apart from the others, as he fell on to his knees beside it.

He scraped at the thick layers of leaf mould and rotten twigs that nature had scattered there so carelessly. His breath came in excited gasps as he felt the cold damp sandy soil beneath his fingertips.

He started to laugh and to dig faster, licking at the bubbles of spittle collected in the corners of his mouth. He had to have the Hand of Glory. He had to sever it above the wrist and steal it in the dead of night. The voices were shrieking at him, urging him to be quick or the magic would not work.

The trowel snagged on something solid. He threw it aside and scraped at the crumbling soil with his fingers. In a moment he exposed a blackened corner of heavy hemp sacking. He worked faster, scattering the soil in every direction until the outline of the rough hemp winding sheet lay uncovered in the ground before him. He sat back on his haunches and reached for his leather bag. Tipping it up he scattered his dissecting tools beside the shallow grave.

Ludo Strewth trembled with excitement – to have found the grave so easily. He was about to tear open the shroud when he felt eyes watching him. He rose and slowly searched the darkness. A movement above his head made him look up. A barn owl, its face ghostly white, stared back at him from the branches of the oak.

'I'll set you rigid in that branch for ever if you so much

as hoot, and I will never whisper you back to life. Never,' he hissed threateningly.

He picked up a scalpel and cut through the hemp winding sheet. The rotten fabric fell apart at the touch of the blade to reveal the blackened shrivelled corpse that lay inside. Ludo hesitated and caught his breath, drawing back from the staring, empty eye sockets and dried-up sinews and scraps of leathery flesh that still clung to the yellowing bones. What dark magic had preserved this corpse? Even so, perhaps the body was too old, too withered and shrunken with decay – what if he had desecrated this grave for nothing and the spells and chants didn't work? But the voices cackled and shrieked:

'Everything the devil touches works. Sever the hand. Use the dark and powerful magic that dwells within a Hand of Glory and gives burglars supernatural powers to unlock doors and put people to sleep. Speak the chant in reverse and awaken everything that you have created. Chant the spell forwards and backwards.'

The voices died away and Ludo glanced furtively around him. Suddenly he laughed and clasped the withered, blackened hand of the corpse and lovingly caressed it. Pinpoints of madness shone in his eyes in the pale moonlight. Of course the spell would work; the voices had promised it. He had prepared so carefully for this moment. He had collected the oils and fats with such care, ready to rub into the dried-up hand, to preserve it. He knew the spell by heart. He had stolen exactly the right name from the Ledgers of the Dead. Everything was ready and tomorrow night was the full moon.

Anxious to begin his magic, Ludo Strewth picked up his bone-cutting saw and quickly began to cut through the crumbling bones of the withered forearm.

2

Impressions in the Dark

Tuppence Trilby reached the bottom step of the echoing iron staircase and hesitated. The light from the
street lamps above highlighted her startling beauty
with soft shadows. Before her stood a narrow doorway.
She could hear the soft melodic notes of a piano and laughter and the rise and fall of murmuring voices.

'In here?' she asked in her soft American drawl as she
turned away from the door of the nightclub to the large,
round-faced man who was a pace behind her.

Richard nodded and smiled eagerly, his ascending
shadow engulfing her as he transferred the heavy bundle
of property folders from beneath one arm to the other.

Tuppence turned back and pushed her slender fingers
against the brightly painted door, which creaked open. As
she stepped inside she sensed the familiar shadowy, smoky
nightclub atmosphere that masked so many shabby secrets
and easy lies, so many adulterous meetings that had taken
place in gloomy alcoves. She frowned and turned back.
'Perhaps a different place . . .' she began, then stopped,
catching the look of disappointment on Richard's face.
Behind her the murmur of voices at the bar had fallen
silent. She could feel men's eyes on her, glancing from her
to the large estate agent. They were watching, judging,
painting her with a brush dipped into their own sordid
secrets. Slowly she turned back towards them and swept

her gaze across their shadowy figures at the bar. She saw that look of desire in their eyes, that lecherous envy that stripped her naked. Then somebody at the bar waved and called out to Richard, the spell was broken, the drinkers were turning back to the bar and laughing and whispering amongst themselves.

Tuppence felt her anger rise, she wanted to curse at them, shame them for mentally stripping her, but she swallowed the anger and felt her shell harden a little more. These guys were no different from any of the other thousands of forgotten faces that had leered at her and desired her beauty, and, after all, they were only showing those very emotions that she had traded on to build her career as a model.

Tuppence sighed and glanced back at Richard and she saw by the way he fidgeted and nervously shuffled the property folders in his large hands that he was thrown off balance by her reluctance to enter the nightclub. Perhaps he had even guessed that she realized he had brought her here to parade before his friends, to swell his own ego. Her anger momentarily flickered again. He was no better than the rest of them, despite his courteous and attentive English ways. He was merely using her as they all tried to do.

She opened her mouth then hesitated. Perhaps she was judging him too harshly. After all she *had* given him one hell of a run around all afternoon in her search for a property to buy. They had visited just about every apartment for sale in the city. Perhaps one drink wasn't too much to go along with. Though it would have been nice, really nice, if just for once there hadn't been a hidden motive behind the offer of a drink, or a crowd of leering onlookers. But maybe she could play them at their own game; she was probably much better at it than they were anyway.

'Make it a straight soda with plenty of ice,' she smiled, slipping easily into the image that her public relations firm had spent a fortune promoting worldwide; of the glitzy, glamorous, paper-thin beauty that stared out from every billboard and every magazine stall. Now she made the play perfectly, touching Richard's arm with just the right ease of familiarity as they crossed the nightclub floor, setting the barflies buzzing; they could not take their eyes off her.

As Richard went to the bar, Tuppence, with a lazy animal grace, moved, slipping between the tables and chairs, towards an alcove with a deep leather sofa. The watered silk of her clinging dress and matching jacket shimmered in the misty tobacco light. Reaching the sofa she sat down and sank back into the soft hide and let its cool chamois smoothness mould itself around her slender figure. Holding the gaze of the watchers at the bar she slowly crossed her long silk-stockinged legs and began to draw off her deerskin gloves one finger at a time. The crowd around the bar stirred and seemed to jump as she snapped the gloves taut and then dropped them carelessly on to the couch beside her. With that sharp snap Tuppence had broken the spell that her beauty had held over them. They shuffled uneasily, glasses scraping on the polished surface of the bar, turning away now as if they had been caught peeping at some secret show. She had triumphed in the silly game, yet it gave her little pleasure. She was sick of the lust, the envy and the jealousy that always seemed to be reflected in the eyes of these anonymous voyeurs. It made little difference whether they were men or women, there was always that moment's glance when people devoured her outer image, when she became part of their fantasies.

She sighed and sank deeper into the soft leather sofa. Perhaps she was being too sensitive again. Perhaps only a fool would want something beyond those covetous stares. After all, the fragile beauty that fuelled their imaginations was her own creation and she would just have to live with it.

Richard was moving clumsily towards her through the jumble of tightly packed chairs and tables, balancing their drinks and the bundle of property folders on a small round tray. Behind him, the crowd at the bar had drawn closer together, the hum of conversation and the clink of glasses blending into the background noise. More people were crowding through the doorway, Tuppence's entrance had been forgotten now, lost in the thickening atmosphere. She smiled warmly and took her drink. It wasn't Richard's fault; he wasn't to know how much she hated these gloomy nightclubs.

She gathered the property sheets into a pile and began to leaf through them, casting them down one by one on the couch between them.

'No,' she sighed, 'I'm sorry but none of them were quite what I'm looking for.'

Richard frowned helplessly. He had shown her flats over the new shopping precinct, penthouse flats with wonderful views, a wide selection of studio flats that overlooked the river. Every one of them had been a stone's throw from the city centre. He couldn't understand. He had chosen them so carefully, trying to suit this beautiful, young, sophisticated American woman. In fact, from the moment she had first entered his office with instructions for him to find her a property in Norwich, he had done little else but organize today's viewing, and he had spent the afternoon and most of the evening showing her around just about everything on his books that could possibly impress her.

'They were all very nice, but I've decided I want something very *old*,' Tuppence laughed, bringing the glass to her lips. 'You'll probably think me very silly, but I would like something really English, with beams and . . . and a history.'

She took a sip from her glass and then added thoughtfully, 'I seem to have been living out of a suitcase all my life, in hotels, apartments, moving from one film location to another. I want to put down some roots, I want to feel somewhere, somewhere with the sort of atmosphere this city has, is where I belong. I want somewhere to make me want to hurry home.'

Richard blushed and fidgeted uncomfortably. He wasn't used to sitting so close to somebody so beautiful. 'Oh, there are plenty of older properties in this city. I could compile a list tomorrow morning and we could look over them in the afternoon.' He watched her finish her glass. 'Ah, I'll get you another drink,' he stammered, pushing the bundle of papers aside and clumsily rising to his feet.

Tuppence shook her head. 'Perhaps another time,' she murmured, brushing her fingers through the thick waves of auburn hair that tumbled across her shoulders. She smiled and stood up, gathering up her gloves in one sweeping graceful movement.

'It's been a long day,' she smiled. 'Filming for the new magazine cover means being up at four thirty to catch the sunrise, and we'll be at the coast all day tomorrow if the weather holds. Leave a message at my hotel if you find anything older, then perhaps we'll take a look another time.'

Without waiting for an answer she turned, slipped

between the tables and vanished through the doorway in a rustle of watered silk and a waft of expensive perfume.

'Wait! Wait, I'll show you back to your car. You'll never find it on your own,' Richard called after her, scattering loose leaves of property details as he hurried after her.

Figures at the bar turned and stared, laughing and leering at his discomfort as he hurried to catch up with her. Above him on the spiralling iron staircase he could see her silhouetted against the starlight. 'Wait!' he shouted, climbing the stairs two steps at a time. 'I'll show you the way back to your car!'

Tuppence paused at the head of the stairway. Behind her she could hear the estate agent puffing his way up. She took a deep breath and let the sight and the night sounds of the city soak into her; the hum of the traffic, the shouts and laughter of people thronging the pavements, the bright lights in the shop windows and the long, moving shadows that the passing crowds threw across the streets. She was Brooklyn-born and had always loved the noise and bustle of cities.

Richard reached the stairhead breathlessly, breaking into her thoughts, and she turned to him and smiled. 'Perhaps we'll have that drink another time. When we've found me a home. To celebrate.'

'Yes, of course. Look, we left my car near the bottom of Elm Hill,' he added quickly. 'We can reach it by walking through the old part of the city, you might like to see it. It's through the old city gate over there. It will only take us a few extra minutes, but we'll pass some beautiful mediaeval houses. Then I'll drive you back to where we left your car, outside the office.'

'Right! That sounds great,' Tuppence laughed and she fell into step with him as he set off towards a high archway of weathered stone further down the street. She paused and glanced up and read the street sign.

'Look! That's what I mean about having atmosphere, all these wonderful street names. Castle Meadow, and . . .' She peered through the archway and up to the street sign in the dimly lit and narrow cobbled street beyond the ancient gateway.

'Lobster Lane,' Tuppence read slowly as she passed beneath the archway, her soft voice melting into the moon shadows as she traced the pitted, black-painted letters on the street sign with her fingertips. 'Lobsters? How can this steep narrow lane have gotten a name like that when the city is so far from the sea?' she asked frowning.

Richard laughed softly. There was an air of innocence in her questions and an infectious delight about her curiosity. 'I think there was once a fish market in Castle Meadow and I am sure that this lane used to lead directly up from the Wensum Quay before the museum was built in Elm Hill. Perhaps the lane got its name from the fishermen hauling their baskets of lobsters up to the market.'

'There's so much history here,' she murmured, letting her fingers brush over the smooth red mediaeval bricks of the first house in the lane. Richard nodded and smiled as he turned to lead the way down to where he had parked his car at the bottom of Elm Hill.

'Wait,' she called, making him stop and turn back towards her. 'Can't you feel the history?' she asked breathlessly. 'Can't you just smell where all that salt water from the fishermen's baskets must have soaked into the worn cobblestones beneath our feet?'

Richard gazed up at her beautiful, graceful figure, silhouetted in the light of the street lamps that filtered through the archway. History was the furthest thing from his mind. He shivered and fought to get a grip on himself.

He wanted to stride back to where she stood and wrap his arms around her, to hold her and possess her. He blinked and shook himself. A cold sweat had beaded his forehead and he stepped hastily back into the shadows to hide the moment's raw lust. But he need not have worried, she had not seen it. Tuppence was glancing over her shoulder through the lighted archway, oblivious of him.

'I was there, nearly there for a moment. In the market with barrows and stalls and bright-coloured awnings,' she laughed.

Richard had retrieved his composure and he wiped his sleeve across his forehead. 'Yes, yes there must have been hundreds of stalls,' he answered quickly from the shadows.

'This lane is so magical,' Tuppence laughed as she turned back. 'It is as if by stepping through that archway we have passed into another time. The noises of the city have faded to almost nothing, and look at the way the shops and houses lean against one another, it's as if they are whispering to each other in the silence. Look how the moonlight reflects on all the tiny panes of glass in the windows, and how it shines on the steep roofs like a sheet of glistening frost. This is where I want to live. In Lobster Lane, nowhere else.'

'It's getting late,' Richard murmured as he glanced at his watch. 'You said you had an early start.'

Tuppence laughed softly and linked her arm through his. 'Could you just find out if any of these houses are for sale? There are lights in some of the windows, people must live here. Perhaps one of them would sell to me.'

Richard trembled at her touch, her scent was making him giddy. Yesterday he would have killed to be this close to Tuppence Trilby. 'I . . . I . . . I don't know. Few of these properties ever come on to the market, they are mostly owned by trusts,' he stammered, trying to hurry her down the steep narrow lane towards Elm Hill before he said something stupid. 'But I could make some enquiries for you tomorrow.'

Tuppence stopped him and pulled away, pointing across the lane. 'What about those archways on the other side? Where do they lead? They look so mysterious. Would there be houses for sale down there?'

'Yes, possibly,' Richard answered, hunching his shoulders and sinking his hands deep into his jacket pockets. He glanced briefly towards the dark archways. There might be something of interest in one of them but it would need a lot of renovation. He knew they led into a rabbit warren of old courtyards and crumbling alleyways filled with warehouses and workshops. Slowly he withdrew his left hand from his pocket and spread his blunt fingers in a dismissive gesture. 'Anything you found in one of those alleyways would be more trouble than it's worth though.'

Richard paused as he sensed her frown and felt her flash of anger. 'But I could take a look tomorrow if you want me to,' he continued quickly.

'Yes, sure, take a look at everything for me,' she answered firmly. She was about to move on when she noticed a patch of light beyond one of the archways.

Quickly, in three whispering steps of watered silk that shimmered in the lamplight, she crossed the lane to peer down through the low archway. 'The sign reads Goats Head Alley, but it looks more like a small courtyard.' She hesitated uncertainly on the edge of the shadows and then she felt her way down beneath the archway.

It went further than she expected and its leaking, rough brick walls seemed to deaden every sound. Solid shadows, thicker than the darkness, seemed to cling to the crumbling mortar. Tuppence shivered. She drew back and glanced over her shoulder towards the estate agent but he was oblivious to her fear as he jingled the loose change impatiently in his pocket and peered into a dark shop window.

'Damn you, Tuppence,' she breathed to herself. 'How can you be afraid of a few shadows? It's only the atmosphere, only the history pressed between the bricks.'

Gathering her courage she reached out again and grimly felt her way, touching the sharp brickwork with her fingertips through the dense shadowy silence. She stepped down into the courtyard and blinked in the sudden bright moonlight. She stopped abruptly. It wasn't at all as she had expected. The old houses crowded in on her, casting claustrophobic shadows across the cobbles, and the air was shiver cold and made her breath billow as white as frosted winter vapour. There was a faint smell, a sour-sweet odour, that seemed to cling to her skin and cut dryly into the back of her throat as it burned her nostrils. It carried the hint of corruption, of death, the exhalation of old, stale, dusty breath. It was all around and it made her afraid. The whole atmosphere was unwelcoming and the silence prickled at her ears.

Shading her eyes against the moonlight Tuppence could just make out the darker shapes of the low doorways and small-paned, bow-fronted windows that blindly reflected the moonlight. Feeling she had seen more than enough of these brooding houses, she began to turn back towards the archway, when she caught sight of a narrow strip of light beneath a door in the furthest corner of the courtyard. There was a sign above, its faded gilt letters faintly illuminated in the silver light. The first letter was a T, its ornate tail curving away into the darkness. The second letter looped into the shape of an A while the third looked like an X. Curious to trace the rest of the word that melted into the shadows she took a hesitant step forward and out into the centre of the courtyard. A hiss broke the silence and made her freeze. She glanced up at the darkened window above the lighted door and saw a face – a long, thin face with wild, staring eyes looking down at her. She blinked and tore her gaze away. Her heart was pounding in her chest and fear shouted in her head, telling her to run, to turn and run as fast as she could.

A blinding flash of light suddenly filled the window; it flickered and blazed for a moment and made the pressing shadows rear and plunge. Tuppence stumbled backwards and cried out as she watched the beam of light shoot up across the steep, weather-bleached roofs, over the broken, tooth-shaped ruins of a church tower that hemmed the courtyard. There were eyes, green luminous eyes, staring down at her from every ridge and gutter.

'What's that?' she gasped, feeling the hairs on the nape of her neck prickle as she picked out strange, statue-still shapes, their frames silhouetted black against the starlight. The closest figure hissed and spat at her, its meowing shriek cutting through the blanket of silence. 'Cats! It's only an alley full of cats,' Tuppence sighed with relief, but there was something in their stillness, in the way they stared unblinkingly down at her, that made her feel they were poised to . . .

A shadow darted across the yard towards her. She cried out, then turned and fled towards the archway as a large ginger-striped tom cat, its fur ridged along its back, over-took her and vanished into Lobster Lane in a shriek of terror. Tuppence reached the furthest end of the alley and ran into Lobster Lane, her breath coming in short gasps. Her fingers were trembling and her teeth chattering uncontrollably. The estate agent was staring at her from where he had been waiting on the far side of the lane.

'What's wrong?' he asked anxiously as he caught sight of her pinched white face and strode towards her.

Tuppence stopped and gathered her composure. 'Just cats. I'm not afraid of cats,' she whispered to herself. But the cats and the dusty old atmosphere in Goats Head Alley had made her spine tingle and she couldn't quite shake the feeling away. 'Nothing's wrong,' she said, glancing back at the dark archway. 'A cat startled me, that's all.'

'This city's full of cats, especially the old quarter,' Richard laughed. 'But was there anything in the courtyard that interested you?' he asked as she fell into step beside him. 'Perhaps one of the empty workshops or a town house? I could enquire if there was something . . .'

'No!' Tuppence answered, shaking her head. With each footstep they took away from that dark shadowy archway the feeling of uneasiness diminished. She laughed, her voice softening back into its soft Brooklyn tones as she continued, 'There was nothing in the yard for me, just a run-down watch-mender's shop and a gallery, I think, at the far end, next to a ruined church tower. There was a store, something to do with tax?'

They walked on in silence towards the bottom of Lobster Lane. Tuppence was slowing now and then to peer in darkened windows or crane her neck to look up at the overhanging galleries.

'There's a house in Elm Hill that was for sale a while ago. You might like it,' Richard murmured. 'I remember seeing it advertised in the *County Press*. It's that one on the right-hand side, but I think we may just have missed the auction date.' They had entered Elm Hill and stopped in the centre of the steep, cobbled lane.

'That's exactly the house I want!' Tuppence cried as she followed his pointing finger. They were looking at a tall, narrow, galleried house that looked as if it had been squeezed in between two adjoining properties. 'Look, at the beautiful carving on the door. You *do* mean this one, don't you?'

'Yes, the Watchgate.' Richard frowned as he took a step towards the house. 'You know, it still looks empty. I wonder . . .'

'Watchgate? Why is it called the Watchgate?' Tuppence asked curiously as she stared up at the darkened, narrow leaded windows.

'Because hundreds of years ago a curtain wall enclosed the whole city to keep out robbers and invading armies, and these watchgates were set into each wall at right-angles for the guards to watch over the surrounding countryside and to warn of any approaching dangers. This is the only one that has survived the ravages of time.'

'Do you think that is the original door?' Tuppence interrupted, hurrying into the shadow of the overhanging gallery.

'It certainly looks old enough to be the original door, doesn't it?' he admitted nodding.

'It's so huge, it almost takes up the whole front of the house,' Tuppence murmured. 'And look, there are pictures carved into each of the panels.'

She fell silent and by the faint light of the street lamp on the far side of Elm Hill she began to pick out the bolder details. There was a castle in the central panel, but the carving seemed to depict its death throes; the corner turrets had collapsed and its outer wall had been breached by lines of tall siege engines that filled the foreground. There was a forest of ladders thrown up against every wall. Tuppence shivered and was about to look away when she saw that the castle gates were thrown open. Knights on their horses were galloping out and there were warriors crowding every parapet. She looked to the left and the right of the central carving and saw that each of the panels depicted parts of that same scene, but in greater detail. Squadrons of knights on their chargers, their pennants floating out behind them, all rode into battle. There were lines of archers defending the parapets, their bowstrings drawn tight, the feathered arrow flights touching their cheeks. Armies of pikemen were surging forward to stab at the invaders. In some of the smaller panels near to the bottom of the door there were single figures; strange beasts, winged monsters and serpents. Tuppence's eyes travelled up the door and into the shadows that almost hid the top and there she saw in soft outline what looked like a resurrection scene. There was a host of angels surrounding a figure rising from a tomb and on either side of them knights knelt or stood, offering up the hilts of their swords.

She moved to one side of the door and ran her fingers up the doorpost as far as she could reach and she found that there were letters, or runes, chiselled into the doorpost. Their loops and tails were joined together into an unending ribbon of words that crossed and re-crossed the surface of the door between the carvings. She stepped back uneasily into the lane and looked up into the darkened apex of the stone archway.

'Why *is* the door so huge? It's much bigger than any of the others in the street.'

Richard smiled at her in the darkness. 'A watchgate door had to be big enough for mounted knights to ride through so that they could gallop out and defend the city in times of trouble. But if you look more closely, you will find a smaller door set into the centre.'

'Yes, I've found it!' she cried, tracing the carved stiles of the smaller door with her fingers, finding more letters and signs chiselled around it, smaller ones that had been almost smoothed away by the rub of countless fingers, and just inside the right-hand side she found an iron ring to open it.

'Tell me, what do all the carvings mean?' she asked, turning excitedly towards the agent.

Richard peered at the mediaeval carvings and shrugged his shoulders. 'The pictures probably tell the story of the sieges of the city and the great battles that raged around it, but I couldn't tell you what the letters mean. They could be either Latin or early mediaeval English. I'm sorry, but I've forgotten the little Latin I learned at school, they mean nothing to me. But there is probably a translation in the museum just across the road in Castle Walk if you are really interested.'

Tuppence sighed with disappointment. The Watchgate and its huge doors of pictures and secret runes had caught her imagination, and she had wanted to discover its story here, where she could touch its smooth-polished wood and listen beneath the moonlight rather than in some dry and dusty museum. 'Yes, sure, I'll take a look some day,' she murmured, turning slowly away.

'Wait,' called Richard, moving to the right-hand corner of the archway. Bending down he started sifting through a pile of wind-blown litter close to the door. Tuppence watched, suppressing a smile at the dignified estate agent rummaging amongst the litter of leaves and crumpled cigarette cartons. He gave a grunt and rose to his feet, clutching a torn sheet of dirty paper. Muttering something, he narrowed his eyes and moved quickly to the nearest street lamp and then gave a triumphant cry.

'What is it? What have you found?' she asked, following him into the light.

'I thought the Watchgate had already been auctioned. I remembered seeing it in the *County Press* some time ago, but while you were looking at the door I thought I recognized the corner of the auction notice amongst the litter in the doorway. This was the notice that was stapled to the door, someone must have torn it down and the wind . . .'

'When? When is the auction?' Tuppence cried. 'Let me have a look at that!'

Richard crouched and smoothed the torn auction notice on his knees. 'It says that the auction will be on the 11th July,' he read aloud and his face broke into a broad smile. 'That's tomorrow. The auction for the Watchgate is tomorrow!'

'You mean the Watchgate really is for sale? How much do you think it will go for?' Tuppence asked incredulously as she gazed up at the tall dark narrow building with its giant's door of secret carvings, its overhanging gallery and tiny leaded windows.

Richard looked up at the tall narrow building and clicked his tongue against the roof of his mouth as he took a wild guess. 'Somewhere between £100,000 and £130,000, if it hasn't been renovated,' he answered as he held out the auction notice towards her. He added, 'The auction's at twelve o'clock tomorrow. It's to be at the Crown Inn, Castle Walk. That's just around the corner, by the museum.'

'Can you buy it for me?' she cried.

Richard hesitated. 'You really need a lawyer to do that. I could recommend one.'

Tuppence shook her head. 'I'd prefer you to do it. I'll wire my bank in New York from the hotel, it's just after lunch there, they'll confirm I've got enough to buy it if you're worried about that.'

'I never doubted you had the money,' Richard stuttered in embarrassment, 'but you haven't even seen inside it. Surely you'll want a surveyor's report or to see the deeds to know if there are any special convenants? You'd be buying more than just a house; the Watchgate is a part of the city's history.'

Tuppence smiled up at the estate agent and melted his opposition. 'I really want the Watchgate more than anything else. Please say you'll bid for it for me. Please.'

Richard found himself nodding helplessly as he led her to where he had parked his car. 'But you'll have to sign the authorization, I can't bid without it.'

A movement away to the right in the entrance of Lobster Lane made them both glance across the road to see a ghostly white barn owl flying in widening silent circles up towards the roof tops of Elm Hill. It hovered for a moment and then alighted on the steep weathered tiles of the Watchgate and paused to stare unblinking down at them.

'Owls are supposed to be lucky, aren't they?' Tuppence murmured, touching Richard's arm. 'I'll bet that's a good omen. I'll bet that means I'm to have the Watchgate.'

'Of course,' Richard answered, avoiding her eyes and busying himself unlocking the car. As far as he could remember owls were a bad sign and to see one foretold a disaster. He drove with a feeling of uneasiness and they covered the short distance to his office in silence.

Tuppence had made up her mind that she wanted the Watchgate and she watched impatiently as he sifted through the filing cabinets in his office. He eventually found the documents that he was looking for and indicated to her where she should sign to authorize him to act on her behalf at the auction. After she had telephoned New York with all the relevant details she turned towards him. 'It's all set then,' she smiled, drawing on her gloves and moving gracefully through the outer door to her black Lotus, Richard following.

Opening the door, she slid easily into the driving seat and turned the ignition key. 'I'll be back in my hotel at about seven thirty tomorrow evening after the film shoot. I'll meet you in the bar and you can tell me all about it, OK?'

Her words faded in the wind as the engine roared and she slipped the car into first gear and accelerated away.

Richard stood for a moment, savouring the rich exhaust smoke and the fading roar of the Lotus as he fished for his own ignition keys in his jacket pocket. 'Americans!' Richard smiled to himself as he unlocked the car door. 'They certainly make the heart beat faster.'

3

A Moment of Madness

It was the perfect night for magic, but Ludo Strewth had hesitated on the threshold of his darkened preparation room above his taxidermist's shop in the furthest gloomy corner of Goats Head Alley. For a moment he had frozen at the sudden sound of footsteps, light woman's footsteps, in the entrance of the moonlit courtyard below his window.

'Who dares to spy on us?' he hissed, slamming the door behind him and snapping home the bolt with quick fingers.

He waited with bated breath, listening for the footsteps to draw closer, pressing himself back until only his hawk-like sharp nose could be seen in the wreath of black shadows between the two huge brown bears that he had mounted as guardians to watch over his secrets.

Anxiously he searched the crowded preparation room, casting his piercing gaze amongst the mahogany cabinets and glass cases, around the tall bell jars and the forest of elongated animal shadows that reached out towards him from every corner in the moonlight. Nothing moved, blinked or so much as trembled amongst the hundreds of creatures he had so lovingly resurrected with his taxidermist's skill to crouch or snarl. He let his stale, pent-up breath of alarm escape through the gaps in his long yellowing teeth and reached up to caress the glistening cold coils of the boa constrictor that he had woven around a dead branch and placed above the doorway of the room. The footsteps had stopped beneath the low entrance to the courtyard. Nothing now broke the night silence save the faint tick of the six clocks in the shop below, each one racing the next to be the first to tell the time.

Ludo frowned and turned towards his marble preparation slab. He realized that what lay there was his greatest secret, exposed in the watery moonlight that shimmered through the jars and bottles of formaldehyde and pickling alcohol crowding the wide window sill. A cat hissed and then meowed in the courtyard, its voice splitting the silence. Ludo spun towards the sound, scattering the neat trays of razor-sharp scalpels and curved skinning knives that lay ready on the cold marble. He snatched up the Hand of Glory he had stolen from the grave of Thomas Dunnich who had been hanged on Gibbet Hill. He hugged it to his chest, caressing the blackened waxy fingers with his own fingertips.

'No one must know that I am going to awaken you but us. I am going to resurrect the life that once pulsed beneath your petrified hides,' he muttered at the blind unblinking eyes of the animals that crowded every corner of the room. 'The magic won't happen and you will stay forever frozen, mimicking nature, just as I have mounted you, if anyone spies on us or catches so much as one whisper . . .' He swallowed his words and hunched his narrow shoulders so sharply that the starched collar of his long white coat crackled.

He crept towards the window and looked out to the stuffed cats he had mounted on the ruined wall by the church tower. 'Why did you not warn me of the trespasser in the courtyard?' he snarled.

He stood on tiptoe and stared down between the tall jars of formaldehyde into the inky black shadows of the low archway. There, someone was moving in the shadows, creeping as stealthily as a thief into the courtyard. Watching the figure emerge, Ludo clenched the mummified wrist in anticipation. A breath of surprise hissed between his teeth as a beautiful woman stepped out and hesitated on the edge of the shadows. He stared down at her, transfixed by her loveliness. He watched with bated breath as Tuppence took another cautious step. The watered silk of her clinging dress shimmered in the silver moonlight that flooded the tiny courtyard and threw a long slender shadow across the uneven cobbles behind her. The cold light traced every graceful line and secret curve of her body beneath the glistening fabric.

Women had never interested Ludo Strewth. They were manipulative creatures who thought nothing of draping the precious skins of his beautiful animals around their necks. He had always shunned their company, preferring to quench his passion here in the secrecy of his preparation room, where he created works of startling beauty from the bloodied carcasses that hunters and trappers sent him. But the woman standing in the courtyard was different. She radiated such beauty, such perfection.

'I must preserve her,' he murmured, feeling his hands beginning to sweat and tremble with excitement and the blood to roar and thunder in his ears. His fingers twitched and tingled uncontrollably, still gripping the hand, and he felt the madness possess him, just as it did whenever he saw rare creatures and beautiful specimens in zoological collections. Creatures that the madness compelled him to steal and add to his own secret collection of the rare and beautiful that crowded the rooms above his shop.

Ludo licked his lips, anticipating that special moment when the waft of chloroform made his head spin and the latest of his treasures lay unconscious and still upon his marble slab, waiting for the first careful kiss and touch of his scalpel that would make it his for ever.

'I . . . I . . . I must have you here amongst my most secret treasures,' he hissed, dizzy with madness to capture this beautiful woman, but he hesitated, licking at the bright bubbles of spittle that had formed at the corners of his mouth. A voice was whispering against it somewhere inside his head – the slender thread of sanity that still remained. He shook his head with quick bird-like movements.

'No, no, it would be murder and quite different from stealing animals. The hue and cry would be louder. Someone would be bound to trace her and then people would come prying, asking questions, searching amongst my treasures.' Ludo shrugged and began to turn away from the window, muttering to himself. 'Anyway her skin would look dry and stretched in no time at all, no matter how long I soaked it in the pickling solution. With no fur or feathers to cover it . . .'

Below the cat hissed again, its meow rising to a shrieking yowl as it darted across the courtyard, making the taxidermist rush back and stare down into the patch of bright moonlight where the woman now stood. He gasped and almost dropped his mummified hand. Her eyes seemed to stare back at him out of the webs of shadows, her soft lips were pencilled by the moonlight and were opening in a cry of fear. Her hair sparkled, each strand catching the silvery light.

'I must have you. You must stand here amongst my treasures,' he cried, finally stifling the whispers of reason inside his head. He pressed himself against the window pane, rubbing the blackened waxy fingers of the dead Hand of Glory against the cold glass. They left greasy smears from the animal fats and Lapland sesame that he had massaged into the dry crumbling fingers to make them burn slowly when he chanted the black-magic spells that he hoped would bring his creatures to life.

'The magic,' he suddenly whispered, gripping the hand tighter. 'Yes, perhaps the magic will draw you to me. Perhaps you will come just as a moth is drawn to flutter against the candle's flame.'

He had no real way of knowing what the magic would do, but he fumbled frantically in the pockets of his white coat for his box of matches.

'Wait, wait for the magic,' he hissed, as Tuppence turned away. The match flared and he held it with trembling fingers beneath the index finger of the blackened hand. He coughed and choked on the stench of burning flesh and blinked his eyes as stinging curls of smoke enveloped his face. Quickly he began to chant.

> *Burn, burn and sparkle bright,*
> *O Hand of Glory shed thy light,*
> *Let those it touches start awake,*
> *Let those who see it my bidding take*
> *And once awake let them follow my will.*
> *Bright sparkle and burn, burn,*
> *Light thy shed Glory of Hand O,*
> *Awake start touches it those let,*
> *Take bidding my it see who those let,*
> *Will my follow them let awake once and.*

A voice growled somewhere behind him in the darkened room, making him spin around.

'Who? What?' he cried as the match scorched his fingers. He cursed and flung it away, catching his elbow on a tall glass jar of formaldehyde. The jar toppled sideways, smashing into jagged pieces on the window sill. Formaldehyde washed across the sill and splashed up against the taxidermist, reflecting the flickering flame that now burned at the tip of the index finger of the mummified hand, magnifying it a thousand times in the bright shafts of moonlight. Evil magic dripped from the burning Hand of Glory, hissing and diffusing amongst the glistening droplets of formaldehyde and rising up in a brilliant flash of light. Stark shadows from the crowding creatures leapt back against the far wall. The two brown bears that guarded the door seemed to growl and flex their claws and lumber forward. The boa constrictor appeared to slither and slide, uncoiling itself along its branch. The searing light reflected in the polished glass of the cabinets and the rows of bell jars that flanked the room momentarily blinded the taxidermist as it blazed around him and out through the window. It lit up the steep weather-bleached roofs of the courtyard and etched the broken tooth-sharp ruins of the church tower stark white against the dark night sky.

The beam of evil light briefly stroked that sky before it shrank back across the roof tops, its dying rays touching the tall fluted windows of the museum at the far end of Elm Hill. One by one the elongated panes of hand-made glass absorbed the light, trapping it within the tiny flaws and ancient prisms of the window, illuminating the simple mediaeval rhymes and crude symbols that the glaziers had scratched there long ago as a protection against evil. The glass frosted over and grew hot as the evil from the Hand of Glory was purged out. Names and symbols etched with a craftsman's hand began to melt together. The glass shook and trembled, the light blazed anew and reflected backwards and forwards to escape suddenly. Each flute in turn broke in a zig-zag, hair-line crack, and a band of pure white light poured down into the darkened museum, sweeping over the rows of silent, life-sized, dusty soldiers, awakening them and throwing long shadows across their waiting mounts. The light diffused beneath the overhanging galleries and, tread by tread, crept up the broad staircase to exorcize every shadow. Old heads creaked on age-worn shoulders; grey eyes blinked in every marionette, and stiff, straw-filled hands reached for rifle butts and sword hilts as they heard a woman's voice, no more than a whisper on the night wind, in the shadows of Goats Head Alley, as it cried out in fear. Chargers snorted and pawed at the polished floorboards as they caught the sound of Tuppence's voice wavering through the awakening light. Unknown to the taxidermist, his meddling with magic had awoken far more than he could possibly imagine.

Ludo cried out in terror at what he had seen in the blaze of light, and he dropped the Hand of Glory, leaving the chant half-finished. He crouched huddled against the wall, his hand held tightly over his eyes, until the light had stopped burning his eyelids and darkness had crept back into his preparation room.

'Everything moved,' he whispered to himself. 'I swear that everything in this room moved . . .'

Slowly he took his long fingers away from his eyes and stared anxiously around the room. The silence prickled his ears and was broken only by the crackle of the flames that still licked at the blackened tip of the index finger of the dead hand where it lay beside him, half-submerged in a puddle of sharp-smelling formaldehyde.

The flame suddenly hissed, spluttered and flared up, making the crowded jumble of shadows cast by his creations seem to sway and dance eerily on the low ceiling.

'I am sure the magic worked for a moment,' he muttered, reaching down and pinching out the guttering flame with his finger and thumb.

Frowning, he raked his soot-smeared hand through his thinning hair, leaving black finger trails across his high forehead. He desperately wanted to believe that the magic had worked, that the black arts he had dared to use had breathed new life into his creatures. He wanted to leap to his feet and rush amongst the snakes and lizards, the sabre-toothed tiger, the wolves and brown bears, and all the other rare and beautiful wild creatures that crowded every corner of his rooms above the shop. He wanted to touch them and feel for a heartbeat or a racing pulse beneath their fur and feathers. Yet caution made him hesitate. What if the magic had restored their wildness? Would they attack, clawing and snarling to be free of their eternal prison? What if they stung and bit him and tried to tear him bone from bone? Nervously, he looked from beast to beast, searching the dark moon shadows for a sign that his magic had worked.

Suddenly he caught his breath. He felt his hair prickle on the nape of his neck. Their eyes were watching him, following the slightest movement that he made. The dead glass stare that he had never been able to overcome in any of his preparations had gone.

'The magic has worked!' he gasped, letting his breath escape through trembling lips as he slowly rose to his feet.

As he moved, one of the huge brown bears that guarded the doorway growled, reaching up and clawing awkwardly at the withered branch above the lintel. The boa constrictor hissed at the bear's claws, its skin glistening wetly with new life as it tried to slither forward. It moved less than an inch, its backbone twisting, its head thrashing from side to side. Muscular ripples rose and fell, travelling backwards along its body, fighting to break free from whatever invisibly held it trapped to the branch.

Ludo frowned and turned his gaze back to the bear. It had stopped clawing towards the branch and both bears had turned their attention towards the other creatures that

filled every inch of the floor space on either side. The closest, a rare banded linsang, barked in alarm, crouching down as the bears' claws scythed through the air above its head. A wolverine snarled, baring its teeth at an aardwolf mounted behind it. Monkeys chattered and shrieked as all the animals, large and small, that crowded the long low room, began to bay and yelp, bellow and roar. Birds flapped their wings and beasts strained and fought to break free from their mounts. Butterflies fluttered their wings in a blaze of bright colour shining on the glass doors of their shallow show cases. Humming birds, sand grouse, quails and every other bird that the taxidermist had ever imprisoned in the tall bell jars rapped and hammered with their beaks, begging to be set free.

Ludo stumbled backwards, looking everywhere at once, his mind filled with confusion. He bumped against the window sill and felt the sharp prick of the broken formaldehyde bottle. Reaching back he carelessly swept the shards of glass aside and slumped down, sitting heavily in the cold wet pools of formaldehyde that had gathered on the old warped wooden sill. But he didn't even feel the cold liquid soak through his coat and trousers, he was numb to everything as he stared open-mouthed at the pandemonium that filled his preparation room. He could see that the magic had worked, but somehow it had gone dreadfully wrong. It was making all his beautiful creatures, his rare treasures, move unnaturally and struggle frantically. If he couldn't think of something to stop the magic he could see that they would tear themselves apart and rip open his careful stitching. But what could he do? He had never thought to search for a spell that would stop the magic. Helplessly he watched the sabre-toothed tiger, which it had taken him so long to steal from the Natural History Museum, tear one of its front paws into ribbons as it tried to break free from the display of logs where it was mounted. Somewhere near the far end of the room a giant forest hog snorted in alarm and elk and reindeer mounted side by side roared and locked their horns together, beginning to rock back and forth most dangerously. The animals' voices were growing into a bedlam of noise. Owls, egrets, bitterns and pelicans were flapping their wings and sending a gale of loose flight feathers dancing through the shafts of moonlight.

'Quiet! Quiet!' Ludo shouted in despair, clapping his hands over his ears to muffle the animals' noise.

As suddenly as it had begun the deafening howls and shrieking bellows stopped. The room fell as silent as a neglected churchyard on a Monday at midnight.

Ludo let his hands fall slowly to his sides and he stared at the now quiet but still struggling beasts.

'You obeyed me! You all obeyed my voice,' he whispered in awe. A movement caught the edge of his sight and he turned to see a large white barn owl that he had mounted years ago on an old beam beside the window. Its talons were tearing from its legs as it frantically beat its wings.

'I must free you all from your displays. I must cut the steel rods and binding wires,' he muttered urgently to himself as he raked his fingers through his hair.

But he hesitated, wondering if the animals would obey him so readily once he had released them. The larger animals were making the floorboards tremble and shiver and they would soon bring the preparation room and all his secrets crashing down into his shop below if he didn't do something quickly.

'Be still! Stop moving!' he cried, leaping to his feet. He looked everywhere at once, and one by one as he repeated his cry and the struggling animals turned towards his voice and their eyes met his wild glare, they stopped moving and became still. Now only each rigid pose reflected their wild urge to be free and grotesque shadows of arched backs and twisted heads spread long across the low ceiling.

Ludo sucked in a shallow breath and thoughtfully let it whistle out between his teeth as he surveyed the petrified creatures that filled his room. He pinched himself sharply to prove that he wasn't dreaming, to prove that this was really the moment he had dreamed of and planned for, and in three quick steps he crossed to the marble slab and sorted through his skinning knives, scalpels and forceps, until he found a pair of heavy surgeon's bone-cutters. With a cry of triumph he snatched them up and turned towards his statue-still collection. He glanced at the two brown bears who guarded the doorway and shook his head. He would try something smaller at first, something with less tooth and claw. Anyway he would probably need bolt croppers or a welding torch to cut through the thick steel rods he had used to fix the bears on to their plinths. Slowly he scanned the room, probing every gloomy corner and letting his eyes flit over all the beautiful creatures that he possessed. His eyes alighted on the barn owl beside the window and he smiled and nervously licked his lips.

'You shall be the first. Just hold still, very very still, or I might damage your talons further,' he murmured at the bird as he reached up on tiptoe.

He worked the sharp jaws of his bone-cutters underneath the talons of its right foot and squeezed and twisted them until he felt them grip around the strong stainless-steel wire that protruded from the underside of the feet, securing the bird to its perch. Clenching his hand tighter on the handles of the cutters he felt them bite into the steel and with a sharp twist a crack sharper than a pistol shot sounded in the silent moonlit room and he felt the cutters shear through the steel. The owl began to beat its wings and struggled as the taxidermist reached up and clutched its soft feathered body in his free hand to hold it still while he prised the cutters beneath the other foot and squeezed the jaws closely around the wire.

Clenching his hand on the cutters he snapped them shut. The owl flapped its wings and broke free from his hands, flying straight towards his face, its talons opening and closing, its wings spreading clouds of dust and loose feathers. Ludo ducked and fell on to his knees as the bird hovered above him beating its wings in the moonlight. Slowly it rose, reborn, upon the night air, and skimmed over his head towards the far end of the room.

'You can fly, you can really fly!' he cried with delight, rising to his feet and turning, following the owl's swooping flight as it winged its way between the other, static animals, passing in and out of their shadows before it turned towards the window.

At that moment Ludo remembered the beautiful woman he had glimpsed as he began the magic. What if the spell had worked on her? What if she was trapped, frozen to the cobbles in the courtyard? Forgetting for a moment the bird and his room full of watching creatures, he rushed to the window, flung it open and stared down into the empty yard. The owl suddenly hooted and flew past his head out through the open window before the startled taxidermist could utter another word or slam the window shut to stop its flight.

'Wait! Wait! Come back,' Ludo shouted. But the owl had vanished, swooping down into the darkness of the low archway that led out into Lobster Lane.

For a moment he fretted and worried at the old metal catch and relocked the window securely. He paused and frowned, raking his fingers through his hair. The owl had taken the first opportunity to escape. He glanced over his shoulder to the silent host of animals and, watching the moonlight reflecting in their eyes, he wondered if he would really be able to control them.

'I must be careful,' he muttered to himself, wringing his hands together, 'or every one of my beautiful beasts will be roaming through the city before this night is over.'

Shivering, he stooped and picked up the mummified hand, carefully brushing at the charred tip of the index finger. It felt hot, as though the flame had vanished within it. He reached the door and paused between the two huge brown bears, feeling them stir in the darkness on either side of him as he drew back the bolt.

'Patience. Patience,' he whispered as he looked up into their solid black shadows and saw the gleam of the moonlight on their teeth and claws.

'I'll be back in a moment to shear through those steel rods that keep you both prisoners but you must promise to stay here within the safety of my shop. I'll be less than a moment and then you will be free,' he added in a cackling laugh as he slipped through the doorway and ran down the narrow stairway.

He moved quickly and heard nothing of the bears' blood-curdling snarls. He did not see the murderous gleam in their eyes. A single lamp lit the stairwell, and as he reached the bottom his long, thin shadow overtook him, hideously distorted. Unknowing, he reached up and began to unbolt the outside door.

4

A Key to the Door of Giants

'Well, how did the auction go? I've thought of nothing else all day,' Tuppence called as she hurried across the snug bar of the White Hart Hotel to where Richard was waiting for her. She was aware of, but ignored, the enquiring glances from the other tables.

Richard rose to his feet and signalled to the barman to bring the bottle of champagne he had ordered.

'As from one o'clock today the Watchgate was yours,' he said, with a grin spreading across his face as he handed over a heavy and ornately forged iron key.

Tuppence laughed with relief and grasped his arm as she gave him a light kiss on the cheek. 'You really pulled it off, Richard. Oh, that's great. But how much did it cost me?'

Richard's grin broadened. 'There was a lot of interest in it but I eventually secured it with a bid of £125,000.'

'That's wonderful. Come on, I can't wait to get over there and take a look inside.'

Tuppence swung her legs out of the Lotus and rose gracefully to her feet, smoothing out the rucks in her slim pencil skirt with a downwards sweep of her long fingers.

'I can hardly believe it,' she murmured to Richard as she swept her eyes up across the beautiful carved door of

37

giants, to the rows of mediaeval bricks set in such wonderful decorative patterns between the wooden beams, to the
overhanging gallery with its tiny leaded windows set
beneath the steeply gabled roof.

'At last I have a place to call home,' she breathed, crossing the narrow uneven pavement in two whispering steps
of shimmering silk.

'Thanks,' she smiled to Richard as she fitted the key into
the lock.

Richard swallowed and smiled to himself. He never
mixed business with pleasure, but he knew that he was
falling helplessly in love with this beautiful American
woman. Her smile and her soft melting accent sent his
blood on a backward journey through his veins, and his
legs felt as weak as jelly whenever he was close to her. Her
exotic perfume made his head swim.

Tuppence paused. She could sense that Richard was
standing directly behind her, a little too close for comfort,
and briefly she wondered if somehow she had given him
the wrong signals, but she shrugged it off, determined that
nothing should spoil this moment. She smiled to herself
and traced her fingertips over the smooth age-darkened
carvings on the door. 'My door of giants,' she whispered,
feeling the mediaeval knights and their proud chargers
trampling the invading hordes beneath their hooves.

On closer examination in the evening light she saw there
was much the shadows had hidden the other night. There
were strange animals and forests of petrified trees, ships
floating in stormy seas in every knife's cut. History was
slipping beneath her fingertips and she could almost hear
the snorts and whinnies of the horses and the cries of the
figures that had been carved there. The wood of the door
was as hard as glass, yet the grain felt as soft as silk and

somehow protective and welcoming in the evening sun-light.

'I'll find out everything there is to know about the legends and the folk tales that have been recorded here. I'll discover everything that has ever been uttered about this beautiful house,' she whispered at the door as she twisted the heavy key and heard the iron levers of the lock drop one by one into place. The sound echoed through the empty building.

The door groaned and gave an inch on its hinges. Tuppence pushed hard and it creaked open to reveal the lower room of the Watchgate. She hesitated on the worn threshold stone. The welcome seemed to have melted away and a shadow of apprehension darkened her eyes as she looked into the low-beamed and gloomy narrow room. Leaves and torn-up scraps of paper littered the cold stone-flagged floor. At the far end a huge open fireplace that almost filled the wall gaped at her like an open mouth, choked with black cinders and mounds of grey ash that had been allowed to spew out into the room. Beside the fireplace a steep winding wooden staircase, overflowing with bundles of yellowing newspapers and sacks of rubbish, vanished towards the rooms above. A large housefly broke the sti-fled silence, buzzing at the small leaded window pane, its iridescent wings trapped in a shroud of long-forgotten spiders' webs. The air smelt stale as if history had sucked it dry and then breathed a hollow emptiness into every corner.

Richard filled the doorway directly behind her. 'I made a few enquiries before the auction. It seems that the last owner, an old lady named Peabody, was moved into a nursing home three years ago. It hasn't been lived in since then but I'm sure with just a little work the kitchen area could be improved . . .' The optimism in his voice faded into silence as his eyes followed her gaze around the gloomy room. He swallowed a little awkwardly. The Watchgate would never have been his choice. But for a moment he thought that he saw the room through her eyes.

Tuppence was unaware of his misgivings. She was home at last, in the first real place she could call her own, and Richard had faded into the background. While she stood there in that empty room the echo of those bleak years welled up inside her and touched a hidden chord. It all came flooding back – the shouts and the bustle of the crowded pavements of Manhattan, the noise of the yellow cabs packed bumper to bumper. She remembered the ice-cold wind blowing off the East River, cutting through her threadbare clothing, the gnawing hunger and the hopelessness, the feeling of desperation and the thought of never getting that real break that would lead to a proper career. There had been endless rounds of those seedy photographic studios on the East Side with their stale cigar smoke and the smell of cheap perfume; the procession of girls who had already sold away their dreams for ever as they got ready to pose, to expose their nakedness for the callous leering eyes and rough touch of the guys who worked on that side of Poverty Street.

She could still hear the echoes of those years of despair. The helplessness in the girls' voices as they tried to retain a little dignity and the cruel unfeeling demands of the photographers as they set up those pitiful creatures of circumstance in their pornographic poses. It all came back so clearly to her. How vehemently she had refused to join, to have a little fun, as they called it, to sell them the rights to her body for a handful of money.

She shuddered and pushed the ugliness, the sheer despair of those years, back into the darkest corners of her mind.

It was a beginning she wanted to forget. Suddenly she smiled, and in her mind's eye she caught a glimpse of herself, the innocent, standing in the doorway of Klein's Photographic Studios on 23rd Street, the gangling and determined child, clutching so tightly to her handful of dreams. She realized in that instant where that penetrating look in her eyes had come from and why Harry Klein had wanted to photograph it so badly. It was the reflection, the mirror, of all that misery and all those failed dreams; all that despair and hopelessness that had almost claimed her and kept her in its grip. The way Harry photographed that look had taken people's breath away. That moment, hovering on Harry's doorstep, had been the ending of her journey through a nightmare world and the beginning of the career that was to lead her here, to the threshold of the Watchgate. Harry's studio had been the nearest to a place she could call home that she had ever known. He had looked after her like a father and she felt a sense of guilt that she had only telephoned him once since she had come to England.

This place was good for her, it put things into perspective and she knew that she was going to enjoy it. 'I'll phone you, Harry. I'll phone you and let you know that everything's OK the moment I get back tonight,' she whispered to herself as she let the memory of Harry and all that he had done for her fade.

She sighed and watched as the late evening light lit up the door of giants and spilled through the open doorway, casting long shadows across the flagstones. The low-beamed room gleamed with warm colours but as the sunlight moved across the carvings it threw them into deep relief, making the knights and their horses seem to leap forward and shimmer with a dark richness.

Tuppence turned to Richard and laughed softly. 'Just

think of all the history that this place must have seen. Why, that door that we just walked through was old before the first explorers had even set out to discover America. Think of all the hands that have held and turned the key in that lock, and all the footsteps that it has taken to wear these flagstones smooth beneath our feet. Just think of all the years, the summers and the winters, the days and hours, the minutes, that have ticked away here in this room. The journeys that must have begun and ended through that doorway. I'll bet that every traveller who set out from here touched those carvings for luck on those journeys, just as I touched them the other night and wished for luck in the auction.'

Tuppence slowly turned and crossed the room towards the huge fireplace. The fly had stopped buzzing at the window pane and the low-ceilinged room stood wrapped in silence as the fading light shone through the insect's wings and showed the iridescent colours where it hung suspended in its shroud of webs. She could feel the sheer weight of all the history of the Watchgate crowding the silent room, just waiting to be retold. She reached the fireplace and put her hand up on to the old twisted and blackened mantel beam that centuries of heat and smoke had made as hard as hammered iron, and she leaned forward and looked into the grate.

'There's a whole load of old-looking implements amongst the rubbish, hooks and rusty chains, and what looks likes a spit, and kettle trammels hanging from a beam or something inside the chimney. Come and see, oh and . . .' Tuppence paused and picked her way through the piles of ash and cinders that had overflowed the hearth.

'And there's benches inside the fireplace, as upright and uncomfortable as church pews. Just think of all the tales and stories that must have been told across the crackling flames!'

She laughed and ran her fingers across one of the dusty seats, her excitement at owning the Watchgate flushing her cheeks and giving her eyes a girlish innocent sparkle.

'I think there's a date carved on the side of this bench,' she called out. 'It's been chiselled on the beam that fixes the bench to the wall and there's a funny-looking cross shape and some strange carvings that run down the beam. They feel like ribbons that have been all bunched up together.'

'What's the date? Can you see?' Richard asked, crossing the room in long strides.

'I can't quite see it in all this dust and shadow. I'll need a light to read it properly, but it feels as though there are two narrow upright lines and a funny-shaped four with a tail, and what feels like a three that curves well below the other numbers.'

Richard whistled through his teeth. '1143! That makes that bench worth a fortune,' he exclaimed, trying to see her in the haze of ash and soot she had stirred up in the chimney.

He crouched down a few steps from the hearth and watched her exploring the fireplace. 'I think you had better come out of that inglenook before you look like a chimney sweep's apprentice,' he laughed.

Tuppence stopped exploring the hearth and looked down at her blackened hands and laughed with him. She hadn't had this much fun for a long time. 'Inglenook? Is that what you call it? Well, I tell you, there's a whole treasure house to explore in here,' she laughed and then coughed as the dust caught in her throat.

She stepped carefully back out of the fireplace and took

the handkerchief that Richard offered to her and began to wipe her hands.

'There's some smudges of soot on your chin and up above your right eyebrow. Here, let me wipe them away for you,' he offered, moving closer and reaching to take back the handkerchief.

'No. No thanks. I'll be just fine,' Tuppence retorted, sensing a note of familiarity, an intonation in his manner that she wished was not there. She sighed inwardly. Why did everyone come on so strong at the slightest opportunity? The laughter evaporated from her eyes. In an instant the penetrating gaze was back, forcing Richard to keep his distance.

He hesitated, almost overbalancing in an effort not to touch her or to cross that invisible line that she had suddenly thrown up. Tuppence saw the look of confusion, almost embarrassment, flicker in his eyes. It wasn't that she disliked him that much, he just really wasn't her type.

'Shouldn't there be another door?' Tuppence asked quickly, trying to remove the tension as she moved to the other side of the narrow staircase.

'Door? What door?' He frowned.

'The doorway at the back of the Watchgate,' she answered, pointing to the fireplace and the steep winding staircase. 'The one the knights and all those ancient warriors must have used to get into this room. How else would they have reached the giant's door at the front? It must have been where this fireplace is but what has happened to it? Why was it blocked up?'

Richard followed her pointing finger and shrugged his shoulders. 'I don't know, but it must have been a long time ago by the look of the brickwork in that inglenook. I'm sure that someone in the museum across Elm Hill will know,' he offered helpfully.

Tuppence nodded and picked her way over the bag of rubbish that littered the stairs to take a look upstairs. She reappeared moments later. 'There's just two rooms up there, a bedroom a little smaller than this and an old-fashioned bathroom. But there's not a single window at the back of the Watchgate, not even in the bathroom, just a tiny vent and fan that must work with the light when you turn it on.'

Richard glanced from the dusty ash-filled inglenook to the worn treads of the steep wooden staircase that climbed up beside it.

'Well, even if the original doorway still existed it wouldn't lead anywhere now except into those dingy alley-ways and decaying courtyards that we passed by on our way down Lobster Lane the other night. They back right up against the Watchgate.'

Tuppence shivered. Richard's words reminded her of the claustrophobic black shadows of the courtyard with the cats, and the stark staring face she had glimpsed at one of the upper windows.

'Perhaps it is a blessing in disguise . . .' she began to say, when a flash bulb suddenly exploded with a pop in the doorway, its blaze of light blinding them.

'What the hell . . . ?' Tuppence snapped, spinning around quickly. Richard turned angrily towards the door, stuttering to find his voice.

The photographer had stepped back and vanished out of sight before she could blink, and in his place appeared a small balding figure with a ferret-shaped face and wearing a crumpled tweed jacket and threadbare corduroy trousers. His notebook was open and he had a pencil poised and ready.

'Glover of the *Eastern Daily*, Miss Trilby,' he rattled quickly, without a hint of an apology in his voice for his unwelcomed intrusion. 'It *is* Miss Trilby, Miss Tuppence Trilby, the most celebrated face of the nineties, isn't it? Is it true that you have bought the Watchgate? Is it true that you plan to settle here in the city?' he asked, his mouth breaking into a well-rehearsed smile, while his eyes hunted the room, prying and probing for the flesh and bones to fill out the story.

'Get the hell out of here, Glover. Just get out before I break every bone in your body,' Richard snarled, advancing menacingly towards the reporter.

Glover swallowed and stepped back. He hadn't expected this reaction. Surprise, yes, and confusion, those two reactions coupled with his forthright quick questions usually drew out all their secrets. People usually hesitated, stuttered and then fell apart. He had to act quickly if he was going to get a story before the door was slammed in his face. Sidestepping the large untidy estate agent he spoke directly to Tuppence. 'There's a lot of interest in this place. The National Trust had an agent at the auction. It's the oldest house in the city apart from the castle and everyone wants to know what you, an American and a fashion model, intend to do with it. Remember, this is a small city and if you intend to live here . . .'

Tuppence stared at him, her eyes blazing with anger.

'But perhaps you don't care. Perhaps you are planning to dismantle the Watchgate and ship it out to the States. Is that what I shall write?' he fired at her as he retreated out of Richard's reach and through the open door.

Tuppence hesitated. He had taken her completely by surprise. She didn't care much for tabloid reporters, especially ones from the gutter press who were always trying to barge their way into your private life, to take you by surprise as they hoped to catch you wrong-footed and shock you into allowing something to slip. Any story would do, anything to sell their cheap newspapers, and she'd had her fill of them. She'd had armies of them digging through her life after Harry had given her that break. They had been looking for the pornographic photographs they were sure she must have posed for. They had tried to link her romantically with Harry and a hundred other guys; in fact they never seemed to stop looking, never gave up the belief that one day they would find something with which to tarnish her. But perhaps this guy was different. She had hated his manner and the cold predatory look in his eyes, but perhaps all he wanted was to know what she was going to do with the Watchgate. Perhaps she should tell him after all.

'Wait right there for a moment,' she snapped. She turned to Richard and asked if he knew the reporter and what sort of paper the *Eastern Daily Press* was.

'The *EDP*? That's a good local newspaper,' he replied. 'It covers quite a lot of the national news stories as well. But I'm surprised that Vince Glover barged in here like that. He usually reports murders, crimes, that sort of thing. I didn't know he ever wrote for the society pages.'

'Well perhaps I'd better explain why I bought this place, before he makes up a major crime story to go with the photograph he's already taken,' she muttered crossly as she turned back towards the reporter.

Glover grinned, but his eyes stayed hard as he exposed a mouth crowded with metalled and dirty teeth. 'Miss Trilby? I'm grateful you can spare me the time. Our readers are always interested in new faces in their city, expecially ones as famous as yours.'

Tuppence gave an inward shudder. Like all his kind, Glover made her flesh crawl and the fine hairs on the nape of her neck prickle, but she forced a welcoming smile and allowed the professional model to take over. It was best they got on with the interview as quickly as possible. She explained that her move to England was a result of her taking on much more location work in Europe and that during a film shot near Norwich she had fallen in love with the Watchgate and she had bought it to live in.

'So there's no truth in the rumour that there has been a split between you and Harry Klein?' Glover probed. He remembered hearing a vague whisper of something like that earlier in the year when she first came over. He had hoped to find something to build a good story on.

Tuppence's eyes narrowed and hardened, but she controlled her temper. 'I do more work for Harry now than I ever did. We're great friends. Does that answer your question?'

Vince sighed and nodded, pushing the pencil behind his ear as he snapped his notebook shut. He wasn't going to get anything more, she obviously was giving nothing away. But he gave it one more try. 'What about your future work? What's in the pipeline?'

Tuppence held his gaze with that special look she had and smiled. She had spent hours in front of the camera perfecting this and she could make it seem that you were the only person in the world to her. 'Harry wanted me to come to England. He saw that it was the next step and that I should establish myself in Europe.'

Glover thanked her and asked if the photographer could take just one more shot of her with the inglenook in the background before they left.

'Why didn't Jones do this story? He normally does the society pages,' Richard asked the reporter as they moved towards the fireplace.

Glover laughed coldly without a trace of humour. 'We were following up a murder that happened just up the road last night – in the Castle Narrows.'

'Murder?' Tuppence cried in alarm, 'A murder? Near here?'

Glover grinned at her obvious alarm and explained, 'It was only on the other side of Castle Meadow, just above Lobster Lane. And since we heard from Jones that Miss Trilby had bought the Watchgate we thought we would finish up the film and take him back a story.'

Tuppence could have laughed. It was a long time since she had been on the tail end of a strip of celluloid. Normally each click of the shutter, each frame she posed for, was worth hours of negotiation and a few thousand dollars in the bank. But the word murder made her shiver and the blood chilled in her veins. The room seemed suddenly cold and airless in the fading sunlight; the warmth and friendliness that she had felt earlier had melted away in the darkening shadows.

'What are the Narrows?' she asked quickly.

Glover had watched the shadow of fear darken her eyes and his mouth curled open. He knew he was going to enjoy the next few moments. 'The Narrows, Miss Trilby, are a warren of old lanes and alleyways, dark gloomy places that lie in the shadows of the castle walls. They were once the haunts of murderous gangs, highwaymen and smugglers, but now it's mostly warehouses and old shops. It's only ten minutes' walk from here.' He paused and watched his words sink in, and he savoured the pictures that he had painted in her mind. 'But if you think the Narrows sound creepy, Miss Trilby, just wait till I tell you about the murder!'

'No! No, I don't want to know about it,' she gasped, stepping backwards, but Glover wasn't letting her off that easily. His tongue flickered over his lips and made them glisten as they tightened into a whiter smile.

He hunched his shoulders and took a step towards her.

'It was a medical warehouse, Miss Trilby. You can imagine it, bottles of formaldehyde, scalpels, bandages, sterile dressings. Packed from floor to ceiling. It was completely wrecked. You couldn't believe the stench. I tell you, the place looked as though it had been torn apart by wild animals. But it was the body of the night watchman that really made my stomach turn over. That is, what was left of it.'

'You can say that again,' interrupted the photographer, fiddling with a flash bulb. 'I've taken some snaps in my time, but what happened to him didn't look possible.'

'It looked as though he had been crushed,' Glover carried on, forcing the photographer to shut up. 'As though every bone in his body had been broken. The skin was so badly torn the police pathologist reckons that he must have been flayed alive. I tell you, lady, it was hanging off him in strips.'

'That's enough!' Tuppence snapped. 'I don't want to hear any more about it.'

Richard saw how upset she was and moved threateningly towards the reporter. Glover gave Tuppence his most brilliant smile. 'Oh, I'm so sorry, miss, I thought you would want to know what's going on in your neighbourhood now that you've moved in.'

'It's a funny thing, though,' muttered the photographer, quite oblivious to what had been going on as he finally gave up on the battery pack that hung from his shoulder. 'There were two drunks, actually they looked more like derelicts, in the outer office of the paper when we left this morning. They were trying to sell some kind of wild story that they had seen a couple of huge bears, brown bears, lumbering through the Narrows in the early hours. They reckoned they were going in the direction of Castle Meadow.'

'Bears?' whispered Tuppence, her eyes wide with fear. 'But there aren't any wild bears in England, are there?'

Richard laughed, trying to break the tension. 'No, of course not. There haven't been wild bears around here since the Middle Ages. It was probably students from the Art School, they get up to all sorts of stupid pranks.'

'Well I'd like to see the student who's clever enough to imitate a leopard or some sort of big cat,' smirked Glover, foiling Richard's attempt. 'We had one of those reported last night, as well, roaring and running about in Castle Walk.'

'Damn, I think the battery chargers are shot,' interrupted the photographer with a final sigh as he squinted at his light meter and then let it dangle from the cord around his neck. 'It's far too dark in here to take another photograph without the flashgun. Perhaps I could drop by tomorrow?'

'No, that won't be possible,' Tuppence retorted sharply, trying to get a grip on the fear that had made her mouth so dry; trying to force away the vivid images that the reporter had painted in her mind of the murder in the Narrows and the wild animals loose in the city.

Glover shrugged his shoulders, well pleased with his visit to the Watchgate. He moved casually towards the door. 'Never mind, Miss Trilby, we'll just have to use that first picture. Thanks anyway for the story. We won't take up any more of your time.'

He paused for a moment, his hand resting lightly on the ancient door of giants. 'You should be safe enough behind a door this thick. Mind you, I'd make sure it's securely locked and bolted at night. At least, until the police have caught the murderer.'

Richard took an angry pace towards the doorway as the reporter and photographer vanished, his fists tightly clenched. 'He had no right to scare you like that. No right at all.'

Tuppence shivered, glad that they had gone. 'Oh, reporters are all like that. They are all searching for a weakness, a way to use you,' she muttered stiffly. 'Look, I have to go north, to Scotland, for a few weeks,' she added, without pausing for breath. She was in a hurry now, a hurry to leave the Watchgate before the sun set. Inwardly she knew it was silly, but right now she needed people, crowds of people, lights and noise to dispel the pictures that the reporter had so carefully drawn to scare her.

'Can you recommend someone, perhaps a firm I could hire, to clean this place up and supply a new oven? I would like it decorated while I'm away – and get the lights fixed, oh, and a telephone laid on.'

'Yes, there's a firm we often use for the rented properties. I can give them a ring first thing in the morning for you,' Richard answered as he followed Tuppence out over the threshold and into the darkening twilight.

Tuppence paused and glanced back over her shoulder before closing and locking the door. 'I think white would be the best colour with all those dark beams, don't you?'

'Yes . . .' Richard was saying as he reached for the door handle of the Lotus, when a blood-curdling howl from somewhere in the maze of alleyways and courtyards behind the Watchgate split the early evening silence, and a huge lumbering shadow appeared in Lobster Lane.

'Bloody hell! What's that?' Tuppence cried, wrenching open her door and scrambling in.

Richard stared for a moment into Lobster Lane, but the shadow had vanished and the howl had died away into an echo. 'I . . . I . . . I . . . don't know,' he stuttered. 'I've never heard anything like it before.'

'Well it's scared the hell out of me, whatever it was,' Tuppence hissed, slamming the door and firing the engine. Richard leapt back as she dropped the clutch and left burning rubber all the way up Elm Hill.

5

Shadows in the Taxidermist's Shop

Dawn was breaking across the city. Its cold, bleak light silently probed every hidden corner, melting away every secret shadow that clung between the close-crowded houses. Brick by brick, cobble by cobble it spread, bringing a blaze of colour to the tall fluted windows of the old museum on Elm Hill. It touched and brought life to the knights and prancing horses carved in stark relief on the Watchgate door. The dawn moved on across the narrow alleyways and ruined courtyards, spreading as relentlessly as the tide breaking across a beach of pebbles. It flowed beneath the night-dark archway into Goats Head Alley, to grey the cobbles of that claustrophobic courtyard and wash away the shadows. It painted the new morning across the taxidermist's open doorway.

Ludo Strewth hovered in the courtyard, wringing his hands together helplessly and listening, following the eerie dawn chorus of the animals that barged and stampeded their way past him and into the darkness of his shop. He could hear the two bears howling somewhere in the Narrows.

'You're making enough noise to wake the dead,' he hissed, as their shrieks echoed between the steep weather-bleached roofs all around him.

But there were other sounds that made him anxious, other sounds that broke the dawn silence. The faint wail of police sirens in the direction of the Castle Narrows and the clamour of an ambulance crossing the city, but closer, much closer, somewhere in the vicinity of Elm Hill or Castle Street, he could hear the sound of a car.

'Quickly. I command you to get back to the shop. I command you to do as I say,' he hissed at the shadowy animal forms that suddenly emerged from beneath the archway and streamed all around him towards the open door.

Their unshod hooves and clawed feet echoed in the courtyard, cats hissed and birds flew around his face as Ludo counted the hurrying shapes through the doorway.

'The bears! Where are the bears?' he cried as he realized that the sound of the car he had heard was getting dangerously close. He heard the squeak of brakes and doors being thrown open. The car must be just beyond the low archway. Now there were voices and the sound of boots on the uneven cobbles. They were moving towards the courtyard. He retreated back into his shop and securely bolted the heavy door.

'Quiet! Hush, be quiet!' he hissed, raising his long arms high above his head to clap his hands furiously together, making the heels of his palms sting as he tried to calm the baying, howling and restless animals that crowded the shop.

Twisting and turning, he forced his way through the milling crush of animals and slipped out into the unlit passageway behind the shop. The rear door stood open and he stepped out into the darkness of the narrow alleyway behind his shop. His heartbeat quickened with a moment of fear as he saw two large bears at the far end of the alley hurrying towards him, a murderous gleam in their eyes. They could easily crush him or tear him apart; he must stay in command.

'Into your places. Be quick, there are strangers in the courtyard,' he snapped, turning on his heel and running back into the shop, only to halt abruptly and stare at the pandemonium that greeted him.

He raked his fingers helplessly through his thinning hair, cursing his impatience to begin the magic before he had given a moment's thought to how it would affect his collection of beautiful animals. All he had wanted the magic to do was to make his animals more real, more lifelike. It had never crossed his mind that it would resurrect their primeval instincts, that they would stampede out into the streets as the sun set to stalk their prey in the dark city. He knew that they could not possibly be hungry or thirsty; the shreds of logic that still clung to his mind told him that it was not possible – their skeletons were now made of wood, wire and rods of steel, they were stuffed with cotton batting. Some even had bodies carved from balsa wood or Styrofoam; they had no lungs to breathe with or stomachs that needed food. Yet the magic had made them breathe, and howl at the moon and claw at his doors.

The magic from the Hand of Glory had possessed them and made them so real, so frighteningly real. And the worst of it was he knew he couldn't stop the magic. He had tried when the animals first barged past him out into the darkness. He tried everything he knew to quench the flame that still smouldered in the index finger of the mummified hand but nothing would extinguish it. The magic had a dark sinister power of its own that drove the animals out to hunt and kill each night. He began to realize that he could barely control what the animals did even here in his taxidermist's shop.

'Be quiet and get to your places,' he cried, trying to snatch at a hovering eagle owl, his frantic fingers clutching at a handful of loose flight feathers.

Dawn was growing stronger, sending fingers of grey light through the chinks and folds of the heavy black curtains he had drawn across the windows of the shop to hide the magic that he had awoken from any prying eyes.

'Be still! All of you be still,' he hissed, stumbling forward as a hartebeest, its hooves skidding on the polished floorboards, nudged him sharply in the small of his back.

An antelope snorted and threw back its head, spinning Ludo off balance against a musk deer as it caught its smooth spiralling horn in the pocket of his long white coat. Crows squawked and owls hooted as the taxidermist scrambled back on to his feet.

'Quiet! There are strangers in the courtyard. I can hear their footsteps,' he whispered.

At last the shop began to fall silent, the animals to freeze back into their lifeless poses. Only two monkeys still chattered, swinging from beam to beam across the ceiling.

'Quiet! Quiet!' snapped Ludo, making the swamp monkey spit at him, its ruff of whiskers bristling from its ears to its mouth. The other monkey, a russet-coloured howler, curled its lips back across its fangs to howl, but at the last moment seemed to think better of it and froze, its long fingers ridged as it clutched at a knot hole in the beam and slowly swung backwards and forwards.

Ludo caught a movement in the corner of his eye and spun round, his white coat tails flying out behind him. He saw a mass of frogs and toads hopping in every direction and at least a dozen snakes slithering out of the dark corners in pursuit of them. A bandicoot rat, a great jerboa and a leopard frog hopped between his feet.

'Get out of sight,' Ludo whispered frantically as the footsteps stopped outside his door.

One by one, the snakes slithered away, climbing the curtains and lacing themselves around the outer casings of the six antique clocks that noisily measured the time beside the door. The rear door of the shop slammed shut. Heavy footsteps made the floorboards tremble.

First one and then the other of the two huge brown bears lumbered into the shop. They growled softly at the taxidermist and took their places on either side of the door.

'This is the place, I'm sure of it.' A gruff voice suddenly spoke just outside.

Ludo took a step towards the door, then froze as he saw blood on the bears' claws. A fist hammered on the door. The noise of the bolts rattling made him jump.

'It's the police. Is there anyone in there?' a muffled voice shouted through the door and again it shook as someone hammered on it.

Ludo stared desperately around the shop. It looked like chaos and panic holding their breath. Everything was in a jumble and nothing was in its place. The animals stood statue-still but their eyes looked alive, watching, following every movement. He dared not open the door. One glance would be enough to unmask the secret of the magic that he had awakened. He began to creep across the shop towards the door at the back when the voices in the court-yard made him stop.

'There hasn't been any sign of the old boy for a couple of weeks now. The shop's been shut up and blacked out whenever I've put my head into the courtyard. He's a bit of an eccentric, but I'm worried about him.'

'Yes,' agreed another voice. 'You'd have to be crazy to live in a dismal-looking place like this, perhaps we should break the door down and take a look. You never know with all these murders going on in the Narrows. It's only a stone's throw away after all.'

'Right. There's a crowbar and a sledgehammer in the

boot of the car. I'll just go and fetch them,' called out one of the policemen.

All the blood had drained out of Ludo's face. His lips twitched and trembled. The police were going to break down his door and peer and pry into all his secrets. He would have to stop them. He would *have* to stop them. He must open the door himself before they forced it.

'All right. All right, I'm coming, hold on,' he shouted testily, muttering loudly enough so that the police officers could hear him, 'making enough noise to wake the dead and bring honest folks out of their beds before the sun is up.'

But as he drew back the top bolt on the door he remembered the sticky blood on the bears' claws.

'The bottom bolt sticks a little. I'll have to get a hammer to tap it loose,' he called to the two police officers as he fought to keep his voice level.

Quickly he scrubbed the bears' claws with his handkerchief, cleaning off the blood as best he could before he stuffed the bloodied rag into his pocket. He gathered up a claw hammer from a box of tools that lay on the floor behind the counter and moved back towards the door.

'Not a sound. Not even the slightest movement. Not even a blink,' he whispered, raising his free hand and putting a long trembling finger to his lips as he swept his wild staring gaze across the animals that crowded every shelf and corner in his shop.

'Rigger. Detective Sergeant Rigger, sir,' smiled the larger of the two policemen standing on the doorstep. 'And this is Constable Thorn.'

Rigger held out his warrant card towards the taxidermist as he slowly swung open the door of his shop.

'Yes, officer? How can I help you so early in the morning?' Ludo frowned, his eyebrows rising into bushy arches as he looked expectantly from Rigger to the constable and back again.

Rigger shivered in his thin coat and hunched his shoulders against the chill dawn wind that had risen from the River Wensum. It was blowing straight through the low archway against his legs, tugging and rippling his trousers with icy fingers, lifting forgotten piles of leaves and scraps of litter from the corners of the dreary courtyard to eddy and dance up against the ruined wall of the church tower.

'We are concerned for your safety, sir. We are checking on everyone who lives in the old part of the city. Do you mind if we step inside for a moment?' Rigger asked as he took a step closer to the doorway.

Ludo tried to hold his ground and glared at the two policemen as he clutched the claw hammer in one hand and thrust his bloodied handkerchief deeper into his pocket with the other. He knew there could be no reason not to let them in if he had nothing to hide. To allow them in out of the cold would be natural. To insist that they stayed outside would only make them suspicious.

Rigger's smile thinned as he stood out there in the cold wind. Talking to this wild-looking eccentric was making him impatient and he continued quickly. 'Constable Thorn informed me that he hadn't seen you recently, and as the only resident in this courtyard of derelict lock-ups he was concerned about your welfare.'

'My welfare? Well, I'm safe, why shouldn't I be?' Ludo asked in mock surprise as he reluctantly retreated back over the threshold to let the two police officers into his shop.

Rigger didn't answer immediately; he was staring spellbound, transfixed by the host of exotic animals that crowded the rooms.

'Where on earth did you get all these specimens from? I've never seen so many rare and beautiful creatures, not even in London Zoo,' he gasped, looking from the huge bears to the leopards, cheetahs, antelopes and all the other beasts and birds that he could barely see in the gloomy shop.

'This must be a treasure house,' he continued, his eyes round with interest. 'Would you turn the light on? I'd love to see them more closely. What is the name of that snake, the one that's coiled around the carriage clock closest to the door?'

Ludo's heart sank. Of all the policemen in the city this one wanted to take a closer look at his collection of animals. He was sure that the officer would notice that none of the beasts was mounted and it was with reluctance that he reached out and pressed the old brass light switch, his mind racing for an answer to the inevitable probing questions.

The lights flickered on. Rigger gasped aloud and blinked in amazement at the richness and brilliance of the colours, at the fine detail in each beak and claw. Thorn, on the other hand, was turning pale.

'They are so beautiful, so lifelike,' Rigger exclaimed.

He paused and let his eyes wander from animal to animal. He was about to ask why none of them were in the bell jars or glass cabinets when he took another step and almost trod on a tiny bright orange frog.

'Oh, I am sorry,' Rigger exclaimed. 'I almost squashed this little fella,' and he bent down and smiled as he admired how the glistening animal sat back on its powerful hind legs as if it was ready to spring across the room. Before the taxidermist could do anything to prevent him, Rigger had picked up the tiny frog.

Rigger frowned and quickly handed the creature to

Ludo. Holding it had made the hairs on the nape of his neck prickle. He hadn't liked the cold slimy feel of the skin, it was as if it was still alive despite everything that the taxidermist must have obviously done to preserve it.

'Thank you. Thank you very much.' Ludo smiled a little breathlessly, stuffing the frog into his pocket on top of the bloodied handkerchief. He had been holding his breath, expecting the frog to croak at any moment and spring out of the policeman's hand. He had been willing it with all his mind to keep perfectly still.

'It is a golden arrow-poison frog. It is quite rare to find one in a collection like this.'

'It's poisonous!' Rigger gasped furiously, rubbing his hand on his coat and trying to dispel the cold sliminess that clung to his fingers.

Ludo laughed and shook his head. 'I removed the poison sac. It can't possibly harm you if you touch it, officer. The South American Indians extract the poison to use on the tips of their arrows.'

'But it felt so cold and slimy. It was as if it was still alive. I had expected it to feel dry, even dusty . . .' Rigger fell silent. He was beginning to feel uneasy, his instincts were nagging at him. There was something out of place in this menagerie of stuffed animals. Something that he couldn't quite put his finger on.

'Oh, that's nothing to worry about,' exclaimed Ludo, showing his yellow teeth in a broad smile. 'The damp sensation you experienced is easy to explain. I have been spraying all the frogs and toads in my collection with a preserving solution of powdered borax and formaldehyde. It takes a day or two to soak into the animal's skin. I started spring-cleaning the whole of my collection a couple of weeks ago; that is why the shop has been shut and everything is in such a muddle. Look, there's a rain frog by that empty cabinet in the corner. I sprayed that at about the same time as the arrow frog; its skin will feel just as cold. I have also sprayed the snakes. Why don't you feel that coral snake, the one coiled around the carriage clock at your elbow?'

Rigger shuddered and stepped away from the clock. 'No! No thank you!'

Constable Thorn had not really been listening to the taxidermist. He had been staring up into the eyes of the huge brown bear standing to the left of the doorway. The creature seemed to be watching him with its mean, murderous eyes. But Thorn caught the word formaldehyde and felt his throat tighten as he immediately identified the sweet dry smell that overpowered this shop. He had always hated that smell at school in the laboratories and had only found out after three miserable years studying biology that he was allergic to it. The allergy had stopped him becoming a pathologist, and made him hold his breath for as long as possible whenever he had to take someone to the public mortuary to identify a corpse. Now he felt his stomach churn over and the midnight coffee and rolls that he had taken from the mobile canteen set up near the scene of last night's murder began to climb back up his oesophagus. He had to get out of this shop. He had to get away from the stench of formaldehyde and he had to do it fast.

'Air,' he gasped, 'I must have some air,' and he clutched at the door handle and wrenched it open, forgetting his fear of the bears as he staggered over the threshold. He fell on to his knees, retching and sucking in mouthfuls of cold morning air.

'Oh dear, what's wrong?' soothed the taxidermist. 'Is there anything I can do?'

Rigger frowned irritably and shook his head as he stared for a moment at Thorn, watching his shoulders convulsing where he knelt on the rough cobbles of the courtyard just outside the door.

'No, no, there's nothing you can do to help. He's got some sort of aversion to medical solutions or something. I had better get him back to the station before he throws up all over your doorstep.'

'Oh, what a pity,' Ludo smiled as he tried to mask the relief in his voice, 'and I was going to show you the rest of my collection of snakes and toads. Some of them are quite rare, you know, and I don't get many visitors.'

Rigger hesitated in the open doorway and turned back towards the taxidermist. The man was grinning and rubbing his hands together, and a wildness, almost a look of madness, seemed to reflect in his eyes. Really, there was something not quite right here.

Sighing, he smiled coldly. 'I'd be extra careful if you have to go out at night, sir. There was another ugly murder in the Castle Narrows last night.'

'A murder? How awful,' exclaimed Ludo, throwing up his hands in dismay. 'I had no idea there had been any murders. You see I'm much too busy with my collection to go wandering through the city after dark.'

Rigger took a last slow look around the shop at the menagerie of exotic animals and stepped out into the courtyard. 'These murders, officer, have there been many?' Ludo asked, a frown of concern wrinkling his forehead as he followed the policeman out over the threshold of the shop and into the courtyard, carefully pulling the door almost shut behind him. 'Only I don't have a radio or go out to buy a newspaper all that often.'

'I have some old newspapers in the car, they will tell you all about the murders. I'll let you have them. I won't be a moment,' smiled Rigger, as he turned across the courtyard towards the low archway, Thorn staggering close behind.

The frog suddenly croaked in Ludo's pocket as the policeman vanished beneath the low brickwork. 'Hush,' Ludo hissed, clamping his fingers over its throat as the car door slammed shut in Lobster Lane and Rigger reappeared with a bundle of papers under his arm.

'They're rather crumpled, but I think they cover all the murders, sir.'

'Thank you, thank you, officer. It's so kind of you . . .' Ludo began, when the door of his shop flew open and then slammed violently shut. Something inside the shop crashed to the floor with a sound of splintering glass.

'What was that?' cried Detective Sergeant Rigger as Ludo spun around towards the noise.

'Oh, nothing, nothing, officer. It's just the wind. It's quite all right, I can deal with it,' he called over his shoulder as he fled back over the threshold, his coat tails flying out behind him, before he firmly bolted the door in the policeman's face.

Rigger had tried to follow but was too slow. He could hear the taxidermist's voice on the other side; he was muttering and cursing to himself. Abruptly the shop fell silent. Nothing but the distant hum of the early morning traffic broke the silence of the courtyard. It was beginning to rain.

Sergeant Rigger shrugged his shoulders. He had wasted too much time already in this gloomy and depressing hole. He had a thousand more pressing enquiries to follow up on the murder in the tobacconist's shop. But he hesitated beneath the shadowy archway and glanced back to the dilapidated shop front. There had been some really strange reports of sightings during the last few weeks. Bears and all manner of other wild animals had been seen roaming through the city under the cover of darkness – animals just like the ones that crowded the taxidermist's shop. All the pathology reports on the murders had indicated gouging and tearing wounds, as if the victims had been mauled by wild animals.

Rigger laughed and shook his head as he turned towards the waiting car. The idea that those stuffed animals in the taxidermist's shop could hurt anyone was ludicrous. They were only models. They were made of wood and wire with cotton stuffing, no matter how lifelike they looked.

Ludo breathed a sight of relief as he heard the prying policeman's footsteps vanish and the car draw away. He leaned heavily on the counter and glared angrily at his collection of animals.

'You almost had me caught,' he hissed, pulling the arrow frog and the handkerchief out of his pocket.

He dropped the frog carelessly on the counter and mopped his brow with the handkerchief, leaving streaks and smears of dark blood on his forehead. He knew that he had fooled the police this time. He knew that his secrets were still safe – for the moment. But how long would it be before the police came back? How soon before they trapped one of his animals and discovered the dreadful truth?

Wearily Ludo rubbed his hand over his face, scratching at the drying smears of blood that were beginning to itch, and spread the bundle of crumpled newspapers out on top of the wooden counter. As he began to sort them into chronological order he muttered and tutted to himself at the grease stains and tea rings that seemed to mar almost every front page. He smoothed out the creases and well-thumbed corners as he read them and stopped now and then to dwell on a banner headline, frowning and raking his fingers nervously through his hair.

MADMAN LOOSE IN NARROWS

THE MAD SLASHER STRIKES AGAIN

VAGRANT MURDERED AND TORN TO PIECES

He swallowed and bent closer over the spread of newspapers and read of the nightly murders. The earlier reports had labelled them the 'vagrant killings' and thought they were the work of some madman, but in the last two articles there was mention of the pathologist's report which suggested that the victim's horrific injuries might have been inflicted by some sort of wild beast that must have escaped from a zoo or a travelling circus. All police leave had been cancelled and marksmen had been put on special alert.

Ludo clenched his fist and smashed it down on the newspapers, making the arrow frog leap high into the air, croaking in alarm. He had never realized that his animals were killing every time they escaped out into the city. 'This has to stop,' he snarled angrily at the crowded room. 'I didn't bring you back to life to cause this . . . this . . . this catalogue of murder and mayhem. It has to stop. It must stop before the police catch you.'

He paused for breath, his lips quivering with emotion. Yellow specks of spittle clogged the corners of his mouth. 'No wonder you sometimes come back spattered with blood,' he muttered.

He suddenly caught his breath as he saw the photograph in the bottom right-hand corner of the newspaper dated two days after the first murder. He felt in the top pocket of his coat and fumbled with frantic fingers for his gold-rimmed spectacles to examine the picture more closely. He pulled them on and let a sigh of excitement escape his lips as the photograph leapt into focus. It was that woman.

The beautiful specimen that he had glimpsed standing in the moonlit courtyard on the night when he had first awoken the magic.

Pushing his thin-rimmed glasses up on to his forehead he read the headline and then quickly scanned the rest of the brief article below the picture:

AMERICAN BEAUTY BUYS THE WATCHGATE

Miss Tuppence Trilby, the international model and the most glamorous face of the nineties, has purchased the Watchgate, the oldest surviving house in the city, and plans to settle . . .

Ludo glanced up from the lines of type to his menagerie of animals and rubbed his fingers together. Perhaps the magic had touched her after all. Perhaps it was keeping her close to hand until he was ready to kill her and preserve her. He frowned and rubbed his chin thoughtfully as he wondered what he should do. He barely had a moment to think of anything but how to control the animals now the magic had resurrected them, but he could clearly remember the shimmering silk of her clinging dress and every graceful line and secret curve of her beautiful body as she stood in the moonlight.

He wetted his lips in anticipation and shivered with excitement to imagine preserving the perfect human specimen. Then he shook his head as he remembered that he had never tried to preserve human skin beyond simple mortuary embalming in his student days. Anyway, it would be far too dangerous. He would have dismissed the idea from his mind right there, but a sudden chilling thought struck him. The magic had responded to his desire for her and was probably keeping her close to him, caging her in the Watchgate, until he was completely ready to preserve her. He knew the magic had enough power to keep her there for ever. He shuddered as he realized that she would grow old before his eyes, in time her skin would yellow and wrinkle, her breasts would pucker and sag, if he didn't obey the magic and preserve her beauty before the years left their scars.

Ludo's eyes narrowed into cunning slits of madness as he reached beneath the counter and carefully fingered the ice-cold bottle of chloroform he kept there. He would have to kill her, but he hesitated. He would have to tread carefully, prepare everything thoroughly. She would have to vanish without a trace.

'I'll take a cast of her body in wax to make a perfect model before I skin her, then her skin will fit perfectly over it, but . . .' He paused and shook his head. He would have to experiment, to check that his preserving, degreasing and pickling solutions didn't harm the texture of her skin. And he wasn't even sure of the best way to stretch the skin over its new body. He didn't want a single bruise or blemish. How could he obtain human skin to experiment with? He had plenty of wood and wire to construct a dozen skeletons in the preparation room upstairs, but he still needed skin.

He wished now that the bears had brought back the bodies of those they had killed, but glancing at the murder reports, he realized that they would have been of no use. They had flayed and torn each victim to pieces; their skins would have been too bruised to have been of any use to him. No, he needed the recently dead, and he needed them in good condition.

And then in a flash of inspiration he realized where he could find an almost endless supply of corpses. He laughed a shrill maniacal shriek and almost danced around the counter.

Mortuaries and undertakers – even hospitals – had a constant supply of bodies. 'I can drive there in my van and wait until the dead of night and steal them.'

Ludo paused, unaware that the evil of Thomas Dunnich, smouldering in the Hand of Glory, was eating away at his sanity. His eyes were bright with lunacy as his mind raced ahead – to preserve human skin, to make it look and feel lifelike, would be the greatest challenge. A voice whispered inside his head: he must use the magic in the Hand of Glory to resurrect the dead. Ludo laughed. 'No time to waste. I must be quick, there is much to do,' he cried, scrabbling through the deep drawers of the counter, scattering their contents carelessly on to the floor as he searched for the keys to his ancient van.

He suddenly stopped and looked up at the two brown bears that waited on either side of the locked door, and slowly swept his narrowed, calculating eyes across the host of animals that filled the shop. Perhaps if he commanded them to watch her . . . perhaps it would keep them from wandering through the city.

'As from tonight, when darkness smothers everything, you shall keep guard for me on the Watchgate. You will shadow the American woman's every move. She must not escape.'

6

Echoes of Yesterday

Tuppence let the aroma of freshly ground coffee beans waft over her. She moved up to the narrow counter of the delicatessen stall and breathed in slowly through her nose, savouring the smell with her eyes tight shut, before she looked for her favourite blends. She leaned slightly forward on tiptoe, her fingertips gripping the counter for balance as she carefully searched the shelves of battered tins and glass jars. She had to study hard to decipher the spidery handwriting on the faded labels until her eyes alighted on a tin on the top shelf.

'Ah, you do have my favourite blend,' she cried, flashing a brilliant smile to the old man behind the counter as she pointed. 'I'll take a half-pound of that Colombian dark roast. Oh, and will you grind it fine for making filter coffee?' she added, stepping back and rummaging through her shoulder bag for her purse.

She glanced casually at her wrist watch. 'Damn,' she muttered as the coffee grinder whirred into life. She remembered she had agreed, under protest, to meet Richard in the entrance hall of the museum at the bottom of Elm Hill at 4.30. He had telephoned her three times since she got back from Scotland – he could always find one excuse or another – and she had the uneasy feeling that his motives were not professional. But he just wasn't her type. It would have been easier if he hadn't done so much for her, she could have just given him a straight 'no', but somehow she felt she had to let him down gently. Allowing him to show her around the museum seemed the best way to do it, but she would have been happier exploring it by herself. She preferred doing things like that on her own, just as she was enjoying wandering through the steep narrow walkways of the old Cattle Market.

She had first glimpsed the bright tented awnings from the bottom of Lobster Lane. She had seen them crowding the steep terraces of Castle Meadow between the weather-beaten roofs of the old city and she had caught the distant shouts of street traders plying their wares. The sights and sounds of the old market had fascinated her and drawn her to explore, in the first free afternoon that she had since she had got back from filming in Scotland.

The clattering whine of the coffee grinder rose to a shriek then abruptly stopped, and the old man emptied the ground coffee into a brown paper bag. Tuppence glanced up and smiled as the sounds of the market filled the silence and she heard again the flap and crackle of the awnings above her head, tugged about on the tall wooden frames of the stalls by the afternoon breeze. The castle clock struck four. She had lost all sense of time as she wandered through the steep narrow walkways of the market, follow-ing the exotic smells of spices, oiled leather, cabbages and cucumbers amongst the crowded stalls. It had seemed a magical place where the warm sunlight filtered down through the flapping sea of canvas and cast a thousand fleeting shadows over the ever-shifting crowds who drifted between the stalls.

'Your coffee, lady,' the stall-holder called, wetting his lips and smiling at her. He rattled her change and slapped it down hard on the counter beside the bag of coffee. Tuppence blinked and turned back.

'Oh, thanks, thanks a lot,' and she scooped up her change and let it tumble noisily into her purse. 'Your English money is heavier than ours. I reckon it sounds so much richer than the money I'm used to,' she laughed.

'I wish it was, lady,' the old man replied, following her with his eyes as she turned away and suddenly realizing where he had seen her before.

'Hey, you're that American – Tuppence Trilby – you are, aren't you? I've seen you on television, luv, an' I've seen your picture in the paper only a couple of weeks ago. You've bought that old house.'

Tuppence turned back. 'That's right,' she smiled.

The stall-holder stared at her for a moment and pushed his flat cap to the back of his balding head. His smile broadened.

'Well, miss, I don't get many famous people, celebrities and all that, buying their coffee here. I'll tell you straight, lady, there's none as beautiful as you so you make sure and come back here when the coffee's all gone.'

Tuppence looked at the market trader with surprise. His face was weather-roughened and coarse and his smile was all gaps and broken teeth, but there was a warmth and a genuine twinkle in his pale blue eyes that she hadn't expected. She laughed easily. 'I'll make a point of buying all my coffee here, only . . .' Tuppence paused and glanced over her shoulder to the maze of narrow walkways that crisscrossed one another in their steep descent towards the bottom of Castle Meadow, 'only I'm completely lost and I have to get to the museum on Elm Hill. You couldn't point out the way, could you?'

The trader laughed loudly. 'It's easy, luv. As long as you keep going downhill you can't miss it. Wait a minute, I'm going that way to make a delivery. I'll show you.'

*

Richard had arrived early at the Elm Hill museum. He glanced up at the large white-faced clock that hung in the vaulted entrance hall and checked it against his watch.

'Half an hour early,' he muttered nervously to himself, thrusting his hands into his pockets.

He began to pace slowly backwards and forwards just inside the tall wood-and-glass doors. The attendant who sat in an alcove beside the doors coughed and smiled up at him, but Richard shrugged off his advances into conversation and studiously ignored him. Quickening his pace, he muttered brisk apologies to the visitors he brushed against as he repeatedly paced the entrance hall.

He was impatient to meet with Tuppence again. He was more eager than he would have ever openly admitted and he sensed that she had seen through his pretence of wanting to discuss the work done on the Watchgate while she had been away in Scotland. He had parked quite close to the museum and noticed her sleek black Lotus outside the house. He had knocked on the door, but there had been no answer, and now, as he paced the echoing entrance of the museum, he glanced regularly out through the bevelled panels of glass in the swing doors, expecting to see her cross Elm Hill towards him.

The white-faced clock ticked away the seconds with leaden slowness. He broke the monotony of his pacing and moved up to the right-hand door to press his nose against the cool glass. Idly, he traced the patches of sun and shadow up Castle Street towards the bustling market stalls that stood in the kaleidoscope of shadowy colours that the sun had cast through the gaudy awnings of the Cattle Market. He caught his breath and stared harder as he saw Tuppence emerging from between two of the crowded stalls. He smiled, feeling his cheeks flush and the blood stir in his veins. He knew he was being a fool, but there was just something about her animal grace, her beauty, that ran riot with his emotions, and he knew he was out of his depth, but he couldn't help himself. Fumbling at his collar, he straightened his tie and ran his fingers lightly back through his hair to tidy the straggling ends that had fallen across his forehead. But as she crossed the last of the broad cobbles of Castle Meadow, leaving the crowded market behind, and walked into Castle Street, his smile stiffened and his face became an impassive mask. She was not alone.

One of those street traders was walking at her side in his tatty, soiled brown coat and greasy flat cap. They were laughing and talking as intimately as old friends. The man looked old enough to be her father and he was constantly touching her arm and pointing out the spires and churches of the city between the roofs of the houses. They walked so closely together that the crowds thronging the narrow pavements had to split apart to allow them to pass through side by side.

Richard trembled with jealousy. Tuppence had only once treated him with such familiarity, on the evening of the auction, and that was because he had secured the Watchgate for her. He ground his teeth as he gripped the ornate brass handle of the museum door and swung it open forcefully. Below the museum steps he heard Tuppence's soft bubbling laughter. She had her hand on the trader's arm and she was thanking him for something.

Richard couldn't quite catch the words but as she ran lightly up the steps she called across her shoulder, 'I'll be back in a couple of days for some more of that dark roast.'

The trader nodded eagerly as he waved his cap above his head, and for the briefest moment he looked up as if he would speak to Richard where he stood holding open the door. But then he smiled and winked, and turned away, whistling noisily as he disappeared amongst the crowd.

'Hi!' Tuppence called out, catching sight of Richard at the top of the steps, but her welcome smile evaporated as she realized that he was glaring at the retreating figure of the street trader.

In fact, Richard's large face was a trembling mask and as she drew level with him she could almost smell the jealousy oozing out of every pore. He blinked and tried to recover his composure but it was too late, his smile looked as though it had been cut out of crumbling cheese and his eyes still burned with anger.

Tuppence swept past him through the door without a word. Her instincts about him had been right. It had been a mistake to try to let him down gently. She sighed inwardly, wondering if she would ever meet anyone who was strong enough to rise above these petty jealousies. Her feelings for Richard hardened as she turned towards him. She was damned sure she wasn't going to allow him to spoil such a great afternoon. She paused beneath the museum clock and felt the atmosphere of the place close in all around her.

Richard noticed the blaze of anger in her eyes and realized that she must have seen his moment of jealousy.

'The Watchgate,' he started, quickly trying to shift himself on to safer ground, 'I thought that we had best meet to discuss the decorating.'

'Richard, I'm sorry, I can't stay, something's come up. Perhaps another time.' Her voice was hard, her dismissal final.

Richard hesitated. He had let his imagination build up something that wasn't there; he recognized her attempt at the gentle put-down and immediately tried to cover his embarrassment by pretending another engagement.

'Yes, of course, I'm rather busy, too. I'll telephone you when we both have more time, in a couple of days.'

He shrugged his shoulders, turned on his heel and hurried out of the museum. The doors swung behind him, their stiles rubbing against each other, masking his vanishing footsteps as they creaked shut.

Tuppence frowned and then let out a soft sigh. She hadn't meant to dismiss Richard quite so abruptly, but now he had gone she felt a sense of relief. Now she could savour this lovely old museum without interruption. She moved on through the open inner doors and suddenly stopped. The atmosphere of the huge vaulted building seemed to come alive. She listened and heard a whispering silence that spread out from where she stood. It was the strangest sound that she had ever heard and it filled the dry dusty museum, twisting and floating in the shafts of sunlight that flooded down through the tall fluted windows. It reflected from every polished riser of the wide wooden stairway that rose in graceful banistered curves to the long echoing galleries that flanked the broad aisle. Tuppence held her breath and listened more closely. She caught the echo of a thousand forgotten voices in the dusty light, she felt the rasp and clip of iron-shod hooves, the creak of leather and the musical jingle of harnesses.

The shadowy places beneath the galleries suddenly seemed crowded with tall uniformed figures. There was the flash of sunlight on cap badges, the glitter of epaulettes and gold braid in the darker edges. There were sword hilts everywhere, bayonets and slender polished lance tips all seemed to catch the light. Tuppence let her breath escape in a gasp and almost stepped backwards as she brought her hand up to shield her face. It was as if a great army had stirred all around her, yet the sound was so transparent it didn't even distort the specks of dust that danced in the shafts of sunlight or rustle as loudly as the summer leaves in a gentle breeze. It was less than the dry coughs and shuffles of the sleepy attendants who patrolled the upper galleries.

Tuppence blinked and the sounds melted away. Everything became still in the drowsy afternoon light. She sighed softly and breathed in the atmosphere. The moment of awe had vanished. She didn't feel afraid, yet her heart was racing, her fingers had tensed and were tingling. Indeed, somehow she felt safer than at any time in her life; she felt warm and protected. She stood on the threshold of history. If she listened hard she could still catch the whispers that ran through the silence all around her; she could eavesdrop on a million yesterdays that had been gathered here in this cathedral of the past.

Gradually her eyes were growing accustomed to the gloomy velvet light and soft shadows of the cavernous hall, and the faint sounds and movements of the summer visitors wandering through the galleries overhead fell into place. The ghostly army that had stirred in her imagination shrank slowly back and she let out a sigh of relief as she peered into the darker shadows beneath the lowest galleries and saw that the figures that she had thought had moved were nothing more than life-sized wax or cloth and wooden figures. They were soldiers and horses, skilfully sculptured into realistic poses that captured a last moment of heroism. She let her raised hand fall gracefully back to her side and realized as she did that she had been holding up the brown paper bag of coffee as if ready to hurl it at her imaginary attackers.

'You guys really had me going there for a moment,' she laughed, imagining the angry attendants' shouts had she thrown it, and the mess of finely ground beans spreading

out across the old pitched and polished floorboards of the museum.

Tuppence frowned and bit her lip. Her laughter and flippancy seemed out of place, almost harsh and piercing amongst these serious, grey-faced statues that crowded the aisle on either side of her.

'You people certainly knew how to dress to die,' she muttered sadly, letting her gaze wander amongst the glittering gold braid on their scarlet and royal-blue jackets, the rich dark bottle-green and sky-washed faded grey uniforms. If she half-closed her eyes she thought she could see every colour in the rainbow painted there, amongst the dark mahogany display cases that were piled high with the maps, the dispatch satchels and all the trinkets and bric-à-brac that had been harvested from the killing fields of war.

Tuppence frowned. She thrust the coffee into her shoulder bag and moved across the aisle into the shadow of the gallery, stopping beside a set piece of a cavalry officer in a splendid uniform of blue and gold in the act of mounting a chestnut charger. His left foot was thrust into the stirrup, the reins were gathered tightly in his left hand while he gazed ahead, his grey eyes straining into the darkness. The horse seemed almost crouching, waiting for him to spring into the saddle. Its neck was arched, its nostrils flared, and it looked as if it had caught the scent of battle.

'You look so real. I almost thought . . .' Tuppence hesitated, the words died on her lips. Standing this close she could see what looked like six patched-up bullet holes in the horse's chest, and the rough sabre slashes that had been darned in the cavalryman's uniform.

'Such a tragic waste,' she whispered, feeling a wave of revulsion flood over her at all the senseless killing encapsulated in these heroic figures.

The museum was not at all what she had thought it would be. She had expected to see suits of armour propped against the walls, swords and shields, and even the artefacts of torture from a bygone age, they couldn't be left out, they had to be there somewhere dotted amongst the museum's relics. But she didn't expect to see this echoing shrine to blood and brutal butchery, this Colossus to the glory of war. She began to turn away, eager for the shouts and bustle of the Cattle Market and the throng of life and the hot sun's shadows beneath the flapping awnings, when something made her stop and turn back suddenly. She could have sworn that she had seen the horseman move, out of the corner of her eye. She stared at the rucks and creases in his crimson trousers, where his left leg reached for the stirrup, and the tight swell of his buttocks and the bulging calf muscle in his right leg pushed against the coarse cloth.

The model-maker had captured the moment so realistically, balancing the cavalryman on the toes and ball of his right foot, that the closer she looked the more lifelike the figure became. It seemed as if he had merely paused, waiting for her to move away, before he sprang lightly up into the saddle. Her eyes were drawn down to the steel scabbard and to the crimson dispatch bag that hung by three leather straps from a thin waist belt of scarlet leather overlaid with gold lace. The dispatch bag was moving. It was brushing gently against the sword scabbard as it swayed slightly from side to side.

'NO! Oh no, this is not possible,' she hissed, her eyes widening in alarm.

'It's the draught, miss, it makes everyone look twice.' The sudden voice right beside her made Tuppence jump and cry out.

'What? Oh, yes,' she gasped, struggling to regain her

composure. She was too startled to be angry with the old white-haired attendant, who must have crept up on her from the alcove beside the swing doors. He was now standing close by her, his thumbs in his waistcoat pockets, a beaming smile wrinkling the ends of his moustache and a bright twinkle in his eyes.

'Beautiful, ain't they, miss, so real and lifelike.' His voice seemed to swell with pride as he swept his right hand out across the broad aisle. 'And it's the biggest collection of uniforms in England, you know. The director of the museum here has been collecting them for years and you won't find them set out like this anywhere else in the world. You know, the model-makers have spent months sometimes setting up these displays, and each one represents a heroic deed or a moment of glory.'

The old attendant's enthusiasm for the exhibits was beginning to infect Tuppence. 'I really thought I saw it move,' she whispered darkly.

The attendant chuckled and drew closer to her. 'I've heard people say there's an atmosphere in here – ghosts and the like. Sometimes I've even heard voices, well, sort of whispers, echoes in the silence.' He paused and glanced cautiously over each shoulder and then quickly scanned the rails of the galleries overhead. 'You can touch him if you like. Go on, feel the cavalryman's sleeve or the horse's neck, that'll prove they can't move, miss. Only be quick, before my guv'nor sees you, he's very touchy about visitors handling the exhibits, but I don't see the harm in it if it puts your mind at rest.'

Tuppence gingerly reached out to touch the horseman's arm. The cloth felt old and threadbare and she noticed a fine layer of dust in the creases. She ran her hand along the horse's neck and felt the cold hard stuffing that lay beneath its soft silky skin.

'I'll walk you through the museum, miss, and point out our best exhibits, if you'd like me to.'

Tuppence smiled at the old man and nodded. 'Thank you, that would be nice, but,' she hesitated, 'do you have a floor where you keep the really old stuff, some time around the Middle Ages, only that's what I came in here to see. I'm looking for some information on the Watchgate, the house across the road.'

The old man smiled and shook his head as he began to move slowly forward. 'There are a few suits of armour, pikes and swords and things on the upper galleries, but the early artefacts are kept on display up in the castle. There are a few books for that period in the vaults of this museum, but you'll have to write and ask permission if you want to see them.'

Tuppence glanced back over her shoulder and let her gaze linger for a moment on the cavalryman before she followed the attendant. There was a trace of disappointment and a wistful shadow of regret in her eyes that the fantasy wouldn't last a moment longer.

'Who was he?' she asked quietly, hearing her voice echo eerily between the silent figures as if they were pressing in closer to listen on either side of the aisle. 'The cavalryman back there. You said each model told a story – who was he?'

The old attendant stopped in his tracks and slowly turned back towards her. There was a haunting softness in her voice that made him want to tell her everything he knew about each of the silent figures.

'It's called "mounting up before the battle", miss. The handwritten label that's tied to the cuff of the uniform says it belonged to a Captain Chard of the 11th Hussars, but I doubt if that was the horse he rode because that one came with a whole batch from the Imperial War Museum some twenty years ago. I saw them arrive and I'll never forget it. They looked most strange all piled up in the back of a removal van, their legs and heads wrapped up in swathes of soft packaging to stop them getting damaged. It seems some enthusiast had skinned the lot of them after a battle in the Crimea, and he'd gone and stuffed them or pickled them or whatever it was they did to preserve them right back in the 1850s. Anyway, the Imperial didn't have room for them so they were sent here, and that's how the whole exhibition began. The horses are the real things. The ones with manes are officers' chargers and the ones with their manes hogged were either troop horses or gun-carriage horses.'

The old man paused and drew in a rasping breath as he swept his hand across the crowded figures that lined the museum. 'You know, I've never told this to anyone before, but sometimes I feel a great sadness when I walk amongst the horses. Their eyes seem to shine – no, not shine, glow, yes, glow with a lustre that I can't explain.'

'Perhaps that atmosphere comes from so many bright beginnings being cut short by death,' Tuppence murmured, shaking her head sadly.

The attendant laughed awkwardly and clapped his hands. The sound echoed like a pistol shot in the silence.

'Now I have made you all morbid, miss. I'm sorry, I didn't mean to do that. Look over there to your right. That display of guardsmen in their busbies and grey greatcoats, they are from the Battle of Inkerman, and that gun carriage and six horses ahead of us are the Royal Horse Artillery going into action. And there's two of the Taplow Lancers bringing their lances down to charge, and there's a dozen more hussars at the trot beyond them and . . .'

Tuppence glanced down at her watch as the old man spoke and realized that it was almost six o'clock.

'Oh, I'm really sorry, I've talked the whole afternoon away,' he exclaimed, 'and there's still one exhibit you really must see before you leave, that is if you'll allow me to show it to you.'

Tuppence smiled at him. He was so gentle, so considerate and so in love with the place that she would hate to disappoint him. 'Yes, why not, I'm not in a rush. Lead on.'

The old attendant's enthusiasm for the exhibits in his care ran away with him as he led her in amongst them, gesticulating and pointing excitedly, first to a troop of lancers, their bright pennants stretched out in an imaginary breeze from their lance tips, then to a galloping dispatch rider crouched low across his horse's neck.

Skirmish scouts and gunners crowded on every side. The figures were set closer together beneath the gallery and it was becoming difficult for Tuppence to see a clear route between them in the fading early evening light.

'Hey, slow down, you're leaving me behind,' she called out, almost stumbling over the prone figure of a rifleman that lay behind a hastily arranged pile of wooden ammunition boxes. He was staring over the barricade, measuring his field of fire, perhaps looking at his range marker. The breech of his carbine was open and he was reaching with his free hand into his ammunition pouch for another bullet.

'Oh, sorry,' Tuppence murmured to the rifleman, hesitating, and then she stepped back, feeling a little foolish the moment the words had left her mouth. What on earth was she doing apologizing to a dummy, for Chrissake? Nevertheless she skirted the redoubt of ammunition boxes rather than step over them and then paused and looked back at the rifleman, feeling the hairs on her neck prickling.

'I'll swear there wasn't a smile puckering the corners of his mouth when I almost tripped over him. I wish there

85

was enough light to take a closer look,' she whispered to herself as she glanced anxiously up at the towering silent figures in the busbies and plumed shakos. As she did so she became more aware of the glistening bayonets and lance tips and the darker shadowy shapes of the men and horses that stood so statue-still around her. The atmosphere felt tense and electric, as if everything in the museum was holding its breath and waiting for something to happen.

'Wait where you are and I'll turn the light on,' the attendant called out helpfully.

She heard the click of a light switch and stark shadows suddenly flickered and danced between the figures. For the briefest second, no more than a flash, she would have sworn that everything moved. Eyes blinked and heads turned towards her, chargers tossed their heads, their nostrils flared and pinpoints of light reflected from their polished bridles as their tails swished. She breathed a sigh of relief as one by one the white fluorescent tubes flooded the area beneath the gallery with bright light, banishing the moving shadows.

Tuppence hurried between a group of lancers who were gathered around a realistic-looking cooking fire and two loaders in scarlet coats from the African wars breaking open an ammunition box to where the old man waited for her. In the distance Tuppence heard the last of the afternoon visitors passing through the swing doors of the museum. The attendant sensed her impatience and hurried on.

'It's only a dozen steps, miss. You won't be disappointed, I promise you. It's the most dramatic exhibit we have and this is the best time of day to see it, with the evening sunlight streaming down through the west windows.'

'Well, OK, but it's getting rather dark in here,' she muttered reluctantly.

'There's nothing to be afraid of, miss. Just keep close to me,' he whispered.

His beaming face vanished in shadow as he flicked off the light switch. He turned on his heel and hurried towards the far end of the museum.

'I'll lose my way again if you don't wait for me,' Tuppence called, reaching out to feel her way along the wall as the area beneath the gallery plunged back into gloomy half-light. She was afraid of losing sight of the old attendant, who moved surprisingly quickly between the exhibits.

'Damn!' she muttered to herself as she almost bumped into a group of troopers bivouacked against the wall, and she almost tripped over the attendant's heels as she barely noticed him in the gloom where he was waiting for her at the end of the gallery. Ahead of her she could just make out the dark bulk of the main staircase, sweeping up and away from her. There were shafts of sunlight streaming down to her right on to what looked like a jumble of figures in the centre of the aisle but she couldn't quite make out what they were supposed to represent through the rows of display cases and the figures that blocked her view. The attendant took her arm and led her forward to the foot of the stairs.

'Now turn around very slowly, miss,' he whispered.

The sound of his voice melted away into the vast electric silence and she felt his hand touching her arm as lightly as silk, as he rotated her towards the shafts of sunlight.

Tuppence blinked and caught her breath and then let out a cry as she instinctively crouched down to avoid the galloping hooves. She would have fallen backwards on to the first tread of the wide wooden staircase had not the old man firmed his grip on her arm and steadied her.

Struggling to regain her balance she stared up at the Guards officer who was galloping his horse over the gun carriage straight to where she stood.

Gradually Tuppence overcame the sensation that the horse was going to land on top of her. The exhibit was unnerving and she found the impulse to step back almost impossible to ignore. In the shafts of sunlight the dapple-grey horse seemed to be rushing at her, its mouth gaping open, the bars of the bit pressing brutally down on its lolling tongue. Its nostrils were flared and flushed bright pink with blood and the whites of its eyes, ringing the dark brown irises, were red with panic. She imagined she could hear its rasping breaths, the thunder of its hooves and the shouts and screams of war as the charger bore down on her, galloping at full tilt through the wreaths of battle smoke to leap wildly over the gun carriage.

'No! Surely it's not possible to paint death so vividly and in so much bloody detail,' she whispered sadly, shaking her head. She wanted to turn away, to shut her eyes to the horrors of war that the galloping horse portrayed, yet her eyes were drawn towards it and she found herself studying every crease in the faded uniforms, every detail that the model-makers had put in those butchered gunners that lay strewn in shadow beneath the wheels of the gun carriage. She studied the regimental drum, the trodden shakos and the shattered lances and rifle butts that choked the wheel ruts in the artificial mud. Slowly her eyes travelled upwards towards the barrel of the gun, dwelling for a moment on the body of a gunner who lay spreadeagled across the breech clutching at the broken lance that pierced his chest. The flying hooves of the dappled charger were stretched out just above him, almost grazing his dirty face, casting stark shadows from the evening sunlight across his bloody uniform.

Beyond the breech of the gun and on the edge of the sunlight, she could see a dense press of uniformed figures who were surging forward against the rider, thrusting their bayonets and sabres at him. She frowned and looked up at the rider. He was unarmed, his blue uniform was torn and bloody and he was reaching out as far to the right of his horse as he dared, to snatch at a battle standard, thrusting his outstretched fingers down into the forest of steel bayonets and sabre blades to retrieve it.

Tuppence felt a quickened, uplifting heartbeat. Although she had never set foot in this museum before, and certainly she had never set eyes on this exhibit, she wanted to cheer the rider, to see him snatch the standard free and escape. And yet, as she opened her mouth, the shout of encouragement choked in her throat and tears for the tragedy sculpted there before her wet the corners of her eyes. As she looked more closely she could see that the bayonets had pierced the rider's legs and sides and there were cuts and slashes in the horse's neck and flanks that the taxidermist's needles had not quite managed to disguise. The saddle cloth and sabretache were both scarred with sabre cuts and the epaulettes and gold lace on the high collar of the rider's uniform were torn loose and darkened with blood. She realized that the long red weals from the horseman's spurs along the flanks of the horse had been cut there for nothing; their race in amongst the enemy had been in vain.

Tuppence sighed sadly and glanced beyond the wounded horseman into the gloomy, echoing museum, to where a solid wall of soldiers in scarlet coats was set in the shape of a horseshoe waiting for the onslaught of their enemy, some crouching, some kneeling and some standing. They were shoulder to shoulder and they rose in tiers to the depth of three men. As the last rays of sunlight poured down through the west window it lit up their sombre faces and reflected on their rifle barrels and the spent cartridge cases that littered the floor and were piled up against the legs of the front rank of soldiers kneeling at the base of the human redoubt.

'The atmosphere! I felt their breaths, I heard their whispers dying away,' Tuppence breathed softly, her lips barely moving. 'I heard the sound of the endless sadness trapped here in these figures.'

The old attendant blinked suddenly and turned his head towards her. The sound of her voice had brought him back from some far-off memory.

'No, it's not all sadness and death,' he answered quickly, pointing up at the leaping horseman, then he swept his age-flecked hand out across the redoubt of Rourke's Drift to the thousand and one other shadowy figures on either side of the vast gloomy hall.

'No, they reflect hope and moments of great sacrifice and . . .' The attendant paused, his lips trembling slightly and his eyes searching amongst the silent statues as if he was willing them to shout back the answers he was looking for.

'Hope! How can that poor wretch up there on the leaping horse give you hope? He's being cut down, torn from the saddle by those bayonets. And what the hell are those guys waiting for if not to die?' she demanded, pointing angrily at the redoubt, her voice sounding harsh and sharp in the darkening silence.

The old attendant suddenly laughed, the sound chuckling in his throat. 'No, miss, you've got it quite wrong. If the light was better I would insist that you read the plaque; that would tell you it's not all about dying. Why, the horses here carried our history on their backs, it's through them and the men who rode on them and marched behind them that today is what it is. But I didn't bring you here, miss, to learn about history, no. It was to experience the thrill of seeing Colonel Hawkesbury leap out of the half-light over that gun carriage, because at this time of day you can't see the steel rods that support the horse.'

Tuppence looked up again at the horseman and caught her breath. She was sure that neither she nor the attendant had moved since they had turned to look at the exhibit and yet the horseman was now staring down, his sea-grey eyes looking directly into hers. There was the ghost of a smile on the corners of his lips. She felt her spine tingle with panic.

'He's moved! I'll swear he's looking right at me! Let's get out of here before it gets any darker,' she hissed, gripping the attendant's arm quite fiercely and dragging him with quickening footsteps towards the far end of the museum and the swing doors that opened on to Elm Hill.

'I'm sure it was only the changing light that made the figures look as though they moved, miss,' the attendant offered apologetically as they neared the exit.

'What do you mean, the light plays tricks? That Colonel was staring right down at me as bold as brass. It was unnerving the way he was looking right inside me, and statues, dummies, call them what you like, they can't do that.'

They were getting quite close to the entrance hall. The evening light was shining through the glass doors, making it easier to see. Tuppence heard the attendant's breath rasping in his throat and she eased her pace a little. She felt safer now they were closer to the exit.

'Tell me, why did that Colonel jump his horse over the gun carriage?' she asked as they reached the swing doors to the street.

The attendant smiled and sucked in a shallow breath.

'He rescued the colours and turned defeat into victory just as it's portrayed in the exhibit.'

'But the French are hacking at him. And look at the horse, surely they must have killed them both?' Tuppence exclaimed.

The old man had pulled the door open for her and now stood there, smiling broadly. She could hear the hum of the city and catch the smells of the market on the warm evening breeze. 'No, miss, they both got clean away from those French butchers, and legend has it that the dapple-grey charger the Colonel rode that day stayed with him throughout his military life and eventually died of old age and was laid to rest beneath a cherry tree in his garden.'

Tuppence laughed with relief and flashed a brilliant smile at him. 'He must have been quite a guy, that Colonel, but . . .' she hesitated, peering over the old man's shoulder back into the gloomy depths of the museum, 'but what about the grim-faced circle of soldiers in red coats all crowded together, one on top of the other? Were they staring out into the shadow of death? Were they only moments from eternity?'

The attendant followed her gaze and absently combed at the ends of his moustache. 'Oh, no, miss,' he laughed when he realized which exhibit she was looking at. 'That's what's left of the second battalion of the 24th. The exhibit portrays the moment when that desperate band of only one hundred men brought the full might of 4,000 charging Zulu warriors to a dead halt, and they were the fiercest warriors in the world. The tale goes, miss, that in the sudden awful silence that spread through Rourke's Drift you could have heard a pin drop as the 24th stared out at that sea of black faces and then, would you believe it, they began to sing their battle hymn, "Men of Harlech", to give themselves the courage to face the next wave of the attack.

But the Zulus never charged again. No, miss, they just stood there, rank upon rank, as far as the eye could see in the fading twilight, and then, without a sign or a signal, they began to beat their assegais on their shields in honour of the brave handful of soldiers in the redoubt. While the echoes of their salute rumbled and thundered through the surrounding foothills the Zulu warriors vanished, they just disappeared. What do you make of that?'

Tuppence breathed a sigh of relief. This old museum attendant could really tell a story. She searched the cavernous shadows of the broad aisle over his shoulder and smiled as she picked out the mass of scarlet coats and the forest of rifle barrels that bristled from the redoubt. She touched the attendant's arm and thanked him for sharing the museum with her. 'You Brits sure have a lot of style! It's a pity that the best of them are just history now – I would have just loved to meet them.'

The old man laughed. 'Don't you be so sure, miss. There are new heroes born into every age.'

'Yes, that's right.' She laughed with him before she turned and ran easily down the stone steps of the museum, calling across her shoulder, 'And it's also true that every dame in distress needs one!'

'Call again,' he shouted after her as she crossed over Elm Hill towards the Watchgate. 'We're open from ten a.m. every day.'

He listened for a moment to the fading tap of her footsteps on the cobbles and then sighed softly. He let the door of the museum swing slowly shut as he absently smoothed his moustache and stared thoughtfully into the shadows of the broad aisle. The American woman had stirred up feelings inside him that he had thought were long dead. She was the most beautiful, graceful creature he had ever set eyes on and if he had only been forty years younger . . . He smiled as the possibilities painted themselves in his mind, then he shook his head and scattered the brief pictures. It wasn't her beauty, or her melting smile, or even the soft drawl of her voice that had unsettled him; it was the way her presence had seemed to electrify the atmosphere of the museum. It was as if she had almost brought the exhibits to life as she passed between them. She had even noticed that Colonel Hawkesbury was staring right at her and although he had passed it off as a trick of the light he frowned to himself as he thought of it. Now that he was alone he could almost hear the uneasy whisperings that seemed to fill the darkness, and for the first time in all his years of shuffling to and fro through the darkened museum, locking and unlocking doors, he hesitated to leave the lighter entrance hall. He was afraid, and he felt that he was standing on the threshold of some awesome power that moved between the exhibits. He hadn't dared admit the worst of it. Every figure that the American woman had passed had seemed to follow her with its eyes.

He shivered and fumbled with the heavy key ring for the key to the swing doors and purposefully locked and bolted them. He was being an old fool – getting goose bumps over a beautiful woman young enough to be his grand-daughter and jumping at shadows. He was letting his imagination run away with him.

'Heroes indeed,' he muttered as he let the keys jangle noisily from his right hand to give him confidence as he made his way slowly up the broad aisle towards the back entrance. He had parachuted into Arnhem, he had fought on the beaches at Normandy, he had already walked through the shadows of death and he had never faltered. He knew what courage was all about but still his scalp tingled and his flesh crawled with each footstep.

The creaking and whispering, the jingle of harness and

the murmuring of a thousand voices could be heard all around him. It abruptly stopped as he passed by and then started up again even more urgently behind him. It was as if orders were being passed from mouth to mouth amongst the whisperings. Twice when he stopped and spun round he was confronted with a wall of utter silence that was even more awful than the echoing whispers.

The rear doors to the museum were set behind the main staircase and he hurried towards them as fast as he could manage, giving the leaping Colonel at the base of the stairs the briefest of glances as he passed by. The horseman was silhouetted against the west windows and the setting sun had hazed the fluted glass with molten rivulets of fire. It looked as though the city was burning fiercely and gave a fitting backdrop to that desperate ride to snatch back the regimental colours.

'I don't know what this is all about – frightening visitors and all – but it really has to stop,' he shouted at the vast echoing room as he fitted the key into the lock and slammed the door shut.

7

The Nightmare Begins

It wasn't just the eerie atmosphere of the museum that had made Tuppence impatient to leave. She had a film shoot on the east coast in the morning; that meant an early start and she wanted to catch a bite to eat before she returned to the Watchgate for the night. Earlier, while she was exploring the Cattle Market, she had caught sight of a row of cafés and bistros on the far side of Castle Meadow and they had looked so inviting, so festive, almost Mediterranean with their crowded tables and bright umbrellas sprawling out across the cobbled pavements.

With these in mind she had hurried into Lobster Lane thinking that it would be the quickest route, but now less than a hundred yards into the steep, badly lit road she had begun to regret her haste; she felt as if someone was following her, watching her. She slowed her stride and caught the distinctive sound of a set of footsteps behind her. Her skin crawled and quite clearly she remembered the morning's headline telling of yet another murder in the old part of the city. She had been a fool to think of short cuts with a murderer loose in the neighbourhood. She increased her pace again, listening intently, and immediately heard the following echo quicken, too.

She felt panic tighten into a knot in her stomach. This wasn't the England she had imagined, this was meant to be a quiet, safe city. She wanted to kick off her high-heeled shoes and run, but the lane became darker and steeper ahead of her and her legs felt as weak as jelly. It had been a long time since she had allowed herself to get into a situation like this.

'Damn! Damn! Damn!' she muttered under her breath as she fought to pull herself together.

She had to think fast, she had to stay cool. She tried to act naturally before she looked over her shoulder. She had to look as if nothing was wrong and she knew that once she turned her head she would have about five seconds to act, to dodge, strike out, run like hell, scream, whatever it took. She had grown up on the East Side, she knew all about body language and how important it was to give nothing away. She must not let him know that she knew he was following her. Casually, as if she didn't have a care in the world, she stepped off the narrow pavement into the centre of the lane and loosened her shoulder bag, gathering up the long leather strap tightly around her hand so that she could wield it like a club. The bag felt heavy, weighed down with the coffee and the other groceries she had bought. She withdrew the key to the Watchgate and gripped it tightly in her other hand.

She glanced over her shoulder, half turning as she did so. To a casual onlooker she was merely looking back at some architectural feature that had caught her interest amongst the crumbling brickwork. But her eyes were glitter sharp and scanned every shadow and dark opening that stretched away behind her to the bottom of Lobster Lane.

'Damn!' she hissed again. The lane was empty, ominously empty, and there were at least twenty, maybe more, dark alleyways and low archways for an attacker to hide in between the houses on either side of where she stood and the junction with Elm Hill. And there must be even more before she reached the safety of the Watchgate.

A car drove slowly along Elm Hill and she willed it to turn up the lane, but its engine faded and blended with the hum of the city. Right now Tuppence would have given anything for a street full of people, a crowd of party-goers even, filling the lane, but even one solitary old bag lady trailing along in the gutter would have been enough. The shadowing footsteps had stopped the moment she turned. She didn't have a clue on which side of the lane her attacker waited and that steep hundred yards of uneven cobbles looked about as treacherous as the north face of the Eiger.

Quite suddenly a cat meowed in the alleyway closest to her and a white barn owl silently swooped down low across her head, touching her with its wing tips. 'Jesus Christ!' she cried, striking out at the bird with her bag, knocking it fluttering to the ground as she leapt forward.

All around her shrieks and animal howls were issuing from every black archway. Her heart pounded in her chest, her feet flew over the cobbles. As she fled she saw huge shapes crowding out of dark archways, pushing forward, reaching out as if to touch her. Breathlessly, she reached the corner of Elm Hill. Behind her, the lane was echoing to howling screams, the scrape of claws and the clatter of unshod hooves. She could also hear the dragging of unhuman footsteps.

She knew she dared not look round and she threw herself around the corner, stumbling over the gutter as she ran for the door of the Watchgate. Sobbing and fumbling she inserted the heavy iron key in the lock and twisted it open with all her strength. Something was touching her back, gripping at her arms and her legs. She screamed and hurled herself against the carved door, breaking free from whatever it was that was trying to catch her. The door creaked open and she fell headlong over the threshold.

The howls and shrieks of pursuit were now less than a

footstep from the open doorway. They were pouring after her over the threshold and with the screams hideous misshapen shadows fell across where she knelt, hiding the light from the street lamps, blackening the flagstones and paralysing her with terror.

'I must get up. I have to lock the door somehow!' she cried, scrambling away from the advancing shadows, but the more she struggled to escape into the Watchgate the louder the howling grew behind her until it echoed so violently in the inglenook it dislodged an avalanche of soot that cascaded in black clouds down the chimney and billowed out across the hearth.

'Help! Oh help me, someone . . . help me, for Chrissake!' she shouted, clawing desperately with her fingernails at the smooth cracks between the flagstones.

Behind her the door creaked noisily on its iron hinges and something quite heavy landed on the floor beside her, bouncing once with a metallic ring. Tuppence turned her head and stared down to see the ornate iron key that she had inserted in the outside of the door. She could have wept for joy. But that moment withered inside her as she fought the panic within. She must still find the strength and courage to pick it up and turn and face whatever nightmares had swarmed out of those dark alleyways to chase her. She had to do it herself, there was no one else. She had to throw her weight against the door and slam it shut to lock it.

But before her hand could close around the cold metal shank of the key a sudden gust of air blew through the Watchgate. It ruffled her hair, knotting and stringing it across her face. It pulled at the rugs scattered on the flagstones and caught up the open pages of the magazines, left carelessly scattered on the two low coffee tables, making them flap and crackle. The air felt dry and warm against her skin and yet it smelt old, thick and musty as if it had lain dormant, shut away in some dark cupboard compressed between pages in a library of ancient books. It swirled around her, tugging at her sleeves, rippling at the silk of her skirt. It touched her hair just as a blind man would touch each fold and curve, each graceful line of her face or hand to know her. So the wind sighed and whispered through the Watchgate. It wove through itself the sound of the echo of iron-shod hooves, neighing horses and the tapping of leather boots; it drew together all the noises from a long-forgotten age. The sounds in the wind eddied faster and faster around her. Now the horses were galloping, the sounds grew shrill and rose into an earsplitting screech and swept right past her.

Behind her, the heavily carved door of giants slammed violently shut. The gust of wind fell away to nothing, whispering as it vanished across the bolts at the top and bottom of the door, pushing and rattling the hasps firmly into the staples on the door jamb. The Watchgate was plunged into darkness without the orange light of the street lamps that had flooded across the open threshold.

Tuppence huddled where she knelt just inside the door, wrapped in a tight ball on the floor. Her eyes were screwed shut and she was trembling uncontrollably from head to foot. Her breaths came in short sobs, her heart was pounding so loud that its sound was the only thing she could hear. Gradually the thudding lessened. She blinked and opened her eyes to find that the darkness was thick enough to touch and it was wrapped so claustrophobically around her that she couldn't even see her own hands if she held them up against her face. She slowed her breathing and listened, straining her ears against the smothering blackness, realizing that the room was wrapped in an eerie silence, that the howls of the chase, the hum of the city and every little scrape and scuttle of sound that made up normal silence had vanished into the dark. She wanted to laugh out loud, to blink and find everything back to normal. She wanted to pinch herself and prove that it wasn't a nightmare. But she was afraid, afraid that the sound of her own voice would be sucked away from her and drowned in the clinging silence. She remembered the light switch on the wall beside the door.

She reached out and felt for the wall and her hand seemed to stretch on for ever through the darkness. Suddenly her fingers found and touched something cold and hard. She explored the blackness until she felt the worn threshold stone and then the grain of the wood at the bottom of the door. She rose slowly to her feet, pressing herself flat against the grainy surface of the wood, clinging with her fingers to the rough iron hinges as if she would drown or slip backwards into a bottomless quickmire if she so much as eased her grip. Now she could search for the light switch.

Reaching out inch by inch her fingertips journeyed across the landscape of the ancient door, touching knot holes as deep as craters, following wandering thunder-cracks and warps in the timber. At times the cracks felt as wide and meandering as river gorges and at last she found a ribbon of carvings, flowers, petals and sheaves of summer corn, that she remembered crossed the door just above the latch. She followed them to the door jamb and felt the cold plaster and brickwork of the wall next to it. She paused; the darkness was thinning. She could see vague shapes in the room, the high-backed chairs, low coffee tables, pictures on the wall, but the far end of the room was still as black as the mouth of hell itself.

The inglenook gaped back at her. She searched the wall and quickly found the light switch close to her hand. She

flicked it on. As light flooded the low-beamed room she breathed a sigh of relief and quickly scanned the room for any of her pursuers, but it was empty. It looked exactly as she had left it, except for the magazines that lay scattered haphazardly across the floor where the gust of wind had left them. Smuts of soot dirtied the hearth. Sinking down, she sat on the threshold stone and rested her back against the door as she wiped her hand across her forehead.

'What the hell's going on . . . ?' she began, when the door shook violently with the sound of hammering.

Tuppence cried out and leapt away from it, her spine tingling, and then spun round to face the doorway, her hands held up to protect her face. Beyond the door she heard a savage growling and what sounded like claws raking across the carvings of the knights and their beautiful horses.

'No . . . no . . . leave me alone,' she sobbed, backing away from the door. She felt so helpless, so alone and vulnerable. It would only be a matter of time before the door gave way.

She was sure that whatever had swarmed out of those alleyways and courtyards in Lobster Lane to chase her was not human. The monsters she had glimpsed as she fled were like nothing she had ever seen before – huge lumbering creatures, armed with teeth and claws, devils with horns that towered over her and beasts running on all fours trying to overtake her, filling the night with their wild animal screams. She shuddered and looked around desperately for something to defend herself with.

Step by step she retreated to the inglenook and armed herself with the only implement that she could see, a heavy brass and iron poker. The clawing at the door was getting louder and whatever was hammering was rattling the locks so that the staples were beginning to splinter on the door jamb. It wouldn't last more than a few minutes now. Soon, whatever was outside would break in. Tuppence sobbed and raised the poker.

'What I need right now is one of those heroes from the museum. Someone help me!' she cried.

The wind that had slammed the door rose again behind her. It came from the inglenook and scattered the layer of soot and carried it in eddies into the room. It caressed her arms and legs, bringing with it the sharp odour of soot and a thousand whispering wailing voices. It hissed and shrieked between the chairs, billowed the curtains and pressed hard against the door and held it firmly shut. Suddenly there seemed to be hoofbeats in the road outside. She could hear shouts and the sound of shots. The clawing and the hammering on the door stopped and the howling of her pursuers grew faint and then faded completely away. Tuppence stood rigid, still clutching the poker, and listening to the silence. The hoofbeats, too, had faded into the distance and the wind that had risen in the inglenook had melted away.

'What sort of place is this? What the hell's going on?' she muttered, instinctively keeping a firm grip on the poker as she slowly retraced her steps across the room towards the small leaded window that looked out on to Elm Hill.

Stooping, she peered through the glass and looked to the left and the right. A car was climbing the hill, shifting noisily through the gears, its headlights throwing long, moving shadows across the uneven cobbles and illuminating every nook and cranny. As its glow passed the Watchgate she saw that the street was empty except for her Lotus parked outside, and nothing moved or seemed to be hiding in any of the dark doorways. It all looked safe and ordinary in the orange light that shone down from the two wrought-iron lamps set high on the wall opposite.

'Well, that's just not possible . . .' she frowned, 'there's nothing out there, nothing to show anything happened at all. I'd be hard pushed to convince anyone that the door just locked itself . . .' she muttered as she glanced down to where the key lay on the floor. She took another look through the small leaded window and then hesitantly drew the bolts.

Those creatures, whatever they were, must have left claw marks on the pavement and scrapes and gouges on the door. There must be some sign outside that would prove they had been real; that they had really attacked the Watchgate.

'I've got to know. I've got to see for myself,' she whispered as she screwed up her courage and lifted and pulled on the latch. The door refused to budge an inch. It seemed stuck fast, as if held by some strange power. She stepped back and frowned as she glanced anxiously over her shoulder and stared into the room. There was something supernatural about the place. She couldn't quite understand it; there was something in the atmosphere, something that she had been much too busy to take heed of, that she had casually written off as 'history' when she had sensed it on that first evening. No, that wasn't altogether true. It had always been there on the edges of her sight, half seen, half heard, only now it seemed to be pressing right up against her. She had felt something similar in the museum as she walked amongst the exhibits that afternoon, similar and yet completely different. In the museum the feeling had been more urgent, more vital, almost directed at her personally. Here in the Watchgate the power, or whatever it was, felt older, more a part of the fabric of the building.

'It can't be ghosts, or certainly no ghost I've ever heard of,' she muttered, shaking her head.

Ghosts were once people. They appear and disappear in

some sort of semblance of whom they once were, and the temperature is supposed to plummet. The atmosphere in the Watchgate was too solid to be full of ghosts and the wind had touched everything with that musty smell and had barred the door against whatever was chasing her. Tuppence shivered; it was unnerving being so close to something so old that she didn't understand.

She reached out and lifted the latch and the door opened. She frowned and glanced anxiously around the room again, not quite knowing what to expect. This was the strangest haunting, if it was a haunting. The door swung easily towards her with barely a creak from its hinges and she gasped as she saw the gouges and scratchings that now spoilt the beautiful carving.

'I have got to take a quick look outside,' she gasped to herself, stepping up on to the threshold and leaning out as far as she dared without leaving the safety of the room. She didn't altogether trust the atmosphere inside the Watchgate; it might slam the door against her or crush her fingers if she tried to venture too far outside. She wanted to keep her options open until she knew a few of the answers.

Elm Hill had looked so safe, the quaint old houses leaning against each other as they climbed up the hill towards Tombland and the galleries, their black beams creating magical shapes and patterns in the light from the hanging lamps that lined the hill. To Tuppence it now looked a steep, treacherous street, with too many black cracks and narrow openings for her howling pursuers to leap from. She thought of making a dash to her car and racing out of the city, but where would she flee to? She didn't know anybody in England well enough to turn up on their doorstep late at night. Then something caught her eye, a movement at the far end of the street. Something was passing slowly through the lamplight into the shadows near the museum entrance. That made her mind up for her. She ducked back into the Watchgate with her heart pounding and slammed and bolted the door. She would not risk trying to escape at night, she would wait until the sun was up. Nothing ever seemed so bad in the daylight. But she hesitated and slowly unlocked the door again. There had been something about the figures she had seen at the far end of Elm Hill in the lamplight. Something familiar that made her want to open the door a crack and peer out again.

'You must have been dreaming,' she muttered crossly to herself, 'unless those are ghosts in the lamplight.'

She gulped a deep breath and put her head out of the door. She caught sight of half a dozen tall figures mounted on horseback slowly cross the lamplit cobbles at the end of the street. She frowned and turned her head and saw another company of horsemen cross the lane at the top of the hill. She blinked and they were gone, but not before one of them had raised his hand as if to wave a salute to her. She quietly closed the door and relocked it. She found herself smiling foolishly and she spoke out loud to the empty room, spreading her arms wide as she did so. 'I don't understand one bit of all this. First these monsters, demons, call them what you will, chase me home from Lobster Lane, then this "atmosphere" rises as a wind and slams the door and protects me from these creatures. Now there's horsemen that look as though they have stepped directly from the museum, guarding or patrolling at either end of the street. Things like this just don't happen, at least not to me, not in real life. Am I going crazy?'

She shrugged her shoulders helplessly. Perhaps the atmosphere in the Watchgate was a whole history of endeavour to protect the good from evil. 'I've got to speak to somebody – anybody, before this place drives me crazy,' Tuppence muttered to herself as she bent and gathered up the scattered magazines from the floor, depositing them in an untidy pile on the coffee table in front of the inglenook.

She rubbed at the soot smuts on her fingers, making a face as she glanced at the telephone that had been installed in the smaller of the disused bread ovens to the right of the fireplace. A smile touched the corners of her mouth as she moved towards it; it looked so incongruous, so out of time, a shiny black plastic sculpture, a statement of today, squatting at the end of its ribbon of flex amongst so much history. She reached out for the receiver but hesitated to pick it up, wondering whom she could dial, with whom she could share her experiences.

Mentally she flicked through the pages of her address book. Faces and names blurred together. Mostly they were just acquaintances, friends for as long as the film shoot lasted or even only for the time it took a shutter to click. Briefly she stopped at Richard's name, she had his home number, but she shook her head and let the pages in her head continue to turn. Harry Klein's name came to mind and she smiled, her eyes softening as she thought of him. She had promised herself that she would phone him and he was someone she could really talk to, someone she could trust. She glanced down at her watch and calculated the time difference in New York. It would be early evening, the city would be leaving noisily from work, the traffic would be grinding to a halt in Fifth Avenue and the tugs' sirens would be wailing mournfully across the Hudson River. She could imagine the pink evening light filtering down through the skylights into the busy photographic studio in Vestry Street.

For a moment as she stood there, remembering, she felt really homesick, and her fingers trembled as she picked up the receiver. She hadn't told that English reporter the whole truth. Harry had been against her going freelance, he felt she wasn't ready, and he thought her move to England was foolish. He had acted just like a jealous father at the first hint of a serious relationship, as if he sensed that he might be losing her for ever. They had had cross words and she had walked out, packing her bags, ready to spread her wings. There had never been a binding contract, Harry didn't operate like that, he had just smiled sadly and let her go, and she had flown.

'Any time, kid, if you need a friend just phone.' Now, as she dialled the international code, she remembered his last words and the way he had looked in that departure lounge, and she felt like crying. As she had looked into his sad eyes she had felt that she was betraying him, betraying everything he had ever done for her, and she reached out and gripped both of his hands.

'I have to chase these rainbows now, Harry. I got to prove to everyone I'm good enough. You know what this business is like, I daren't wait around too long.'

And he had smiled and nodded his head. He had never married or had children, but she knew that he loved her as a daughter and that without him she would have vanished among the thousands of hopefuls trying for a career.

She dialled the area code and the number and after a short pause she heard the purr of the ringing tone and remembered how the sound would be echoing in the studio. She let the phone ring and ring, imagining him cursing and muttering as he shuffled towards the phone and then she began to worry that something might have happened to him. But perhaps he was making himself coffee in his untidy kitchen. Perhaps she should call later, give it another hour until he had settled down after work, and she was about to put the receiver down when the ringing tone stopped and a gruff voice called.

'Yup, Harry here, who is it? What the hell do you want?'

Tuppence felt herself smile at the harsh sound of his voice. He sounded so close, as though he was right there beside her. She wanted to laugh, to cry with relief, reach out and throw herself into his arms.

'Harry! It's me, Tuppence,' she said, almost breathlessly. 'I'm sorry, did I stop you doing something?'

For a long moment the line was silent. Tuppence frowned. 'Harry – Harry, are you there?'

Then she heard him laugh, the deep and easy guttural laugh that was so typical of him, and he quickly called out her name. For a moment she detected complete surprise and then a touch of hurt, even anger, in his voice. He was upset that she had left it so long before calling. But the anger disappeared quicker than frost in sunlight as he asked her a thousand questions, without pausing for breath, about her film locations, the light, the shadows of the English countryside, everything and anything rather than touch on that moment as she had boarded the airplane.

Tuppence laughed and pushed her hair back out of her eyes as she listened to his voice, savouring his New York drawl, and for a few brief moments she almost forgot the silent atmosphere of the Watchgate pressing in all around her and the hideous creatures that had chased her home.

'Tuppence! Tuppence, is something wrong? Are you still there?' he suddenly called out as he realized that apart from his name she had said nothing and yet there had been a trace of anxiety in her voice.

'Tuppence – answer me!' he shouted into the receiver, making her jump.

She gripped the phone tight and cradled it close against her cheek. 'Harry,' she whispered into the mouthpiece, her voice sharp and urgent as she glanced over her shoulder towards the door. 'Me leaving you and coming over here – do you still hold it against me?'

'Hey, kid,' he laughed, 'that's history, it's forgotten. I was just being an overprotective fool. What you did was right for your career and you know it.'

'I don't give a damn about my career right now. It doesn't matter who was right and who was wrong. What's important is, do you forgive me for going? Do you forgive me for leaving you after all you did for me? Answer me truthfully now.'

Harry frowned and glanced up at the skylight. She hadn't spoken to him properly for months, she had only left the briefest messages with his answering service to let him know that she was fine, and now out of the blue and in a voice crackling with panic she was almost pleading with him to forgive her for doing what they both knew she had to do.

'What is it, Tuppence? Tell me, kid, what's wrong?' he rasped, knuckling his free hand into a fist. 'Come on, spill it out, you know I've always loved you like a daughter. Sure, we argue sometimes, that's what families do. Now tell me, has some bastard been bothering you? Just give me his name and I'll break his legs for you.'

He heard Tuppence sob with relief at the concern in his voice. 'No, no, it's nothing like that. Harry, it's . . . it's . . .' She hesitated. She felt foolish, childish, as if she was trying to run home at her first brush with the big wide world. Just talking to Harry, hearing his rough voice, had lifted the oppressive atmosphere and lightened the shadows that pressed in around her. Somehow, to tell him that hideous monsters and horned demons had chased her home and mounted horsemen were now guarding each end of the lane seemed so ridiculous, he would probably laugh her off the phone.

'It's this place, it's so different,' she replied, searching for the words to try to explain. 'It's so old and so much has happened here. There's so much I don't understand about it. I feel so lost and so alone.'

But Harry didn't laugh or scoff at her. He could hear the real fear in her voice and could sense the terror in her quickened breaths. He did a quick calculation. It must be night-time in England. He realized that she must have been really frightened by something and that he would have to keep her talking until she calmed down.

'Start at the beginning. But first give me your number and the international code in case we get disconnected,' he soothed, reaching for a pen.

Tuppence gave him the number and then started to tell what had frightened her, beginning with the eerie atmosphere in the museum.

'Ghosts?' he rasped after a short pause. 'England's supposed to be full of them. You probably stumbled into some sort of haunting in that Lobster Lane or whatever you called it.'

'But they were so real, so solid, and their claws gouged marks in my door. How do you explain that? And those horsemen – they cast real shadows, I could see them.'

Harry shrugged and spread his free hand out in a hopeless gesture. 'Who can explain anything, kid? Ghosts do the weirdest things. But if I was you either I'd call the cops or I'd barricade the door until morning and then get the hell out of there and catch the first plane home.'

Tuppence smiled. Harry was always so black and white, so sharply in focus. He would have enthused over the beams and the inglenook, drunk in the atmosphere and then he would have shot a couple of rolls of film before catching a plane back to New York.

'No, Harry, it's not that simple. I love this place, it has a special feel about it. I really want to live here, only sometimes it scares me.'

'Well, if you wanta stay in England, Tuppence, guess you'll just have to get used to all those ghosts and hauntings. But remember, there's always a place here for you at home.'

'I know, Harry, but . . .' She began turning towards the window as a scratching noise behind her intruded on her consciousness.

She gave a cry and almost dropped the phone. There were two faces at the small leaded window. They were staring at her, their mouths hanging open to show rows of razor teeth. The larger face was edged in red hair and its small piggy eyes seemed to bore right through her. The other face had a ugly ruff of grey hair that sprouted from the corners of its leering mouth. Both faces looked hideously inhuman and their blackened fingers were scratching at the tiny panes of glass as if seeking a way in.

'No! Get back, get back,' Tuppence cried, snatching up the poker that she had replaced in the hearth.

Elm Hill was suddenly filled with the sound of hoofbeats. The two faces briefly chattered and shrieked and spat at the window and then vanished, and Tuppence saw the shapes of horsemen gallop past, their iron-shod hooves kicking up sparks on the darkened cobbles.

'Hey, what the hell's going on there?' Harry shouted at the confused jumble of sounds that suddenly erupted from his earpiece.

'Wait! Wait right there!' Tuppence hissed into her mouthpiece before she roughly thrust it down into the bread oven beside the telephone.

She ran across the room and was just in time to glimpse two small figures, one running in leaps and bounds, the other scuttling on all fours, duck into the dark entrance to Lobster Lane. The noise of the hoofbeats made her turn her head to see a line of horsemen sweep past the entrance of the Watchgate. There was a brief blaze of colour, blues and reds, and the flash of loops and knots of gold braid in the lamplight, and they were gone, cantering past Lobster Lane, out of the light and on towards the museum and the junction with Castle Street.

Tuppence pressed her cheek against the tiny squares of cold leaded glass to catch another glimpse of them, but they were already gone beyond her line of sight, their hoofbeats slowing as they faded into the distance. A crackle from the telephone receiver made her glance back over her shoulder. She frowned and hurried back across the room. She had forgotten all about Harry.

'You're just not going to believe this!' she laughed tensely into the telephone, 'but this place is going mad, no, it's worse than that, it's turning into a zoo. Harry, I'll swear I just saw two monkeys scratching and chattering at my window and then a crowd of horsemen dressed up in uniforms, the ones I saw this afternoon in that museum, came cantering along and chased them into Lobster Lane. You know, it really would be quite funny if they hadn't scared me half to death.'

Harry soothed and calmed her as best he could. There wasn't much he could do from three thousand miles away. He tried to promise to take the first plane over but she was dead against it and he half guessed that he knew why. She was afraid that she would cut and run and return with him to New York and leave her dreams behind her along with the independence that she had worked so hard for. Her career would be lost for ever, left to gather cobwebs of regrets in England. No, he knew that she had to stick it out on her own. She had to beat this haunting or whatever it was scaring the hell out of her, so he gave her the best advice he could.

'Bolt the doors. Pile everything in the room against them,' he advised her, 'and then retreat upstairs and make sure that the windows and the bedroom door are firmly locked. Then sweat it out until dawn and get the hell out of there the moment the sun comes up. Call a priest, call a whole cathedral of priests, in the morning and let them deal with it. They're good at exorcizing ghosts. Call them in the morning anyway, they'll know what to do.'

Harry checked her number before he rang off, and promised to phone her on the hour every hour until the sun came up. 'Remember, kid,' he shouted as she disconnected, 'I'll be by the phone all night.'

The line went dead and then crackled and the dialling tone hummed in the silence. Tuppence listened to its monotonous sound for a moment, shivered and then replaced the receiver. Harry's voice had given her courage but now that he had gone she felt even more alone. Quite suddenly the lights on the wall of the museum across the lane went out. Tuppence glanced at her watch; the hands stood at 12.30.

'Damn!' she muttered, remembering that Richard had told her that the street lights went out just after midnight in the old part of the city. She checked the bolts on the door, gave the key a final twist in its huge lock and hurried up the winding staircase to her bedroom. It mirrored the room below with its low beams and small leaded windows that looked out into Elm Hill, but the bedroom was smaller, having been partitioned at some time in its recent history to allow the installation of an en suite bathroom. Tuppence smiled as she entered the room and pulled the door closed behind her, swiftly locking it. White paint against the dark beams was exactly right, and the print on the curtains exactly matched that on the duvet and counterpane. Combined with the brass bedstead, dressing table and chairs that she had chosen before her trip to Scotland it all looked so good, so comfortable. The room was exactly how she always imagined her own bedroom should be.

She crossed to the window and checked that the catch was securely fastened. Pausing, she glanced out across the steep roof tops and spires of the old quarter of the city. They looked so mysterious, so magical in the weak silver light of the fingernail moon that hung so low in the night sky amongst the flickering stars. It cast long night-shadows of velvet black between the tall chimney stacks and blind-eyed dormer windows.

She was about to draw the curtains and shut out the darkness and the pale moonbeams that filtered into the room, when she caught the faint echo of hoofbeats on the cobbles below. They were coming closer, up the hill towards the Watchgate. Tuppence felt her heartbeat quicken. She wanted to jump back to hide in the safety of the shadows beneath her bed, but she forced herself to stay at the window, gripping the wooden sill with both hands. If she wanted to stay in England living in this beautiful old house she would have to face it out with these ghosts, or whatever they were, who haunted the old quarter of the city. This time she wasn't going to hide, she was going to get a good look at one of those horsemen.

The rider came into sight, trotting fast up the centre of Elm Hill, but he slowed as he reached the Watchgate as if sensing her presence at the window. He looked up at her and although he was mostly in shadows she thought she saw a smile cross his face. He raised a gloved hand as if to salute and involuntarily she raised her own hand and would have returned the acknowledgement, but at that moment a shrieking howl broke the night silence somewhere in the maze of alleyways that led off Lobster Lane. The horseman unsheathed his sabre, reined his mount to a halt and pirouetted, sending up a bright shower of sparks. He cantered back towards the entrance of Lobster Lane. Tuppence used the brief seconds before he vanished from her sight trying to study his uniform, seeing if she could recognize it from her visit to the museum. The jacket was of a deep dusty blue with bands of gold across his chest and the cuffs and collar were red and edged with braid, but the breeches were a plain faded grey colour. The sorrel horse wore a deep scarlet saddle cloth edged in white beneath its saddle, that rippled and floated in the wind the horse stirred up. Behind the saddle, strapped across the saddle roll, was a carbine rifle. She tried to see more details but they cantered away from the patch of moonlight and into the darkness.

She thought hard and tried to remember if she had seen that uniform in the museum earlier and then shook her head. She couldn't think; there had been so many figures crowding beneath the galleries. The horseman below had looked dirtier, more travel-stained than any of the exhibits, but then he had looked so real out there trotting along the street, his fast-moving shadow flowing over the uneven cobbles, the bit rings jangling in the darkness. Tuppence frowned crossly and looked down into the empty lane. This haunting was getting ridiculous; she had almost welcomed the sight of the horsemen. They had made her feel safe – she had even waved to a ghost for Chrissake!

The telephone in the bread oven downstairs suddenly burst into life, its shrill double tone echoing through the Watchgate. Tuppence stared around her for a few moments before she realized what it was.

'Damn! I should have had an extension put in up here,' she muttered as she ran to the bedroom door and unlocked it, but she smiled with relief as she leapt two at a time down the steep twisting stairs. It would be Harry. Good old dependable Harry, ringing back just as he promised. God how she loved him; she couldn't wait to hear his rasping voice.

Ludo Strewth crouched beneath the low archway that led into Goats Head Alley. He was gesticulating frantically at two monkeys who were leaping and scuttling erratically towards him up Lobster Lane. Then he heard the clatter of horseshoes on Elm Hill behind them and he cursed, then turned, ready to flee back into his taxidermist's shop. The monkeys reached the low archway just as the rider appeared at the bottom of the lane. Ludo roughly pushed them both towards the open door of his shop.

'Get inside and keep silent,' he hissed.

Ludo started to follow, then hesitated beneath the dark archway, hugging the shadows. He had to get a better look at one of those horsemen. He frowned and raked his long fingers absently through his hair. He couldn't understand where they could have sprung from or why they had so suddenly appeared. Twice now since darkness fell they had driven his creatures back into Lobster Lane whenever they had tried to follow the American woman or venture near the Watchgate. He had caught a brief glimpse of them earlier, when they had galloped the length of Lobster Lane, scattering his animals at lance point and forcing them to hide in every dark crack and alleyway. He was certain that they were not mounted policemen; no, they hadn't blown police whistles or summoned up reinforcements. Indeed, they had acted very strangely.

Searching in the darkness of the archway close to the damp brick wall his fingers closed around a fragment of broken brick, and he hurled it out into Lobster Lane in the hope of drawing the horseman towards him. The brick bounced and spun, clattering noisily down the narrow lane. The horseman turned his head towards the noise, then spurred his horse into a trot and advanced, carefully searching each of the alleyways that he passed. Ludo leaned forward and studied the figure in the saddle.

His thin face greyed in the moonlight and a knot of fear clutched at his stomach. He sank back into the shadows beneath the archway and held his breath until the sound of the clattering hoofbeats had receded. What he had just glimpsed was not possible. No one else knew the secret of the magic that he had used to resurrect his animals, no one else had touched the severed Hand of Glory. The horseman could not have been real. Ludo blinked and rubbed his eyes, then crept back to the entrance and stared at the shape of the retreating rider in the pale moonlight. He hadn't imagined it. The cavalryman looked exactly like one of those old soldiers from the museum, as if he had sprung from one of those displays in the museum at the bottom of Elm Hill.

Ludo rose to his feet and, keeping to the shadows, he followed the horseman to the bottom of Lobster Lane and on along Elm Hill. He followed him until he disappeared through the rear entrance of the museum. Ludo looked up the hill and saw other horsemen patrolling in the lamplight before he fled back to the safety of his shop in Goats Head Alley and slammed the door behind him.

Breathlessly he crouched in the dark. A cold sweat was damp on his forehead. Perhaps it wasn't his magic that had brought those museum exhibits to life, perhaps some other force was working against him. Then he remembered that the American woman had been in the courtyard on the night that he had awoken the power. She had seen him light the Hand of Glory. Perhaps she had conjured up some magic of her own to protect herself. That must be it. That would explain the appearance of these horsemen. They weren't anything to do with his magic; she had called them up against him. Bleakly, as he huddled in the darkness, he realized that he would have to destroy the soldiers before they hurt his beautiful animals.

'I'll burn that museum down. Yes, that will put an end to whatever has awoken in there,' he muttered grimly, wiping the cold sweat from his forehead with the palms of his hands.

'You are all being watched,' he hissed at the restless menagerie that crowded his shop. 'You must tread with infinite care until I have set light to that museum in Elm Hill and burned it to the ground. I must destroy every one of those troublesome horsemen.'

He paused and stabbed an irritable finger up in the air, pointing towards his preparation room. 'I'm far from ready to snatch that American woman, so don't frighten her and bring those horsemen nosing into my affairs. Watch her from a distance. Carry on shadowing her every step, but do it more discreetly, don't make her suspicious. Do you hear me?' he hissed.

The bears growled, the monkeys shrieked and chattered and the snakes hissed, gliding silently to entwine themselves around the six hanging clocks. Ludo turned towards his wooden counter, his voice trailing off into barely audible mutterings as he bent and rummaged through the deep drawers. He pushed aside bundles of swabs and scattered packets of curved sewing needles, hammers, bone-cutters and saws as he tried again to remember where he had stored his old notebooks. He was sure they contained jottings, forgotten notes and vital clues, for preserving human skin. There were notes he had taken during his apprenticeship days beneath the watchful eye of the Master of Taxidermy, Edward Mokes, who had also been an embalmer for the Royal College of Surgeons, and now he cursed himself for not taking more notice of the master's words. The more he thought about it the more sure he was that Mokes's knowledge held the key to the secrets he now sought. If only he could remember where he had put those notes. His fingernails scraped the bottom of the drawer and he straightened up, pushing the drawer firmly shut with a sigh. He had searched everywhere, he had ransacked every dark cupboard, cellar and hiding place in the ramshackle old building, and all to no avail.

The animals were growing restless. He unlocked the outer door, opened it a crack and put his ear to the gap and spent a moment listening to the night silence. The horsemen appeared to have gone.

'Watch her with caution,' he whispered, selecting the stealthiest of his creatures, sending out the snakes, the lynx, an Australian water rat and a snowshoe hare with the snowy owl into the dark courtyard.

'The rest of you will remain silently in the dark court-yard and warn me if the horsemen come back,' he said, beckoning the bears to follow him up into the preparation room.

Quickly he climbed the steep staircase, feeling the treads shake and tremble as the bears followed on his heels. It was better to keep them out of sight until he had destroyed those cursed horsemen. He paused a step inside the room and stared down hopelessly at the neat rows of human preparations that lay head to toe on the floor.

'Useless! Utterly useless!' he muttered, stepping over

and between them on his way towards his marble slab. He shuddered and swept his hand across the rows of bodies.

'Move them to the far end of the room. Stack them on top of each other, as close together as possible,' he ordered the two bears without looking back.

They had all been dismal failures. Even the skeletons that he had hurriedly built from wood and wire seemed to be deteriorating. The wood looked wormy and the steel was pitted with rust. But it was the preservation of the skin that had most disappointed him. Every one of the bodies had begun to putrefy, to turn yellow or brown, to take on the look and texture of drying parchment. And they had bruised so easily wherever he had accidentally touched them. His stitching tore through the skin wherever it was stretched too tightly over the skeletons, and the slightest distortion of their faces had given them the most hideous-looking snarls or smiles. They were monsters, hideously deformed, and he had firmly refused the whispering voices in his head, which tempted him to light the Hand of Glory and attempt to resurrect them.

He bent over his marble slab to inspect his most recent figure, wrinkling his nose at the sweet smell of corruption and frowning at the dark purple bruising that showed all too clearly where he had gripped the skin and peeled it back from the cadaver's face. There was one thing that he was sure of, one thing that every experiment had taught him: the art of embalming was a trick, an illusion. It would only last for days, perhaps weeks at best. He had studied every treatise on the ancient art that he could find, only to realize that with all the Egyptian methods the corpse was wrapped in linen or cotton bandages after it had been soaked in preserving oils and that never thereafter was the skin exposed to the atmosphere.

He sighed and motioned to the bears to remove the

body on the slab and replace it with the last of the cadavers that he had stolen from the Uppington undertakers. The whole business of trying to preserve human skin was becoming a nightmare, but he couldn't stop trying. The magic was possessing him, driving him mad, filling his mind with the vision of that beautiful American woman. To preserve her body had become an obsession that filled his every waking moment and echoed through his fitful dreams as the skin and bones that he stole each night piled up in his preparation room. He had to find the right solution, the right formula and mixture of oils, acids and alkalines, and there were so many thousands of combinations, each one a droplet different. He threw his hands up helplessly and cursed the bears as they dropped the new corpse on to the slab too roughly.

'Carefully! Carefully! Can't you do the simplest of tasks?' he hissed. 'Even the most delicate touch bruises the skin,' he frowned and bent closer to examine the dead face.

As soon as he was close enough he realized that the morticians at the undertaker's had beaten him to it and beautified this corpse for viewing. Touching the puffy cheeks he smeared the layers of make-up. He pulled back the shroud and saw that the chest had been opened and the skin at the edges of the wound was already showing purple blotches. He turned away in disgust.

'It's useless, it's already been spoilt. Put it with the others. There's just enough time before dawn to find another mortuary,' he muttered grimly, opening out a large-scale map of the city and poring over it, looking for another undertaker, one that he hadn't already plundered.

Ludo was meticulous, scrupulously careful in his body-snatching. He chose the mortuaries and funeral parlours with infinite care. He had become an excellent locksmith, slipping in and out of these houses of the dead as quietly as a shadow in the night, and he only stole from caskets that had already been sealed up for burial. He made notes of the dates of interment or incineration on the other coffins in case he needed to return. Until tonight he always managed to have the skin of at least two corpses soaking in different baths of solutions, but now he needed a body to replace the one the morticians had ruined and he needed it quickly if he was ever going to solve the riddle of preserving human skin.

He didn't quite realize that it was the evil within the Hand of Glory that made him hesitate to destroy his failures, that whispered him into hoarding the hideous pile of humanity that was growing with each experiment in the gloomy preparation room. The blackened mummified hand that possessed him smouldered silently, waiting for its darker magic to flower.

Tuppence wearied of pacing out the long hours of darkness in the bedroom. It had meant a headlong rush down the winding stairs each time Harry called and she knew that she had to snatch a few hours' sleep or she would look a wreck on the film set in the morning. Finally, well after 2 a.m., she had wrapped herself up in a blanket and, armed with a poker, slept fitfully in the high-backed chair beside the inglenook. As she had drifted into sleep she thought of that horseman and the way he had looked up and smiled, and in her dreams she heard the soft jingle of the bit rings, murmuring voices and the tramp of marching feet. It was a sunny morning and she could feel the heat of it through the billowing dust that blew across the road. There were hazy figures, knights in armour, moving carts, travelling towards her through the curtain of dust. As she spread her arms to greet them she found she wanted to laugh, but the dust filled her mouth and stung her eyes. She tried to move but she was trapped; the figures were looming close, threatening to tread on her.

The shrill double tones of the telephone jarred her awake. She blinked and sat bolt upright, scrabbling in the mouth of the bread oven for the receiver. The brass poker fell from her lap and clattered noisily on the flagstones at her feet.

'Tuppence! Tuppence, are you all right, kid?' Harry's rasping voice growled at her through the receiver from three thousand miles away.

'Yeah,' she answered, glancing anxiously around the room. 'Everything's quiet here now. An old rattletrap of a van drove past since you last phoned, but now it's quieter than the grave.'

Harry laughed. 'Well don't lose your sense of humour, girl. But what about that horseman? Is he still hanging around? Take a look, will you, before I ring off!'

Tuppence hurried to the window and steeled herself to look out beyond the reflection of the light that the room threw through the glass. Elm Hill was wreathed in cold black mist and shadows; there was nothing to see in either direction. She shivered and returned to the telephone, gathering the blanket more tightly about her shoulders.

'I think he's gone,' she answered in an uncertain voice. 'At least, I can't see anything. It's pitch black outside now that the moon's gone down.'

'What time is it there?' Harry asked and Tuppence glanced at her watch, yawning.

'It's three thirty a.m., just about one hour before dawn here, I guess.'

Harry paused a moment and when he spoke his voice was soft with apology. 'Listen, kid, I've got to go out. I've got to meet some guy in Pete's Tavern to set up a film shoot. You remember Pete's, don't you, 129 East 18th? The phone number's Gramercy 2312 if you need me, but I'll ring you the moment I get back, say in about two hours.'

'No,' Tuppence answered slowly, looking out at the darkness through the small leaded window panes, 'it will be light enough in about an hour for me to make a dash for it. If I leave then it'll mean I'll get to the coast a little early, but it'll be better than being cooped up here. I'll ring you at Pete's if I need you, OK?'

'Sure thing,' Harry's voice rasped. 'Take care now and don't forget to see a priest the first moment you get. I'll call tomorrow . . .'

'Harry, wait,' she cried as he was about to disconnect.

'What is it?' he asked quickly, his voice hardening. 'Are the creatures back?'

'No, no, I just wanted to say thanks, Harry, thanks for being there,' she whispered into the phone.

Harry smiled. 'We're family, kid. Now remember, watch your back as you leave that old house of yours. Stay sharp, stay safe and ring me the moment you get back from the coast.'

'But it will be early morning in New York,' she exclaimed.

'So, I'm a light sleeper – ring!' he retorted, disconnecting before she could reply.

Tuppence felt too tense and anxious about the impending dawn and the dash to her car to try to catch another moment's sleep. She paced the Watchgate planning her escape, going over every detail a dozen times. She had to lock the door of giants, it would be madness to leave it open, a clear invitation to every burglar, but should she run to the car and unlock that first before she locked the Watchgate, or should . . . The sound of a car engine slow-

126

ing, shifting noisily through its gears, made her jump. It was coming to a halt just outside her door. She ran to the window to see who the hell it was and momentarily her spirits lifted at the thought of company, but it was only that old van, the one she had seen earlier. It was slowing down as it passed the Watchgate and turning into Lobster Lane. Tuppence tried to read its faded lettering but it disappeared too quickly, and she stayed at the window watching the dark night sky turn grey and the dawn break slowly across the roof tops.

As the light strengthened she saw a thin shifting mist was creeping up Elm Hill. It was only about a foot deep but it hid the cobbles and the raised drain covers and in places boiled up to block the lane with thicker bands of fog. It clung with glistening dampness to the mediaeval brickwork on the doorways and the narrow entrances to the alleyways.

'Damn!' she muttered, watching the wheels of her Lotus vanish and the mist begin to smother the low bonnet. It would be suicide to try to drive at any speed through this mist, especially in a low-slung sports car. She would smash the undercarriage on those raised drain covers before she had driven a hundred yards. She might as well put on a blindfold.

She turned and began to pace the floor again, wondering how long it would take for the mist to clear. Normally she hadn't left her hotel in the city for early morning sessions until 5.30 or even 6 o'clock. Perhaps it was always misty this early. Perhaps it would clear. With hope in her heart she returned to the window and looked out. The greyness in the sky had turned eggshell blue, dawn was bleeding new colours into the roof tops. The red, weatherbeaten tiles sparkled with dew and the covering of grey-green moss that clung to every ridge and gutter spout had the look of wet coral spores. The mist was breaking up as she had hoped; it was swirling in the dawn breeze, clinging to the windows and brick walls of the buildings opposite and making them glisten, painting them in shrouds of wetness. She could just make out the cobbles in the lane.

'I'm going to risk it,' she breathed, running her hands through her tangled hair.

She didn't dare glance in the mirror, she could clearly imagine what a wreck she looked with dark rings beneath her eyes, her cheeks tense and slightly hollowed with fatigue.

'Thank God for make-up,' she sighed as she pulled on a warm suede jacket to protect her against the damp breeze. Gathering up her shoulder bag she fished out the ignition key of the Lotus.

She took a deep breath and threw the bolts on the Watch-gate door. Immediately that was done she turned the heavy iron key in the lock and withdrew it. She reached for the latch and then she paused and retraced her steps to where she had left the poker on the window sill.

'If there's anything out there I'm going down fighting.' She steeled herself as she lifted the latch and pulled the heavy door open towards her. The long night had seemed to take for ever and she was glad that it was finally over. She was as scared as hell of what might lurk outside but she just couldn't sit and wait all day hoping it would go away. Fear always had worked like that with her; nothing was ever as bad if you went out and faced it and began to make things happen.

The door swung inwards easily with barely a creak of its iron hinges. 'Now or never,' she cried, thrusting the key in the lock on the outside of the door. She stepped up on to the pavement and pulled the door shut behind her as she turned the key. She was on her own now, there was no one to protect her. Watch your back. Stay sharp.

She dropped the key to the Watchgate into her bag and ran across the pavement. Half clawing, fumbling with trembling fingers, she tried to fit the key of the Lotus into the door lock. It slipped, skidding on the paintwork. She tried again and it slid easily into the lock, but she almost bent the key in her haste to unlock the door. She wrenched the door open and shoehorned herself into the driving seat, slamming and locking the door shut. Her skirt was rucked up high above her knees and her suede jacket was balled uncomfortably in the small of her back but she had made it. She was safely locked in her car. She breathed a sigh of relief and glanced up at the Watchgate as she pushed the key into the ignition.

'Oh God!' she cried in horror.

The whole front wall of the Watchgate was a crawling mass of snakes. Every inch of brickwork between the beams had vanished beneath their writhing, glistening skins. Vivid oranges, speckled yellows, iridescent blues and greens slithered and wound together, and countless gleaming black eyes and flicking forked tongues were turned, reaching down towards her.

The scream froze in her. She wanted to get the hell out of there, to drive as fast as she could away from the Watchgate, but she had to fight down the rising panic and stop the urge to stamp on the accelerator. She knew if she followed her instincts that she would only stall the car and then she would be trapped. Her skin was crawling with revulsion, her breath was coming in short shallow gasps.

'I'll do it slowly,' she wept, but her fingers were paralysed with terror. Try as she might she couldn't move.

Something ran up across the bonnet of the car and came towards her. The movement broke the spell that terror had cast on her and she pressed herself back into her seat, staring out at a small brown shiny lizard. It stopped and lifted its head, staring back at her through the windscreen, its long tongue flicking in and out of its mouth. A shadow passed over her and made her look up through the glass roof of the car to see that the entire roof was crawling with lizards. Tuppence heard the scrape of their tiny claws and felt the hairs prickle on the nape of her neck. A shiver of fear ran down her spine. She turned her head and looked out of the car window and saw that the pavement was alive with lizards, frogs and toads; they were everywhere, smothering everything with their scaly bodies. The snakes were beginning to slither silently down the front of the Watchgate towards the ground. She had to start the car now.

She forced her fingers to turn the ignition key, the dials lit up and flickered, the engine turned over, coughed once and stalled as her foot stamped in terror on the accelerator.

'Damn,' she hissed, realizing that she had flooded the engine. She had to stay cool or she would be trapped there. She had to keep her right foot off the accelerator pedal until the engine had fired. Her nerves were taut and jangling as she reached for the key a second time; it seemed to take an age for her fingers to close on the key and turn.

'Come on! Come on!' she hissed as the engine whirred then roared into life. Gripping the gearstick with white knuckles she slammed it into first gear. Her right ankle was aching with tension, her toes were tingling, cramped from the desire to stamp on the accelerator. Another lizard much larger than the one on the bonnet suddenly appeared at the window beside her, its scaly feet suckered to the glass. Its gleaming black eyes were only inches away from her face.

The whole car shuddered as she touched the accelerator

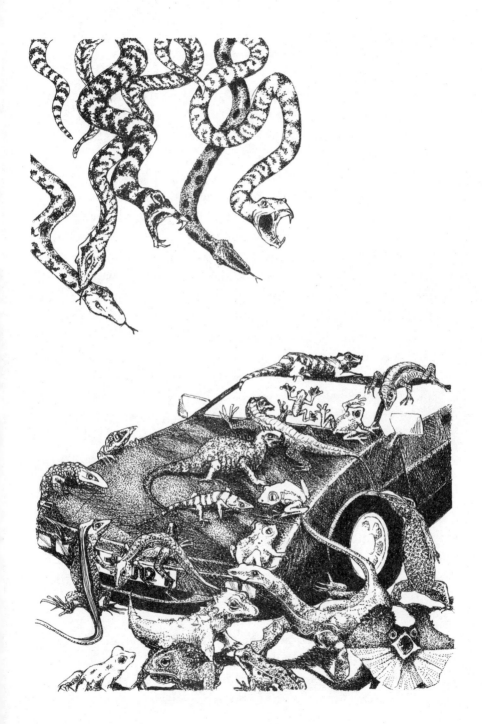

and pressed it down. The needle on the rev. counter swung to 3,000. She let the clutch out in one sudden jerk and the car leapt.

'Jesus Christ!' she shouted over the roar of the exhaust as the car lurched forward, trying to shake the steering wheel from her hands as it bumped over the bodies of the lizards and the first of the snakes.

She hung on to the wheel and ploughed the car through the reptiles. The lizard on the bonnet was plucked off by the sudden rush of wind as the car gathered speed. The glass canopy above her head lightened and she heard the shriek of claws scraping across the sunroof and the thud as the creatures hit the aerofoil and dropped away behind her. She steered erratically between the drain covers, the tyres screaming. The engine was over-revving wildly in first gear, the vacuum gauge was almost off the dial and she was forced back in her seat as the needle touched 60 mph. The tortured roar of the engine made her wince and she dropped it into second.

As she passed the entrance to Lobster Lane, a large cat, a lion or a tiger, sprang from the shadows and for a moment loped along beside her, making her stamp harder on the accelerator as she ploughed forward into the remnants of the mist that still lay thick at the bottom of Elm Hill. She had to feather the brakes to slow down quickly, and flick on the windscreen wipers to clear away the film of moisture. She was just in time to see a company of horsemen, galloping towards her, line abreast, up the hill. As they emerged from the mist she braked hard and the wheels locked.

'Oh no!' she cried and the sleek black car began to slew around and slide out of control, ending up broadside across the cobbles. Tuppence hung on to the wheel knowing she should steer into the skid, but she was too frightened to do anything and she sat there helpless as the car turned itself around. The horsemen raised their lances and scattered. For a moment their neat line milled in confusion, and then they re-formed and swept on up the road towards the Watchgate.

The Lotus hit the low kerb with a violent bump, juddered to a halt and stalled. Tuppence banged her head hard on the side window and for a moment she sat there dazed, confused and trembling, vacantly staring at the riders as they brought their lances down and began to spear the snakes and the larger lizards, which were streaming back into the entrance of Lobster Lane. Gradually she began to pull herself together and rubbed at the side of her head. The pain brought everything sharply back into focus and she quickly reached for the ignition key again and restarted the engine. But she held the car on the clutch for a moment and frowned. In the dawn light she recognized the horsemen's uniforms as they mounted the pavement in front of the Watchgate and picked off with their lance tips the last of the writhing snakes that clung to the eaves and guttering. They were the soldiers from the museum, she had walked between them yesterday.

'These guys really are protecting me,' she laughed, letting the clutch out slowly as she pulled across the hill to turn the car. 'But why is Lobster Lane haunted with all those animals?' she frowned as she slipped the car into reverse to complete the turn.

Backing up, she glanced out of the passenger window. The horsemen were now crowding the entrance to Lobster Lane, prodding the repulsive reptiles as they slithered away into the shadows. She didn't understand any of it, but she sure wasn't going to get out of the car and start to ask questions even if the ghosts were friendly. She pushed the gearstick forward and was about to let in the clutch when a dull-yellow hare as large as a dog broke cover from an alleyway just beyond the Watchgate and ran towards the entrance of Lobster Lane. It saw the horsemen and momentarily froze, crouching, its ears twitching to the scrape and clatter of the milling horses. Then it zigzagged between the horses' hooves and darted back into Elm Hill, running towards her, its round eyes wide with terror, its ears flat against the side of its head.

One of the horsemen wheeled round and, leaning forward in the saddle, brought his gleaming lance tip down as he cantered after the hare. Tuppence watched in horror as the gap closed and the shadow of the galloping horseman overtook the animal. The lance tip pierced its neck a finger's width from its left ear and swept it screaming and convulsing high into the air. The rider reined his horse to a skidding halt and sent up a blaze of sparks from the wet cobbles ten paces from her car. He saluted her with his reins hand and let the lance with its helplessly skewered, squealing hare rest easily against his right shoulder.

Tuppence looked up and saw the cavalryman's face break into a stiff, almost manufactured smile, his grey eyes softening as he spoke: 'The way ahead is clear, madam. The road is yours.' The voice sounded muffled and distorted as if he spoke through a bundle of rags.

'Thanks, thanks a lot,' she shouted back to him, trembling from head to foot.

He certainly looked real, real enough to reach out and touch, and she had not imagined his voice. She tried to smile at him and, hesitantly, gave a small wave as she steered the car away from the kerb and past the museum.

'You should have spoken to him. You should have asked him what all this is about,' she told herself, regretting her lack of courage as she realized that she had allowed a unique moment to slip away for ever.

She sighed to herself as she tugged at her jacket and tried to free it from the small of her back. There would be plenty of other opportunities to see this haunting if the ghosts that hung around the old quarter of the city did so as obviously as they had last night.

She drove slowly through the city, going over in her mind everything that had happened during the night and carefully following the signposts for the coast. There wasn't much traffic on the roads, just the infrequent farm lorry and an occasional delivery van bringing produce to the shops and markets. Red post vans seemed to be crossing every junction and rattling milk floats crawled along in the gutters. It was going to be a clear morning. The leaves on the avenues of trees looked freshly painted and the sun was just edging up over the roof tops and touching everything with its sparkling light. She smiled. The terrors of the night were beginning to recede. She was leaving the city behind her.

8

A Trip to the Coast

The crowded tenements and rows of houses packed back to back had vanished in the wing mirrors. Beyond the thin ribbon of squat bungalows and shops that clung on to the side of the twisting road, the countryside was opening up. Cows were being herded out into the emerald fields. There were acres of yellow, ripening corn, each dew-coated, full-eared stalk glistening in the sunlight, and stretches of dark, secret woodland marching away across the landscape, softening the contours of the hill tops and filling the hidden valleys. And far in the distance shone the pencil-thin line of shimmering sea. Thin wreath-tails of mist still clung to the dips and hollows but otherwise the road ahead snaked away clear and empty, a driver's road that urged her foot down harder on the accelerator.

She switched on the cassette player and the sound of Billy Joel's '52nd Street' filled the car. It was pure New York – the shadowy canyons between the skyscrapers, the glittering Manhattan lights at night, the jostling crowds endlessly threading their way to somewhere else. She could hear the noise of the traffic, the rush of the subway trains and to her it was all the good and the bad times blended into one haunting melodic sound. The needle on the speedometer dial crept easily past seventy to seventy-five, the car responded to the slightest touch and ate up the tarmac, clinging to the curves of the road as if it had been painted on it. Tuppence began to laugh and to sing along with the tape. Elm Hill was seeming so far away, almost forgotten, when suddenly a bird swooped from nowhere and hovered twenty yards in front of her car.

'Bloody hell!' she cried, stamping her right foot hard on the brake.

The seat belt cut into her shoulder as the car skidded. She fought to keep it straight as the tyres churned up a cloud of smoke and rubber seconds before she hit the bird with a sickening bang. It rolled up across the bonnet and slid up the windscreen, leaving a smear of blood and a handful of white feathers clinging on to the wiper arm as it rose up. Then it slid over the engine cover, hit the aerofoil and spun in a feathered arc on to the road behind her. Tuppence quickly brought the car to a halt and sat still for a moment, her fingers locked on the steering wheel, her stomach knotted with shock. One moment the road ahead had been empty, curving away towards the crest of a low hill, and the next the bird had been right on her.

She let the side window down and looked back at the wretched little creature lying there on the crown of the road, the light breeze ruffling its feathers. She reached for the door catch and hesitated, scanning the road in both directions. She wasn't sure if she expected to see a line of galloping horsemen or the roadside crawling with slithering snakes, but she looked and listened carefully all the same.

'I am losing my mind,' she muttered crossly to herself. 'This isn't Lobster Lane and this isn't a haunting.'

She pushed the door open and climbed out. The grey-black tarmac wound away from her in both directions, desolately empty between the ripening cornfields. Skylarks sang in the vault of blue above her and the leaves of the oaks and elms that sporadically lined either side of the road rustled in the morning breeze. In the distance, perhaps a mile or two away, she could see a large truck crawling slowly up a hill, otherwise the road and the morning were hers. Brushing the creases out of her skirt she walked to the front of the car and examined the damage.

'What a mess,' she exclaimed as she bent and looked at the blood and feathers clinging to the number plate. Luckily the bird hadn't done much damage to the car.

'Poor thing, you didn't stand a chance,' she murmured as she slowly moved around the car to where the bird lay. 'I've got to take a closer look.' She glanced up at the rustling leaves in the roadside trees and listened to the skylarks and the hedgerow birds' song, trying to convince herself that everything was normal, that there was nothing sinister about the owl. This poor creature couldn't be one of those ghosts from Lobster Lane. Ghosts didn't bleed and die.

She looked down at the bird and gingerly prodded it. It felt dead, but there wasn't the slightest trace of the impact on the back of the carcass. The pale yellow feathers ruffled up in the breeze, the broken wings lay twisted beneath its body.

'Well, you'll never fly again, that's for sure,' she whispered as she flipped the bird over with the toe of her shoe. It was an owl, a barn owl, she recognized its heart-shaped white face, beak and hooked talons. As she pushed it across the road with her foot she saw that the left wing had almost been severed from its body and was only attached by a piece of torn skin.

Bending closer, she was examining the wretched creature when a faint noise in the distance, different from the other sounds of the countryside, made her look up. She listened, straining her ears, trying to shut out the other noises, and then she heard it again: a distinct scream of tyres biting into the tight bends of the road. It was closer now and she could pick out the thunder of an engine. A car was approaching from the direction of the city, using the empty morning road as a race track. It would reach her in moments, powering out of the bend, hugging the centre of the road, crushing and scattering the carcass of the owl beneath its wheels. She didn't like to touch dead things but she crouched down and grasped the bird in both hands. Its head fell backwards and she saw that the beak had been shattered by the impact; one eye was hanging by its optic nerve, gritty and bruised on the owl's cheek, while the other stared blindly at her. It looked a sad and pathetic mess and the feathers on the torn wing felt sticky, blood-sticky, between her fingers. She let a sigh of relief hiss between her teeth as she ran back to the car holding the owl at arm's length. It was just an ordinary owl after all. Just as she thought, she had been jumping at shadows.

The roar of the approaching car swallowed up her specu-lations. She pressed herself against the driver's door of the Lotus as a Porsche rounded the bend and hurtled towards her. She caught a brief glimpse of the driver's startled face, his tight knuckles gripping the steering wheel, as he swerved to avoid her and her car, his tyres squealing on the warming tarmac. He was quickly past her in a rush of wind and a dazzling flash of sunlight reflecting on his windscreen. There was a thundering roar and a blur of bright red paintwork before the car vanished in a haze of exhaust fumes and a sound of shifting gears over the brow of the hill ahead.

'I hope you catch up with that slow old truck on a blind bend, mister, that'll scare the shit out of you,' she shouted angrily, tossing the hair out of her eyes and blinking at the cloud of gritty dust that the car had stirred up.

She took a deep breath and looked down at the owl,

wiping the sticky drying blood from her fingers with a tissue from the box she kept in the glove compartment. She didn't want just to leave the wretched thing to rot on the roadside. She felt sorry that it had killed itself on her car but the bloody mess was nothing that a bucket of water wouldn't clean. No, she felt she ought to bury it or dispose of it somehow. Then she remembered the stuffed eagle owls and peacocks that Harry kept in his studio on Vestry Street to use as props. This bird wasn't quite as glamorous, but perhaps if she had it stuffed, she could keep it in the corner of the inglenook. She reached into the car down beside her seat and pulled the boot catch, then went round and laid the carcass of the bird carefully in the boot. Someone on the film set was bound to know where she could have the bird stuffed. Yes, and then she would have her own owl to guard the Watchgate against the haunting. She laughed softly, relieved that the incident had been nothing more sinister than a simple accident. She fired the engine and drove on towards the film shoot and the coast.

'Oh yes, it's definitely dead and that eye looks a real mess,' nodded the photographer, gravely peering into the boot of the Lotus at the owl as he adjusted the aperture on his camera.

'But do you know anyone who will stuff it for me?' Tuppence asked, pouting as the light of the flashgun momentarily burned her eyes.

The photographer shook his head and listened to the whirr of the battery charger before he answered. 'It looks too badly damaged to me, love, I'd throw it in the rubbish bin if I were you. It's only a common barn owl.'

Tuppence sighed and brushed her hair out of her eyes.

She looked down at the pathetic little creature. Somehow it seemed such a waste just to throw it away.

'There used to be a taxidermist in Goats Head Alley,' the cameraman added slowly after a few moments' thought. 'I remember, I took some stills of his collection of rare animals for the *National Geographic* – but that's a few years ago now.'

Tuppence glanced up quickly at his mention of Goats Head Alley. The name rang a bell, she had seen it or heard it quite recently, she was sure of it.

'Yes,' he continued. 'I can remember the old boy quite clearly. His name was something like Sleuth and he fussed around us continually in his long white coat, flapping his arms wildly in the air above his head. He was quite adamant that we were not to use our arc lamps to light his collection, said the heat would affect the animals' skins. Silly if you ask me, but he made us do everything on time exposures. It took us ages to get the shots we wanted. Yes, he was a real eccentric, but he might just be able to do something with the remains of that owl if he's still alive and hasn't retired.'

Tuppence suddenly remembered where she had seen Goats Head Alley. It had been when she had found the Watchgate on that very first evening and she had crossed the lane to explore beneath one of those low archways. She caught her breath and shivered as the memory flooded back, of that claustrophobic courtyard and the hissing cats that guarded it, the stifling silence and the door in the far corner with the faded letters above it. Yes – they had begun with T, A and perhaps an X, yes, that must have been the taxidermist's shop that the photographer was talking about. But it had looked deserted that evening, inhospitable and wrapped up in its own brooding secrets.

'Don't you know of any other animal stuffer in the

city?' she asked hopefully but the cameraman shrugged his shoulders impatiently.

It was the last day of shooting for this soap commercial. Everyone was packing up to get home and he wanted to get away. There was something depressing about this location and he really didn't want to be still there when the technicians were clearing up the scaffolding and the miles and miles of electric cable and stowing all the other accessories of filming away in the huge articulated trailers.

'No,' he said finally, stepping back as she closed the boot of the car. 'He's the only one I've ever heard of around here. There's bound to be others dotted around the country but I haven't a clue where they are.'

'It's crazy – I feel more nervous about going back into Goats Head Alley than I do about going to the dentist,' Tuppence muttered irritably, pulling up at the first telephone kiosk on her way back to the city.

She felt exhausted and her eyes were sore with tiredness but she knew she must follow up Harry's advice before returning to the Watchgate. She was sure the telephone operator must have thought she was mad wanting to talk to a priest about ghosts, but she managed eventually to connect her with some bishop or archdeacon in the Cathedral Mews who knew all about hauntings and exorcisms. The guy had soothed her, assuring her that hauntings were rarely harmful or dangerous and advising her to return home, promising her that the local vicar would be round to see her before nightfall.

The Vicar of Cripplegate Church sat on the edge of his chair, sipping at his coffee with shallow, bird-quick motions. He was smiling and nodding his head at Tuppence, his gold-rimmed spectacles catching the afternoon sunlight each time his head moved as he listened to her explanation of the nature of the haunting.

'No, no, there's never been any sightings of ghosts in either Elm Hill or Lobster Lane, Miss Trilby,' he soothed in a rather supercilious voice, carefully putting the half-empty cup down on the coffee table and pressing his fingertips together as if he was about to pray. 'But the Watchgate is quite another matter. It is so full of history you see, I'm sure it's positively teeming with ghosts.'

His smile seemed to thicken as though he was enjoying the look of alarm that showed in Tuppence's eyes, and he allowed the tension to tighten while he sipped at his coffee again.

'But you need not worry about evil ghosts haunting you in the Watchgate, Miss Trilby, you have witches' barriers built into the fireplace and a door that has been carved to protect you against demons. I am sure you are quite safe here.'

'What do you mean – witches' barriers and carvings on the door against demons?' Tuppence asked, trying to ignore the Vicar's irritating habit of joining his hands together piously before each answer. It was as if he believed his replies came straight from heaven.

'I have made a special study of mediaeval reliefs and carvings,' he replied haughtily over the rim of his cup before he replaced it on the coffee table, and he paused as he deliberately joined his fingertips one by one. He pointed with the reverence of a water diviner into the depths of the inglenook to the high-backed wooden benches.

'The previous owners of this historic house allowed me to examine the rare carvings on those benches. If you look at them closely you will see that they are witches' barriers.

There are twelve horizontal bands carved beneath a cross of St Andrew, and they are the only surviving examples that I know of in the whole of Norfolk. A few carvings still exist in Yorkshire and Lancashire if you know where to look.'

Tuppence leaned forward with new interest and looked at the rough polished carvings. 'Yes, there, I can see them, but what do they do?'

The Vicar chuckled and pressed his praying fingertips to his chin.

'Do?' he murmured thoughtfully. 'They don't actually *do* anything, Miss Trilby, but they were originally carved as a defence against witches entering this house. You see, in mediaeval times, and later of course, right up until the late eighteenth century, the common mass of people believed that a witch, or indeed anything evil, could not enter or cast a spell over or harm anyone within a dwelling that had a witches' barrier carved on it.'

'Is that right?' Tuppence exclaimed, crossing to the fireplace and staring up towards the small clay chimney pot that she could just see beyond the bend in the brickwork. 'And I thought those carvings were for decoration. But why put a barrier in the chimney? No one could squeeze down through that small round hole, surely?'

The Vicar laughed out loud at her ignorance and drained the dregs in his coffee cup, rattling both cup and saucer as he put it down.

'Chimneys were a lot larger, proper thoroughfares, in those days, Miss Trilby. Why, children scuttled up and down them sweeping them clean, and I'm sure if you look closely you will still be able to see the bricks that were set slightly proud of the wall – they were used as steps. And don't forget people believed that witches could change themselves into the shapes of their familiars. No, they had to protect the chimneys as much as the thresholds in the doorways. That's why the door of the Watchgate is so intricately carved; each panel is an essay against evil.' He glanced down at his watch and rose to his feet.

'You must know the stories. Why don't you stay and have another cup of coffee and tell me some of them?' Tuppence asked quickly. His knowledge of customs and of the Watchgate's carvings fascinated her.

'It's rather late I'm afraid, perhaps another time,' he muttered apologetically. 'I have to rush, there's an evening service in twenty minutes. But why don't you come? Cripplegate Church is almost as old as the Watchgate and it's only just around the corner. The main entrance is in Offal Street and there's our ruined tower. That backs on to Goats Head Alley.'

Tuppence shivered at the mention of that claustrophobic courtyard as she followed the Vicar to the door. 'There used to be a taxidermist called Sleuth or something who lived in Goats Head Alley. Do you know if he's still there?' she asked.

The Vicar nodded. 'Oh yes, yes, that would be Mr Strewth. He's in the corner next to the ruined tower. Kindly old chap, but he's a bit of a recluse you know. Thinks of nothing but his collection of animals. We normally allow him to display his stuffed cats on the broken wall of the tower if the weather's fine. But why do you ask about him?'

'Oh, I hit an owl early this morning on my way to the coast and I wanted to have it stuffed rather than throw it in the trash.' She tried to keep her voice level and easy. 'And I just wondered if you knew the guy.'

'Well, he's perfectly harmless, Miss Trilby, if that is what you are bothered about. If I were you I would take that owl round to him first thing in the morning. Now I really must be going or evensong will start without me.'

Tuppence smiled and thanked the Vicar as he hurried out into the street. 'But the ghosts,' she called after him anxiously, making him pause. 'Are you really sure they won't harm me?'

The Vicar smiled and pressed his hands together once more. 'I sprinkled holy water over the threshold some years ago, Miss Trilby. Any evil presence in the Watchgate would have been exorcized. I assure you that whatever you experienced, ghosts, spirits, call them what you like, they cannot harm you. Please remember the atmosphere in the Watchgate must be thick with history – after all it has stood watching over the safety of the people of this city for almost a thousand years. But I would be careful venturing out into the street at night with that murderer on the loose. He's much more dangerous than a street full of ghosts.'

'Thanks,' Tuppence called after him.

She stood there for a moment in the open doorway and looked down the hill towards Castle Street. It all looked so peaceful in the soft early evening sunlight that it was difficult to imagine the horsemen or the creatures that had terrified her the night before. She frowned and brushed her hair back off her forehead. Perhaps she was letting her imagination run riot. Perhaps she had turned a common prowler into an imaginary hoard of creatures and then dreamed up horsemen to protect her in the dark. But that didn't explain away the scratches and splintered gouges in the carvings on the door.

The phone rang inside the Watchgate, breaking into her thoughts and making her jump. 'Hi, Harry. I was going to phone you in an hour,' she smiled, cradling the receiver against her cheek. She heard the concern in his voice.

'Yes, I did call a priest and I spoke to a bishop or someone. And the vicar of the church out back of the house came and visited, he's only just left after putting my mind at rest. He assured me that the city isn't haunted and that I'm quite safe.'

But Harry wasn't easily convinced by her bravado and he pressed her for answers, making her go all over it again. 'OK, OK. I'll visit that museum first thing tomorrow morning and check out those horsemen, if that will make you feel better,' she retorted, her voice irritable with tiredness.

'I'm sorry that I kept you up most of last night, Harry. Perhaps I over-reacted, jumped at a few shadows because I was too tired. I just don't know how much of it was real any more. I'm too exhausted to even think about it right now. I thought I'd just catch a bite to eat up town and then get an early night and have a good sleep. I'm sure everything will be fine.'

'Sure, sure,' Harry answered. 'But promise me two things, kid. First, you don't walk about the city after dark – take the car. And secondly, you phone me tomorrow.'

Tuppence smiled and suppressed a yawn. 'Sure, of course, Harry. The car's parked right out front, I'll take it.'

But after Harry disconnected she hesitated with her hand on the door latch. She was undecided where she would go to eat. She was as hungry as hell. The cafés and bistros on the edge of the market were the closest, but after last night she wanted somewhere brighter and safer – away from the old quarter. Then she remembered the hotel she had used before she bought the Watchgate. Sure, their food wasn't the best in town but their restaurant was bright and busy. Yes, she'd feel safe in the White Hart.

She parked the car with its wheels almost touching the

hotel entrance and charmed the doorman into keeping an eye on it for her. The head waiter found her a table, facing the bow windows that looked out on to the street, without any trouble. She sat down wearily and stared out into the busy street, barely noticing the waiters who brought her the food. She sat huddled over her plate, eating fast, oblivious to the hum of conversation and the clatter of plates all around her. She wanted to believe that last night hadn't happened, she wanted to believe that she had imagined it all, but her knuckles were white where she gripped her fork and her eyes kept scanning the crowded pavements. Darkness was falling and deepening her doubts as the shadows thickened.

'Is everything to your liking, miss?' The head waiter's voice made her jump. He was bending over her and looking anxiously down at her pale, drawn face.

'Yes, everything's fine, thanks. It's just been a long day and I'm in a bit of a hurry . . .' she explained apologetically. She paid the bill without waiting for her coffee and hurried out through the lobby towards her car.

The receptionist smiled and greeted her by asking how she liked the Watchgate. She slowed. It would be so easy to stay here, all she had to do was ask for a room. There were doormen and porters and there was someone at the desk all night. She would be so safe.

'Oh, the Watchgate's great – really great,' she replied, banishing the desire to run. 'It's what I always wanted, all those beams and the big fireplace. It's so beautiful.'

And she hurried out, unlocked the car and shoehorned herself behind the wheel before the temptation to stay overwhelmed her.

She slowed as she crossed the bridge over the River Wensum and felt the rumble of the uneven cobbles beneath the wheels. It was as if the bridge marked an imaginary gate. The crowds thinned out, the architecture changed and the buildings drew together in a conspiratorial silence. Alleyways and lanes led off on either side of the main thoroughfare into a warren of dark secret places. She turned into Castle Street, the brick and flint wall of the rear of the museum on her left. Further up the street she could see the entrance to Elm Hill and ahead, beyond that, she could make out the striped awnings of the market and the dark openings of the Castle Narrows that brooded in the shadows of the castle walls. A cat streaked out across the road ahead of her and ran into Elm Hill; another broke cover twenty yards further up the road, meowing as it vanished into an alley crack.

. 'Cats!' she muttered. 'It's only cats.' But there was still time to change her mind. She could accelerate up into Castle Meadow, turn left and drive until she met Tombland, and from there she could recross the bridge over the river and leave – or she could face up to her fears. She slowed and turned the Lotus into Elm Hill and stopped, keeping the headlights on main beam. Her heart was hammering in her chest, her hands were gripping the wheel as she searched the shadows. She let her eyes move slowly from the doors of the museum and up towards the Watchgate, studying each dark archway and opening. Nothing moved. Elm Hill looked innocently empty.

Here and there, lights burned dimly in shop fronts, casting eerie shadows amongst the displays. Tuppence gave a sigh of relief and eased her sweating grip on the steering wheel. Much as she wanted to believe that the previous night had been a figment of her imagination, she half-expected hideous creatures to erupt from the alleyways on either side of the hill – or horsemen to materialize around the car. She let in the clutch and accelerated swiftly up the hill to park right outside the Watchgate. She studied the eaves and the guttering, the window frame and the over-hanging gallery, and satisfied herself that there were no snakes or lizards clinging to the house. Then she dashed across the pavement with the key all ready in her hand and let herself in.

As soon as she was inside she switched on all the lights, feeling a wave of relief as the feeling of safety closed in around her, but she was tired, exhausted, too bone-weary to realize that there was more than peace offered to her by the atmosphere in the Watchgate. Her eyes felt raw from the tension over the previous twenty-four hours.

'Well, magic carvings, if you have the power to keep out evil then use it – please. Keep me safe tonight,' she yawned as she threw her bag into the chair by the inglenook and crossed towards the stairs.

She fell asleep the moment her head touched the pillow, a deep dreamless sleep that shut out the scratchings at the windows and the faint tapping on the door. She slept through the scrape of clawed feet on the cobbles and the hoot of owls hovering around the chimney pots. Twice she turned restlessly and cried out in her sleep and twice the horsemen cantered swiftly through the darkness to patrol the road outside.

Tuppence awoke refreshed and listened to the noise of the city as the morning sunlight filtered through the chink in the curtains. She stretched, throwing back the duvet as she reached for her watch. It read 11.30.

'Jesus, I must have been tired,' she murmured, tumbling out of bed.

She drew the curtains open a finger's span and blinked at the bright sunlight on Elm Hill. It looked so peaceful, the tall mediaeval houses leaning shoulder to shoulder up the hill, cars and vans trundling slowly across the cobbles as they passed the museum, browsers peering in the galleries and antique shops.

'So much for ghosts!' she laughed as she drew the curtains and moved to the bathroom.

She switched on the light and the extractor fan came on as she went to brush her teeth. It whirred, shuddered, stopped and then juddered slowly into life, spitting out bits of brightly coloured feathers that fluttered down to the carpet at her feet. She stepped back and frowned – what the hell was going on? The fan had worked perfectly the day before; she had noticed that you could see the lights on the castle parapets through the spinning blades. She bent and stared at the feathers. They were from a tropical bird, vivid greens and blues. She shivered and it was as if the shadow of the haunting darkened the sunlight in the bedroom behind her. She looked anxiously over her shoulder and listened. The bell of Cripplegate Church struck twelve noon, the hum of the city went on uninterrupted.

'Pull yourself together, you're jumping at shadows again. This has got nothing to do with those ghosts,' she muttered to herself in the mirror. 'It's only some old feathers that someone must have stuffed into the fan some time. They could have come from anywhere.'

She picked up a handful of the shredded feathers and turned them over in her hand; they felt real enough. She crushed them in her palm before dropping them into the bin. After a shower, she dressed herself in faded denim jeans and a loose silk top and hurried down the stairs in old trainers to start the day. She rang the photographic agency first while her coffee was percolating.

'No, I need a short break. Yes, now. I want a rest before I start filming in Cairo. That's right, nothing for the next couple of days. I want to explore this city, get to know it.

Yes, of course, I'll phone you on Monday about work!'
She laughed as she replaced the receiver and put the telephone into the disused bread oven.

She hadn't taken a few days off for ages. It felt good not to be rushing some place, searching her reflection before she set out, looking for those telltale signs of wear and tear that age insisted on etching on her face. The details that the camera's savage eye showed as the feather edge of ruin, the beginnings of history.

9

The Substance of Dreams

Tuppence walked down to the museum, crossing Elm Hill to enjoy the warmth of the sun on her face and the hot summer breeze ruffling through her hair. Holidays were a tonic and she was eager to explore the city and discover its secrets. She thought she would do the museum first and lay those ghosts before she delivered the owl to the taxidermist in Goats Head Alley. She climbed the worn stone steps to the museum entrance and reached out to push open the door, but she hesitated, her optimism for adventure evaporating as she reached the vaulted entrance hall. She could just make out the shapes of the exhibits that filled this echoing cathedral of the past.

'Damn!' she muttered, glancing over her shoulder towards the bright awnings of the covered market in Castle Meadow. Her courage was failing before she had even started. She wanted to retrace her steps and vanish anonymously amongst the crowds who jostled for space on the pavements of Castle Street. She wanted to slip unnoticed beneath the crackling, flapping awnings of the market instead of getting to the bottom of this haunting.

'Get a hold on yourself,' she whispered. 'You're only going to be looking at a load of dummies, for Chrissake.'

She pushed against the doors and entered the cool, whispering silence of the museum. 'Hey, I've come back to take a closer look at . . .'

Her voice fell away to nothing as the museum attendant sitting in his alcove near the entrance turned and rose to his feet, gazing enquiringly at her. 'Yes, miss? Is there some way I can be of help to you?'

'No, no, I'm sorry, I thought you were someone else,' she apologized as she realized that he wasn't the kindly old man who had shown her around on her last visit.

'I'm not allowed to leave my chair here, miss, but there's an information desk just inside the main hall if you need assistance,' the attendant offered.

'Oh, no, not at all, it's OK,' she murmured. 'Thanks anyway.'

She turned thoughtfully towards the huge echoing hall and screwed up her courage. She would have liked the old attendant guy as her guide, he would have known exactly where she could find those horsemen who had ridden up Elm Hill in the middle of the night. All she would have had to do was describe the uniforms that they wore. He had known so much about the place.

'What the hell. I'll just take a quick look inside,' she whispered as she left the entrance hall behind her and walked into the depths of the museum.

The hum and bustle of the city vanished. It was cool and the shadows seemed dark and secretive beneath the galleries after the bright sunlight outside. The air was breathlessly silent, even the soft, squeaky tread of her trainers seemed muffled by the atmosphere. Tuppence widened her eyes against the gloom and moved as cautiously as a cat down the long line of exhibits. She paused frequently to read the legends on the brass plaques closest to her, or to sweep her gaze across the further silent, statue-still horses and soldiers who filled the outer aisles, marching away in endless ranks on either side of her towards the grand staircase at the far end of the hall. There were so many exhibits, hundreds, perhaps thousands. It would probably take her all day, or even longer, to inspect them all.

She stopped, defeated by the enormity of the task. The chance of finding those few horsemen amongst all the exhibits was slender. She stood in the centre of the main aisle, her hands on her hips, and slowly shook her head as she regarded the glittering brass and braid, the bright colours of the uniforms and the forest of bayonet points and lance tips which crowded her on both sides.

'OK,' she murmured, more to herself than to anyone who might be listening, 'I was jumping at shadows the other night. There's nothing here for me to worry about. You don't scare me, you're just a beautiful collection from the past . . .'

She paused as she realized that she had raised her voice. Now she was actually talking to the statues! How ridiculous! She glanced round anxiously to see if any of the other visitors to the museum had noticed and breathed a sigh of relief to find that she was alone. She began to retrace her steps towards the entrance when a figure over on her left, well away from the main aisle, caught her eye. Frowning she stopped and stared at the rider. He was wearing a dusty blue jacket with bands of gold braid across the chest. She could just see the head of his horse, the rest of the figure was blocked from her sight by the other exhibits. From the colour of the horse's jowl it looked like a sorrel. She felt her spine tingle. It looked like the horse that she had dreamed about the other night. She couldn't be sure, at this distance, whether it was the rider who had saluted her in her dreams, but he looked too damn like him for her to leave the museum without a closer look.

Reluctantly Tuppence left the main aisle. She had come here for reassurance, not to add further doubts, and she felt cold with fear as she threaded her way between the crowded exhibits and passed close to a coloured drum horse and its drummer, and a team of gun-carriage horses in the act of being led away by two troopers. She quickly moved around the uncoupled gun carriage and skirted an officer and two mounted lancers who blocked her path. The closer she got the more she was sure the figure resembled the guy who had saluted her in her dream. Another couple of steps and she knew for sure. This *was* the man. She stood right beside him, holding her breath in anticipation. The silence of the museum suddenly became stifling, it seemed to crackle with tension, yet it wasn't frightening or hostile. It was as if the whole place was holding its breath and waiting while she looked up at the mounted figure.

'How could I have dreamt about you in such detail?' she whispered.

The travel-stained rider was exactly as she remembered, even down to the scarlet saddle cloth edged with white and the saddle roll with the carbine rifle strapped across it. The horseman was sitting slightly differently, leaning forward, taking his weight on the balls of his feet in the stirrups. His right hand was upon the hilt of his sword and he was gazing into the distance and frowning slightly, a troubled look in his sea-grey eyes. Tuppence moved to the side of the exhibit and bent to read the small brass plaque on its wooden stand.

'Scout and outrider – 10th Hussars. 1824.

'The uniform and saddle belonged to Trooper Dibble of the 10th Hussars who was twice mentioned in dispatches for his bravery and selfless devotion to duty while gathering intelligence of the Russian advance on Sebastopol.'

Tuppence straightened up and frowned as she looked at the horseman. It was uncanny that she had created him in her dream in such fine detail, even down to the splashes of mud and dirt on his boots and breeches. And the colour of his horse matched her dream exactly.

She smiled and murmured thoughtfully, 'I couldn't have chosen anyone better to protect me from those creatures than a horseman who lived and slept in the saddle, who survived on his wits as he travelled by the roughest roads to get his dispatches through. You must have been always ready to shoot your way out. I bet . . .'

She paused, her eyes focusing on the carbine, and glanced quickly around, listening for the sound of other visitors. The heavy silence told her she was alone. She stretched up and worked the gun loose from the straps on the saddle roll and carefully lowered it with both hands.

'If you really had ridden up Elm Hill to protect me and it wasn't all a dream then this rifle will be loaded. You wouldn't have gone anywhere unprepared.'

She examined the rifle closely, turning it over in her hands. The wooden stock was scarred and scratched with age and frequent use, but there were fresh traces of oil on the breech as though it had been recently cleaned. Tuppence knew a little about guns. Harry had insisted that she learned to shoot, it was good for her balance and it helped to concentrate the mind. Tuppence also enjoyed the sport and had become a crack shot. But this rifle was older than anything that she had ever handled before and she had to figure out how to open the breech. Keeping her fingers well away from the trigger she worked the bolt and it suddenly slid open to reveal a bullet lying there ready in the breech. The colour drained from her face and her fingers fumbled as she closed the rifle. She hadn't wanted to see the bullet lying there, that only gave credibility to her nightmare. She had wanted to believe that she had dreamt everything. It would have been much better if the breech had been rusted up from disuse and not freshly oiled.

She stood there, trembling with confusion, not knowing what to think or who to turn to. She wanted to stop the nightmare happening again but she did not know how. Children's voices suddenly broke the silence and their light, quick footsteps broke through her thoughts. Tuppence reached up and thrust the rifle roughly back under the straps of the saddle roll. The barrel caught; it refused to go any further and stuck out untidily to one side.

'Damn!' she hissed. The noisy children had reached the gun carriage, in another moment they would see her tampering with the rifle and she could just imagine their shouts of delight if they thought they had caught her doing something underhand.

She turned on her heel and began to slip noiselessly away when she realized what the children were doing. They were running between the exhibits, pulling roughly at the horses' manes and tails and snatching at the soldiers' dispatch bags, trying to dislodge their lances and unsheath their swords. Two of them were clambering up on to the gun carriage while a third had managed to mount the riderless horse and was using the loops of the reins to whip the horse's neck, swearing and kicking savagely at the creature's flanks with his heels.

Tuppence stopped, her face tight with anger at the senseless way the boys were mauling the exhibits.

'Hey, you!' she shouted, advancing towards them. 'Get off! Get away from there!'

For a moment the children stared at her, their mouths hanging open in surprise. The tallest boy, sitting on the gun carriage, recovered his composure first and swore at her, then jumped lightly to the ground and ran off. The other two cursed and laughed but looked a little shame-faced as they quickly followed on his heels. Tuppence turned as she heard heavier footsteps hurrying towards her. It was a red-faced attendant who had heard the children's shouts from the top of the main staircase and had run down to investigate.

'Three brats were climbing all over everything. They ran off that way,' Tuppence answered his breathless enquiry and pointed away to her left. She watched him lumber off in pursuit.

'Bloody kids,' she muttered as she made her way into the entrance hall.

She paused, her hand on the swing door, and looked back for a moment, picking out the serious faces of the scarlet-coated soldiers in the redoubt. Behind them, at the foot of the broad staircase, she saw the leaping figure of Colonel Hawkesbury, dramatically stretching out his open hand to snatch back the captured colours from the French. She had returned to the museum to lay the ghosts of her dreams but her visit had left her feeling more unsettled and more anxious to escape from what she did not understand.

She shivered, as if cold fingers had run down her spine, and pushed her way out into the sunshine. There she stood on the top step and soaked in the warmth from the sun's rays. She was undecided about what she should do next. Should she visit the taxidermist before lunch or explore the Castle Narrows?

'The owl,' she decided out loud. 'I had better get rid of that next, before it goes rotten in the trunk of my car.'

Tuppence clutched the plastic carrier bag containing the mangled remains of the owl and hurried up Lobster Lane. It looked peaceful enough in the sunlight but she kept a sharp eye on the narrow openings that lay on either side. She found Goats Head Alley easily enough and passed beneath its low echoing archway, then hesitated on the threshold of the small courtyard beyond it. It looked quite different from how she remembered it. Before, the bright moonlight had cast black mysterious shadows into every corner. Now it just looked cold and dreary, the tall overhanging warehouse fronts with their gantries and pulleys crowding out the small patch of summer sky. The courtyard was as quiet as a tomb and the air smelt foul and damp.

Tuppence stepped across the patch of sunlight and saw again the faded gilt letters above the shop window by the ruined church tower. It read 'Taxidermist', but the place looked deserted, the window smeared with years of grime.

'That vicar was wrong. The old boy must have died years ago,' she sighed as she reached the shop front, twisting the handles of the plastic carrier bag between her fingers.

She bent down and pressed her nose against the window pane, cupping her hand beside her face to cut out the reflection of the daylight, and stared into the gloomy interior of the shop. 'Jesus,' she murmured as she narrowed her eyes for a better look.

The place was stuffed full of animals, thousands of them were crowding every inch of space. She saw foxes, eagles, owls, crocodiles, roe bucks and just about every species that she had ever dreamed existed, and more besides.

'This place is a regular Noah's Ark. Perhaps this taxidermist isn't dead after all,' she gasped as she glanced at the jumble of tools and books and papers that were strewn across the top of the counter.

She straightened up and tried the door handle. The door gave easily and a bell that hung on the inside jangled noisily as it swung open. She stepped over the threshold and stopped abruptly, wrinkling her nose at the sharp dry smell that closed in all around her and made her want to sneeze.

The door swung shut behind her and the bell rang again as the latch clicked.

'Hello – is there anybody here?' she called anxiously as she stepped backwards and swept her gaze across the menagerie that almost crowded her out of the shop.

Something sharp dug into the small of her back and she stopped and spun round, crying out and almost dropping the owl as she stared up at the huge brown bear that stood to the right of the shop door. She had backed against its rigid outstretched claws. Its mouth was set in a snarl and its small murderous eyes seemed to be staring straight down at her. She stumbled away from it and backed against the counter. All the animals in the shop seemed to be watching her. The silence had become stifling. Everywhere she looked, sharp eyes stared back. The only sound was the racing irregular tick of the clocks on the other side of the doorway.

Tuppence looked up at the clocks and shuddered as she caught her breath. She saw the mass of glistening snakes, wound together in a frozen knot. The more she looked around the shop the more snakes she saw, coiled on the display cases, hiding in dark corners. They were just like the ones she had seen clinging to the front of the Watch-gate, the ones that the horsemen had picked up on their lance tips in her dreams.

'No, no, no, it's just not possible,' she hissed, clenching her trembling fingers so tight that her knuckles bled white and her nails bit painfully into the palms of her hands.

She wanted to run for the door and escape, but a tiny, brave part of her wanted to look more closely at the snakes, to trace along their glistening bodies for telltale signs of lance wounds. The thought that these long-dead creatures might be a part of her nightmare made her thoughts career out of control. Black crows perched forward from a high rail that ran the length of the shop so that they seemed to be staring inquisitively straight down at her.

Tuppence swallowed and fought to pull herself together. It was ridiculous to be afraid of a shop full of stuffed animals. They were all dead, after all, for Chrissake. She took a step towards the door then saw that the floor between the larger animals was literally solid with every imaginable kind of reptile.

'Oh, no . . .' she began as the door at the back of the shop swung open and a tall stooping figure in a dirty white coat hurried in.

'I thought I heard somebody snooping around. The shop's closed. Can't you read the sign in the window?'

He stopped muttering abruptly as he saw her and his wild eyes narrowed into cunning slits. His mouth split open into a wet, brittle smile and he licked his lips as he advanced across the shop towards her. He reminded her of a stork as he picked his way over and between his menagerie, moving with an awkward high-stepping gait, his head thrust forward on a neck of scrawny, wrinkled skin. But she didn't laugh. The closer he came to her the more she sensed some shadow of darkness lurking just beneath the surface of his calculating smile. There was some threat lying hidden behind his yellowing teeth and cunning eyes. He circled behind her, patting the huge brown bear's arm and whispering to the animal as he stopped between her and the door, effectively cutting off her only means of escape. He looked out into the courtyard as if he was searching for someone, before he spoke to her.

'Why, Miss Trilby, this is a surprise. How nice of you to call on me alone,' he soothed, rubbing his long dry fingers together with a sound like the rasp of fine sandpaper.

Tuppence shivered. He had spoken as if he expected her,

as if he knew her. How had he known her name? He leant closer, his face only inches from her, and she recoiled at the stench of death and decay that clung to the fabric of his clothes. He was staring at her, stripping away her loose top and jeans with his wild eyes, but he wasn't undressing her sexually. She could have coped with that, it disgusted her but it happened all the time. No, this frightening-looking guy was trying to look underneath her skin. She could have sworn that he was mentally measuring her muscles and bones, just as an undertaker would measure up a corpse before making the coffin to put it in. He made tiny clicking sounds with his tongue against the back of his teeth and licked absently at his thin lips before he spoke.

'You have come too early. I am far from ready to preserve . . .' He stopped with the sentence unfinished as he caught sight of the plastic carrier bag that she was clutching in her right hand. His experienced eye picked out the shape of a bird lying in the bottom of it. He frowned and stepped back a pace, realizing that in his surprise at seeing her standing in his shop he had almost blurted out his secret.

He blinked and raked his fingers through his hair as he recovered his composure. She was alone. Now was the perfect moment to capture her. He knew he must be careful not to frighten her or give her an inkling of his true intentions, at least not until he had securely tied her and held the chloroform swab an inch from her nose. She could struggle as much as she liked then; she would be dead long before her cursed soldiers reached his courtyard. He smiled to himself. She would thank him when he mounted her as the centrepiece of his collection, he was sure of it. She would thank him for giving her the chance of immortality, for halting the creep of the years that age was writing on her skin. But now, this minute, he must reassure her, make her see him as her friend. He must dispel the look of fear in her eyes while he moved behind the counter and picked up the ice-cold bottle of chloroform.

He smiled as he edged back, raising his arms, stretching out the tails of his dirty white coat behind him as though they were stiff, featherless wings, as he pointed at the crowd of animals that filled the shop.

'Do you like my collection? There are some of the rarest animals in the world here. I have saved them from crumbling away into dust. Yes, I have stopped them from getting another moment older. Isn't that wonderful, miss?' He smiled at her.

Tuppence shuddered. The thought of being trapped here for ever in this dirty, dusty, stinking shop appalled her. She wanted to get out of here fast, get right away from this creepy old guy with his wild staring eyes and his collection of the dead, but she fought down the urge to try to rush past him or nimbly side-step around him in a dash for the door. She sensed danger, so instead she began to try to charm her way out. She smiled back at him.

'Yes, they're really beautiful. It must have taken a lot of work to get them looking like that, and here I am taking up your valuable time. Perhaps I ought to leave right now and let you get on.'

Ludo laughed, his voice shaking as he answered, 'Oh no, miss, there's no need for you to rush away, it's spring-cleaning time around here, that's why my collection are all out of their cases. They're being oiled and sprayed to keep them looking their best. We don't want any fleas or mites infecting their fur and feathers, do we?'

Tuppence felt the smile tighten with panic. The taxidermist seemed to want to keep her there and the smell of the place was beginning to make her light-headed. Her instincts screamed at her to get out of there quickly.

'No, I really must go.' She took a step towards the door. 'Look, I've got to meet my agent for lunch,' she added quickly as a shadow of anger crossed his face.

He was reaching for something beneath his counter. His lips twitched as he glanced sideways up to the huge bear and muttered something beneath his breath as he moved back towards her, the bottle of chloroform and a wad of cotton wool in his right hand. Tuppence saw that the pupils of his eyes had shrunk to mere pinpoints, giving him a wild demented look.

Tuppence caught a whiff of chloroform and, in an instant, realized what he was intending to do. She suddenly remembered the owl in the plastic bag and hurled it at him as she grabbed at the door handle with her other hand.

Strewth cursed under his breath and swept the bag away angrily as she fled. The bear growled and turned towards the open door, flexing its claws. The snakes began slithering around the casings of the clocks.

'No, be still!' he hissed sharply, standing the chloroform bottle down on the counter. 'We've missed the perfect opportunity. We'll never catch her in the streets, they are too crowded. I am far from ready to preserve her skin, but we'll have to take her tonight. We cannot afford to let her get away. You must help me. First, I must destroy her soldiers and burn down the museum.'

Tuppence slowed beneath the archway and glanced back over her shoulder. Beyond the still-open shop door she could see the tall thin taxidermist in his dirty white coat, waving his fist, and apparently talking to thin air.

'He's not a harmless old eccentric, he's a bloody

madman. He should be put away,' she sobbed as she tried to pull herself together.

She hurried up Lobster Lane towards the crowds of Castle Meadow and the market place but she couldn't shake off the memory of that horrible place. It made her flesh crawl. The dry, sharp smell of those dead animals still seemed to cling to the back of her throat and the airless, gloomy silence, broken only by the erratic ticking of all those clocks, seemed to echo in her head. She remembered how the clocks had been swarming with snakes. It wasn't only the crazy taxidermist who had frightened her; the stuffed animals had really set her nerves on edge. They had seemed so real, so lifelike, and they held an awesome menace. She would swear that their eyes had followed her every movement. It was funny how none of them were in their display cases; you would have thought that the old guy would have replaced them as soon as he had cleaned them rather than leave them crowding out his entire shop.

'I'll keep well away from Goats Head Alley, that's for sure,' she promised herself as she left the market and waited for a gap in the traffic before she crossed over into Tombland.

Richard had just finished a late lunch and was heading back towards his office when he caught sight of her. 'I'm . . . I'm . . . I'm so sorry about the other day,' he stammered after he had greeted her.

Tuppence was glad of a friendly face after her ordeal in the taxidermist's shop and she laughed easily. 'Oh, forget it. I'm just going for a cup of coffee, will you join me?'

Richard hesitated and glanced at his watch. He had a client due in his office in five minutes. 'Look, I'd love to, but I really have to rush just now. Perhaps I could buy you a drink later, say this evening around nine thirty?'

Tuppence shook her head. She had promised Harry she would be in when he phoned.

'Perhaps another time then?' Richard answered, trying to mask his disappointment with a smile.

'Wait!' Tuppence called after him as he turned to go. She didn't relish spending the whole evening alone. 'I've got to wait for a transatlantic call, but I'd love it if you could drop in for a coffee.'

10

Driven into the Flames

Tuppence ate early, a hot chilli in La Mexico on the south side of the Meadows, and then she had returned home to wait for Harry's call. It was a warm airless evening, without even the slightest breeze to ruffle the curtains of her window. She felt hot and restless and would have liked to leave the door of the Watchgate open to allow the air to circulate while she percolated some coffee, but she thought better of it and slipped the bolts securely. She yawned and glanced at her watch. It was only nine, but she was tired, and half regretted inviting Richard to drop in. The percolator hissed and bubbled from where it stood on the left-hand side of the inglenook, close to the fire basket, and the rich smell of coffee slowly permeated throughout the low-beamed room.

She picked up one of the magazines from the coffee table and idly leafed through the pages before heading towards the stairs. As her hand reached for the banister rail she heard loud crashes behind her, as if someone was hammering on the door of the Watchgate. There was a muffled voice crying out, begging her to open the door.

'Richard, is that you?' she gasped, dropping the magazine and running to the door, not daring to open it. Again the voice came, this time almost screaming with panic.

'Richard – Richard, what's wrong?' she cried, throwing back the bolts, feeling the old door tremble and shake as someone hammered frantically on the carved wooden panels.

'For God's sake open it!' Richard screamed and then other noises, snarls and growls, swallowed up his voice and made Tuppence's blood run cold as she lifted the latch. Casting around, she saw the brass poker lying beside the door. She snatched it up and gripped it tightly in her right hand as the door suddenly burst open with such force that it sent her reeling backwards.

'Jes . . . Jesus Christ!' she gasped in horror as she regained her balance and looked up at the hideous figure that filled the doorway.

'*Oh my God, Richard, is that you?*' The words screamed in her head but no sound passed her lips except the rattle of her teeth chattering together. She was paralysed with terror as she stared at the struggling figure on the threshold. She knew the voice had been Richard's but the face was barely recognizable. It had been torn apart; a flap of skin hung across his bloody eyes, deep gouges split his cheeks and his lips frothed bright bubbles of spittle and blood as he tried to scream. His untidy tweed jacket and corduroy trousers hung about him in tattered ribbons.

'Tuppence, help me, help me,' he whimpered as he thrashed and flailed his arms furiously like a drowning swimmer.

Something was trying to pull him away from the Watchgate and he fought to find a purchase on the smooth spiralling columns that stood on either side of the wooden door frame. Tuppence raised the poker and stared up into the dark shape of a huge towering creature, silhouetted against the lamplight, its vast shadow falling on the wall of the street opposite. It snarled and tightened its glistening and bloody claws around Richard's chest and throat and wrenched his clutching fingers free of the columns.

'Tuppen . . .' he gurgled as he tried to reach out for her with jerking fingers before the claws tore out his windpipe and dragged him away into the darkness.

'Richard! Richard!' Tuppence shouted, forgetting caution as she ran over the threshold after him.

Too late she saw that the darkness on either side was crowded with menacing inhuman shapes. She stopped abruptly and turned back, leaping towards the open doorway of her sanctuary, but a second huge bear stepped in front of her and blocked her path, its bloody claws reaching out for her. She screamed out in terror, trying to duck beneath its outstretched arms and dive through the open door. She was a footstep from safety, almost over the threshold, when she saw the percolator rock backwards and forwards on its stand in the hearth. Suddenly it toppled sideways in a cloud of soot and ash. She felt the wind from the inglenook ruffle her hair, the pages of the magazines on the table turned in the wind and she smelt that same dry musty odour that had risen on the night of the last haunting of the Watchgate. The door of giants began to swing towards her, shutting her out from the light and safety within.

'No! Oh no,' she cried, dropping the poker and reaching out with both hands to try to stop it closing. But the bear was there first, snarling and rearing up, shifting its clawed feet on the threshold and pushing its shoulders against the closing door. The musty wind rose to a shrieking gale within the Watchgate, the magazines flew up in the air, tables overturned and chairs fell crashing to the ground. The iron hinges on the door creaked and groaned and the door slammed violently shut, throwing the huge brown bear out across the pavement. Tuppence crouched down, trembling with terror, pressing herself against the intricately carved panels at the bottom of the door. She could hear the howls and snarls of the creatures filling the darkness all around her and she pushed hopelessly against the door. But it was shut fast against her.

The bear rose slowly to its feet. Tuppence had to do something, and quickly. A lizard ran across her hand, making her leap up and look round desperately. The other, larger animals were moving towards her now. The Lotus was useless, even though it was only a few strides away, for the keys were in the Watchgate. Something sharp pricked her leg and she looked down to see a porcupine rattling its spines against her.

'I've got to escape. I've got to get out of this nightmare,' she hissed, backing away from the Watchgate.

The bear snarled and moved towards her, the other closed in beside it, out of the darkness, its mean, murderous eyes shining in the lamplight. Their huge shadows stretched out to engulf her.

Then Tuppence heard hoofbeats at the bottom of the hill. The soldiers, it must be the soldiers. She turned and ran down towards the sound. She tried to cross the road, desperately dodging between the animals, but they pushed and barged, herding her roughly towards the entrance of Lobster Lane. A gazelle raked its horns across her arm and a large black panther almost tripped her up. The bears were catching up with her, she could hear the scrape of their claws on the cobbles only a footstep behind.

At last she could see the horsemen. There were a dozen of them, spread out on the crown of the road, galloping hard towards her. The leading rider was suddenly in amongst the milling animals, his lance tip brutally skewering the panther, sending it crashing sideways. A second rider was standing in his stirrups, shouting something and pointing wildly towards the museum entrance with his sword.

Tuppence barely had time to glance at the museum as the swirling mass of animals crowded around her, surging towards Lobster Lane. A rider appeared beside her and reached down and grasped her arm, lifting her up on to his horse. She saw claws tear at the horse's flanks, slowing and stopping him as he struggled to break free from the mass of creatures. The rider twisted around in the saddle, slashing desperately at the huge bear. Tuppence slipped sideways on to the ground as the horse collapsed and when she regained her balance, she ran towards the museum. Breathlessly she leaped up the stone steps and threw her weight against the heavy glass and wooden doors. She had to get away. The doors creaked and moved but she slipped and fell on to her knees.

The bears had cast the rider aside and were after her, lumbering up the stone steps, snarling and clawing, as if to stop her entering the museum. They were close enough now for her to catch the dry sweet odour of the taxidermist's shop on their fur. The mass of animals howled and bayed and swarmed after her up the steps. The horsemen rode amongst them, hacking to left and right with scything sabre strokes.

'Get away from the museum,' shouted one of the riders as he pirouetted and spurred his horse up the steps in a desperate bid to reach her, but his warning was lost in the howling shrieks and growls. Tuppence screamed as a bear's claws grazed her arm, catching fast in the cuff of her silk blouse.

It snarled, curling its lips back across its teeth, as it pulled her towards him. She struck out at its arm but she felt weak and helpless against its strength as it lifted her up off the ground. Her sleeve began to tear at the shoulder seam. She heard hoofbeats on the top step and saw the flash of lamplight on the rider's sabre as he lunged at the huge animal. The bear growled and swung around to face the horseman. Tuppence felt the sleeve tear free and slip from her arm as the creature turned. She fell, tumbling sideways, hitting the doors on the way down, so that they gave against the force of her fall, opening inwards a crack.

She scrambled on hands and knees through the narrow slit and found herself in the darkened entrance hall. Looking back she cried out as she saw the two bears attacking the horseman, clawing him from the saddle and sending the horse crashing backwards down the stone steps. The bears grunted and turned back towards the doors, their huge, grotesque silhouettes blocking out the lamplight. Their claws smashed the glass and tore into the woodwork, the doors splintered and sagged on their hinges as the bears lunged into the museum and lumbered towards her. Tuppence crouched, paralysed with fear. She wanted to scream, to cry out for help, but her lips only trembled with terror. Behind her, the vast main hall and the rising galleries echoed to the clatter of hooves and whispering shouts.

She glanced wildly behind her into the dark echoing museum. She had no choice but to try to lose those foul creatures by hiding in the warren of display cases. There must be a door at the back of the museum; she would have to find it. She snatched a panicking breath and ran headlong into the dark hall.

She didn't see the tall stooping figure of Ludo Strewth, standing directly in her path, until it was too late. He was hunched over a lighted match, shielding it as the flame took a hold. She didn't see him, and she didn't notice the smell of the petrol that he had just finished pouring across the wooden floor. When she ran, blindly, straight into him, she sent him sprawling on to his knees. He cursed as the match flew out of his fingers and fell amongst the pools of petrol, its flame guttering and then flaring up as it ignited

173

the heavy liquid, and tongues of hungry flames fled away amongst the exhibits.

Tuppence stared down at him for a moment, recognizing him in the light of the flickering flames, mesmerized by his wild staring eyes.

'You're mad! You are stark raving mad,' she hissed, backing away, stepping into the rivers of orange flame as the bears lumbered up to stand on either side of him and the whole menagerie of animals began to stream into the museum.

Ludo Strewth stared up at her, his wild eyes blank with confusion. He blinked and twitched his fingers then sneered as he recognized her in the light of the flames.

'You're too late, Miss Trilby, too late to save your precious horsemen. They're all going to burn, burn to a cinder.' And he shrieked with laughter.

Suddenly the laughter died on his lips as he realized the danger. 'Come here, you, before the flames scorch your skin,' he hissed at her as she turned and fled deeper into the museum.

Turning on the bears he cursed them and beat his fists on their arms. 'You useless fools. You were to capture her and carry her into Goats Head Alley. Now she'll be ruined, destroyed.' He shrieked and raved in anger, snatching up the silk sleeve from where it was still hooked on to one of the bear's claws. The bears snarled at him and roughly pushed him aside, striding through the flames after Tuppence. The mass of animals swarmed after them, howling and baying as if for blood.

'No! No, don't follow her, you fools. The fire will consume you, too. Come back! Come back!' Strewth screamed.

He crushed the remnant of silk dementedly between his

fingers and gesticulated wildly at the horde of animals pouring into the rapidly spreading flames.

Tuppence looked around desperately and saw her pursuers swarming after her. Beside her, the uniforms of the closest of the exhibits had begun to burn, and were sending up plumes of dense black smoke. The fire was spreading across the whole of the interior of the museum and the entire floor was bathed in a flickering orange light. Everywhere she looked, new flames were racing over the floorboards between the stationary soldiers, following the wet trails of petrol and devouring everything in their path. But the exhibits seemed to be moving in the dancing light. All around her, horses and soldiers were fleeing from the flames. She heard the clatter of hoofbeats and the scrape of boots on the wooden floor. She tried to look more closely but the searing heat made her raise her arms to shield her face. She began to choke on the thickening smoke as she ran blindly through the maze of display cases.

She knew she had to find the door that lay somewhere at the back of the great hall, before the creatures from the taxidermist's shop caught up with her. They terrified her even more than the heat and smoke of the fire. They struck a terror in her deeper than anything she had ever encountered, and she would rather die than let them touch her. The smoke was thicker now and it made her cough and gasp; her eyes stung and gritty tears streamed down her cheeks. She stumbled dizzily against the sharp corner of a display case and sank on to her knees. She tried to rise but her head was spinning, her lungs felt as though they were about to burst and her legs buckled.

'Help me. Help me someone. For God's sake help me,' she wept against the roar of the flames.

The fire had spread throughout the great hall of the museum as it fed on the tinder-dry exhibits encircling her.

The heat was by now so intense that it was beginning to buckle the columns that supported the galleries, cracking the ceiling joists and bringing down whole sheets of crumbling plaster. The exhibits were, one by one, becoming bright torches of flame, toppling and crashing to the ground as the fire ate through their supports, and sending up showers of hot sparks into the darkening fog of smoke.

Tuppence choked and reached out to clutch at the leg of the display case that she had fallen against. She knew that while she had breath she must try to escape, that if she stayed kneeling where she was she would be burned to death. She closed her fingers around the leg of the case and screamed as the fire-hot varnish scalded the palm of her hand. She snatched it away and wept bitter tears of anger as she realized that it was hopeless, knowing that she could not even stand up. She was trapped. She looked up through the smoke and frowned, blinked and rubbed at her sore eyes. There were figures moving towards her through the smoke, bright-uniformed figures with horses. They were closing in from every direction. The exhibits had come to life.

She wanted to laugh, to shout, but her breaths were coming as whispered gasps. She tried to reach out her hands and fell helplessly forward in a near faint. Far away, on the edge of consciousness, she felt strong hands catch her and break her fall as they gathered her up. She heard voices, urgent voices issuing orders, commanding that she be taken to the door at the rear. Beyond the soldiers' voices she heard the howls and snarls of her pursuers; they were closing in. She could hear their bloodthirsty baying and she knew she must warn her rescuers. She tried to shout but all she could do was to cough. The hands that held her strengthened their grip as her body convulsed, racked with the effort of trying to get a breath in the smoke.

A horseman loomed over her, his face serious with concern. He looked down at her and then glanced quickly at the pursuing mass of animals. Tuppence frowned and blinked as he swam in and out of focus. It was the Colonel, the one from the large exhibit who was vaulting over the gun to snatch the colours from the French gunners. He was shouting orders to the soldiers who were carrying her and marshalling a company of lancers and riflemen to defend them.

'Send a runner to the fountain on the first gallery. Tell him to bring wet cloths and cover her head.'

Tuppence felt the soldiers who carried her stagger and sway and slow down as a mass of Ludo Strewth's creatures overran them. She struggled and managed to raise her head, and she cried out in terror as she saw the hideous creatures swarming over the soldiers, snapping and clawing at the horses in their efforts to reach her. She saw a dozen rats, their hides burned through to their skeletons, a mass of sparks, running across the soldiers' uniforms, leaping from man to man and setting them alight.

The Colonel reappeared, spurring his horse through the milling crowd, thrusting his sabre through a burning rodent and hooking it away from her. 'The doors have been blocked from the outside. Head for the main staircase, there is a fire escape on the first floor,' he shouted to the soldiers carrying her, and she felt them turn and slowly begin to fight their way step by step through the smoke and flames, towards the main staircase.

As she felt herself slipping away into unconsciousness, she was dimly aware of a blue flashing light reflecting into the smoke and the wail of sirens growing louder and louder. But the last things she remembered seeing were the two brown bears, their fur ablaze, lumbering towards her, crushing and trampling the soldiers in their path in their effort to reach her.

11

Inside Hell's Kitchen

Night had pulled a shroud of silver shadows over the tiny hamlet of Thieves Bridge on the outskirts of the city. Owls hunted in the moonlit churchyard and hedgehogs foraged between its unkempt graves. A car, its headlights picking out the deserted green, shifted gears and slowed as it crossed the narrow bridge towards the lights of the city. Dec Winner turned fitfully in his sleep, trapped in his nightmare in the upstairs front bedroom of Number Two, Church Cottages, and he clutched at the tangle of bedclothes.

He was falling, spinning helplessly through the darkness, tumbling over and over, away from the dull black belly of the aircraft. The drone of its engines was fading too rapidly, he knew that something was wrong. His stomach churned with panic as he realized that his body was paralysed, stretched taut as it spun through the cold empty void. He forced himself to look up and he stared at the revolving ice-cold stars. The parachute! It wasn't there, stretched across the sky above him. It hadn't opened! He forced his mouth open to shout as a strangling knot of terror tightened in his throat but the rushing wind sucked out his words in a ribbon of wailing screams.

He was dropping faster now and every nerve and twitching muscle in his body was crying out to him to snatch at the D-ring on his harness, to grab at the rip-cord on the emergency chute. He could hear his own voice above the roar of the wind, echoing inside his head, shouting and cursing at him, begging him to grip the cord. The bare black earth was rushing up to meet him, the open-armed trees thrust their spear-sharp branches up towards him. With one last desperate effort he clawed with both hands at the rushing wind and touched his chest. The harness had vanished. There was nothing. He was falling naked to earth. He arched his back and jolted awake, to find himself sitting upright in a tangle of sweat-damp bedclothes.

Dec sucked in short rapid gasps of air as he blinked and tried to focus on the bedside cabinet, searching for the blinking red eye of his fire brigade alerter. He listened for the second set of bleeps that would send him racing across his bedroom, gathering tracksuit and trainers, hopping and stumbling to pull them on as he took the stairs three at a time . . . and he let out a sigh of relief as the night silence lengthened. He had everything ready for a quick dash to the fire station on the far side of the green because he was expecting a shout. He had listened into control earlier in the evening on their VHF frequency and it sounded as though it was going to be a busy night. Fire had broken out in the Corn Hill Hotel and there had been a serious accident on the ring road. Just before he had switched off his radio a call had come in that part of Gibbets Common was ablaze. The long hot summer weather was causing a rash of fires; so many they could barely cope with them all.

Dec yawned. It wasn't the alerter that had awoken him this time, but he knew that it might go off at any moment as control began to move the outlying volunteer crews and water tenders into the city, spreading the net of fire cover as thinly as they dared in the tinder-dry countryside. He didn't envy them their task of choosing which stations to cover and which to leave unmanned. He sank back against the pillows and felt the cold damp sweat of his nightmare on his neck.

Slowly he released his grip on the tangled sheets. 'It's always the same dream. Always the bottomless drop,' he whispered, touching the edges of the bed to reassure himself that there was something solid beneath him before he reached up and rubbed at the beads of sweat that had formed upon his forehead.

He shivered and tried to push away the images that his nightmare had seeded so vividly in the darkness; the brief, bright flashes of panic, the claustrophobic blackness of the fuselage, the faltering roar of the engines, that always led to the blind scramble for the escape hatch. Dec shook his head and tried to focus his eyes on the ripple of moonlight that flooded through the gap in the curtains, spreading its silver patterns and solid shadows across the rumpled ridges of his counterpane. The falling nightmare occurred too often. It always haunted him in that moment of waking with a feeling of dread. Half of him wanted to step back into the dream and find out why he was in the aircraft, why it was crashing, and why he had jumped without a parachute, and yet the other half made him afraid to shut his eyes, afraid that the next time the nightmare seized him he would hit the ground before he woke.

Dec laughed softly in the darkness and broke the feeling of terror that had gripped him so tightly. The fear was ridiculous, he was never going to jump from an aircraft. He had a passion for planes, yes, and he loved nothing better than the thunderous roar of their engines, and the sheer sense of power that they gave him. But to hurl himself out into that black void . . . He shook his head and peered at the blurred dial of his alarm clock as he felt on the bedside cabinet for his glasses. Faintly in the distance he caught the drone of an aircraft, high up and heading out across the North Sea.

'You craze me. You bring me bad dreams,' he muttered, following the whispered throb of the plane as his fingers closed on the thick rubber band that he had tied to the broken frame of his glasses.

Fumbling in the dark he pulled the band down over the top of his head, cursing as it snagged on his untidy hair and pinched his ears. 'I'll try welding on another piece of plastic tomorrow instead of taking them to the opticians,' he murmured absentmindedly as the shadows in the bedroom leapt into focus and he swept his gaze over the clutter of long-ago boyhood, the memories that filled the corners of his bedroom, until his eyes settled on the dial of the noisy alarm clock. 'Only eleven thirty,' he yawned, stretching his arms then pushing the broken glasses on to his forehead. He smiled to himself as he remembered how his colleagues in the farm chemical laboratory had teased him about the rubber band and had said that it made him look like a skier, and how the rest of the volunteer crew at the fire station had been quick to pick up on the idea and christened him 'Downhill Dec'. The name had stuck.

He yawned again and pulled the glasses up over his head. Perhaps he wouldn't mend them after all; he rather liked the image of a downhill skier, it had more dash than being a poisons chemist and it was a lot better than the constant teasing that his passion for tinkering with everything mechanical brought on him. He pushed his glasses on to the cabinet beside the alerter and settled back amongst his pillow. Yes, Dec Winner, downhill skier, had a certain ring to it.

He had barely closed his eyes and begun to drift back to sleep when the alerter on his bedside table burst into life. He jerked upright in the bed as if he had touched an electric wire. The red lens on the top of the alerter was blinking furiously at him in the darkness; this time it wasn't a dream. He threw back the covers and leapt out of bed, pulling on his tracksuit trousers before the first set of shrill bleeps had finished. Stumbling in the hurry he trod his feet into his trainers and snatched up his glasses as the second set of bleeps began. He cursed as he collided with the bedside table, remembering to drag on a thin sweatshirt as he ran for the door.

Amy, Dec's mother, awoke with a start in her bedroom to the noise of the front door slamming and the rush of footsteps receding across the gravel drive. She waited, listening for the click of the front gate, and then sat up in her darkened room and reached out for her dressing gown. She shivered despite the hot airless night and gathered her gown tightly about her shoulders. It didn't matter how many shouts he rushed off to – she feared for his safety and she knew she wouldn't sleep until he was home again. She heard the roar of the fire engine starting up across the other side of the green and watched the blue light from its flashing revolving beacon.

Figures jostled and ran into the fire station. Bedroom slippers, unlaced boots and shoes were hastily kicked off, quick greetings and anxious questions were thrown around in the crowded room as the firemen stamped and trod their feet into their black rubber boots and hoisted up the yellow waterproof leggings.

'Gibbets Common's on fire,' John called as he struggled and forced his arms into his heavy navy blue tunic then reached up for his yellow helmet and debris gloves from the shelf above his peg.

'I bet it's the Corn Hill Hotel, that went up earlier tonight,' Dec shouted back, his tunic flung carelessly over his shoulder and his helmet and gloves in his hand as he ran into the engine bay to open the up-and-over doors.

'The museum on Elm Hill is on fire and there's persons reported,' Vic the sub-officer called as he scrambled up into the crew cab and the engine moved off. Turning he glanced back into the crew compartment and counted the men before he reached for the hand set of the VHF radio fitted into the dashboard in front of him and informed Control that they were rolling with seven riders.

The radio was alive with voices, it was obviously turning into a busy night. After a slight pause the static crackled and the controller's voice came clearly over the air, shutting out the buzz of voices as Control acknowledged, 'Thieves Bridge received at 23.27, VF standing by.'

There was a moment's silence in the crew cab broken only by the rattle of the webbing straps that held the black metal first-aid box secure and the swish and clatter of the yellow plastic tallies, torches and personal line pouches that hung attached by clip- and D-rings to the breathing apparatus behind the seats, as the fire engine gathered speed.

'Jesus, that museum is a hell of a place to catch fire,' Paul muttered.

Vic frowned as he replaced the hand set and shook his head, thinking of the task before them. This wasn't a make-up, the brigade was at full stretch. They were to be the first pump in to the museum and there were persons reported.

For a moment he clutched on to the seat as the driver flung the machine around a tight corner. They were in the suburbs of Norwich now and there was plenty of traffic about. They jumped a set of red traffic lights, leaving the sound of squealing brakes behind them.

Vic flicked on the crew cab's light on the dashboard and

turned his head towards the men. He chose carefully from the four firemen sitting in the back.

'Dec, Geordie, get rigged up in breathing apparatus and get into the building if you can, to search for the persons reported. John, you're their BA Control Officer.'

Dec nodded silently as he and Geordie began to raise the back rest of their bench seat to get to the BA sets.

John pulled out the control board from where it was stowed in the BA compartment and checked that the clock set into the top was working and showed the correct time.

'Look through the one one D cards and see if there's one for the museum,' Vic continued, turning to the Leading Fireman who sat beside him. 'We'll need to know where the hydrants are in that part of the city if we're going to do more than just piss on the fire when we get there.'

Vic fell silent and looked anxiously through the windscreen, searching for a glimpse of the blaze or a column of smoke above the roof tops. He had taken his kids for a visit one Sunday at the beginning of the summer; the place was the size of a cathedral, it would be easy to lose a whole brigade in its great hall let alone their one pump and seven men. He knew from the babble and buzz of the voices on the radio demanding extra men and machines to tackle the other fires raging in the vicinity of the city that they would be hard pressed to get any extra help tonight.

It was difficult getting into BA in a swaying and crowded crew cab. The cylinders of air were heavy and tended to topple you over as you tried to pull them on. Dec cursed as he forced his arms up through the webbing straps and pulled them over his shoulders. He felt the weight of the cylinders pulling him over backwards and he bent forward, his face almost crushed up against the middle partition, while he pulled the cylinder as high up on his back as he could and tightened the straps.

Buckling and tightening the waist-band strap he pulled the face mask out of its canvas protective bag before drawing the large rubber strap over his head.

'Bloody hell, just look at that pall of smoke hanging over the place,' the driver shouted as they turned into Castle Street.

Dec didn't have time to look up, he was filling in the tally for his BA set. He switched the demand regulator valve on his mask to negative pressure before turning on the cylinder to charge the set with air. The pressure gauge was attached to the air line at chest height on the right-hand side by a short but strong flexible tube sewn on to the webbing strap. Dec looked down at the gauge and watched the needle swing through the red quadrant that marked off the last ten minutes of air in the cylinder until it stopped just proud of 190 atmospheres. He smiled to himself; the set was almost fully charged. It would give him twenty to twenty-five minutes of air before the warning whistle sounded to tell him that he was down to the red quadrant and if he didn't get out fast he would be sucking rust. He scrawled the pressure reading on his tally and adjusted the distress signal unit attached to the webbing strap on the left-hand side of his chest.

The machine swung sharply across Castle Street to avoid the swelling crowd of onlookers that had spilled on to the road and the tyres rumbled over the cobbles. Dec slid helplessly into Geordie as the machine slowed and turned into Elm Hill.

'Save the dancing 'til later, mate,' Geordie shouted through his mask, disentangling himself from Dec as he pointed ahead of them to the thick black smoke pouring out through the broken museum doors.

Dec's gaze followed the pointing finger. 'Jesus Christ,' he muttered under his breath. It was one thing to do smoke exercises in the smoke house but quite another to roll up to the threshold of Hell's kitchen. He blinked and took off his glasses, slipping them into a gap beside the first-aid box. He then took a deep breath and pulled his face mask down over his head. He knew from experience that sharp focus wouldn't be that important once they were inside the museum. In smoke as thick as that a sense of touch would be all there was to go by, and keeping a cool head and courage in the dark was essential.

'I'll lead. You tie off the guide line,' he shouted to Geordie who was just finishing checking his set.

Geordie nodded briefly as Dec tightened the four rubber straps on the mask until he had an airtight seal on his face. Quickly he switched the valve on the cylinder off and ran through the low pressure test, sucking in the last of the air to create a vacuum that made the mask cling as tightly as a limpet to his face. When he was satisfied that no poisonous fumes and smoke could seep into the mask he opened the valve and charged the set with air as he breathed again.

The fire engine stopped with a jolt and the rest of the crew leapt out. Vic called Control to inform them of their arrival and immediately asked for assistance making pumps 5. The crew began running out the first length of hose and set a jet to work through the broken doors into the entrance lobby of the museum. Dec took a moment to adjust his helmet strap then gathered up the cylindrical leather bag containing the 200 feet of guide line and held it securely under his arm. It would be their lifeline to the world outside. Without that to follow they could flounder in the dense smoke and become lost in moments. He scrambled down on to the pavement, awkward beneath the weight of the cylinder on his back, and, standing hunched slightly forward, waited for Geordie, glancing up Elm Hill. There were police cars and ambulances with beacons flashing, hampered by the traffic jam created by people drawn to the fire. The traffic stretched as far as he could see and blocked the hill completely. Sightseers thronged the opposite pavement and the police were trying to erect barricades and move them further back.

Windows on the west side of the museum, which faced on to Castle Street, began to shatter and explode from the heat of the fire and shower hot glass on to the parked cars. Faintly Dec could hear the roar of the fire above the clack-clack sound of the demand valve, which he had now switched on to positive pressure. Geordie had climbed down and touched his arm; it was time to go.

Together they turned towards the museum steps where John had set up the BA control board but an agitated old man with snow-white hair blocked their way. He had a museum attendant's jacket thrown hastily over his pyjamas and bedroom slippers on his feet.

'There's a woman trapped in there. I saw her when I was putting out the cat,' he cried, gesticulating frantically. Vic tried to calm him, asking him exactly where he had seen her and which was the best way for his men to get to her.

'There, there – in the great hall. She was silhouetted against the flames,' the attendant cried, his eyes glazed with shock, his lips trembling as the incoherent words tumbled out.

'We'll find her, don't worry,' Dec shouted through his mask as he and Geordie moved past the attendant and handed their tallies to John who checked that their cylinder pressures matched what they had written before he slotted them into the grooves on the control board. He glanced at the clock and wrote 23.37 as their 'time in' before securing the end of the guide line to the railings. That done he did a quick calculation and wrote 00.02 under 'time out'.

'Don't get lost in there,' he shouted to Dec and Geordie as they began to climb the museum steps, feeding out the guide line as they went, 'because I haven't got enough men out here to make up a rescue team.'

Dec raised his left hand and waved in acknowledgement. He knelt beside the right-hand side of the broken doors and peered around into the boiling smoke, while Geordie clipped his own personal line on to the belt strap of his breathing apparatus set. Now they were joined by a thin umbilical cord of rope.

'We'll search to the right,' Dec shouted over his shoulder.

Geordie knotted the guide line securely on to the broken door and tapped his shoulder twice, giving Dec the signal that he was ready, and slowly, keeping hard contact with the right-hand wall of the vaulted entrance hall, they moved forward. Dense smoke and solid darkness closed in around them. They moved as cautiously as blind men on a cliff ledge, stretching and sweeping the backs of their left hands out all around them in the claustrophobic blackness. They stamped and worked their feet well out in front of them testing each treacherous footstep. The roar of the fire, the crash and splintering of glass and moulded plaster-work was getting louder. They reached the attendant's alcove and Dec quickly searched it while Geordie tied off the line.

'Nothing in here,' he shouted and they moved forward again.

Dec felt a moulded woodwork door surround; the paint or varnish had bubbled and become sticky from the heat. 'We must have reached the entrance to . . .' he began to shout when orange flames suddenly erupted away to their left and leapt up twenty, perhaps thirty feet, licking and curling around the galleries.

Both firemen staggered as the wall of heat hit them. 'We'll never get any further,' Geordie shouted, tugging at Dec's shoulder. 'The place is becoming a raging inferno. Nobody could survive in here.'

'Wait!' Dec shouted urgently. 'Look over there, through the smoke. I'm sure I saw someone move at the foot of that stairway.'

Geordie leaned forward and peered through the swirling smoke between the charred, skeletal exhibits, the burned-out display cases and the ruined treasures that lay amongst a sea of smoking ash and debris. He frowned and wiped the front of his mask with a gloved hand.

'Well I'll be damned, I think you're right. But there's more than one person – no, I'm not sure, it's almost impossible to see through this smoke. But how are we going to get to them? We won't have enough air to get to the stairs and back if we keep to the right-hand wall and the whole place looks as though it is about to burn up or collapse.'

Dec glanced down at his pressure gauge. The numerals were fuzzed without his glasses but the needle was a long way from red quadrant.

'We've got enough air if we hurry. We'll go to the right, tie off here on to the door jamb and then cut straight across the hall to that column, the one supporting the end of the right-hand gallery. The fire's burning mostly on the left of the great hall and if we keep beneath that gallery it should protect us if any of the ceiling caves in.'

Geordie picked out and measured the distance to that first column away to the right; he could just see it through the swirling smoke.

'You're a crazy man,' he shouted back as he shook his head. 'We're supposed to keep a contact with the right-hand wall, it's madness to dash out recklessly when the place is like this. If the flames die it will be pitch dark and we'll be lost in this smoke or crushed when the roof collapses. No, it's a crazy idea. Anyway they'll die of smoke inhalation long before we ever reach them.'

'We're their only chance,' Dec shouted back. 'They'll die for sure if we don't get to them.'

Geordie measured the gap to the column again and licked his lips as he looked through his mask at Dec. There wasn't a braver man than Dec in the crew at Thieves Bridge nor one to whom he would trust his life so utterly in a tight spot. He laughed. 'How did you know I always wanted a George Medal to prop up on the mantelpiece?' he laughed as he lashed the guide line to a stout hook on the door jamb. 'OK, let's do it.'

Dec took a last quick look around the smoke-filled hall, engraving every hazy detail, every half-hidden landmark in that cauldron of heat and fire, on his mind before he sprang forward away from the relative safety of the entrance hall. The flickering tongues of flame were dwindling, folding in upon themselves and then erratically blazing up. The smoke was getting thicker by the second, swallowing up the landmarks and leaving only memories. He had to go *now*. Now or never.

'Go for it!' he shouted over the clack-clack of the demand valve and, hunched slightly beneath the weight of the cylinder, he suddenly began to run into the swirling smoke.

Jets of water poured down through the broken windows. The flames hissed and spluttered and thick yellow smoke from the smouldering debris shrouded them completely. They were running blind. Dec had measured off the distance to the column with his eyes, ten paces, and he was rarely wrong. He counted seventeen strides and realized that he must have missed it.

'Damn,' he muttered. 'Damn, damn, damn.'

It was as hot as a blast furnace and rivers of sweat were pouring down his forehead and stinging his eyes. He had calculated that if he missed the column that supported the gallery then another couple of paces should take him right in amongst the crowded display cases and exhibits that he had glimpsed so briefly beneath the gallery. But there was nothing in front of him, nothing that he could touch with his left hand. He could feel the shattered, burned-out remains of wood and glass crunching beneath his boots and realized that he must have veered to the left and led them out into the main aisle as the smoke had thickened. He hesitated and, sensing Geordie close up behind him, put his hand on his shoulder. He half-turned and was about to shout, to warn Geordie that they should turn back, when a burning face suddenly appeared in front of his mask and two hands in charred, once-white gloves snatched the leather cylindrical bag containing the line from beneath his right arm and vanished with it into the smoke.

'Hey! Hey, come back!' Dec shouted in startled surprise as he stumbled, trying to clasp the line in both hands to pull it back.

A cold tingle ran down his spine as he realized that what he had just seen simply wasn't possible. No one, no one human, could survive and breathe in this smoke.

'Geordie – Geordie, for God's sake, there's ghosts,' he cried as shadowy figures appeared on either side of him in the smoke.

A voice shouted at him to hurry and firm hands grasped his elbows and jostled him forward. Briefly he felt Geordie's hand tighten on his shoulder. He was shouting something and trying to pull him backwards and away from the figures who were urging him through the smoke.

His fingers clutched at the fabric of Dec's tunic but they faltered and one by one they loosened and were torn away. Dec tried to turn and call back; he could feel the tug of Geordie's personal line where it was attached to the waist belt of his set. But there was nothing he could do to stop them both being dragged into the heart of the fire by these grisly creatures.

'There is a woman on the stairs. You must rescue her,' a muffled voice rasped close to his ear.

He twisted his head towards the sound and cried out. Through the visor of his mask he was staring straight into a soldier's face. Flames were licking at the eyeballs and smoke erupted with each strangled word through charred holes in the cheeks. The lips and nose had shrivelled away to reveal the teeth and septum bone, which showed stark white in the swirling darkness.

'Hurry, you must hurry,' the figure urged, moving closer.

Dec felt panic rise. This had to be a nightmare, this couldn't be real. He wanted to screw his eyes tightly shut and block out this hideous sight. He could feel the bile rising in his throat and fought it down. If he was sick in his mask he would drown in it. He wanted to scream but he couldn't open his mouth wide enough. Ahead through the shifting smoke and flames he saw the staircase, it was alive with struggling figures. There were soldiers dressed in bright uniforms of scarlet and blue, embroidered with loops and knots of braid and rows of brass buttons that reflected the light of the flickering flames. It looked as if the ghost of every exhibit in the burning museum had come to life. But they couldn't be ghosts, ghosts wouldn't burn or seem as alive and solid as these smouldering figures. He could make out burning animal shapes, some with horns and claws, fighting with the soldiers, and he realized that into whatever nightmare he had blundered, it was brutally real. Something collided sharply with his legs and he would have fallen but for the strong, vice-like hands that were propelling him.

He glanced down and cried out, shuddering. The floor beneath his feet was alive, swarming with animals of every shape and size. They were scattering, scrambling over each other, fleeing now from the soldiers and the fire. Some were no more than blazing skeletons. A rat, its tail a ribbon of sparks, ran over his boots and he instinctively kicked at it. Voices shouted orders all around him. He heard the rattle of rifle bolts and the scrape of sabres being drawn and with a great shout the soldiers charged after the fleeing animals. In that moment, with the soldiers milling around him, Dec saw the woman. She was lying on the second step of the staircase, her head swathed in steaming wet rags. He rushed forward and knelt beside her and tore the rags aside. Her face was smoked black and smeared with soot, her hair was a matted tangle, half covering her face. He felt in the angle of her jaw and found a faint, stumbling pulse. He sensed Geordie kneeling close beside him.

'She's alive. She's unconscious but she's still alive,' Dec cried. 'It must have been the wet rags . . .' He stuttered as he stared up at the mountainous shapes of two huge bears lumbering through the soldiers, tossing them aside as though they were toys. Their hides were a mass of smoke and flames and their eyes glowed as red as hot coals. They snarled as they advanced on the two firemen, reaching down to claw at their hearts. Geordie screamed as claws tore through his tunic, shearing neatly through the right-hand webbing strap of his breathing apparatus. The claw caught in the metal-armoured air-line sewn into the strap and lifted him up off his knees. The bear snarled with rage and hurled him down amongst the milling soldiers. The

194

air-line went taut, stretched a fraction, and then snapped and the precious air escaped in a shrieking hiss. Geordie clutched at his mask, his eyes wild and staring, his mouth opening and closing, and then he slumped forward.

Together the bears turned towards Dec and growled and opened their arms to claw at him. He cowered over the prostrate body of the woman in a helpless gesture to defend her, and tried to ward them off. A volley of rifle fire suddenly crashed all around. He looked up to see two lines of soldiers in scarlet uniforms advancing at a run through the smoke, firing in quick succession at the bears. An officer with sword in hand led them up the stairs right in between the bears to where Dec knelt. The bears staggered, faltering in their attack beneath the hail of bullets, and thin wreath-tails of smoke erupted from the ragged bullet holes in their burning hides.

Dec seized on their hesitation and scrambled back a pace across the stair, dragging the woman with him, but the snarling bears saw him escaping and strode after him, lashing out at the riflemen, crushing and clawing them down. They were through the soldiers in moments and towering over Dec again who tried helplessly to avoid their lashing claws. He snatched at his torch, pulling it free from his belt, and flung it at the closest hideous snarling face. The bear suddenly howled and threw its arms out, its great bulk blocking his view. It seemed to rush towards him and smother him, and he tensed, covering his masked face with his hands, shrinking down, waiting for the crushing impact.

Then he heard the clatter of hoofbeats on the stair right beside him and a screaming howl from the other creature followed by a roaring cheer from the besieged soldiers all around. There was a roar and crackle of gunfire and Dec looked through his opened fingers to see six horsemen, three to each of the murderous bears, charging them, skewering them on their lances. The sheer force of their charge was driving them backwards away from the stairway and into the heat of the fire. The creatures were fighting back, clawing at the steel lance tips, howling and snarling as they lashed out with all their rage and strength towards the horses' heads. But pace by pace the lancers spurred their mounts bravely forward and forced the bears into the flames.

A horseman cantered up the stairwell through the smoke and leapt down beside Dec. 'Is she alive?' he shouted, his voice muffled and choked as though he was speaking through a bag of rags.

Dec felt for her pulse again; it was weaker and stumbling even more erratically. 'If she doesn't have air now – immediately – she'll die,' he shouted back against the clacking of his demand valve and the roar of the fire.

The horseman sank down on his knees and took the woman's delicate hand, holding it tightly. He looked up at Dec, his smoke-blackened forehead crinkled into a frown. 'You must save her, you must.'

The warning whistle in Dec's breathing set suddenly sounded. He only had ten minutes of air left. He glanced down at the gauge. The needle was touching the top of the red quadrant. John would know that they were running out of air. If more fire engines had arrived and he had managed to get together a rescue team they would be on their way in. Dec remembered hearing Vic make five pumps and he prayed that at least some of them had arrived as he pressed the switch on the top of his DSU, distress signal unit, to guide them to him.

He quickly glanced across to where Geordie lay, unconscious, the blood from the claw wounds staining the front of his tunic. He had to think fast, he couldn't just kneel there hoping and waiting to be rescued. The whole attack on the staircase had only lasted moments. Geordie and the woman could both still survive if they got air. He knew exactly what he must do. He reached up and began to unfasten the chin strap on his helmet. The leather bag that contained the guide line caught his eye where it lay on the bottom step below and for a second he followed the thin white strand of rope to where it vanished into the smoke. At intervals of six feet along the line there were two sets of tags, one long and one short. If he made a run for it and abandoned Geordie and the woman he could follow the short tags and might just make it back to the museum steps. But he shook his head and dismissed the idea before it had properly formed. He had never ducked out on anyone in his whole life and he wasn't going to start now just because the going was getting a little tough.

He unclipped the last press stud on his chin strap and tossed the helmet aside. Pointing to Geordie he shouted to the horseman beside him to get his ruined mask off his face. He had to shout loudly to be heard over the wailing shriek of the DSU and the horseman didn't seem to understand.

'You must rescue the woman!'

'No,' Dec shouted back angrily, 'I am going to rescue them both or we'll all die in the attempt. Now get your soldiers, or whatever they are, to carry them out. I'll walk between them and share what remains of my air.'

Dec took a deep breath and switched the demand valve to negative pressure. To take off his mask in an unbreathable atmosphere meant going against all his training. Every nerve in his body, every ounce of common sense and self-preservation instinct shouted at him to keep the mask on. He screwed up his courage and loosened the rubber straps. He had to take it off if he was to save their lives. He turned towards the woman and dragged the mask off his face. The heat and the stench of the fire hit him and he gasped and almost choked as he roughly brushed aside the tangled knots of her hair and clamped the mask down over her face before turning the valve to positive pressure. The air hissed into the mask and her chest moved slightly as she coughed and inhaled the air. Her eyelids flickered. Dec felt his head beginning to swim and the pent-up breath burned his lungs. As he gazed down at her he glimpsed the beauty of her fine features through the soot and filth that coated her face. He blinked, his mind was wandering already, he had to concentrate if he was going to keep them all alive.

He switched the valve back to negative, covered her face with the wet rags and snatched another breath before switching it back and putting the mask over Geordie's face. The air forced its way into Geordie's lungs and he groaned and clutched at his chest as half a dozen soldiers began to lift and carry him towards the entrance, closely followed by the horseman carrying the woman. Dec stumbled and reeled dizzily along between them. Twice the mask slipped from his hands and he wasted precious air before he caught hold of it again. He was suffering from oxygen starvation and heat exhaustion and he moved as if in a dream; nothing seemed real any more. The wail of the DSU and the shrill warning whistle had become music and he struggled to keep up with the eerie soldiers who neither felt pain from the fire nor needed air to breathe. The hiss of air in the mask was growing weaker each time he clumsily switched the valve to positive. He was dying on his feet and there wasn't anything he could do about it.

Somewhere ahead in the thick swirling smoke he thought he caught the clacking sound of the BA sets of the rescue team. He staggered, choking and gasping, and tried to point as he crumpled on to his knees. Tears were running down his blackened cheeks and he tore at his tunic collar, desperate for air. 'Rescue, rescue . . .' he gurgled, dragging his mask from the woman's face and pushing it against his own.

He clawed at the valve, switched it to positive and sucked wildly on the empty cylinder. The vacuum he created made it cling on to his filthy cheeks. Crying out he tore the mask away and collapsed forward amongst the hot ash and the charred remains of the display cases. The noise, the heat of the fire, the hopelessness of failure and the choking, gasping pain in his chest began to fold over him, covering him in smothering darkness.

The cavalryman laid the woman down and crouched over him. He had begun to lift him up when he caught the sounds of the rescue team. He looked up and glimpsed the beams of their torches and their yellow helmets and black face masks appearing through the smoke. He called urgently to his fellow soldiers, ordering them to lay Geordie down beside the other unconscious bodies.

The rescue team was now only a footstep away. The horseman could hear their leader calling back to the others that he thought there was something just ahead of them as he worked his way forward, searching along the guide line. Quickly, the cavalryman stooped and grasped Dec's wrists, stretching out his limp arms, placing them around the other two so that it looked as though he had been trying to carry or drag them out of the fire. He noticed that the guide line was lying close to Dec's face. Quickly he forced the line in between the fingers of Dec's right hand.

'Quickly, back into the smoke. Hide yourselves,' he hissed at the escort of soldiers and they silently melted back into the billowing smoke.

Colonel Hawkesbury retreated with them but once the smoke had completely enveloped him he stopped and waited, listening. He heard an excited shout from the leader of the rescue team and he crept back as close as he dared to reassure himself that the woman whom the magic bound them to defend was safe. He absently rubbed his gloved hand across his smoke-blackened forehead and saw that a spark had clung to the calfskin glove and burned through it, causing a deep smouldering hole in the coarsely sewn-up fabric of his hand. He frowned and crushed out the edges of the glowing burn as he shook his head. He didn't understand all the pieces of this nightmare magic that had resurrected him. He knew that it wasn't real life, not a life of flesh and blood. He had memories, half glimpsed, of what his life had been, but they were overshadowed by this overwhelming urge to protect this woman whose voice, whose cry of fear, had first awoken him.

He blinked, dispersing the memories as he took a step through the thickening smoke towards the rescue team and saw them struggling beneath the weight of three spare BA sets. The team leader had fallen on to his knees beside Tuppence, feeling for her pulse as he clamped a mask over her face and switched the set on. Immediately he reached over and felt for the pulses of the two men and shouted, 'They're alive! Let's get them out as quickly as possible before the whole roof caves in.'

One by one the limp bodies were lifted and carried out through the swirling smoke.

Colonel Hawkesbury watched them vanish and then glanced up at the roof. The fire was spreading through the rafters, it was time to evacuate his men. He turned on his heel and hurried to where they were waiting.

12

Recovery and Regrets

Dec was slowly regaining consciousness, climbing painfully up out of the black swallowing hole of oblivion. First he was aware of the lights, blue flashing lights, that beat against the inside of his eyelids, then gradually a jumble of noise faded in and out of focus. Static crackled and popped in his ears, voices shouted, there was laughter and people speaking all around him. He heard footsteps and the dragging of hose across the cobbles, the roar of diesel engines and the wail of sirens. Everything was getting sharper. He felt the drift of mist from the water jets fall on his forehead, a hand touched him and then shook his arm and above him voices called out his name. He was aware of his tongue and the taste of acrid fumes on his blistered lips. It made his stomach tighten and he wanted to retch. The taste triggered the memories of himself blindly stumbling through the smoke and sharing his last mouthful of air. It all came flooding back.

He gasped, his back arched in convulsion, his mind screaming in a panic for air. The mask was still clamped down over his face, he could feel it pressing on his cheeks and the bridge of his nose. He was sucking and drowning on the vacuum. He had to tear it off his face but strong hands were gripping his arms, stopping him. Voices called to him, told him to lie still, breathe slowly. Suddenly a hiss of cold air filled the mask and entered his mouth and nose. He gasped, it tasted so sweet, so pure, and he sucked greedily at it and made himself cough and choke. His lungs felt as if they were on fire, steel bands of pain were tightening around his rib cage. The air hissed into his mouth again. He choked and retched and became aware through the burning pain that someone was calling at him and tapping his cheek.

'Dec, wake up. Dec, can you hear me? Dec, wake up.'

He tried to open his eyes but his eyelids were stuck together with a mixture of his own tears and the grit and filth of the fire. He screwed them up, blinked and forced them open and looked at the blurred ring of faces staring down at him. Blinking again he began to focus. He saw Vic and John to his right and two ambulance men kneeling on his left, one of them holding an oxygen mask firmly over his nose and mouth while the mobile ventilator pumped more air into him. He inhaled it gingerly, coughing as it entered his lungs.

'You're the luckiest bastard alive,' a voice laughed from behind him.

Dec painfully turned his head to see a fireman he didn't know kneeling just behind him. He was rigged in BA, his yellow helmet still on his head, the face mask hanging down from its neck strap across the front of his tunic. The shape of his mask showed clearly against his blackened forehead, neck and cheeks, the result of being so long in the fire. He grinned at Dec then squeezed his shoulder and began to rise to his feet.

'I had to stick around to check you were all right before I got this set off my back. It's not every day of the week I get to rescue a hero.'

Dec suddenly remembered Geordie and the woman. He struggled violently, breaking free of the ambulance men, tore the mask away from his face and cried out. 'The others? What about the others? We have to go back in there and bring them out.'

The fireman laughed and shook his head. 'It's all done, mate. They went to hospital ten minutes ago. But if you hadn't carried them as far as you did before you collapsed they would have both been goners for sure.'

Dec stared up at the fireman in silence as he took back the mask from the ambulance man without protest and breathed through it again. It was all flooding back. Vivid pictures of the ghostly soldiers and the bear-like creatures that attacked them on the stairs. He coughed and shook his head, trying to explain.

'But I didn't carry them, the soldiers did. I would never have made it without . . .' He stuttered and fell silent as he sucked in another mouthful of air.

Vic, John, the ambulance men and the fireman who had pulled him out of the building were all smiling and nodding and looking down at him. They didn't believe a word. One of the ambulance men checked his pulse and shone a pencil torch into his eyes, then reached for the stretcher that lay just behind them.

'It's the oxygen starvation and the heat exhaustion that's making him delirious. We had better get him off to hospital right away.'

Vic nodded silently and began to help lift Dec across on to the stretcher.

'No, no, I can walk. I don't need to be carried on one of those things.' He coughed and choked and struggled feebly but Vic insisted, so he stopped arguing and allowed them to manhandle him on to the stretcher.

'Just rest,' Vic said quietly. 'I'll call into the hospital when we have finished up here.'

Dec looked across to the museum. The fire was out but thick clouds of smoke and steam were still boiling out of every broken window and through the collapsed roof and open doorways. Five fire engines, a hydraulic platform and four police cars were parked in the gutter along Elm Hill. There were wide puddles of water on the cobbles and lines of red and yellow hose crisscrossed the hill and the junction of Castle Street, snaking and twisting their way into every doorway of the museum. Firemen were beginning to break the couplings on the hoses and roll them up. It was late and the excitement of the fire was over. The crowd who had thronged the area around the museum and hampered the firemen in their work were beginning to break up and move on. Dec clutched at Vic's sleeve as the ambulance men lifted the stretcher.

'But Geordie was attacked in there. You must have seen how his air-line was torn in two. You have got to believe me.'

Vic smiled and nodded encouragingly as he untangled Dec's fingers from his sleeve. 'Yes, yes, of course,' he answered soothingly, 'you saw it all.' He smiled, putting Dec's glasses into his hand as he walked beside the stretcher across to the ambulance which was parked in Castle Street.

He stood watching it pull away, its blue beacon flashing and reflecting in the windows of the parked cars and fire tenders that lined the street.

'These hallucinations he's having, they won't be permanent, will they?' John asked anxiously, falling into step beside Vic as they crossed back into Elm Hill to begin the long task of making up their equipment.

Vic frowned and took a moment to answer before he shrugged his shoulders. 'No, no, of course not. But he can thank his lucky stars that you had the sense to send in the rescue team with those spare BA sets.'

He was privately wondering what had really happened inside that burning building. The rescue team had found the BA guide-line pouch on the stairs and it lay in a direct course from the entrance hall instead of following the right-hand wall. Dec wouldn't normally have taken a risk like that, he wouldn't have stayed in after the whistle had sounded on his set. And what the hell had torn Geordie's air-line in two? There was a handful of troubling questions that needed answering but they would have to wait until Dec and Geordie had recovered.

'Well I reckon they owe me a couple of pints in the Gallows for getting that rescue team in so quickly,' John laughed as he bent down to break a hose coupling.

The doctors kept Dec under observation during the rest of the night but discharged him early in the morning with strict instructions to keep away from smoke-clogged buildings in the future. Geordie had lost a lot of blood and was still in a bad way over in intensive care. Dec slipped into his room and sat beside his bed, watching the saline drip emptying into his arm and listening to the hiss of the ventilator assisting his breathing. The nurses and doctors had no idea when he would regain consciousness.

'The woman I helped to rescue last night,' he asked on a sudden impulse as a nurse hurried into the room to check Geordie's temperature and monitor the drip. 'Is she still here in the hospital? Could I see her for a moment?'

The nurse frowned crossly at him. 'It seems everybody in Norfolk wants to speak to her. We've had the police, the press, television, all pestering us to see her since first light. Don't you think we have enough to do without all their nonsense?'

Dec began to apologize for asking when the nurse quite suddenly relented and smiled. 'But I suppose it's different as far as you're concerned, after all you did rescue her.

Come on, I'll slip you into her room, but only for a few moments, mind, she's not up to seeing anyone for very long just yet.'

Dec frowned and pulled at his glasses, forgetting for a moment the thick rubber band attached to the broken frames. He winced at the pain as the band caught in the knots of untidy hair at the back of his head.

'Why? Why all the fuss over her? Did I rescue someone famous last night?' he asked, bending and quickly gathering up his fire boots, the filthy crumpled yellow leggings and the dirty fire tunic that still stank of the fire.

The nurse barely paused to answer as she pushed her way through the door out into the corridor. 'She's that American model, you know, the one in all the adverts. I'd have thought you would have recognized her last night,' she muttered dismissively.

'I couldn't see much through all that smoke and I didn't really have time to get a proper look at her,' Dec laughed as he hurried through the door and ran to catch up with her, his borrowed hospital slippers flapping with each stride.

Tuppence lay in agony, propped up in a swathe of white pillows in her hospital bed. Her lungs burned with each shallow breath, her skin felt as though it had shrivelled up and burned away to expose a forest of tiny nerve endings on her raw flesh. And someone must have tied her hair back while she was unconscious because it was knotted behind her head so tightly that it hurt to move or even to blink her sore eyes. They had smeared sticky shiny grease all over her hands and face. She felt wretched and she hurt. It was worse than being in hell and her temper was worn thin with the continual pestering of the cops and their endless questions. Why oh why had she been in that museum? She couldn't recall.

The door handle turned and the door swung towards her. She was certain that it would be that weasel-faced guy from some newspaper, he was so sure he was on to a good story. The nurses had cleared him out of her room twice since daybreak but now he was back. Tuppence narrowed her eyes against the searing pain and hissed, 'Get him out of here!'

Dec hesitated in the doorway of her room. He felt his cheeks redden with embarrassment. The brigade didn't encourage its firemen to establish contact with the victims they rescued. It often triggered memories of their harrowing experience and caused trauma, sending them back into shock. The firemen were supposed to remain anonymous, faceless figures in uniforms, freeze-framed for ever at the scene of the tragedy.

'I . . . I'm so sorry,' he stammered, clutching his fire gear more tightly as he backed out of the room. 'It was wrong of me to trouble you.'

'No, wait,' Tuppence coughed, letting her eyes settle on him for a moment as he hovered in the doorway before she turned her head painfully towards the nurse who had slipped into the room.

He sure didn't look like any of the reporters who had bothered her earlier. He didn't look like the policeman who had sat at her bedside trying to get her to talk. No, he looked entirely different from any of them. He was so oddly dressed, with his bare feet thrust into bedroom slippers and a sweat-streaked tee shirt and dirty slacks. His untidy halo of fair hair stuck out in all directions and he was carrying an assortment of filthy clothes clutched to his chest.

'He's the fireman who rescued you,' the nurse

announced coldly. 'He's just been discharged from the hospital and asked if he could see you for a moment on his way out. I didn't think you would mind.'

Tuppence coughed and motioned Dec into the room, wincing at the fingers of pain that seemed to grip and tear at her face and arms as she moved.

'No, no, of course I don't mind. Come right in,' she rasped as she tried to smile, but her lips twitched and tightened and the hint of warmth in her eyes faded away with the pain.

She looked more closely at the bundle of clothes Dec was carrying and tried to imagine him in his uniform. Slowly she shook her head. 'I'm so sorry, mister, I just don't remember you rescuing me.'

She blinked painfully and looked away as she tried to banish the hideous images that suddenly filled her head. She shuddered and ice-cold shivers scattered across her fire-hot skin. Seeing this fireman had brought it all flooding back. The morning brightness of the hospital room momentarily darkened, images of the creatures that had chased her into the museum and pursued her through the flames swam before her eyes. She smelt the acrid fumes of the fire again and felt her throat tighten with panic. Her hands tensed on the bed sheet and her ears filled with the roar and crackle of the flames and the shouts of those eerie uniformed figures who had fought to defend her and carried her to the foot of the broad staircase. The image of the bears advancing, looming over her, made her shrink back against her pillows and cry out. She jerked back to reality as she realized that the nurse and the fireman were both staring at her.

'I'm sorry,' she rasped as she reached out for a tissue from the locker beside the bed.

She didn't want to talk about it yet, the memories were

too raw, too brutal, and she doubted that anybody would believe a word of it. 'I was trying to think back, but I really can't remember a thing, just a blur of smoke and fire.'

'Well I have far too much to do to stand around in here all morning. Just don't you stay any longer than five minutes,' the nurse said sharply to Dec. 'And don't let those reporters in when you leave.' She nodded severely at Tuppence before she pushed her way out of the door.

Tuppence watched the door click shut and rasped, 'I don't know what I've done to her but she seems really upset about something.'

Dec smiled and shook his head. He had never stood so close to anyone so beautiful before. Her loveliness shone out even through the grease and ointments that the nurses had smeared on to her fire-scalded skin. Her bone structure was perfect. But it was her eyes that held him spellbound. He could easily see why the nurse was so frosty towards her, she was probably jealous of all the attention that was being paid to a beautiful American woman while she was run off her feet coping with the drudgery of real life.

'It's probably been a tough night for her,' he answered softly, 'and I expect she has been on duty close to twelve hours without a break. I'm sure it's nothing personal.'

Tuppence glanced up at the soft strong sound of his voice. There was something about this guy, the tone of his voice, the way he was almost apologizing for the nurse's brusque and cutting manner. He didn't have to do that, Jesus, he was the one who had risked his life to rescue her, not that stupid nurse! Tuppence frowned as she realized that she had barely given him a second glance since he had entered the room. Sure, she had looked at him, more out of annoyance at the intrusion than anything else, and on that merest of glances she had summarily dismissed him on account of his filthy appearance. She had done exactly what she accused almost everyone else she met of doing to her, she had judged him purely on his outer shell.

'I want to thank you,' she said quickly, coughing slightly and smiling at Dec through the pain, 'but just saying thank you seems so little for what you did. You saved my life.'

Dec laughed, feeling himself beginning to melt inside from the warmth of her smile. He felt awkward as he stood there clutching his filthy fire gear. He looked for somewhere to deposit it, but the room was so clinically clean, so antiseptic, that he balanced the bundle between his ankles, trapping it with his calves an inch or two off the floor.

Reaching up he pushed his glasses up and eased the rubber band out of his tangled hair before he replied, 'It was nothing, miss, just a part of the service . . .' he hesitated, looking down and twisting the broken frames between his fingers before he continued, 'but I was wondering, miss, if you saw anything in the smoke. It's a strange place, that museum, full of so much history. Did you see anything? Ghosts or . . .'

He stopped again and looked into her face as a shadow of fear darkened her eyes. Tuppence watched him, her eyes narrowing slightly. Perhaps he had seen those soldiers and the mass of animals in the smoke. She opened her mouth to answer him, she wanted to tell him, to spill it all out, but she hesitated. How much had he seen? How much would he believe of the nightmare that had overtaken her?

'Yes, there was something in there,' she muttered grimly, 'something huge and frightening . . .'

The door suddenly swung open and the nurse reappeared. Tuppence fell silent.

'It's time you were going, I have to do Miss Trilby's

charts.' She frowned at Dec as she ushered him towards the door.

'Yes, yes, of course.' Dec smiled at the nurse, and bending down, gathered up his gear. He would have loved to stay for ever, just listening to Miss Trilby's voice and watching her smile as he traced the outline of her beautiful face against the pillows. And she had said that she had seen something in the museum. She could prove that he hadn't been hallucinating.

'Perhaps I could talk to you later when you have recovered and been discharged?' he asked as he backed towards the door, but before she could answer he touched his cheeks and added, 'That red blotching on your skin, you needn't worry about it scarring you, I have seen it before and it always vanishes in a day or two. Then you'll be as good as new.'

'Thanks, thanks for the advice. Yes, that would be nice to talk to you later,' Tuppence called. She started to beckon him to stay but a glowering look from the nurse made her drop her hand back on to the counterpane. The exertion of talking had made her inhale too deeply and she now bent forward coughing as the air entered her sore lungs and by the time she had straightened up he had gone. The door clicked firmly shut.

Tuppence stared at the closed door, a faint smile touching the corners of her mouth. It wasn't often she met someone, anyone, who made her take that much notice of them. What was it about him? He hadn't come on strong, if anything quite the opposite. He was shy, almost apologetic about rescuing her. Sure, he looked OK, as tall, maybe a little taller than her, and physically he was very fit, but he didn't have great looks or the style of the male models and actors she was used to working with. Yet there had been something in his pale blue eyes and open friendly face when he had laughed, something warm about his smile, despite the shadows of tiredness and the smudges of soot. Something that made him different, so much more real than all the other guys.

She laughed softly and sadly to herself and whispered so that the nurse wouldn't hear, 'Tuppence, you're losing your mind. Everyone builds up a hero out of the person who rescues them!'

And she pushed away her fantasies and looked down at the red raw skin on the back of her hands and sighed. It was a pity that he had disappeared before she had even had the chance to ask him his name.

The door suddenly swung open and she forgot the fireman as a doctor walked into her room. The man was brisk and thorough with his examination before he announced that she could be discharged immediately after breakfast.

'But the burns! Don't I need some treatment? My job depends on how I look,' she asked anxiously.

The doctor paused in the doorway. 'The colour and soreness of your skin was caused through exposure to the heat of the fire. Luckily it is all superficial and will dissipate in a day or two. The only treatment your skin needs is to be kept moist by liberally applying the cream I have prescribed. The nurse here will arrange for the pharmacy to have some tubes ready before you leave.'

'But what about . . . ?' Tuppence began, but her words trailed off as the doctor hurried out. She turned to the nurse who was writing up her chart. 'What's the matter with this place, everyone's in such a god-awful hurry?'

A knock on her door made her turn her head back to see the reporter from the *Eastern Daily* back to pester her. 'I have told you already, I don't know who started the fire. I was taking an evening stroll when I saw the flames inside the museum. What do you want me to do, make up some wild story about ghosts or something? Now get out of here.'

Tuppence looked at the museum from the window of her cab as it rumbled down Castle Street, avoiding the piles of ash and burned debris from the fire that filled the gutters. As they turned up Elm Hill she looked back to the cordoned-off building. It looked a ruin. The beautiful fluted-glass windows were all smashed and black smoke stains spoiled the old brick and flint walls. She caught a glimpse through the broken windows of shafts of sunlight filtering down through holes in the roof, lighting up the collapsed galleries, the burned-out staircase and all the charred devastation inside.

'You'll have to wait while I get the fare,' she instructed the cab driver as he pulled up behind the Lotus outside the Watchgate.

Tuppence climbed out of the cab and stood on the pavement, looking quickly up and down Elm Hill. Pictures of the creatures who had killed Richard and chased her into the museum were still vivid in her mind. She had asked the policeman who had questioned her in the hospital whether anyone had been hurt but he had told her that she and the two firemen who had rescued her had been the only casualties. She had almost blurted out the whole story. She had tried to tell him about the creatures from the taxidermist's shop and the exhibits that had come to life in the museum to rescue her but the disbelief in his eyes had made her fall silent.

She noticed that the air smelt of wet soot and charred wood and she smeared the layer of ash on the Lotus and drew her finger right through it. It didn't matter whether anyone believed her or not, it was real enough to her, real enough to make her throw a few things in a bag and get the hell out of there before darkness fell. She knew that the door of the Watchgate had slammed shut, locking her out when the creatures had killed Richard, and when she lifted the latch and pushed tentatively against the carved door, she half expected it to resist. But it creaked easily open. Tuppence stepped over the threshold and the smell of percolated coffee emanated from where it had spilled across the hearth. The magazines were scattered all across the floor and one of the chairs lay on its back, otherwise everything looked exactly as it should. The cab driver hooted impatiently and she crossed the room and picked up her bag and rummaged through it for her purse.

'Hey, don't forget your stuff, lady,' the cabby called after her, holding up the tubes of cream from the hospital that she had forgotten in her haste.

She paid him and ran back to the safety of her house, slamming the door and throwing the bolts to shut out the world, then breathlessly climbed the winding stairs to the bathroom.

'Jesus!' she gasped as the pain subsided in her chest and she stared at her blotchy red reflection glowing through thick layers of shiny ointments and pulled her fingers through the wild knots of tangled filthy hair that surrounded her face.

Her first instinct was to turn away and clean herself up in the shower but she fought it down. The nurse had told her quite definitely that she must keep her skin moist with the ointments and it was important not to wash until her normal colour had returned and the pain had disappeared.

'Treat it like sunburn. Sunburn!' she muttered with disgust as she caught sight of the filthy state of her blouse and jeans in the mirror. She was too careful with her body to burn it with the sun's rays. She quickly changed into clean jeans, dragged a brush through her hair and tied it back again. She felt a little better, a little more human, as she dialled the agency.

'I shan't be able to work for a couple of days, a week at the most,' she said abruptly. 'I was accidentally caught up in a fire last night. No, it's nothing serious but the doctor said that I won't be able to wear make-up until the soreness disappears. Yes, I'm sorry but Egypt's out I'm afraid.'

She thought quickly and asked, 'Say, could you fix me a flight to New York later today – before it gets dark?'

The receptionist asked her to wait while she rang the tour operator on another line. Tuppence glanced down anxiously at her watch; it was already eleven thirty-five and she wanted to get out of there fast. The line crackled, making her jump. The receptionist spoke again.

'There's a flight at six o'clock from Heathrow. Would that one do?'

'Yes, that will be fine. Book me on to it, please, club class. I'll call you in a couple of days from New York. We can sort out a new itinerary from there, OK?' she answered, breathing a sigh of relief as she put the receiver down.

She hadn't the slightest idea why or how those creatures from the taxidermist's shop had come to life or why that madman had wanted to capture her. It was too terrifying even to think about, all she wanted to do was to put three thousand miles of water between them and her. She hurried back upstairs and threw the things she would need for the next few days into a case. She would have everything else crated and shipped out later. She took her case out to the car and stood for a moment on the worn threshold of the Watchgate. She was full of regrets, she didn't want to leave the long, low-beamed room with all its atmosphere and feel of history. She had got to love this old house in the short time she had owned it and she felt in a peculiar way it had tried to protect her from the creatures that had haunted her. But she sighed and ran her hand over the smooth-polished contours of the carvings on the door. She couldn't remain a prisoner walled up behind this door for ever. She would be afraid every time the sun set and the shadows of darkness lengthened across the city.

'Goodbye, my door of giants,' she whispered softly, pulling it shut and twisting the heavy ornate iron key in the lock then slipping it into her bag.

She would get an agent to sell it for her. She need never see it again, but she would have a replica made of the key and keep it to remember. She turned, blinking away the tears, and slipped behind the wheel of her Lotus.

13

Pieces of the Jigsaw

Tuppence fired the engine and worked the windscreen washers while it warmed up and tried to clean away the layer of soot and filth from the fire. She was pointing up the hill in the direction of Tombland, the quickest way out of the city towards her road to London, but as she pulled away from the kerb she waited for a gap in the flow of late morning traffic and swung across the hill instead, reversing up so that the Lotus was heading down towards the museum entrance and the junction with Castle Street. She knew that she should be running, getting out fast, but this diversion would only take a minute. She had to take one last look through those burned-out doors and whisper her thanks to the charred remains of the ghostly soldiers.

She let out the clutch and drove slowly down the hill, glancing anxiously into Lobster Lane, fearful of what might lurk there, waiting to pounce on her as she passed. She pulled up opposite the museum entrance, switched off the engine and hurried across the road, picking her way between blackish puddles, up the worn stone steps and through the blackened tide of sludge that had poured out of the building as the firemen fought the blaze.

The doors hadn't been boarded over, just sealed with half a dozen strips of traffic tape and a 'Danger – Keep Out' notice. She paused, her hand on the tape, consumed with sadness as she remembered the panoply of colours, the forest of lance tips as they caught the sunlight, the proud horses snatching at their bridles and the vaulted, atmospheric hall that echoed the moments of triumph, hope and courage she had sensed amongst the statue-still exhibits. She remembered how they had come to her in her moment of need, striding through the smoke, their uniforms spark-bright and smouldering, the fire gnawing at their bones. She owed it to them to say goodbye in the great hall amongst the ruins of their sacrifice rather than here between the doors.

She made a gap between two of the pieces of traffic tape and slipped into the entrance hall. The dead silence and the stench of the burned-out building engulfed her, she shivered and hesitated. She almost retraced her steps, it was so utterly silent, so forlorn, so desolate.

'No, I *am* going to say goodbye,' she whispered to herself, screwing up her courage and creeping stealthily forward over the deep carpet of ash and sludge that squelched up over the soles of her trainers and oozed into opaque grey puddles to fill the footprints she left behind her. Reaching the doorway into the great hall she stopped. Close up, the devastation from the fire was horrific. The museum had been reduced to a charred shell, the spine of slender gothic arches that ran the length of its roof had been split apart by the fire. Burned and splintered rafters, broken stonework and strips of blackened lath and plaster-work hung down, edging the gaping holes in the roof with jagged teeth. Sunlight streamed down, misty and trans-lucent with wisps of steam and lingering curls of smoke that rose up from the wreckage.

A shadow crossed Tuppence's face and she frowned and looked up. Birds were moving through the shafts of sunlight, squawking harshly in the muffled silence as they circled down into the museum to perch briefly on the buckled twisted columns that had once supported the galleries. They strutted around as if searching for something and then noisily flew up and down the misty length of the burned-out building, alighting on the skeletal armatures that had once kept the exhibits erect. They pecked at the brittle wire bindings as though they were feeding, scavenging on the flesh of the soldiers who had perished in the fire. Tuppence watched as a large shiny black crow picked at a mass of bone and wire and pulled something free. It lifted its head up and swallowed a glistening eyeball.

She shuddered and cried out, her revulsion turning to anger, then rushed forward shaking her fist at the bird still perched on the charred remains of the skeleton. She clapped her hands and shouted, 'Get out! Get out of here, you filthy scavenger.'

The crow turned its head sharply in the direction of her voice and lowered its head, tilting it from side to side, its black eyes carefully watching her. The other birds flocked noisily towards her, swooping between the heaps of fire wrack, to circle around her head, pecking at her hair. Tuppence cowered and raising one hand to protect herself scrabbled with the other in the debris, looking for a length of wood, a metal rod, anything to ward them off. Her hand closed on the smooth ferrule of a broken lance but before she could pull it free the first crow opened its beak and disgorged the eyeball. It bounced down across the mound of rubbish and landed at her feet. The bird squawked and rose lazily into the air, flapping and beating its wings, stirring up the hazy shafts of light and circling up out of her reach to vanish through one of the gaping holes in the roof. The rest of the carrion flock followed it, cawing and squawking noisily.

She realized that in her anger she had rushed halfway

across the museum hall. She hesitated and glanced sadly at the pitiful remains of all that had once held so much atmosphere, all that had represented courage and endeavour. She began to turn back towards the entrance hall when she heard the crunch of a footstep behind her to her left. Her spine crawled, her heart began to race. She imagined those hideous bears, their hides smouldering and crackling with sparks, their claws stretching out as they closed in on her. She wanted to run, dash for the entrance, but her legs felt as though they had been filled with lead. Desperately she raised the broken lance shaft she was still clutching in her hands, and turned, ready to protect herself.

'You hideous bastards. You . . . you . . . foul . . .'

Her voice faltered and she stared open-mouthed, unable to stop the vicious downward stroke of the lance. It was the fireman, the one who had rescued her, his open smile changing to a look of surprise, his eyes widening with alarm. He stopped abruptly and threw his arm up to ward off the blow, staggering as the shaft struck him close to the wrist. He cried out as the pain shot up his arm and his fingers burned and tingled with the numbness spread through them.

'Oh my God, I'm really sorry, I thought you were . . .' Tuppence fell silent as she let the broken shaft fall to the ground. Dec bit his lip to stifle the agony and looked down at his arm, gingerly opening and closing his fingers, letting out a sigh of relief as he realized that she hadn't broken anything.

He didn't believe in ghosts, but he had come back to try to find an explanation for what he had seen. He had hoped to have the ruins of the museum to himself and was certainly not expecting to see this woman in here. He knew the forensic team were due to start sifting through the debris but he wanted a quick look first. He wasn't sure what he was searching for but he couldn't stop thinking about those soldiers and the creatures that had attacked them. He had barely taken the time to shower and change at his home in Thieves Bridge before he had driven into the city, even though he knew that it was dangerous entering a building so near to collapse.

What he was doing was strictly against all the rules. He had heard her footsteps and thought that it was the forensic team arriving and so had begun to make for a breach in the far wall where it had collapsed in the fire, hoping to slip out before they saw him. Then he had heard her shout and had retraced his steps.

'I hope I haven't broken your arm. I'm really, really sorry,' she apologized again, making Dec look up.

'No, I'm sure there's nothing broken.'

He laughed softly, gritting his teeth against the pain though he let his arm fall casually to his side. Tuppence tried to smile but her eyes darted anxiously to the mounds of rubbish.

'So why did you come back?' he asked quietly. 'You know you shouldn't be in here at all. Didn't you see the notice in the entrance hall? This whole building could collapse at any moment.'

'I came to take one last look around, to say goodbye,' she replied hesitantly.

'Say goodbye to what? Those ghosts, phantoms in the smoke, who carried you?' he asked more forcefully, watching for the shadow of fear that he had seen in the hospital. He moved closer and lowered his voice. 'Or was it to check that those other, terrible creatures had all perished in the fire?'

Tuppence stared at him. The colour drained from her face. She hesitated and then asked in a whisper, 'So you saw them as well?'

Dec laughed harshly. 'I didn't only see them, they – one of them attacked the fireman behind me. It ripped his breathing apparatus in half and . . .' Dec paused. He had caught the sound of voices, the scrape of footsteps and the crunch of broken glass underfoot. Figures were moving through the shafts of sunlight, silhouetted in the doorway of the great hall.

'That must be the forensic team. They've come to find out how the fire started. We had better find a back way out, quickly. If they catch us in here we are both in a lot of trouble.' Dec spoke in a hiss, touching her arm, pulling her to follow him between the piles of reeking rubbish.

'Wait a minute,' she whispered fiercely at him, 'we both saw those creatures, didn't we? And I saw that mad bastard of a taxidermist who controls them pouring petrol all over the floor of the museum and then setting light to it. So why don't we tell those officials? Why don't we tell them what we saw?'

Dec stopped and turned back. He laughed softly but there wasn't a trace of humour in his face, it was tense and serious. 'They'll never believe us, nobody will. I've already tried to tell them and they laughed in my face. They think I've been hallucinating, suffering from oxygen starvation.'

Tuppence's look of determination began to evaporate. She hesitated. 'But we both saw them. We know they really existed, they have to believe us.'

Dec shook his head. 'They'll believe what they want, and ghosts and hideous creatures won't look good on their fire reports. And there's nothing here to prove our story's true. The bodies of those animals were all burned up, along with the soldiers who helped carry you and Geordie out of the flames. I know, I've already looked.'

The forensic team were getting closer, working their way across the great hall, flash bulbs popping, rakes and shovels scraping and riddling the charred debris.

'We will need hard evidence if we are going to convince anybody. Come on, there's daylight showing through that break in the wall. That must be one of the alleyways that lead into Castle Street.'

Tuppence hurried after him, moving as silently as she could between the towering piles of rubbish, clambering over the loose bricks and flints and out through the breach in the wall. There she stopped and nearly collided with him.

'Damn,' Dec muttered under his breath, drawing her aside away from the ragged hole. 'It's a dead end, an inner courtyard that leads nowhere.'

Tuppence felt the hot afternoon sun on her face and she shaded her eyes to look across the small neatly mown lawn with its sparkling fountain, shady lime trees and regimented beds of rose bushes. It was warm, with hardly a breath of air to stir the stillness. Doves were cooing and whispering in the branches of the trees and far away she could hear the faint hum of the city traffic.

'Look, there's an arched doorway. Over there on the left-hand side of the courtyard. Perhaps that leads out into the street,' she whispered hopefully.

Moments later Dec was back beside her. 'It's locked I'm afraid. There's no way out of here, all the windows are barred. There's a double trap door on the far side of this lawn but I'm sure that only leads down into some cellars beneath the museum. It looks as though we'll have to stay here until the forensic team have finished for the day and just hope they don't come out here for a breath of fresh air.'

Tuppence glanced down at the hands of her watch in desperation. She would never make that six o'clock flight unless she got out now.

'You've got to help me or I'll miss my plane. I'll go mad

if I have to spend another night anywhere near this place.' She looked desperately around their sunlit prison.

Dec frowned and pulled off his glasses, absently polishing the lenses on his sleeve. There wasn't anything he could do, he had examined the outer walls of the courtyard carefully, they were completely boxed in. He followed her out across the grass and towards the fountain.

'I'm sorry but we're trapped,' he answered gravely.

Tuppence turned helplessly towards him. 'But I have to get away from here before it gets dark, before this whole nightmare begins again.'

Dec pulled his glasses back on and held her with his gaze before he spoke. 'But everything, the ghosts, the creatures, they were all consumed by the fire. There's nothing to haunt you now.'

She shivered as he spoke, as if the sun had vanished behind a cloud, vividly remembering the hideous creatures pursuing her and the clatter of horseshoes on the road. No, it had been too real to vanish in a puff of smoke. She wanted to escape, to run from the possibility of it all beginning again.

'I don't know what happened to me,' she cried. 'I didn't ask to be drawn into this nightmare any more than you did when you rescued me and I just want to get as far away from here as I can.'

She looked so fragile, so helpless and afraid standing there in the sunlight. He wanted to reach out and put his arms about her, to gather her up and protect her from everything that frightened her, but he was far too shy to risk crossing that space between them.

'I saw them as well and you're not going to face the fear of them alone. I'm here, I'll stay with you until you're sure you're safe,' he smiled. 'My name's Dec, Dec Winner,' and he stretched out his right hand, feeling a little foolish at the formal greeting.

'Tuppence, Tuppence Trilby,' she replied with a sudden smile and grasped his hand with both of hers.

Fate had created the most unlikely of meeting places for them but she felt a wave of relief and a slight easing of the nightmare that haunted her as she held tightly on to his hand. There was a warmth and a strength about him that made her feel safe. It made her want to tell him everything that had happened since that night she had first seen the Watchgate.

The words crowded and stumbled over one another. The six o'clock flight to New York was forgotten and her escape was pushed to the back of her mind. Dec glanced at the breach in the wall, afraid that the forensic team would either hear her or see them. He drew her away to the furthest corner of the courtyard and sat beside her on one of the stone benches close to the trap doors.

'I'm sure all those animals burned in the fire,' he reassured her as she fell silent. 'I know the bears were destroyed, I saw them driven, skewered on lances. They were pushed into the heart of the fire, flames poured out of their heads, their eyeballs were like molten coals. Sparks crackled and danced across their shoulders as the flames consumed them.'

'I know that taxidermist started the fire. I know,' she muttered grimly. 'I watched him do it. But if everything, every animal, every creature that he ever touched and brought to life was burned up in the fire people will say that we were crazier than he is – if we go around accusing him without anything to prove it.'

'Yes . . . yes I know,' answered Dec thoughtfully, 'but there must be something . . . something that didn't get destroyed. Something that is just lying there, hidden in the ashes of the fire.'

Tuppence laughed softly and shook her head. 'We'll

never find anything in there. What we ought to do, if we had the nerve, is to take a look in Goats Head Alley to check if the taxidermist escaped from the fire. And if he did we can call the cops and let them deal with it.'

'Yes, perhaps you're right, but what will we tell them?' he smiled at her.

He hadn't expected to meet her again, especially after seeing her picture spread across the front page of the morning paper on every newsstand he passed on his way back into the city. He had stopped and bought himself a copy and read all about her and he counted himself the luckiest man alive to have been the one to rescue her. He caught a sound of voices from the museum and stared across the courtyard towards the breach in the wall.

'It looks as though they're going to find us. I'm really sorry that you've missed your flight. If I hadn't stopped you from leaving you wouldn't be in this mess. I'll explain that I brought you into the museum, that you didn't realize how dangerous it was.'

Tuppence turned her head and looked up at him. There was something charming and old-fashioned about him, an inner strength that showed in the determined angle to his jaw and the laughter lines around his eyes. And there was such an openness in his deep-set eyes. She liked him more for having met him a second time. There was something else about him, something that she had noticed in the hospital but would never have been able to put her finger on if they hadn't met again. She glanced at his glasses and saw how the rubber band which held the broken frames together wove its way through his tangle of curly hair at the back of his head. Neat, inventive, and very individual.

'Thanks, but you don't have to make excuses for me, really,' she whispered back.

Dec lifted his hand to silence her. 'Listen, can you hear

that? It's not those guys inside the museum, it's something closer.' He stood up and spun around, searching the shadows beneath the covered walkway behind them.

'Look! Look at the handle. It's turning, grating,' Tuppence gasped, clutching his arm and pointing down to the wooden trap doors on the edge of the lawn.

Dec drew her back into the shadows but there was nowhere they could hide. They could only wait and watch.

The iron ring stopped turning and the trap doors creaked slowly open. A smoke-smudged face appeared just above the level of the lawn, looking towards them. They saw a white-gloved hand beckon out of the darkness of the cellar steps and heard a muffled voice urging them to hurry. Tuppence stared, white-faced, her fingernails cutting painfully into Dec's arm.

'It's the Colonel. From the museum. But it's just not possible, you were all destroyed, all burnt up,' she gasped.

'Some of us escaped, madam. Now hurry, please, there are eyes watching your every move,' Colonel Hawkesbury urged again.

Dec hesitated. It was possible that some of those ghosts or whatever they were might have escaped from the fire but he didn't relish following one of them into the bowels of the earth no matter how friendly they appeared. Before last night's fire, magic, ghosts and the supernatural were things you spun into stories beside a winter fireside or acted out on Hallowe'en, not something you rubbed shoulders with and followed into the dark.

'Be quick. There are spies,' the Colonel hissed, stabbing his white-gloved hand up to a row of black crows perched in frozen stillness on the broken roof ridge of the museum. Just at that moment two members of the forensic team clambered through the breach in the wall.

14

Lamplight in the Museum Vaults

Dec glanced quickly from the crows to the members of the forensic team. He shrugged helplessly and then grimaced at Tuppence. 'We're probably even crazier than that taxidermist if we follow this ghost into the pitch-black cellars but I don't think we have any choice.'

Tuppence gripped his arm harder. Dec smiled and whispered to her as he led her to the brink of the cellar steps. 'Keep your eyes tightly shut if you're afraid. I'll be your eyes.'

And he followed the Colonel slowly down the steep stone steps that led into a brick-lined passageway. Dec was aware of two military figures both dressed in scarlet coats and white breeches whom they brushed past on the steps and who closed the heavy wooden trap doors, bolting them securely. The last glimpse of daylight vanished and the darkness wrapped itself claustrophobically around them. He felt Tuppence breathe quicker against the back of his neck and her arm tighten around him as she struggled not to tread on his heels.

Reaching out with his right hand he began to feel his way carefully along the wall of the passage. Muffled voices and footsteps echoed around them in the tunnel and everywhere they heard the soft plop and drip of leaking water and smelt mildew, decay and damp in the ice-cold darkness. Dec was counting off their steps, memorizing the twists of the passage and the slope of the tunnel floor just in case these ghostly figures vanished and they had to find their own way back. Suddenly a match flared brightly ahead of them, sending their shadows fleeing backwards across the low-vaulted brick ceiling.

Tuppence cried out with relief and eased her grip on Dec. He halted, blinking against the sudden light, and watched as a figure in front of the Colonel lit a brass hurricane lamp and adjusted the flickering wick before holding it up at shoulder height.

'It is but a footstep further now, madam, just around that corner ahead of us. Perhaps you would do me the honour,' the Colonel smiled and offered his arm courteously to Tuppence.

Dec moved aside to let her past. 'No one's ever going to believe this,' she murmured to him under her breath.

She place her hand carefully through the Colonel's arm and he gently took it and placed her slender fingers correctly on to the back of his right hand, covering the ugly burn in his glove. He bowed slightly to her and then straightened his back and motioned to the soldier carrying the lamp to lead them forward. The soldier's spurs clicked rhythmically and his long leather boots creaked with each measured stride he took as he vanished around the sharp twist in the passageway, closely followed by the Colonel and Tuppence.

Dec frowned and hurried after them in the darkness. Ahead the sound of voices grew suddenly louder and then died away to nothing. He rounded the corner and abruptly halted and stared, open-mouthed, at the scene that lay before him. The tunnel had opened out into acres of cellars that stretched away as far as he could see amongst the forest of thick stone columns and spreading arches that supported the low-vaulted ceilings. The stench of paraffin oil and burnt cloth wafted over him and made him catch his breath, but it was the sight of hundreds of charred and blackened figures crowding every inch of space and the rows of horses picketed beside the stone columns that made him gasp. The soldiers stood or sat so still, their heads turned towards him, their eyes flickering from the hazy light cast from dozens of oil lamps that had been hastily strung up between the archways. Rifles, ammunition boxes, lances, water bottles and countless other articles of war had been gathered in the night from the burning museum and lay scattered or stacked in haphazard piles between the men and the horses.

He felt as if he had stumbled unasked into the last death throes of a great army. He recognized their uniforms, or what was left of them after the fire. He knew that they neither breathed nor felt pain and yet he wanted to turn away, to lower his gaze from their hideously burnt limbs. A slight movement on his left made him turn his head to see that Colonel Hawkesbury had led Tuppence into the centre of the largest cellar.

The Colonel raised Tuppence's right hand and said loudly, 'Our Lady of the Watchgate is safe,' and he pointed to Dec and continued, 'and our rescuer has brought her back to us.'

A sigh of relief echoed in the smoky paraffin light. The horses scuffled and scraped their hooves and the soldiers' serious faces creased into weary smiles.

The soldiers began to stir and shuffle forward, their voices starting to rise. They were whispering Tuppence's name. Dec made to take a step towards her and reached out to shield her but he hesitated as the rattle of rifle bolts echoed through the low cellars and he found himself staring into a semi-circle of rifle bayonets.

'You would be a fool to come between our Lady of the

Watchgate and those who are sworn to defend her,' the Colonel muttered quietly as he swept his hand across the mass of riflemen who were aiming their guns at Dec's heart.

Dec allowed his hand to fall helplessly to his side and he backed away until he felt his shoulder blades scrape against the rough brick of the cellar wall. He knew he was a trigger squeeze from eternity, he could see it in their eyes, and beads of perspiration began to break out across his forehead.

'Wait a moment. I want to know what the hell's going on? I thought you were going to help us,' Tuppence cried in alarm.

'Indeed, madam, we are pledged to it. We are here to help and protect you,' the Colonel answered, turning back and raising his hand and motioning the riflemen back to their places. 'But dealing with the dark magic that has been stirred up against you is not proving a simple matter . . .'

A disturbance in one of the furthest cellars made the Colonel pause and frown as he turned towards a figure hurrying to him. It was Trooper Dibble, Tuppence saw with a shock.

'What news is there, scout? How many of those creatures escaped from the fire, if any?' he asked urgently, beckoning the horseman to follow him.

Turning on his heel the Colonel guided Tuppence and Dec into a small secluded ante-room away to the left of the main area of cellars. 'My temporary headquarters,' he muttered bleakly, sweeping his hand across the crumbling moss-damp walls and forgotten litter of rotting sacks, wooden crates and broken bottles that filled the corners of the room.

Tuppence entered and her stomach turned at the smell

of death and decay. She shuddered to think what might lie hidden beneath those mouldering piles of rubbish.

'You will come to no harm, madam,' the Colonel said softly as if he felt her apprehension and he took a top coat from one of his aides and draped it carefully around her shoulders to guard against the chill of the room.

Dec followed her through the doorway, closely followed by Trooper Dibble, and stopped in front of a table that had been hastily assembled by stacking a dozen ammunition boxes together. A large linen map of the old part of the city lay spread out on top of it, weighed down by two cylindrical brass lanterns whose soft dancing pools of light illuminated every street and alleyway engraved into the textured surface of the map.

Dec bent forward to study the drawing and murmured, 'These cellars, they stretch for hundreds of yards and fork off in all directions. I'll bet there must be at least a dozen exits.'

Colonel Hawkesbury frowned and glanced around at the sound of his voice. 'Yes, and they are linked to the old sewer system. There are far too many exit holes for us to defend but that is only a part of our dilemma . . .' He turned to the trooper. 'Tell us, what news is there from Lobster Lane and Goats Head Alley?'

The horseman frowned and spoke slowly. 'I don't think any of those creatures escaped from the fire into Goats Head Alley, at least there were none to be seen on Elm Hill or the alleyway off Lobster Lane. But I did see the beasts of the air, the black carrion crows, and many other birds circling the roof tops of Goats Head Alley in the first light of dawn.'

'Yes,' muttered the Colonel thoughtfully, 'we have watched those birds flocking to the ruins all day scavenging on the bones of our dead. I'm afraid they spotted our Lady before we could bring her down into the safety of these cellars.'

'Were those birds from the taxidermist's shop?' Tuppence exclaimed. 'I thought they were just scavenging. I chased them out of the ruins of the museum before we climbed through that hole in the wall and into the courtyard.'

The Colonel, his aides and the horsemen turned and stared at her. The scout was the first to break the silence. 'Those birds will carry the knowledge that you have survived the fire back into Goats Head Alley, my lady. The magic will know that you are here amongst us.'

The Colonel nodded gravely. 'Yes, we must act quickly.'

The heavy fabric of his neck chafed on the tight band that edged his high collar, rubbing through to show the weave of the material. Dec watched in fascination. He was so close that he could see every detail, every unnatural crease and fold in his skin. Every one of the soldiers and horses seemed more real than the most real marionettes, a masterpiece of the puppeteer's art. They seemed real enough to bleed, but the disfiguring burns showed the reality by exposing their skeletons of wood and wire and the soft strands of straw and kapok that made up the bulk of each figure. He stared at the deep burn on the Colonel's hand and tried to see what lay beneath the surface. Then he felt the Colonel's eyes bore into him; he looked up and caught his breath. The man's eyes were so alive, so piercing.

'It is the magic that we fear, madam. The dark sinister power that dwells beyond the archway in Goats Head Alley, and we know that it did not perish in the fire.'

'How do you know that it didn't? Your horseman said that he hadn't seen any of those creatures except the carrion crows,' she exclaimed.

Colonel Hawkesbury laughed softly and sadly shook

his head. 'Because, madam, that sinister power resurrected every one of us who now crowd these cellars. If the power had perished our animation would have faded away and those crows would be senseless on the ground.'

Tuppence stepped back from the map table, her heartbeat quickening. Why if the same dark magic had brought these soldiers to life did they not seize her? She looked past the group of figures gathered in the small ante-room to the shifting crowds of soldiers in the main cellars beyond and shuddered as she realized that she and Dec had stupidly walked into a trap. They were now prisoners.

'Madam, you are free to go. No one here would set a hand upon you.' Tuppence blinked at the Colonel's muffled voice, it was as if he had heard her thoughts. She looked back at him. He had drawn his sword and laid it, hilt towards her, on the map table. Every one of his aides and the scout laid down their sabres and revolvers next to his.

'Our awakening was a freak of the magic, an accident, carried in the moonlight that flooded across the roof tops of the city many nights ago. How or why it happened we do not know but when it shone down through the tall fluted windows of the museum and bathed us in its brilliant light its power was magnified by the tiny flaws in the glass and the evil was purged out before it touched us. It resurrected only the good, the endeavour, the sacrifice that still dwells in the dried blood and sweat that stains the cloth of our uniforms and covers the horses' hides.'

'But why did you protect me? How was I drawn into this nightmare?' Tuppence cried.

'You were there in the very centre of the magic at the moment that the spells were cast and the chants were uttered. It was your voice that came to us on that night and awoke us. Your cry for help bound us to protect you.'

'The taxidermist – he must be at the bottom of all this,' Tuppence hissed, gripping Dec's arm tightly as the memory of that moonlit evening when Richard had walked her down Lobster Lane flooded back. She remembered she had insisted on exploring beneath the archway that led into Goats Head Alley and the memory of that cold claustro-phobic courtyard with its hissing cats and secret eerie shadows made her shiver. She could see the sharp, broken-toothed ruins of the old church tower etched black against the moonlit sky and the blind windows and black door-ways surrounding her. Then she remembered the sudden sight of that stooping white-coated figure staring down, his mad eyes greedily devouring her. Yes, she remembered her cry of fear as the brilliant flash of light filled his window, engulfed the courtyard and then vanished away over the crowding rooftops.

'I wish I had never gone snooping around in that horrible courtyard, then none of this would ever have happened,' she muttered miserably.

'No, madam, the magic would have happened despite you. It was too strong to have been an accident,' the scout answered. 'Perhaps it was your destiny to be drawn into it because you have the strength to help us destroy it. You can get far closer than we can to the centre of its power.'

A frozen silence spread throughout the low-vaulted cel-lars. The Colonel, his aides and every lancer, hussar, rifle-man and wild-eyed charger turned and stared at the scout. One of the horses neighed and snorted in alarm, the sound echoing from one of the outer cellars as it scraped and cast up sparks from its iron-shod shoes on the rough brick floor. It broke the spell and the soldiers shuffled forward through the misty paraffin light to crowd the entrance of the ante-room, their burned and soot-smeared faces creased with concern.

'No, no, I will not have it,' the Colonel cried angrily, slamming his burnt hand down on the map table. 'You scouts and rough riders are too reckless. It is our duty to protect our Lady of the Watchgate, not to risk her life. No, it would be madness to even suggest that she venture anywhere near to the centre of the magic.'

The scout quickly stepped back. 'Forgive me, ma'am, I meant no disrespect.'

Tuppence looked across at the horseman and held his gaze as he spoke. He was exactly as she had imagined when she stood beside him in the museum. He was lithe, hardened by the life he had led, and yet there was a gentleness in his sea-grey eyes.

'They seem to know less than you do about the taxidermist's shop,' Dec interrupted suddenly, making her turn quickly towards him.

For a moment she stared at him and then glanced back at the scout. They were so different, yet in many ways they were so alike. 'What did you say?' she frowned, moving closer to him.

'I don't think these soldiers can get anywhere near the taxidermist's shop. They don't seem to have seen him when he broke into the museum and dowsed the floor with petrol even though he was only inches away from where they stood when he set it alight.'

Dec paused and thought for a moment before he turned slowly towards the Colonel. He chose his words carefully. 'Perhaps, Colonel, it is time that we had a council of war, pooled our resources; it might help. Together we may be able to destroy this magic.'

'No, I am totally against it. We must not risk our Lady's life,' the Colonel replied angrily.

'Now just a minute!' Tuppence demanded. 'I decide

what the hell I do or don't do around here. It's high time you all realized that.'

The Colonel stared open-mouthed at her, startled by her outburst. He faintly nodded his head in bleak agreement but still he tried to dissuade her.

'No,' Tuppence replied firmly, 'things have changed a lot since your day, Colonel. Women like me ain't used to being treated like pieces of porcelain. We're used to hand-ling our own affairs. Oh, and can all of you please stop calling me "madam" or "our Lady of the Watchgate". Jesus! It makes me sound like some old matron. Just call me Tuppence – that's my name.'

Dec watched the ripple of surprise as the sound of her outburst spread throughout the crowded cellars.

'Good, I'm glad that's settled,' she smiled. 'Now let's do as Dec suggested and chew over what we know about this magic business. Let's see what facts we've got.'

'The centre of the power is beneath the archway that leads into Goats Head Alley,' offered the scout.

'Yes, and we know the madman who started it and who burned down the museum,' answered Tuppence frowning. 'But what I don't understand is why he was dabbling in magic and why he wanted to attack me.'

'Oh, he probably wants you as a part of his collection,' Dec laughed. But his laughter died on his lips as he looked at the sea of frowning undead soldiers' faces illuminated by the dancing flames of the guttering lanterns.

'Yes, I think you have touched at the dark heart of this magic,' echoed the Colonel gravely as he pushed at the loose strands of straw that were escaping from the hole in the back of his gloved hand before he reached out and trimmed the wicks of the lamps, making them burn more steadily.

'Then those creatures weren't trying to attack me in the

flames, they were trying to capture me. They were trying to take me back to the taxidermist's shop,' Tuppence cried, a shiver of revulsion travelling up her spine. 'He tried to seize me when I visited his shop yesterday. If I had realized I would never have gone within a thousand miles of the place. But why me? Why does he want to make me a part of his collection?' she gasped. 'That guy's a madman, you've got to stop him.'

Dec looked up at her and smiled as he pulled on his glasses. 'Taxidermists preserve beauty. They recreate the perfect specimen out of death. Perhaps he wants to preserve you because he sees you as the most beautiful woman . . .'

'Cut that out,' Tuppence snapped, shivering and gathering the gold-braided edges of the soldier's coat more tightly around her shoulders. Dec seemed suddenly to have developed a habit of touching at the truth of this nightmare and it unnerved her. 'What the hell can we do to stop him?' she demanded.

The scout swept his hand across the map. 'The boldest move would be for our riflemen to storm the courtyard and attack while we deploy the cavalry in the maze of alleyways to ensure that nothing escapes. But . . .' the scout hesitated and clenched his hand into a fist as he lowered his eyes, 'we cannot, madam. The source of this magic is too powerful, it blinds and thwarts us. It prevents us from entering the courtyard.'

'We must assume a defensive position, Miss . . . Miss Tuppence, until we have determined the exact nature of their next attack,' the Colonel interrupted gravely.

'Defensive?' Tuppence cried angrily. 'Jesus, are you just going to hide out in these miserable rat holes and wait for that . . . that lunatic to come looking for me?'

'No, oh no, most certainly not, madam,' Colonel Hawkesbury replied, a little ruffled by her piercing accusation.

He admired her spirit and her show of courage but he could not get used to her directness, but then perhaps all the women of this new age were as forward. 'No . . . of course not,' he continued, regaining his composure and pointing down at his map. 'My plan is to escort you back to the Watchgate as soon as darkness falls. You will be a lot safer in there than in this warren of cellars while the scouts gather more intelligence and find out what this taxidermist plans to do next.'

'Are you crazy?' Tuppence cried in horror. 'Those creatures have been hammering on the door of the Watchgate and climbing all over the place trying to get me ever since I bought it. No, I'm not sticking around there, I'll be a lot safer getting right away from here and catching the first plane I can back to the States.'

'I have a horrible feeling that that madman would follow you and find you wherever you tried to hide,' Dec murmured seriously.

'This evil, or its emissary, cannot touch you while you are inside the Watchgate,' the Colonel added quickly.

Tuppence turned angrily from one to the other of them. She wanted to call the Colonel a fool and to tell Dec that she wasn't climbing into a cage and becoming a virtual prisoner, but she hesitated and asked, 'What do you mean? What do you mean when you say that no evil can enter the Watchgate? You sound like that old vicar. What's to stop this taxidermist taking an axe to the door or sending his creatures to hack it down?'

'I doubt if anything can break it down. It is a fortress,' the Colonel smiled. 'The beginnings of the Watchgate stretch back into the roots of history. It was built upon superstition, built to guard people against everything they feared: invasion, the plague, magic. The fabric of its shell, the very bricks and mortar, were trowelled together with chants and spells, it was built on an ancient site and a child was probably sacrificed and buried where the threshold stone now stands to keep the evil out and shadow-treaders danced beneath its eaves. Its humble builder hid hag stones, squirrel skins and dried toads beneath the wattle plaster of its walls. It is a sanctuary against the darkest evil, strengthened by the superstitions of each new age as new people dwelt there and used its powers. Even the glaziers added their touch to the tiny panes of glass as they set them into the windows and engraved them with magic scratchings.

'Those carvings on the outer door are not mere illustrations from an age long-vanished, they are intricate picture words, signs of magic, symbols, gouged into the wood with ritual tools to ward off all manner of evil.'

'Yes, the place has a magical feel about it,' she murmured. 'But I would be a prisoner. I would never dare to step outside in case that taxidermist was about to try and snatch me,' she muttered thickly, shaking her head at the idea.

'My men would watch over you and escort you whenever you wished to leave.'

'There's another way, a quicker way, to find out what is going on,' Dec interrupted, making everyone in the room turn towards him. 'I could steal a look at what is going on in the taxidermist's shop. His magic or whatever it is doesn't affect me. I could slip into Goats Head Alley tonight under cover of darkness and spy on him for you. I could find out what he is planning to do next. After all he won't be expecting me and there is nothing to connect me with Tuppence, is there? He'd never know I rescued her from the fire.'

Mutterings of interest and disapproval rippled around the map table and vanished out among the soldiers who were crowding the doorway.

'Tuppence is ours to guard and protect. You are not a part of this,' a voice called out in the crowd.

The Colonel raised his hand for silence and stared thoughtfully at Dec before slowly shaking his head. 'No, I fear that would be a rash move. The carrion crows must have spotted you in the courtyard before we brought you down into the safety of these cellars. The magic would have been warned of your presence here amongst us by now.'

'Madness, utter madness,' echoed the scout. 'You, sir, are a civilian. To have you blundering noisily into that courtyard would only serve to warn the magic . . .'

Dec blushed at their brusque dismissal and pulled off his glasses, hastily polishing the lenses to mask his embarrassment.

'That really is a great way to thank Dec for risking his life to rescue me from the fire, isn't it?' Tuppence snapped, glaring angrily at the figures gathered around the table.

She turned towards Dec, her eyes softening into a smile. 'I'm against you going into that courtyard alone as well, so I intend to go with you.' Tuppence paused, her smile widening into a grin.

'No, oh no, you mustn't do that,' dozens of voices called out, rising to a clamour as the ranks joined in. Horses neighed and struck up sparks on the rough brick floors but Tuppence merely folded her arms and declared that they would leave as soon as it was dark.

'Madam!' cried the Colonel, his face a mask of despair, 'I must advise you against such folly. I . . . I . . . I must forbid it!'

Tuppence shook her head and unfolded her arms. She rested her slender fingers firmly upon the map and leaned forward, holding the Colonel's gaze. 'Sorry, Colonel, no deal, I'm not going to hide in the Watchgate while that crazy bastard creates new creatures to terrorize me. I'm going to find out what he's up to so that we can go to the police and have him arrested.'

'The police!' The Colonel laughed harshly. 'And what do you think they could do to stop the magic – put him in prison?' He was angry and frustrated and banged his fist on the table as he spoke.

'I really don't know, we'll just have to wait and see what we find in Goats Head Alley, won't we?' she answered firmly.

The aides and the scout stared helplessly at her while the Colonel rubbed a hand across his forehead. He looked dazed and bewildered and repeatedly shook his head. He wasn't used to being crossed, to having his orders contemptuously countermanded but he knew that neither he nor all the others whom the magic had resurrected to protect her could stop her from doing exactly what she wanted to do no matter how foolish her actions were.

Wearily the Colonel turned to his aides. He ordered them to organize the riflemen into a flying column to accompany them to the entrance of the courtyard while sharp-shooters would be positioned on the roof tops overlooking Elm Hill, to cover their retreat. Turning, he drew the scout away from the table and ordered him to deploy the cavalrymen in every alleyway and dark opening of the length of Elm Hill and Lobster Lane.

Bending close he whispered, 'Keep the best, the fastest two mounts saddled and ready and as close to the entrance of that courtyard as you dare. Let us hope and pray that they can escape from the centre of this magic.'

15

Councils of War

Ludo Strewth was beside himself with rage. He stood in the centre of his shop surrounded by vacant shelves and deserted display cases staring at the utter devastation the fire had wreaked upon his beautiful collection of animals. Only a handful of charred skeletons, their hides a blaze of sparks, had managed to return to him and they now lay in smouldering ruins at his feet.

'You shouldn't have followed her into the fire. I commanded you not to do it,' he muttered bitterly under his breath, kicking out savagely at the tangled mess of wire, burned hide and feathers that lay at his feet, but as he stood there he realized that it was the magic that had driven them. The dark spell had destroyed everything that he had ever created and his desire to possess the American woman began to crystallize into hatred, a raw brutal hatred that would not let him rest until he had ground her bones into dust.

A fluttering movement above his head made him look up. The row of silent, black, hunched crows and fire-stained owls had managed to escape the flames and had flown back to his shop in the first light of dawn to roost on the curtain rails and the tops of the display cases. For a moment he stared up blankly at the birds.

'Find her bones for me,' he hissed suddenly, striding to the door and flinging it open. 'Bring me back an eyeball, a row of teeth, anything that will prove she has perished in the fire. Go now! Go.'

He shrieked at them, flapping his arms wildly, sending the birds swooping and winging their way out before he resumed pacing backwards and forwards in his empty shop. He was still doing this when the crows returned with the news.

'She's alive,' he hissed, his eyes narrowing as he caressed the smooth glossy chest feathers of the huge crow perching on his shoulders.

The crow squawked and twisted its head to one side to stare up with glistening eyes at the taxidermist's face.

'She's alive while everything I created lies in ruins,' he muttered, his voice dripping with hate, his lips thinning into a bloodless line.

He hurried through the shop and climbed the steep staircase to his preparation room. He unlocked the door and threw it open, then switched on the hanging lamp and let his eyes wander over the rows of purple-bruised and hideously putrefying figures that filled the long low room. 'Miserable failures,' he muttered, grimacing with disgust at the stench of rotting flesh and the odour of sweet dry formaldehyde that wafted over him.

It was the heavy reek of corruption that appalled him; it clearly showed his failure to preserve the human form. The smell was so different from the clean musky odour of his beautiful collection. He blinked at the stench and shut out the despair he felt at losing everything. Holding a handkerchief pinched to his nose he quickly and carefully threaded his way between the gruesome human remains and hurried to the window. He threw it open; darkness had buried the courtyard below in black shadows. Silence held its breath in Lobster Lane and only the distant hum of the city drifted through the window on the warm night breeze.

Slowly Ludo turned to his marble preparation slab and reached out and caressed the severed Hand of Glory that lay there, stroking its waxy, shrivelled and blackened skin with his fingertips, feeling the heat of the fire that smouldered within its index finger. He savoured the revenge that he was about to begin. Wetting his lips he whispered to the mummified hand, 'You will avenge what she has done to me.' He turned and raised the hand and waved it above his head. 'I was going to strip off your putrefying skins, one by one, and cremate them,' he whispered at the rows of corpses. 'But now that she has destroyed everything,' his voice rose into a shriek of madness, 'the magic will resurrect you and you will hunt her down and bring her here so that I can tear her limb from . . .'

He paused and spun round. There was a sound beyond the window. A footstep? Not quite, more of a scrape or a rustle of leaves.

'Cats in the tower,' he muttered, irritable at their interruption. He briefly searched the black bulk of the ivy-covered ruins of the church tower that rose up a handspan from his window, standing out against the star-bright sky.

He shrugged his narrow shoulders and muttered under his breath before he turned back to his preparation slab. He drew the crumpled silk sleeve from the pocket of his long, dirty white coat and threw it down savagely beside the mummified hand on the marble. The bears had been of some use, they had torn this piece of clothing from Tuppence's blouse.

'Revenge,' he hissed. 'Her body in a thousand tiny pieces,' he shouted.

Flecks of saliva bubbled on his lips as he snatched up the mummified hand and bound it with the torn sleeve.

He struck a match and held the bright flaring flame against the charred index finger. Acrid yellow smoke curled up to envelop him as the finger began to glow white hot. He let out a shriek of wild laughter and ran between the corpses, chanting over and over the words that had brought his beautiful animals to life.

He paused and frowned as he stared down at the rotting figures. He didn't want these resurrected for their beauty, he wanted only for them to hunt down the American woman and bring her to him alive so that he could wreak his revenge.

'Wake up. Wake up,' he shrieked as the silk sleeve began to shrivel and burn, its pure white smoke mingling and blending with the thick yellow smoke that was already filling the room. 'Scent the accursed woman. Know her and seek her out. Follow her to the ends of this earth and bring her before me so I can destroy her!'

Ludo suddenly stopped chanting and cried out as the last strand of the silk burst into flames and curled around his fingers, burning his flesh. Cursing he backed against the window and dropped the smouldering hand upon the sill as he nursed his burned fingers, scratching off the charred scraps of silk that clung to them and licking them gingerly.

He quickly forgot the pain as the dead figure lying closest to him twitched. He bent forward eagerly. The eyelids flickered and the nostrils flared. Ludo quickly scanned the rows of putrefying bodies that filled the room. They were all beginning to move. They blinked open their empty eye sockets and began to moan, then started to sit up.

Ludo rubbed his hands together and his eyes narrowed to pinpoints as he cackled out loud. 'Revenge, how sweet my revenge.' He moved away from the window and passed amongst the rising corpses, to instruct them of his purpose.

'She is hiding beneath that museum. Find her, seize her and bring her back alive. Bring her to me . . .'

The body near the window suddenly jerked upright and shrieked, its nostrils pulsating as it swivelled awkwardly round and pointed with its decayed arm.

Ludo spun to face whatever the corpse had sensed and stared open-mouthed at the face in the open window.

Darkness blanketed the courtyard. Nothing moved in the shadows beyond the low archway. Silently Dec and Tuppence crept through the ranks of kneeling riflemen who ringed the black gaping entrance and passed beneath the arch. Every breath, every rustle of their clothing seemed to echo loudly in the claustrophobic stillness, yet step by unchallenged step they worked their way forward. Tuppence had barely breathed a sigh of relief to see the stars reappear overhead at the other side when a light sprang on in the furthest corner of the courtyard above the taxidermist's shop and the window was thrown wide open.

'That's the place . . .' Tuppence began when a voice, shrill and cackling with madness, floated down to them.

'Listen,' Tuppence hissed. 'That's him.'

Dec drew her closer and whispered, 'Who is he talking to?'

'He talks to himself all the time. He did when I went into his shop. But from the way he's running on I'll bet that crazy bastard's hatching something evil up there.'

Dec crept across the courtyard and peered into the shop, then beckoned her to follow. 'The place is empty. We've got to get closer. We must get up to that window if we want to find out what's going on,' he whispered.

'You're crazier than he is,' Tuppence hissed, shaking her head. 'That's impossible. The window's well above our reach and nothing on earth is going to make me step into his shop again even if the door stood wide open.'

Dec laughed softly and pointed to the ruined tower. 'That mass of ivy and creeper is as good as a ladder. Come on before he finishes whatever he's doing.'

Tuppence clung on to the creeper and stared through the curling whispers of yellow smoke into the preparation room. She could have reached out and touched the taxidermist as he bent down to pick something up and horror tightened her throat as she realized that the blackened waxy object he was caressing was a mummified hand. She almost let go of the creeper and lost her footing when she watched him set light to its index finger and begin to chant a spell, repeating the words forwards and backwards. She was sure from the words that he was trying to awaken something that lay beneath her line of sight under the window sill.

'Look,' she hissed in alarm to Dec. 'It's my sleeve he's got there.' She felt cold and remote as a great foreboding flooded through her. 'What the hell is that madman trying to do?'

But before she could continue the remnant of silk burst into flames, wrapping and entwining itself around the taxidermist's hand. She cowered back as he ran to the window and carelessly dropped the smouldering hand on the sill as he crushed and beat out the flames that were licking around his fingers. The hand lay only a short reach away from her. Its waxy, shrivelled and blackened skin dully reflected the light from the bare hanging bulb. Tuppence stared at the glowing index finger of charred flesh. Somehow it must be at the centre of this magic. She watched the taxidermist as he moved away from the window. He was muttering about revenge and how he would use the magic to trap her and he bent to examine something that was out of her sight.

'I'm sure it's the hand that's the key. I'm sure we must destroy it,' she hissed at Dec. 'I . . . I think I can just reach it,' she added in a whisper as she tightened her grip on the ivy with her left hand and stretched out with her right across the gap.

She arched her fingers as she reached and touched the blackened waxy skin. It felt cold and slippery and it made her shudder with revulsion. She clutched at the withered thumb.

A shrieking wail suddenly cut through the taxidermist's mutterings. She jumped, her eyes wide with terror, a scream strangled in her throat as a head appeared. She clung on to the hand but nearly lost her balance as a hideous, purple, putrefying face rose up above the sill, its bulging pussy eyes staring directly at her. Its blackened lips were dribbling with preserving fluids. It raised a trembling arm of hanging flesh and pointed in her direction. Ludo Strewth spun round, his eyebrows arched in surprise. He cried out her name and rushed at her, snatching desperately at the Hand of Glory.

'No, oh God, no,' she choked as he tried to wrest the hand away from her. The waxy skin of the thumb tore and it snapped between Tuppence's fingers and she fell back against the tangle of ivy branches. The taxidermist screamed and cursed, reaching across to claw at her through the open window, hatred in his eyes. Tuppence let out a cry of fear as more horribly mutilated figures began to rise, one by one, whispering and shrieking her name as they all shuffled towards the window.

Dec acted quickly, clasping his free hand around Tuppence's waist and pulling her back away from the window. At the same time he kicked out violently with his left foot and slammed the window shut on the taxidermist's arm. Ludo screamed in pain and clasped his wrist as hideous figures crowded around him and filled the window, their disfigured faces sneering and snarling. Clenched fists and outstretched hands pressed against the glass and then suddenly smashed through it. Wailing shrieks filled their ears and splinters of glass scattered down on them in a stinging rain. The vile, stinking creatures began to climb up on to the window sill.

'We're going to jump,' Dec cried, tightening his grip on Tuppence's waist as he let go of the thick creeper. His stomach knotted as he saw the ground rush up towards them. He bent his knees to cushion their fall and gasped as they hit the cobbles and sprawled forward, the impact jarring and numbing his legs.

'Run, for God's sake run,' he shouted as he scrambled back on to his feet. Roughly clutching at her arm he dragged her with him and they staggered to the low archway that led into Lobster Lane.

The shrieks of pursuit were right behind them. Tuppence glanced over her shoulder and saw two of the creatures jump down on to the cobbles; they stumbled and then began to cross the courtyard in giant strides. The shadows of the naked figures were beginning to engulf them. She stumbled and would have slowed and fallen but Dec pulled her on, shouting at her, breaking the trance of fear.

'Run, for Christ's sake run, woman.'

Their racing footsteps echoed beneath the archway. Their pursuers were almost on them, closing on their heels, as they reached the outer arch and broke out into Lobster Lane.

The waiting lines of riflemen silently parted to allow their escape to safety. Orders were shouted to left and right. The ranks closed, bright points of flame lit the dark-

ness and the crackle of rifle fire echoed. Dense cordite smoke drifted across the first kneeling rank as they reloaded and the standing rank behind then fired their volley.

'That must have stopped them,' Dec called, slowing up.

Tuppence leant heavily on his arm and was about to nod in breathless agreement when a shrieking sound behind her made her spin round.

'Jesus Christ,' she hissed as she saw two naked pursuers appear through the drifting smoke and into the lamplight.

They looked huge and almost as powerful as the brown bears that had chased her into the museum. They moved with a similar lumbering gait and covered the ground with long strides, only they were more frightening, more monstrously vile, with their purpling, decayed skin now hanging in ribbons and tatters from glistening steel and wire skeletons. The hail of riflemen's bullets had torn right through them.

Hoofbeats echoed in the lane and a line of lancers swept into view, the lamplight casting glittering reflections from their lance tips and the buttons and braid on their uniforms. Grunting and cursing the two monsters turned and attacked the oncoming horsemen, reaching out, snapping their thrusting lances as easily as stalks of straw, catching hold of the riders and hurling them down from their saddles. The horses reared up and thrashed out with their iron-shod hooves only to be knocked aside with crushing force. The sharp-shooters posted on the rooftops fired single rifle shots, hitting the monsters again and again, but they strode relentlessly on towards Dec and Tuppence.

'Run. Run for your life,' Dec cried. 'Nothing's going to stop them.' He grabbed at her wrist and pulled her after him down the lane towards the junction with Elm Hill. Hoofbeats skidded and clattered in the road close behind them. They heard the scout's voice calling out, urging them to mount the horses that he was leading.

'Be quick. Vault up and I will guide you back to the safety of the cellars,' he cried, drawing level with Tuppence and holding out the reins of one of the horses to her.

'No,' shouted Dec, barely glancing at the horseman. 'They'll get us there. We're better off staying in the open and running for our lives.'

'Then make for the Watchgate. They'll never break in there,' the scout urged, cantering on ahead of them and casting loose the reins of the riderless horses. 'I'll hold those creatures back while you unlock the door,' he shouted back to them over the crackle of the rifle fire and the echo of the hoofbeats in Lobster Lane.

He spurred his horse back to stand between Dec, Tuppence and the advancing creatures, then pulled his carbine free from the straps of his saddle roll and, straightening in the saddle, he put the butt of the gun firmly into his shoulder, calmly took aim and fired.

'Save yourself. Don't ride towards those creatures,' Tuppence shouted as the horseman worked the breech of the carbine to discharge the empty cartridge case and reload.

'Only when you are safe, madam,' he called over his shoulder as he spurred his horse forward into the shadows of the advancing figures.

'Damn,' Tuppence hissed, glancing desperately up and down Elm Hill.

The Watchgate was only a footstep away but she guessed that if they sought refuge in there behind its magic door every one of those soldiers who had come magically to life to protect her would be crushed and torn apart defending the doorway. She didn't want that. She had grown to like them rather in the last twenty-four hours. But what the hell could either she or Dec do to stop this awful carnage?

'We've got to keep running,' Dec shouted, pulling at her arm and urging her to follow him down the hill past the burned-out museum. 'My car's parked in Castle Street.'

His voice broke her moment's hesitation. She turned to follow him and shouted back, 'Hey, wait, my car's here right in front of us. Quickly, get in.'

She was about to fish in her pocket for the key when she realized she was still clutching the piece of broken thumb from the Hand of Glory. 'Well at least we didn't come away with nothing,' she muttered and she slipped the thumb down into the bottom of her pocket. Dec had slithered to a stop and spun round.

'Get in. Get in,' Tuppence shouted, unlocking the car, shoehorning herself behind the wheel and slamming the door as she thrust the key into the ignition and fired up the engine.

Dec wrenched open his door and flung himself at the low seat as she accelerated away from the kerb in a cloud of exhaust fumes and burning rubber, the tyres screaming over the cobbles.

'What's happening behind us?' she hissed as Dec managed to shut his door.

He quickly found the electric window button and stuck his head out of the window as she braked severely for the junction with Castle Street.

'The scout's just cantered out of Lobster Lane. The creatures are right behind him. No, they've stopped. They're wandering erratically backwards and forwards all over the road. They're bending down and crawling and sniffing at the cobblestones. The scout has frozen. It's as if he has turned back into a statue.'

The car stopped at the junction and Tuppence looked

back just as the wild and demented figure of the taxidermist appeared at the entrance of Lobster Lane. He was shouting and gesticulating at the two naked figures.

'Look,' she hissed, gripping Dec's arm. 'It's true what the Colonel said. His soldiers can't get close to the source of the magic. The horseman is frozen because the taxidermist has appeared. Listen, the sound of rifle fire has stopped. But I don't understand why his creatures aren't following us any more.'

For a long moment Ludo Strewth stood in the centre of the road, staring up and down the hill, before he shook his clenched fist at the Watchgate and shouted a string of obscenities at the carvings on the door. He then turned to the two monstrous figures and beckoned them to follow him back into Lobster Lane.

He shouted over his shoulder at the closed door of the Watchgate, 'Run, Tuppence Trilby. Run as fast as you can, but there's no escape. My new creatures know the smell of you, I scented it into the magic that resurrected them. They will find you and hunt you down and bring you back to me no matter where you try to hide.'

He paused, threw his head back and let out a shriek of maniacal laughter. 'Savour your last night of freedom, Tuppence Trilby, because tomorrow night my creatures will find you and bring you to me.'

The scout stirred and gradually came to life the moment Ludo Strewth disappeared from sight. He lifted the carbine, twisted in the saddle and frowned as he scanned the empty hill, before he spurred his horse towards the car. Tuppence shuddered as the taxidermist's words rang in her ears.

'It's hopeless,' she cried. 'The soldiers can't protect us against that madman, the dark magic is much too powerful. What are we going to do?'

'There must be a weakness. There's got to be . . .' Dec muttered, pausing to look up as the scout dismounted beside the car.

'The way is clear, madam, you can enter the Watchgate. The two creatures that pursued you from Goats Head Alley have vanished.'

Tuppence shook her head. 'No,' she answered firmly. 'I'm not going to hide away in there.'

'But you will be quite safe. The Watchgate is a fortress and our lancers will patrol the hill during the hours of darkness.'

'No,' Tuppence answered again, shaking her head, 'not after what we saw in that courtyard. We've got to get right away from here.'

'There were dozens more of those creatures in the taxidermist's shop, we disturbed him while he was bringing them to life. There are more than we could ever hope to stop.' Dec paused and stared thoughtfully at the scout. 'You know, I think those two naked creatures lost our scent when we got into the car. I think we would be safer if we kept on the move.'

'Those creatures could never keep up with this car no matter how fast they can run. Tell your Colonel that we'll come back first thing tomorrow morning. That's a promise,' Tuppence added as she dropped the clutch and spun the wheels before roaring away up Castle Street. The scout's cries of protest and his insistence that he would follow her quickly faded behind them.

'Where the hell shall we go?' Tuppence muttered, slowing as she turned the car into Museum Walk.

Dec looked anxiously into every dark courtyard and alley they passed. 'You could always stay at my place tonight. Take a right and then a left into Tombland, go over the bridge and then follow the main road until you reach Thieves Bridge.'

'Your place?' she asked defensively. They were waiting for a gap in the late evening traffic that was crawling along Tombland towards the bridge and she glanced quickly across to him. She felt a wave of disappointment sweep over her. She had thought that he was different from all the others, she had begun to really like him.

Dec sensed a strange note in her voice and he looked quickly around, expecting to see one of those creatures following them, but the road behind them was empty. For a moment he was at a loss to understand, and then he laughed softly. 'I'm sorry, Tuppence, you must have mis-understood me. I didn't mean for you to spend the night with me, I just meant that we could put you up. But I'll book a room at the Gallows at the first phone box on the far side of the bridge. It should be safe enough to stop there.'

'We? You mean you and your wife?' Tuppence asked, her disappointment deepening.

Dec smiled and shook his head. 'No, I'm not married. I meant me and my mother – and she won't be very pleased if you put up in the pub across the green instead of using her spare room.'

Tuppence felt her cheeks flush hotly at the embarrass-ment of misjudging him so badly. No, this guy wasn't at all like the others and she missed another gap in the traffic as she looked across at him. 'It's me who should be apologi-zing, not you. This whole business has made me edgy,' and she glanced into her rear mirror to check that nothing was creeping up on them before she smiled and reached out to touch his hand, letting her fingertips dwell for a moment longer than she had meant to. 'And I want to thank you for staying with me in this,' she whispered softly.

Dec felt his lips crease into a broad grin. Her touch made every nerve in his body tingle and he wanted to reach across and put his arms around her, to tell her that he would willingly walk through hell to be with her, but he was afraid to spoil the closeness and warmth of the moment.

He blinked and stuttered. 'I think we had better get out of here, don't you? Only that's the second gap you missed in the traffic.'

'Yes,' Tuppence muttered grimly, 'before they work out how we escaped,' and she accelerated out into Tombland amidst a screech of brakes and the blaring of car horns and threaded her way across the bridge, dodging in and out of the narrow gaps between the oncoming cars.

The traffic was thinning as they drove through the outer suburbs. 'Perhaps you had better drive, you know the way,' Tuppence offered as she braked hard for another unexpected turning.

Dec smiled and shook his head. 'No thanks. I've never driven anything as expensive as this and I'd hate to crash it. I'll try and give you the directions a little earlier.'

She glanced across at him silhouetted in the glow from the car's instrument panel and the sweeping dazzle of the oncoming headlights and saw that there wasn't a trace of envy or a moment's jealousy in his eyes. He really didn't mind that she owned such an exotic car. It was such a welcome change from the usual covetous looks she got, especially from men. 'Well it's only a car,' she almost said, but she stopped herself as she remembered that as a fireman it would probably take him for ever to save from his salary and he would never be able to afford a car like it.

She sighed sadly and looked ahead, following the signs

to Thieves Bridge. It was a real pity that they lived in such different worlds because deep down she knew that no matter how much they wanted to be together it could eventually tear them apart.

'Do you think that madman really believes we're hiding in the Watchgate?' she asked.

'Yes,' Dec answered slowly, 'but I don't think it will take him long to work out that we have escaped in your car.'

'How soon, do you think, before he'll start searching?'

Dec shrugged. 'If only we knew the strength of that magic, it would give us some idea of how we could destroy it.' He shifted in his seat and changed the subject as he pointed through the windscreen. 'My village is just a couple of miles ahead, but I'll warn you now that you had better slow down for the bridge. It's very narrow. Our house is across the green on the other side of the river, beside the church.'

Tuppence changed down and drove carefully over the bridge, catching sight of the lights of the pub beside the river on the other side. 'That looks really beautiful. But why is it called the Gallows?'

Dec smiled. 'Because they used to hang the highwaymen in front of it. The place is full of old prints, pictures and bits and pieces from the eighteenth century.'

'I'd love to see it,' she hesitated and swept her gaze across the darkened green, 'when this nightmare is over.'

Dec glanced at the narrow bridge. 'I don't think anything's followed us here. I'll take you over there for a quick drink after supper if it still looks safe enough.'

'Supper? But your mother won't be expecting me. I couldn't just barge in uninvited. It would be rude.'

'No it won't,' Dec insisted. 'There used to be six of us before my father died and my two elder sisters married and moved away. My mother's never adjusted to the drop in numbers, she still cooks for six. She would be mortally offended if you refused. That's our house, no, the next cottage. Pull up into the drive.'

Tuppence released the boot catch and lifted out her overnight bag. 'You make your mother sound quite fierce.'

Dec smiled and shook his head as he picked up her case and headed for the front door. 'You'll like her, I promise, but you might find Bobby, my younger sister, a little on the wild side.'

Tuppence hesitated on the threshold as Dec disappeared through an inner doorway, calling to his mother as he went and telling her that he had brought someone home to stay the night. The house wasn't at all how she had expected; there was the scent of beeswax and flowers in the quiet atmosphere and soft lamplight illuminated the hallway. A tall grandfather clock noisily measured the minutes, its hour hand stood at nine o'clock. Oriental rugs were spread on the polished floorboards. An ornately carved hat-stand and a mahogany inlaid luggage box stood facing the front door, as if guarding the entrance, and there were prints, woodcuts and steel engravings of hunting scenes evenly spaced along the wall that led to the steep staircase. Tuppence caught sight of her reflection in the glass of the closest print.

'Damn,' she hissed, 'I look a wreck,' and she glanced down in horror at her filthy jeans and trainers. They had been clean on that morning but they showed the wear and tear of her visit to the cellars and the climb up the ivy in that foul courtyard and she was still wearing the faded cavalry jacket that the Colonel had given her. She would never have dressed like this if she had known that she was going to meet Dec's mother.

She rummaged desperately through her bag for a hairbrush but it was too late, the door at the other end of the hallway was swinging open and a small, smartly dressed woman, her greying hair drawn neatly back into a bun, hurried towards her. In a flash Tuppence knew that it really mattered to her what Dec's mother thought of her and for the first time since she had stood hesitantly on the doorstep of Harry's photographic studio in New York she felt shy and vulnerable. She made to brush at the tangles in her hair with her fingers but stopped herself and let the hand fall helplessly to her side.

'Tuppence, it's so nice to meet you. I'm Amy,' the woman smiled, and the genuine warmth in her eyes and the firmness of her grip as she clasped both of Tuppence's hands in hers put the girl instantly at her ease. Dec's mother didn't seem to take a second look at her dishevelled appearance or blink an eye at her filthy clothes as she led her towards the dining room.

'I'm so glad you're staying with us. I'm afraid it's only cold meat and salad for supper but it's already on the table.' She suddenly stopped. 'Men, aren't they hopeless? I don't expect Dec showed you to your room when he brought you in, did he? They never think of these things. I suppose he just left you standing helplessly in the hall.'

Dec grinned at Tuppence as he bent to pick up her case.

'Supper will be in here, dear, when you are ready,' Amy smiled at her as she turned towards the dining-room door.

'Thanks, thank you,' Tuppence answered as she followed Dec up the stairs. Her fear of meeting his mother had evaporated. She had been so warm and welcoming, so natural.

The front door suddenly exploded open and slammed shut and an excited voice called out.

'Dec? Dec, whose fabulous car is that parked in the drive? Is he married or what?'

Dec frowned irritably and turned as a dark-haired girl reached the foot of the stairs and stared up at Tuppence in surprise.

'You're Tuppence Trilby, aren't you?' she cried as she recognized her. 'I saw your picture in the paper – well actually I've seen dozens of pictures of you, but you were in the paper this morning. Dec rescued you from that fire, didn't he? Your hair! How did you get it to look like that? It's great. And that jacket! Where did you get it? Is that really your car? It's fabulous.' Her questions tumbled out breathlessly as she took Tuppence's hand and grabbed her case from Dec. 'You must be staying, you are, aren't you?' she cried, pushing past him as she took Tuppence along to her room at the end of the corridor.

'Girl talk,' Bobby announced brusquely as she pushed her brother out of the room when he tried to follow them in.

'Supper's on the table, you had better come down quickly,' he called crossly through the door. The last thing on earth he wanted was for his sister to interfere, she could ruin everything.

'You're never going out with him, are you? He's so *square*,' Bobby demanded incredulously as she stabbed her fingers at the closed door.

Tuppence laughed and shrugged her shoulders. Her eyes were drawn towards the small window and the uninterrupted view across the green towards the city. 'Well, he hasn't asked me, but he's a nice guy, the nicest . . .' she answered absently.

Bobby laughed and dismissed him with a wave of her hand. 'Oh, he's OK, I suppose. My friends call him Dependable Dec. You know, if you ever want any help he'll never let you down, that sort of thing. But he's not a snappy dresser, is he? And he's nowhere near as handsome as those men you model with in the magazines.'

Tuppence smiled as she sorted through the few things she had thrown into her case that morning for something more presentable to wear down to supper. Bobby was as likeable as her brother. The whole family had welcomed her without a moment's hesitation and she already felt at home amongst them. 'Looks, clothes, they're only skin deep,' she answered, 'but Dec's different from all those guys and that's what I like about him.'

She hesitated as she remembered that moment when they first met. She had virtually dismissed him as he stood there in his filthy fire-fighting clothes in the doorway of her hospital room. She suppressed the urge to talk about the gulf that separated their two worlds and instead asked for the bathroom so that she could freshen up before going down to supper.

Supper turned out to be a feast of cold meats and salads laid out on a dining-room table long enough to seat twelve. But all through the meal Tuppence was on edge, listening, half expecting the creatures to burst in.

'No, no, I couldn't eat another thing,' she protested in dismay as Amy tried to load her plate for the second time.

Bobby and Amy laughed and talked and tried to draw her into the conversation so naturally that she felt as if she had always been a part of their lives, and they both chided Dec for being so quiet and distant throughout the meal. Bobby suddenly brought the table talk to a halt by exclaiming, 'Creeping Death called today. I meant to leave you a note, only I forgot.'

'Creeping Death?' Tuppence echoed, half rising from her chair. It was as if the shadow of the taxidermist's shop reached across the table and the colour drained from her face.

Amy saw the alarm in her face and reached out to take her hand. 'Bobby's referring to the farm chemical factory where Dec works. She belongs to a countryside environmental group that is opposed to crop spraying. She's been at Dec's throat about his work ever since she joined, but it's really nothing to get alarmed about, dear.'

'Well, some of those chemicals kill everything they touch even after they're supposed to have been checked and called safe,' Bobby added hotly as she got up from the table.

Tuppence looked across at Dec. 'But I thought you were a fireman. I thought that was your job.'

Dec blushed and smiled as he shook his head. He pulled his glasses off and began to polish absently at the lenses as he explained, 'We're all volunteers. None of us are full-time firemen. I'm really an industrial chemist.'

'I've never understood why he's so embarrassed when he tells anyone he's a doctor,' Amy interrupted.

'A doctor? You're a doctor?'

'No, I'm not a medical doctor, Mother always gets it wrong. I took a doctorate, a PhD, in industrial chemistry at London University a few years ago and I work for the Downland Chemical Institute. They have a small farm-testing site at the other end of the village.'

Dec pushed his glasses back on to the bridge of his nose and dragged the rubber band roughly over the top of his head.

'And it's about time you had those glasses fixed,' frowned Amy as she rose to clear the table.

'Yes, Mother, I'll do it tomorrow,' he muttered absently as he looked across the table and saw that Tuppence was grinning at him. He blinked to cover his embarrassment and suggested that he and Tuppence should get a breath of fresh air and perhaps have a drink in the Gallows across the green.

'That would be great, if you're sure it will be safe,' she smiled, standing up and pushing her chair back, but she hesitated and reached for the pile of empty plates. 'But we ought to stay a while and help clear away the supper things first.'

'Go on the two of you, I've got all night to do these,' insisted Amy, smiling and taking the pile of plates out of Tuppence's hands and shooing them both out of the dining-room.

The green was bathed in moonlight and soft shadows. They stood statue-still beside her car, listening and searching the darkness before they walked across to the Gallows.

'Duck your head,' warned Dec as he held open the door for her to enter.

Tuppence stepped over the threshold and down two stone steps into a large, dimly lit, low-beamed room. She stopped and looked about her. It smelt of years of stale beer and the tobacco smoke that had soaked into the yellowing paint and brown-stained plaster walls. Prints and paintings, yokes, buckets, rifles, gin-traps and articles of bric-à-brac that she had never even imagined existed covered the walls and hung from the beams. Most of the small tables along the edges of the room were empty but a noisy crowd stood at the bar at the far end of the room. The hum of conversation momentarily faltered as the crowd shifted and turned to stare curiously at her and then one by one they turned away again.

'Hi, lads,' Dec called as he descended the step behind her, gently leading Tuppence by the arm towards the bar. 'They're some of the lads from the fire engine who were with me last night,' he told her.

Their conversation died completely as they watched Dec introduce her. 'This is Tuppence, the young lady who we rescued from the museum last night. That's Paul, John, here's Vic and . . .' A chorus of voices erupted along the bar before he had finished the introductions.

'Have you recovered?'

'What do you want to drink?'

'How do you like Thieves Bridge?'

'Geordie's regained consciousness,' Vic informed Dec with a grin, 'and he's shouting blue murder that you led him under that falling beam that tore his BA set in half.'

'But it wasn't a beam,' Dec frowned, 'it was those . . .' He hesitated. The whole crew were grinning at him and nudging each other.

'Did you see anything in the fire, Tuppence? You know what we mean, ghosts or monsters or something?' Paul asked with a laugh as he handed her the ice and soda she had asked for.

Tuppence looked quickly at their mocking smiles and the way they were teasing Dec and her anger rose. 'Yes,' she wanted to say, 'they were twice your size and swarming through the flames to get at us. But what do you know, you weren't in there.'

But what good would it do? She shrugged and muttered, 'I don't know what I saw, the smoke was so dense, it was so frightening. I'd rather not talk about it.'

She looked to Dec for help and he smiled as he sensed her discomfort and guided her away from the bar to an empty table by the window that looked out across the river bank. He half wished he hadn't brought her, he had felt the atmosphere change when they realized who she was, and he had seen them nudging each other.

'Hey, I nearly forgot,' the barman called after him. 'There were a couple of reporters in here at lunch-time, they were from the *Eastern Daily*. They were asking all about you and the rest of the crew. I lent them that photograph of the lads in front of the fire engine. They reckon it will be on the front page of tomorrow's paper.'

'Damn,' Dec muttered as he sat down opposite her. 'That means the taxidermist only has to buy a paper and put two and two together to find out where we are.'

'We'll have to move on before it gets light,' Tuppence replied, 'but we can't keep running for ever, can we?' she added, staring out of the window and across the river.

She suddenly gripped his arm. 'Look! There, on the other side of the river!'

Dec leaned forward, almost pressing his nose against the window. 'What is it? What did you see?'

'I don't know, I just thought I saw some figures moving across the top of the river bank,' Tuppence whispered, twisting her glass anxiously between her fingers and making the chunks of ice clink together. 'I'm so tense that I'm probably just jumping at shadows.'

Dec stared out of the window, cupping his hand against the glass to cut out the reflections of the lights behind him at the bar. He laughed softly and whispered down to her, 'You're not jumping at any old shadow. Look here, look along to the right of the bridge, in the shadows and then further back amongst the bushes and undergrowth, there, that line on the top of the bank.'

Tuppence followed his directions and caught her breath as she saw the glint of starlight reflected from a dozen lance tips. She blinked and waited for her eyes to grow accustomed to the dense shadows beyond the pools of light that were cast by the inn's lamps.

'It must be the lancers,' she whispered, picking out the shapes of their horses against the rough stone wall of the bridge.

'And I'll bet there's more of them in every clump of

trees, every bush and thicket around the green,' Dec added, straightening up in his chair.

'How the hell did they find us so quickly?' Tuppence frowned.

Dec half rose. 'And if they have found us so easily surely those creatures . . .'

Tuppence stared out of the window, her knuckles whitened on the stem of her glass as the horror of what he had just said struck home.

'Yes,' Dec nodded seriously. 'That's why we have to work out how we are going to destroy those creatures before . . .'

'Your friends,' Tuppence interrupted. 'Call them over here and show them the soldiers. Explain everything that has happened to us. They would have to believe you. They would know then that you haven't made it all up, especially if they meet the soldiers and see how real they are.'

Dec glanced at the noisy crowd at the bar and then slowly shook his head. 'There's not a lot of room for magic and ghosts in their world. They'd probably still laugh it all away no matter what we tried to show them.' He paused and looked down to the ring-stained table top, tracing the interlacing curves with his fingertips. 'And do you know, the worst thing is that I would have been just as sceptical as all of them if I hadn't been sucked into it. I still had doubts even after we followed the Colonel into the cellars. Magic belongs in books, fairy tales, not here in the real world. It was only after we saw those creatures come to life in the taxidermist's shop . . .' Dec stopped and stared at her. Talking about it had tugged at some hidden knowledge, had sparked an idea and brought it sharply into focus.

'I'll bet you're right. That mummified hand is the key to this nightmare. I bet if we destroy it then this magic will shrivel to nothing.'

'I've still got the piece that broke off when I tried to steal it. It's in the pocket of my jeans back at your house.'

'I think we'll need to destroy it all,' Dec added thoughtfully. 'Perhaps we can get into that . . .'

'No!' Tuppence cried as she caught his train of thought. 'I'm not going back in there, not for . . .' She hesitated as she threw her hands up in desperation. 'You saw how many of those monsters crowded that room. We'd never get within a hundred yards.'

'We might – with a little help from those soldiers. Come on,' and he stood up and led her out into the darkness.

'What can the soldiers do? You know they can't even enter that courtyard,' she protested.

Dec laughed. 'No, but they can set a ring of fire around it for us and draw the monsters out. And you never know, fire might be the one thing that can destroy them. Remember, fire destroyed those huge bears in the museum, didn't it? And we will have the element of surprise. The taxidermist will never expect us to come back. I'll bet that shop and all the forgotten rubbish in the surrounding warehouses are as dry as a tinder-box.'

'What if you're wrong? What if he's watching out for us and those creatures don't burn? What if instead of burning up they swarm through the flames and come after us?' she asked.

'We've got to try and get that hand,' Dec answered firmly, 'and we have to do it before those creatures start to hunt you down.'

'And how will you destroy it? Answer me that!' Tuppence asked hotly. 'Aren't you afraid of going back there?' She held his gaze as the warm night breeze ruffled her hair.

Dec shrugged helplessly. 'I haven't really thought it through properly yet. Let's just get hold of that foul thing.' He smiled at her. Shyness tied his tongue and stopped him from reaching out and taking her in his arms. He longed to tell her that he loved her and would die before he let any of those beasts lay a finger on her. He felt his cheeks redden and he blinked and shrugged helplessly, blurting out, 'Yes, yes, of course I'm scared to death, but . . .' He struggled for the words.

The scrape of a horseshoe on the gravel made him pause. 'Ask them if my idea is any good,' he urged as he caught sight of the Colonel and the scout silhouetted side by side against the backdrop of the shimmering summer stars at the top of the river bank.

'Tell them everything that we saw in that courtyard and see if they agree with me that we have to destroy that mummified hand.'

Tuppence half-turned and saw Dec framed in the light of the doorway. She smiled to herself. Bobby had got him all wrong, he was much more handsome than all those models she worked with. His jaw was chiselled with real determination and his look held an inner strength that she had never encountered before. 'OK, I will,' she whispered, 'and if the Colonel agrees then I'll go back into that court-yard with you.'

16

Shuttlecock Alley

Now Tuppence regretted the rashness of her promise. She was wearing her dirty jeans of yesterday, shivering despite the faded soldier's coat thrown around her shoulders as she waited beside the Lotus in the cold glimmer of dawn. The light was just beginning to ghost morning colours into the steep roof tops of Elm Hill.

The Colonel had listened to everything they had told him of the taxidermist and his grey eyes had widened when they told him of the Hand of Glory and repeated the spell. He had agreed with Dec that the hand must be destroyed if they were to conquer the dark magic. He had called a battle council and had twice sent rough riders back into the city to gather the latest information from the pickets who had been left to watch the courtyard. Tuppence had been all for doing it right away; a couple of gallons of petrol, some old sacking and a box of matches was all that was needed to create a smoke screen. But the Colonel had insisted that nothing should be left to chance and this took all night to organize, before they had set off for the city.

'It's time,' Dec whispered, touching her arm and making her jump.

'What the hell's all that stuff?' she hissed, pointing to the column of scarlet-coated soldiers moving silently into Lobster Lane laden down beneath the heavy bundles of twigs and bracken balanced precariously on their shoulders.

'It's to lay against the walls on the outer side of the buildings that face into the courtyard. We must complete an unbroken ring of fire that will block off all those narrow alleyways except the main one. Come on, we'd better hurry,' he whispered as he bent down and gathered up three heavy bundles of twigs in his arms.

'Can you bring that can of petrol and those matches,' he added nodding towards the red two-litre can on the pavement beside the car.

The last of the riflemen were piling their bundles of kindling against the old brick-beamed buildings close to the entrance of Goats Head Alley. Two horsemen carried smouldering slow matches, shielding the glowing cords from the unpredictable gusts of dawn wind.

'It really is a shame to burn these places down, they're so old, so beautiful,' Tuppence muttered to herself as Dec stopped beside the scout a few places from the low archway that led into Goats Head Alley.

'Hopefully the buildings won't burn. We just want to create a smoke screen to draw the monsters out . . .' the scout whispered softly.

'Don't forget to give us enough time to climb up to that window before you light those fires,' Tuppence hissed in alarm as she saw the soldiers behind them push their bundles of kindling as close as they could to the low brick archway.

'Come on, let's do it before it gets light,' Dec urged and reluctantly she followed him beneath the arch.

The courtyard was empty, wrapped in its own gloomy secrets. Tuppence shivered and kept close to Dec. 'There's no light in the room above the shop,' she whispered.

Dec took a last careful look around the courtyard and

hurried straight across to the base of the wall. With one eye on the shop he began to search for the best way to climb up. He had just helped Tuppence up to the first foothold when he noticed something.

'Wait,' he whispered in a troubled voice as he turned towards the shop, 'I think the door is ajar.'

He took two quick steps across the courtyard and gingerly pushed against the door. 'It's empty, there's nothing in there, just some twisted wire and burnt feathers scattered on the floor. The place is deserted. I'm going to risk a look through that door at the back.'

'No, come here, you crazy fool, you're walking into a trap,' Tuppence gasped, climbing back down the ivy and following him over the threshold, but he had already opened the door at the back of the shop and disappeared.

'Damn,' she muttered, gritting her teeth and cautiously crossing the room. She heard the stairs creak and a door open above her and she almost jumped out of her skin. Then she heard Dec's voice calling out to her. Her spine tingled and the hairs on the nape of her neck prickled. Every nerve in her body screamed at her to turn and run, run for her life.

'They've gone. Vanished. Come up here quickly and see for yourself. There's nothing here but a few mouldering bones and strips of rotting flesh, oh, and a muddle of empty bottles and jars.'

She knew something was wrong. None of the creatures had tried to slip out of Goats Head Alley. Her instincts shouted that they had blundered into a trap. She froze and listened to the brooding silence, broken only by the stumbling erratic tick of the six clocks that hung beside the door. And then she realized and the knot in her stomach tightened. The taxidermist would never have left his clocks.

He hadn't vanished or spirited his creatures away. They were hiding here somewhere, she was sure of it.

'Dec...' she began, only to catch and swallow the urgent warning as another sound, a loud scrape of footsteps, echoed in the courtyard beyond the open doorway.

The dawn light was creeping beneath the archway, greying the cobbles and melting back the shadows. Tuppence took a hesitant step towards the door and stared out.

'J... J... Jesus Christ,' she gasped as she saw the monstrous figures from the preparation room. They were standing staring at her out of each of the warehouse doorways that surrounded the courtyard.

Throwing her weight against the door she slammed it shut then fled through the door at the back of the shop and raced up the stairs. 'Dec! Dec, it's a trap!' she cried as she reached the stair head and flung wide open the door of the preparation room, almost colliding with him. The stench of putrefying flesh that wafted over her made her choke and gasp for breath.

'What is it?' asked Dec gripping her arm and pulling her further into the room.

'It's a trap,' she cried. 'Those creatures are out there. The courtyard's full of them. They must have been hiding in those warehouses. We crept right past them when...'

A stair tread creaked, making them both spin round.

'The window! Make for the window,' Dec urged, pushing her forward across the room.

Tuppence shuddered with horror as her feet skidded and slipped on the skin and bones and other untold foulness that littered the floor. They sent jars and bottles crashing over in their haste to reach the window. The light suddenly clicked on and wild laughter erupted behind, making them both stop and turn. Ludo Strewth stood in the open doorway. In his right hand he held the smouldering, mummified

Hand of Glory. His demented eyes narrowed into murderous slits of hatred as he advanced mumbling and muttering towards them. A huge purple-faced figure dressed in an ill-fitting tweed suit filled the doorway behind him.

'I knew that you would come back to steal my magic. I knew that once you had touched the hand its power would lure you back!' the taxidermist hissed, caressing the hand as he advanced towards them, blocking off their escape. 'But you have failed,' he snarled triumphantly at Tuppence. 'The magic is mine, mine alone to use as I wish.'

Ludo Strewth threw his head back and let out a shriek of maniacal laughter. Yellow flecks of spittle bubbled at the corners of his mouth. 'Do you think I'm a complete fool, woman?' he sneered. 'Did you think I would sit here and do nothing while you plotted to steal my magic?'

He swept his free hand back across the hideous figures crowding the doorway and sneered at her. 'I have been dressing my new creatures, hiding their nakedness. I have prepared them to blend in amongst the crowds, to hunt you down and bring you to me. But it wasn't necessary for me to go to such lengths, was it? Because the trap was so simple and you walked so readily into it.'

'The soldiers will burn everything in here, you bastard,' Tuppence shouted, backing away from him until she reached the window sill, then quailing as she turned and caught sight of the shifting crowd of hideous figures in the courtyard below.

The taxidermist cackled and shook his head. 'They are impotent, powerless. They cannot enter this courtyard to rescue you and their bonfires cannot harm me or smoke me out. You are my prisoner now and I will savour every scream of agony as I take my full measure of revenge on you for luring my beautiful animals into that burning museum.'

Dec pressed close beside her and whispered to her as the taxidermist gloated and sneered. 'When I say, jump through the broken window and grab on to the ivy.'

'Quiet!' Ludo screamed, glaring at Dec and snapping his fingers at the creature in the doorway. 'Enough of your whispering – seize her!'

'Now,' shouted Dec, grabbing at a heavy glass bottle of chemical that stood beside him on the sill and hurling it at the advancing beast.

Tuppence sprang up on to the sill and ducked through the window. 'Jump! Jump!' Dec urged, scrambling up beside her and giving her a brutal shove as the bottle smashed against the creature's chest. The chemicals hissed and bubbled as they soaked into the creature's clothes and ate into its flesh.

Tuppence cried out as she hit the tangle of creepers. She clawed at the branches but they tore through her hands. She was falling, helpless, down towards the howling, snarling hordes of monsters that crowded below her. The injured creature snarled and rushed at Dec and he felt its wet and slippery hands grip at his leg as he scrambled over the sill. He kicked out savagely and jumped the gap, grasping on to a thick branch with his right hand while he made a wild grab at Tuppence's vanishing arm with his left.

'Climb, for God's sake climb,' he shouted at her as he caught hold of her.

Tuppence felt his grip on her arm break her descent and she grabbed desperately for the closest branches and began to scramble up towards the top of the ruined tower. The howling snarls below her rose to a deafening crescendo of rage, the creatures threw themselves against the wall, tearing at the thick fibrous roots and the wrist-thick tangled tendrils of creeper as they tried to dislodge their prey. The injured aberration in the preparation room lurched and jumped across the gap, clawing wildly at the branches, but the sutures on his arms and hands tore open and he fell heavily into the courtyard. Below, hand over hand, the monstrous creatures began to scale the ruined tower.

'Keep climbing and don't look down,' Dec shouted.

A shriek of rage suddenly rent the air as the taxidermist came to the broken window. 'Don't let them escape, you fools,' he cursed at his hideous beasts as he urged them to swarm up the ivy-covered tower.

Dec reached up, searching with his fingers for a hand-hold on the crumbling tooth-sharp top of the tower. The creeper tentacles were thinner here and tore loose at the slightest touch and the flints and bricks and mortar that he dislodged showered down on their pursuers.

'Come on, we're nearly there,' he gasped to Tuppence as he found a handhold and pulled himself up and over the rough bricks and on to a sloping lead-lined roof. 'Here, give me your hand,' he urged, reaching down to her and clasping her wrist with both hands as he hauled her up to the top of the wall.

'Those monsters – they are still following us, they're just behind us,' Tuppence cried in terror as she scrambled up over the top of the tower and collapsed beside him.

'I'll soon stop them,' Dec hissed, tearing at the thin tendrils of ivy along the top of the wall. He broke and pushed the mass of creeper away from the bricks. For a minute it hung there, swaying backwards and forwards, and then it billowed out and collapsed in a creaking, splin-tering heap beneath the weight of their pursuers, landing in the courtyard below.

'I can smell burning,' Tuppence frowned, rising to her knees. An acrid stench of burning leather, wax and flesh was rising up from the courtyard. 'What the hell's going on down there? Have the soldiers started the fires?'

'Yes, I think so.' Then Dec frowned and shook his head. 'No, I can see smoke rising in Lobster Lane but it's not that you can smell, it's that taxidermist . . .' Strewth was shouting his spells and running backwards and forwards in the courtyard amongst his monsters, waving the smouldering severed hand.

Dec turned his head and looked down at his feet. He remembered the creature in the preparation room grabbing at his leg and how he had twisted and kicked out to be free of it. In the desperate struggle to scale the wall his right foot had felt odd and had repeatedly slipped on the ivy branches.

'He's got my shoe! He's burning my shoe! He's burning it like he burned the sleeve of your blouse,' he cried.

'They'll have your scent as well as mine now.' Tuppence craned forward and peered down into the grey gloomy courtyard, her face drawn into a mask of despair as she watched the monsters' hideous faces become enveloped with the smoke from the shoe. 'We'll never get another chance to destroy the magic now. He'll send those monsters out to find us wherever we try to hide,' she whispered with despair in her voice.

Ludo Strewth paused in his chanting and looked up towards them; his face looked disembodied as the thick yellow smoke curled around him. His eyes mirrored the madness that had possessed him and his lips curled into a pitiless sneer as he called out, 'There is no escape.'

'Come on,' Dec whispered pulling her away from the parapet. 'We've got to find a way down. We're not just sitting here waiting to be caught, we're not giving up that easily. If we can't get to that mummified hand we'll just have to find another way to destroy the magic,' he added thoughtfully.

He quickly scanned the leaded roof of the tower and spotted a small trap door in the furthest corner. 'I'm sure I've been here before. This used to be a bell tower to St Saviour's years ago. I think that's the way down into the church. Come on, there's just a chance we can get out into Cripplegate before those monsters seal off the entrance.'

Dec lifted the heavy trap door and stepped down on to the first stone step. He reached up, grabbed Tuppence's wrist and pulled her in after him. 'The steps are narrow and steep, keep your hand on the outer surface wall where the treads are widest.'

His voice echoed up to her in the swallowing darkness as dizzily they descended, following the worn steps round and round in a continuous downward spiral. Window slits clogged with ivy and forgotten birds' nests appeared and disappeared and the air was dark and musty. Tuppence slipped and stumbled, snatching at Dec's shoulders to stop herself falling.

'Keep to the outside,' he whispered, taking her hand and putting it on the wall.

'You sure know how to show a girl a good time, don't you?' she muttered, grazing her knuckles on the wall.

Dec grinned as he turned his head and looked up at her, the weak light from a window slit reflecting off his glasses. 'This is nothing to some of the places I could show you. Wait a minute, I think we've almost reached the bottom. There should be a door.'

At the next turn of the stairs they reached it. Dec moved forward and ran his hands over the thick, iron-studded wood, smiling and muttering to himself as he peered through the small metal grille.

'Well?' Tuppence asked impatiently as she crowded at his elbow. 'Where the hell have we got to?'

Dec turned his head and grinned. 'To exactly the place I thought – the top of the main aisle just to the right of the altar and the choir stalls. Now keep your fingers crossed that no one has thought to put a padlock on this door.'

'How do you know so much about this place?' she exclaimed.

Dec laughed softly as he gripped and turned a large twisted-iron ring with both hands and heard the latch rise up off the staple. 'Because I went to All Saints' School in Bathgate Street just around the corner. I used to sing in the choir here and we were always messing about in the old bell tower on practice nights, it used to drive the choir master mad. But I had forgotten all about the place, it looks so different from that courtyard. It was only when I was looking for a way down that it began to feel familiar.'

He fell silent as he tugged at the heavy door. It creaked and shifted on its rusty hinges and slowly swung open. Dec breathed a sigh of relief and stepped down into the main aisle. Tuppence quickly followed him.

'Now where?' she whispered, putting her hand to her mouth as her whisper carried, echoing in the vaulted ceiling high above her head.

'Hush, you'll wake the dead,' Dec hissed. 'Follow me, there's a small door hidden behind the screen next to the vestry and it opens into an alleyway that leads directly into Elm Hill. We used to slip in through that door if we were late for choir. Come on, we've got to escape before those creatures surround the church,' he urged, moving quickly along the main aisle.

'It's so beautiful in here,' Tuppence whispered, trying to keep her courage up as she followed him down the aisle.

'Look at those soaring columns of stone, the watching gargoyles, the marching rows of empty pews, the graves and the banners . . .'

'Shut up, here's the door,' he warned, touching her arm and pulling her to the side of a tiny arched doorway. He bent down and took off his one remaining shoe and wriggled his toes. 'It'll be easier to run like this, but I've always hated being barefooted,' he muttered, slipping the bolts on the door and carefully pulling it towards him.

He opened it inch by cautious inch. A gloomy alleyway stretched away from them. There were dustbins and sacks of rubbish piled haphazardly at irregular intervals along its length. Smoke from the soldiers' fire drifted across the end of the narrow alley.

'That smoke may help us to slip past those monsters if they're waiting in Elm Hill,' he whispered. 'My car's much closer than yours, it's parked about ten yards from the church front entrance. Follow me and don't make a sound.'

They reached the end of the alleyway and Dec stopped, then crouched and peered out through the drifting smoke. Faintly in the distance he could hear the wail of sirens. He smiled to himself. Soon Elm Hill would be full of fire tenders and that madman would never dare try anything with so many people around.

But on the opposite side of the hill monstrous shapes suddenly appeared, closing in towards them. Dec realized there was no time to wait for help to arrive.

'Come on, run, now!' he hissed as he sprinted forward.

Tuppence dashed after him across the road but they hadn't covered more than a dozen strides when the air around was filled with dark sinister shapes. Black crows, brilliant exotic birds, owls and bats swooped down on them.

Dec flailed at them with his hands and as he reached the

far kerb he stumbled against a row of dustbins. Desperately he snatched up two dustbin lids and thrust one of them at Tuppence. 'Use it as a shield to ward them off. Come on,' he shouted, and he sprinted the last few yards up the hill towards his car.

Cawing and shrieking the birds hurled themselves at Tuppence in a sinister flock, their beaks snapping, their claws and talons catching at her hair. Dec pulled out his electric key and unlocked the doors as he ran. Two of the crows swooped on him and clawed at his head and he struck out with the dustbin lid making them shriek and flap to the ground.

'Get in, get in,' he shouted as Tuppence flailed at the birds, knocking them to the ground, as she rushed to the car. She wrenched open the door and fell in.

Out of the corner of his eyes Dec could see that the hill was swarming with the taxidermist's beasts. They were streaming out of Cripplegate, out of every arch and alley-way on either side of them. He slammed the car door shut behind him and stabbed with the key towards the ignition. He missed and stabbed again. The birds were clawing at the windscreen, pecking at the glass. Tuppence screamed with terror and covered her ears to block out their screech-ing. At last Dec fired up the engine, it turned over, misfired and caught. Dec slammed it into first gear and stamped on the accelerator, slewing the wheel round as he powered the car up the hill, burning rubber on the cobbles and scatter-ing the attacking birds.

'Look out!' Tuppence shouted as the windscreen cleared and a huge lumbering beast appeared in front of the bonnet and launched itself at Dec through the glass.

The car juddered from end to end and the bonnet dipped as the creature was lifted by the speed of the car and rolled across the bonnet towards them. Both Dec and Tuppence threw their arms up to protect their faces as it hit the windscreen, cracking it into a thousand jagged fragments before it slithered away and fell back on to the road. Dec skidded and drove blind into Tombland, his foot flat to the boards, the engine screaming. He slammed the car into second gear as he punched a hole in the opaque windscreen and roared across the bridge, narrowly missing a fire engine and two police cars who were racing into Tombland.

Dec straightened up, glanced across and shouted, 'Look out, there's a bird trapped in your door.'

She spun round and saw that one of the crows had been caught when she had slammed the door. Its leg was almost severed but its talons were opening and closing as it tried to claw at her head. It was flapping its wings frantically and stabbing with its beak at the roof of the car and the drag of the wind spun it round and round as the car accelerated.

'Open the door,' Dec shouted over the noise of the wind rushing through the broken windscreen. 'It's the only way to get rid of it.'

Tuppence fumbled at arm's length with the door catch as she tried to keep out of reach of the bird's talons and she forced the door open against the pressure of the wind. The crow shrieked and vanished, sucked away in a blaze of black feathers, tumbling over and over on the road behind them.

'Are they following us?' Dec shouted, jumping the traffic lights at the junction with Grove Street and heading out towards the ring road.

Tuppence twisted round and looked out of the rear window. 'No, I don't think so,' she answered hesitantly. 'Well, at least, none of those monstrous creatures, but I'm not so sure about the birds. There's so many in the sky and roosting on the roof tops and in the branches of the trees I'm just not sure.'

'We've got to get rid of this car quickly,' Dec shouted above the noise of the wind and the sudden creak of the broken windscreen as it finally caved in under the pressure and showered them with glass.

'Damn, damn, damn that crazy bastard for trapping us in this nightmare,' Tuppence shouted, violently shaking her head to dislodge the sharp shards of glass that clung to her.

'I'll swap the car. I'll leave it at the garage where I normally have it serviced and borrow one of theirs, I've done that often enough before,' Dec muttered more to himself than to her.

He knew they had been lucky to escape and now they had to stay one jump ahead while he worked out a way to destroy those monsters. And he had to be quick before those birds spotted his car. He stamped on the brakes as he swung the car into Thorn Lane and then took a right into Rouen Street. He glanced down at the clock on the dashboard, it read 7.45. He slowed up. There was no point in getting to the garage before it opened.

'What do you think will happen to those soldiers?' Tuppence asked staring out of the rear window.

Dec shrugged. 'They'll probably retreat into the museum cellar now that we have escaped. But they are the least of our worries just now. They are not the ones being hunted by those creatures, are they?'

Tuppence was about to agree when he braked sharply.

'Thank God,' he sighed as he saw that the huge double doors of the workshops were lying open as he swung the car into Hall Road and on to the forecourt. He threaded his way through the lines of cars parked there and then drove straight into the works.

'I know it's not booked today,' he smiled at the bewildered mechanic, 'but it's important that you keep it under cover until you can replace the bonnet and the windscreen. Could I borrow a car? Now, yes, anything will do, we're late for an important appointment.'

The mechanic shook his head and rubbed a greasy hand across his forehead. 'I'm sorry but we just ain't got the space . . .' he began but stopped as he watched Tuppence begin to rise out of the car.

'I know you, you're that woman on the telly,' he gasped.

Tuppence flashed him a brilliant smile. 'That's right. We're looking for a garage to use in a shot next week. Do you want me to mention this place to the director?'

The mechanic stared spellbound.

'Well, can you help us out? Have you got space for this car and can we borrow another one for a couple of days?' she asked softly, her voice almost purring.

The mechanic hesitated as he wiped his filthy hands on a cloth and glanced quickly round the crowded workshop. 'Oh yes, I'll squeeze it in over there, but we've only got that old Renault, the yellow one parked outside. You can borrow that now or you can wait until the boss gets in, he'll probably find you something better.'

'No, thanks, we haven't got the time. That car will do just fine. Thank you, thanks a lot,' Tuppence smiled, squeezing his arm in thanks as she opened the door and slipped into the old car.

Dec fired the car a dozen times before the engine caught and they pulled noisily away across the forecourt.

'When will your director call? Only the boss will want to know,' the mechanic shouted after them.

'I'm sure he'll ring you tomorrow,' Tuppence laughed, waving and settling back into her uncomfortable seat.

Turning to Dec she grinned. 'Well we must have borrowed the oldest car in England. Now where?'

'I don't know, I'm racking my brains,' he answered thoughtfully, grinding the gears and turning from Hall Road into Queens Road.

'Well you had better think of something quickly, that's the second sign you just passed directing us back to the city centre,' she muttered in alarm.

'We're on the ring road,' Dec answered, slowing the car. 'Every sign to the right will direct you back but . . .' He glanced up at the sign for the roundabout ahead. 'London!' he suddenly announced swinging sharp left into St Stephen's Road. 'There's a bookshop I know in London that might just help us.'

'Bookshop!' Tuppence exclaimed. 'Are you crazy? Why don't you drive straight to Norwich airport? We could take a shuttle to Heathrow and then on to New York, those monsters will never find us there.'

Dec didn't answer her immediately, his mind was racing. He hunched over the wheel and drove as fast as he dared through the early morning traffic towards Ipswich. 'Running's no good,' he answered her at length. 'We've got to stay here and find a way to stop, to destroy, those creatures completely.'

'Oh sure, be a hero, why not? But how's going to a bookshop in London going to help us? And why London, there's plenty of bookshops here in Norwich?'

Dec shrugged. He had caught the glimmerings of an idea as they pulled away from the garage but he wasn't sure how to put it into words or where to begin.

'This whole nightmare is rooted in magic, isn't it?' he began slowly.

'Sure, we know that already, but I still don't see why going to London is so important.'

'Well, perhaps if we could find out more about that mummified hand and the spells that the taxidermist chanted we might discover an antidote, or something. You know, an anti-spell to stop the magic.'

'I don't believe what I'm hearing. We're going to London in search of an anti-spell while those creatures hunt us down?'

'No, it's not as haphazard as that,' he replied braking for a set of traffic lights. 'There's a bookshop that specializes in magic, near the British Museum. It must have a copy of almost every work on the subject. It's in Shuttlecock Alley. I used to spend hours browsing through the sections on alchemy and herbs and mediaeval medicine when I was at the university and I always call in when I have to go down there on business. It's amazing the knowledge that's stored in that shop.'

He paused and pulled away from the lights, changing heavily through the gears. 'You still have that piece of mummified hand, don't you?' he added.

She nodded and dug in her jeans pocket and found the waxy fragment of thumb. She frowned as she pulled it out.

'It's disgusting,' she shuddered, turning it over and examining the blackened fingernail and the withered waxy skin that covered the bony knuckle.

'Can you remember the spell? You know, those words he was repeating backwards and forwards?' Dec asked as he threaded his way through the traffic.

The horror of it flooded back and filled her mind. She glanced fearfully over her shoulder and her skin began to crawl, the hairs on the nape of her neck starting to prickle.

'How could I ever forget?'

'Here, quick, write them down,' Dec insisted, pointing to a piece of crumpled paper that lay in the glove compartment and giving her a pencil stub from his pocket.

'Why? What do we want this for?' she frowned as she started to scribble.

'Because the spell and the mummified hand are at the centre of this magic, we're sure of that. We know that it resurrects the dead but that, so far, is all we do know. The more we know about how that taxidermist made the magic – why he uses it, where he discovered the spell and where he dug up that mummified hand – the more chance there is that we'll stumble on something that will be able to destroy it.'

Dec paused and glanced down at the fragment of thumb in her hand. 'Let's put together the pieces of the jigsaw that we already know. The taxidermist immortalizes beauty, his skill is to recreate an image, an effigy, of the living animal, but for our madman this is not enough, he wants to make his animals live again. To do this he dabbles in magic in order to bring them to life but what he didn't account for when he tampered with the natural order of things was the chain of reactions that would occur. When you wandered into his courtyard and the moonlight reflected his magic into the museum and awakened those exhibits . . .'

Dec suddenly laughed. 'That's it! Of course. He was mad enough to ignore one of the basic rules of physics, that to every action there is an equal and opposite reaction. There's the key to this nightmare. We can neutralize this magic without the mummified hand!'

Laughing he changed lanes and quickly left the suburbs behind as he drove into open country following the signs to Ipswich.

'No, I still don't get it,' Tuppence muttered after a long silence. ' "To every action there's an equal and opposite reaction"? What does that mean, for Chrissake, you've lost me.'

Dec thought for a moment. The way he had associated

the law of motion with the taxidermist was pretty abstract and he looked for a way to explain it to her. 'Right, imagine a cricket bat hitting a ball – action. The ball flies through the air – reaction. Now if that cricket ball hits something then it could cause another reaction, so the cricket ball is then both reaction and action.'

'So . . . OK, I think I understand, but what has this got to do with the madman?'

Dec sighed. 'Well, imagine that the taxidermist has hit the ball by creating the magic to make those creatures. He thinks he is in control because they come to life and obey his orders but what he doesn't realize is the ball has hit something and created another reaction and not only is he not in control of this but he doesn't even know about it. Now I think that is where we can work to counteract this horror but we must approach it scientifically and as methodically as any other piece of research that I would undertake in my laboratory.'

'Scientifically? Give me a break,' Tuppence cried. 'What are you going to do? Capture one of those creatures and stuff it under your microscope? Or will you make a grab for one of those black crows strutting about on the verges?'

Dec glanced at the crows. 'I'm sure that those birds scavenging on the verges are real, the birds from the taxidermist's shop don't need to eat, do they? But seriously I will need to examine one of those creatures if I can get hold of one, or a piece of it. Do you remember how I threw that bottle of chemical at the beast in the preparation room as you were scrambling through the window? Well, whatever was in that bottle ate through its clothing and scalded its skin, and just knowing that something must hurt them is a start, isn't it?'

Tuppence stared at him for a moment and saw a glimmer of what he was getting at. Her eyes softened and she smiled as she reached out and touched his arm, letting her hand linger. 'You're a pretty sharp doc. You know, I reckon you might even crack this nightmare if you can work all that out before these creatures catch up with us.'

Dec blushed, he hadn't meant it to sound so neat and easy. Apart from the fragment of thumb, a jumble of words that made up the spell and a scattering of disjointed ideas, he had nothing to go on and nowhere to start. The only other thing he could think of was to go through the thousands of books in the magic shop. And they were never going to have enough time to do that.

Ludo Strewth tilted his head so that the beak of the glossy black crow perching on his shoulder was brushing against his ear. He rubbed his hands together and licked his lips as the bird cawed and whispered to him and then he leaned over the map which was spread out on his marble preparation slab. With a dirty fingernail he traced the route that the American woman and her accomplice had taken, first to Ipswich in the yellow car and then on to London by train. He laughed triumphantly and sneered.

'You think you can vanish amongst those seething millions but you'll never escape me. My birds are watching you, following your every footstep, and soon my beasts will . . .' He hesitated, the sneer dissolving into a hate-filled frown as his eyes wandered critically from face to face along the rows of hideously putrefying creatures that now crowded eagerly around him.

'Somehow I must hide your faces, cover their ruination from prying curious eyes,' he muttered, shaking his head.

He couldn't understand what was happening to the skins of these cadavers. Even if he had been a complete novice fumbling clumsily in the dark with the preservatives, oils and lotions that he had accumulated during his lifetime's work they still should not be decomposing so quickly or have bruised and rotted wherever he touched them. It had not happened to any of the animals that he had resurrected. There had been no change at all in their hides or the fur and feathers, except he had noticed a fine film of greyish mould in the larger animals. But that seemed no more than a misted breath of degeneration that he had put down to sudden changes of temperature and the damp night air encountered outside the shop.

Snapping his fingers he beckoned forward the largest of the figures, that he had christened Motyka. 'We must be quick and seize that woman and her cursed accomplice before every one of you rots away completely.'

Ludo paused, raking his fingers irritably through his hair as the clattering roar of a motorcycle climbing Elm Hill drowned the sound, staring out of the window as an idea began to crystallize in his mind.

'Of course,' he whispered licking his lips, 'nothing could be more perfect. I'll disguise some of you as dispatch riders. There are thousands of them in every city, no one will ever give you a second glance. You will be completely anonymous and able to come and go as you please. Motyka, pay attention,' he hissed to the lumbering creature that towered beside him.

'Tonight you will take the others to steal motorcycles, helmets, leather jackets and over-trousers, in fact everything that will transform you into dispatch riders. But be careful to take only a little from each motorcycle shop and do not get caught or leave any clues.'

Motyka gurgled and snarled, his putrefying face breaking into a leer as he turned towards the door, the other creatures close on his heels. 'No, wait,' Ludo cried, making them shuffle to a halt. 'Some of you will stay behind to keep those foul soldiers bottled up in the museum cellars. I can't have them escaping and thwarting my revenge. The rest of you are to travel to London and follow the American and her accomplice. Shadow them wherever they go and then close in on them unnoticed. Snatch them and bring them back to me.'

Quickly he moved amongst his creatures, examining their faces closely. He chose the least hideous to stay with him, those he would disguise with hats, cloth caps and overcoats to cover the worst of their decomposition. The more degenerate would become the motorcycle riders while his birds would fly across London and help to search them out.

'No escape!' he sneered, clicking off the light.

'Are you sure this is the right place?' Tuppence asked as the taxi cab turned into Gordon Street and began to slow down. Frowning she glanced from the drab, rundown back street to the name and address of the magic shop that Dec had scribbled down for her earlier in the day as they were leaving the hotel.

'That's the only Shuttlecock Alley that I know of, lady,' the cab driver answered, pointing up to a street sign on the wall of a dark and narrow street beside the taxi, 'but if that's not the place you want I could drive you somewhere else.'

'No, no, it's OK, thanks. I'll find the shop I want, I'm sure it's here somewhere,' she muttered as she paid him off and then reluctantly watched the car pull away in a cloud of diesel fumes.

Oddly enough she felt safe in the numerous cabs she had used to cruise around London in the last couple of days. It had been Dec's idea that they split up to put the creatures off their scent. He was sure that the taxidermist and his beasts would come after them and they had to do everything they could to stay one jump ahead, constantly covering their tracks by changing their hotel every night and only eating in crowded restaurants and staying where the lights were bright. He had also warned her to watch out for strange birds or oddly dressed characters on that first morning as he hailed her a cab before he set off to the magic shop but she hadn't seen anything out of place, nothing that she could put her finger on. Half the people she glimpsed through the cab window seemed oddly dressed and London was awash with flocks of birds, mostly pigeons, starlings and sparrows, that fed on the pavements and perched on every roof top. The only thing she had noticed were the number of motorcycle riders who seemed to follow her cab but Dec had only laughed and dismissed her worry as he pointed out that there were thousands of motorcycle messengers on the streets.

Tuppence smiled to herself as she remembered her anxiety when they had booked into the first hotel near Euston Station as Mr and Mrs Winner. The fear of being alone during the hours of darkness had been pressing heavily on her mind but to share a room just now made her hesitate. She knew that Dec meant more to her than every other guy she had ever met but she didn't want to rush things and spoil it. Dec had sensed her apprehension and blushed in confusion as he dragged off his glasses and polished them studiously while he told her that he felt it necessary for them to divide the night into watches and take turns to sleep in case the creatures scented them out.

He warned her to be on her guard, 'And that's my bed,' he added as he turned and pointed out the couch behind the door.

The roar of a passing motorcycle cut across her thoughts.

She shivered and pulled her jacket more tightly around her shoulders. She was cold despite the stifling afternoon air and she changed her grip on the overnight case that contained the few essential belongings that she had purchased for them both. She had never bought that kind of personal stuff for anyone before and she had rather enjoyed it. She blinked and glanced around. She saw the crumbling Regency façades with broken windows and fading paintwork, the neglected shop fronts and the dirty, litter-filled basement stairways and she sighed. Every city she had ever visited was the same, all glitz, glamour and bright lights on the surface whilst a few blocks away the tentacles of poverty and decay slowly devoured its heart.

She was about to turn into Shuttlecock Alley when a slow, clumsy figure at the far side of Gordon Street caught her eye. He looked out of place on a stifling summer afternoon swathed in his heavy overcoat, the high collar turned up, and a wide-brimmed hat pulled down over his forehead, masking most of his face. There was something about his lumbering gait that tugged at the chords of her memory. She caught her breath and froze. He had the same rolling walk as those huge bears from the taxidermist's shop. The figure turned and crossed the road towards her. He mounted the pavement and walked right beside her and then turned away, his overcoat sleeve brushing against her arm as he passed.

The moment's contact and his smell made her skin crawl. She wanted to scream out loud and turn to run for her life, but the scream ached in her throat and her legs felt leaden with terror. She stood there helplessly, watching him walk away. He passed through a crowd of children who were playing on the pavement and then turned and vanished into a doorway further down the street. She breathed a shallow gasp of relief, wrinkling her nose in disgust at the odour of decay and death that the figure had left behind him.

'Why didn't those kids notice the stench?' she muttered as she glanced frantically up and down the street, afraid that she would see more overcoated figures closing in on her.

But the street was empty apart from the children and a handful of old women who were sitting sunning themselves in their doorways. There were also two dispatch riders sitting on their motorcycles at a distant corner. She hesitated and smoothed out the crumpled piece of paper that she had balled in fear in her hand. She managed to decipher the name of the shop that Dec had written out for her, 'Daruma'.

'I have to warn him,' she breathed as she hurried into Shuttlecock Alley and picked her way around the boxes of jumble piled outside the junk shops, the racks of books put out to attract the passers-by, almost blocking the narrow pavement.

Halfway along the alley she found Daruma, the shop that dealt in books on magic, and she quickly opened the door and slipped inside. A bell jangled somewhere in the back, muffled by mountainous racks and shelves crammed with old books, untidy piles of broadsheets and unbound manuscripts and boxes of papers.

'Dec?' she hissed as she peered through the gloom. She took a tentative step forward, undecided which of the dozen narrow aisles between the crowded bookcases to explore first.

The air in the shop smelt dry and musty, claustrophobically thick with the millions of secrets, chants, spells and magic curses that were stored there, pressed between the endpapers of those countless volumes. The silence seemed muffled and completely enveloping.

'Dec, Dec, where the hell are you?' she whispered urgently as she took another cautious step.

Something soft and furry brushed against her cheek, making her jump and cry out as she staggered backwards and dropped the overnight bag. She stared open-mouthed at the carcass of a shrivelled squirrel that slowly rotated and swung backwards and forwards, suspended on fine copper wire from a beam that ran across the ceiling.

A small, white-haired wizened figure in a long brown coat shuffled towards her out of the gloomy depths. He stooped and retrieved her case and held it out to her.

'You have met my doorwarden,' he smiled, pointing to the squirrel. 'It hangs there to ward off demons.'

'Well it certainly gave me a fright,' she answered, straightening her jacket and taking back her case.

'You can never be too careful, miss,' the proprietor murmured. 'Watching over this treasure house of secrets is a lifetime's work, almost a crusade. We must not allow it to fall into the wrong hands. But what is it that you are looking for, my dear, a good-luck spell or a chant to help you find something that you have lost?'

'No, I . . . a friend of mine told me to meet him in here this afternoon, a tall guy, fair hair and glasses.'

The old proprietor's eyes widened with interest and he tilted his head to one side and smiled, placing his fingertips together one by one into the shape of a pyramid.

He was about to answer when he was distracted by the sight of a large ungainly figure who had stooped into the doorway of the shop. He seemed to be sniffing from side to side, crouching forward, as if he was following a scent, and he pressed his gloved hands against the glass, blocking out the afternoon sunlight.

Tuppence frowned and glanced back over her shoulder as the door opened and the bell jangled.

'No, oh no!' she cried scrambling backwards and colliding blindly with a rack of books, falling to her knees.

She quickly regained her feet, hurrying to get away from the lumbering creature that was advancing over the threshold towards her, its overcoat billowing open, its gloved hands reaching out to snatch her. The carcass of the squirrel suddenly began to spin wildly on its wire, creating a high-pitched hum. Bells and chimes began to clatter and jangle beside the door. The huge menacing figure, disorientated by the noise, hesitated and stopped, snarling with rage as it struck out towards the squirrel.

'*Bezup! Bezar!*' the wizened old man cried at it as he grabbed Tuppence by both wrists and pushed her roughly further into the shop away from the flailing creature.

As he turned back he tore open his long brown dust coat and revealed a shimmering robe of black and gold, and in so doing, he seemed to grow as he strode towards the creature. At the same time the shop darkened into blackest night. His voice rose in an eerie echoing chant and his fingertips seemed to flicker and mould around the powerful magical signs that he drew in the air, and they hung there like quickfire illuminating the creature's hideous face. Its snarls weakened and subsided, its screaming shrieks became howls of pain as the magician opened a ram's-horn flask that hung around his neck on a golden chain and threw the contents into the beast's face. A rich musky perfume filled the bookshop. The creature lifted its hands to fend off the clinging scent and step by step retreated over the threshold. With one final snarl it stumbled across the pavement and vanished out of sight, taking the darkness with it.

The proprietor slammed the door violently shut, threw the bolts, twisted the lock and rattled down the blind, shutting out the sunlight. He paused for a moment to

gather his breath in rasping gulps and then he carefully rubbed off the blackened spark marks from his fingertips. He retrieved his brown dust coat from the floor and slipped it on, buttoning up the front before he turned on the light and thoughtfully turned to where Tuppence crouched, still trembling from head to foot, amongst the overturned piles of books.

'You're a magician, a sorcerer!' she whispered fearfully as she remembered the mad taxidermist and his spells, and she cowered away from him. 'I saw the fire brighten your fingertips as you painted pictures in the air.'

The old man laughed, his voice silencing her abruptly as he swept his hand theatrically across the rows of books. 'To guard such a fountainhead of forbidden knowledge and keep it from evil hands requires many disguises and many skills, my dear.'

His smile dissolved and his piercing eyes grew darker, his voice became urgent. 'So what Dec told me is true, the living dead do stalk your footsteps.'

Tuppence shrank further back amongst the books, the colour draining from her face. A muffled shout from somewhere in the back of the shop made her gasp and glance round.

'Dec!'

'What the hell's going on? What's the terrible commotion?' he shouted, scrambling over the precarious piles of books that blocked the narrow aisle and hurrying through. He came to a dead stop as he saw Tuppence crouching amongst the books and he bent and pulled her to her feet.

'One of those creatures that you described to me tried to follow your young lady into my shop,' the proprietor muttered, his eyes narrowing with concern.

He looked round and saw another huge figure pausing

on the pavement outside as it moved closer, momentarily etching its shadow on the blind as it rattled the latch fiercely.

'Quickly, get back away from the doorway,' he hissed to both of them as he unscrewed the cap on the ram's-horn flask and scattered a fine rain of tiny silver droplets towards the shuttered door.

As the droplets touched the faded paintwork they hissed and bubbled, bursting and emitting the rich scent of musk which wafted through the bookshop. Its pungency made Tuppence's head spin. The crowded shelves seemed to darken and melt away and she found she was standing in an ancient forest of giant trees. Shafts of sunlight filtered down through the ceiling of interwoven branches, doves whispered and cooed and the ground felt moss-soft beneath her feet.

'Quickly, you must follow me,' a disembodied voice called to her from between the trees and she felt a hand close about her wrist and tug her forward.

She blinked and the forest faded. She was back in the shop.

'Come on,' Dec urged.

Tuppence hurried after him, glancing fearfully back to the door as she saw that the figure was still standing there, its shadow spoiling the blind. A motorcycle roared through the alleyway and cast a fleeting shadow into the shop, the beat of its engine echoed in her ears. She stumbled over a set of library steps and unseen stacks of books that littered the narrow aisle before she caught up with Dec.

'It's hopeless, we'll never be free of those monsters.'

'Hush!' the old man warned her, drawing them both into a small windowless room somewhere in the depths of his shop, quietly shutting and locking the door before he switched on the light.

'Time is running against us,' he whispered urgently, motioning them to be seated at a circular table which was carved with magical signs and symbols.

'Who are you?' Tuppence frowned. She sensed a power in the old man that was way beyond the appearance of the humble shopkeeper who had greeted her at the door.

He laughed softly and cast off his dust coat as he spread his arms and held out his shimmering robe towards them. 'I am Theopus, a master of magic and by many births the direct heir of Paracelsus, the guardian of the fountainhead of all dark knowledge. And you must be Miss Tuppence. Dec has told me everything about the taxidermist's evil . . .'

'Have you found a way to destroy it?' she interrupted.

Theopus shook his head. 'The words of the spell seem so familiar, I'm sure the answer is staring me in the face.'

'Doesn't the fragment from the mummified hand help at all?' Tuppence asked, seeing it lying in the centre of the table.

Theopus picked up the shrivelled, blackened thumb and turned it over in his fingers. 'Of course!' he suddenly cried. 'The chant is a thief's spell and this fragment is from a Hand of Glory.'

He paused and carefully putting the thumb down hurriedly pulled one of the ancient books from its place on the shelf and riffled through it.

'Yes, here it is.' He brought the book to the table. 'Tell me, does the taxidermist's Hand of Glory look anything like that?'

Tuppence looked at the steel engraving and shuddered. 'Yes, yes it does, it looks exactly like that,' she whispered.

The magician sat back placing his fingertips thoughtfully together and then slowly shook his head. 'No, the Hand of Glory and the thief's spell alone could not have resurrected those creatures. The words uttered correctly would evoke a drugged sleep in the household that the burglar was entering. It could also open locks and the most powerful of the mummified hands would render the thief invisible. But it would not be able to bring the dead to life, unless . . .' Theopus paused, deep in thought.

'But I saw him light the index finger and heard him chant those words as the creatures rose,' Tuppence cried, breaking the silence.

Theopus looked up at her and said slowly, 'In magic anything is possible. We must search the ancient books and find out everything we can about the Hands of Glory and the thief's spell.'

The magician began carefully to turn the parchment pages of the book in front of him, moving his index finger along the lines of hieroglyphics. 'It is written in code and is difficult to follow even with all my knowledge. It is written thus to safeguard the wisdom,' he muttered.

His eyes suddenly brightened. 'The hand must be cut from the right arm of a gibbeted criminal. The blood to be squeezed out before embalming with the fat from a hanged man, wax from a bishop's beehive, Lapland sesame, salt . . .'

He fell silent as he bent over the book, 'The words are jumbled, it looks as though someone has tried to scratch them out, I cannot read them. No, wait,' he cried turning the page with excitement. 'There is an antidote to the spell. It can only be broken by dowsing the flame that smoulders within the fingertips of the hand with the blood of the thief who lit it or by wetting them with the milk of a barbastelle.'

'What the hell's a barbastelle?'

'It's a type of bat found in Eastern Europe,' Dec answered flatly, staring down at the fragment of thumb.

'Well at least we have an antidote to the taxidermist's magic,' Tuppence offered helpfully.

'But it doesn't explain how a Hand of Glory could hold enough evil power to resurrect the dead,' Theopus murmured, resting his chin on his hand.

Dec pushed his glasses up on to his forehead and rubbed his eyes. The stifling atmosphere in the tiny book-lined room was making his head ache. 'Wait! Wait a minute, let's try and tackle this scientifically. What would have happened if the thief had chanted the spell without one of those Hands of Glory?' he asked.

The magician smiled. 'That's easy to answer. Nothing. The householder would probably have woken up and caught him and then he would have been hanged.'

Dec thought for a moment and then continued. 'So the magic power must have come through the severed hand, yes?'

Theopus shook his head slowly. 'No, well not entirely. For magic to work properly or correctly it must be a blend of all the elements.'

'But what if the elements are unequally balanced? Let us say the gibbeted criminal was thoroughly evil, could that power have distorted the thief's spell?' Dec pressed.

Theopus sunk his head into his hands and thought back over lifetimes of magic. 'Yes,' he answered thoughtfully. 'Perhaps you have touched at the heart of this nightmare. The hand of the gibbeted criminal gives the spell its power.'

'How the hell did that taxidermist know where to look for the body of a hanged man so that he could cut off his hand?' Tuppence cried, her face a mask of disgust as she looked at the shrivelled fragments of skin and bone. 'I thought they stopped hanging people years ago.'

'There must have been records . . .' Dec began when the

magician rose to his feet with a cry, sending his chair crashing to the ground behind him.

'That taxidermist,' he asked urgently, 'is he tall, stooping, with thinning white hair?'

'Yes, he looks exactly like that.' Tuppence shuddered as the magician hurried across the room and began to search along the shelves, looking at the books one by one, twisting his head to one side to read each spine in turn.

'Yes, now I remember him,' he cried, pulling out a huge black volume bound with silver locks that bore the title, *The Ledger of the Dead For the County of Norfolk.*

'It was only when you mentioned the records of the hangings that I recollected him visiting this shop last winter. He bustled in here out of a howling blizzard, he was all smiles and sincerity and told me that he was researching eighteenth-century crime and punishment and the only thing his thesis lacked was a graph to show where the majority of the criminals had been hanged in England.'

'Yes, he was here. I had dropped in to buy some books on fungal poisons, I remember seeing him near the door,' Dec interrupted.

'And you showed him that book?' Tuppence cried turning to the magician.

'Why yes. I have so much to guard and he appeared quite harmless. He masked his true intent so cleverly, how was I to guess?' Theopus retorted, laying the heavy volume down on the table in a cloud of dust.

'The damage has been done, there's nothing we can do about it now,' Dec added softly, calming her anger. 'At least we can see if he left any clue in this book to show us where he exhumed the body and stole the hand. Every scrap of knowledge will help us now.'

Theopus had been quickly scanning the lines on the linen pages, running his finger over the countless names and tiny maps and steel engravings before turning them over carefully. Suddenly he cried out.

'He has defiled the Ledger of the Dead. Look, look, he has torn out a whole page!'

'Damn, now we'll never know,' Dec spat in frustration.

'Wait,' the magician hissed, studying the pages before and after where the missing page had lain, pressed face to face with them for almost two hundred years. He reached into a drawer beneath the table and brought out a sheaf of thin, flimsy blank papers and a thick black pencil.

'What are you doing?' Tuppence frowned, leaning forward as Theopus took the pencil and began to write, mimicking the jumble of copperplate letters that was faintly ghosted amongst the true print on the page.

'I am copying down what time has imprinted from the ink of the missing page. Look.'

He held the piece of thin paper up against the light, turning it around.

'Norwich in the County of Norfolk,' Dec read looking up across his shoulder.

'Wait, there is more,' said the magician as he wrote out a list of names and dates and began to draw the spidery outline of a map, tracing a hill and a gallows that stood in the shadow of an oak tree and beneath the tree a line of shallow graves.

The magician suddenly frowned and his hand began to shake as he wrote the name 'Thomas Dunnich, Gibbet Hill, 1776'.

'Thomas Dunni . . . ?' Dec began, peering at the name the magician had written when Theopus, with a cry of terror, pressed his fingers over Dec's lips and stifled his voice.

'No! No, you must never utter that name.'

'But who the hell was he? What are you so afraid of?'

Tuppence gasped, her words fading unfinished as the flimsy sheet of paper suddenly smouldered in the magician's hand, blackening around the name, and then burst into flames.

'It has gone,' Theopus hissed, screwing the burning sheet of paper into a tiny ball in his closed fist. It dissolved into ashes as green and yellow sulphur-bright flames licked up between his fingers.

'It would have been better if you had never seen his name or known that he had once walked this earth. I would have been content for him to remain lost in the pages of the Ledger of the Dead.'

'But he isn't lost, is he?' Dec interrupted in a hushed whisper, holding up the blackened fragment of skin and bone. 'A part of him is here with us now, in this room. It was his body, wasn't it, that the taxidermist dug up on Gibbet Hill?'

The magician trembled and drew them both close to him. 'He must have chosen him because he was the closest to Norwich. He could not possibly have known whom he disturbed or what terrors of darkness he would stir up.'

'Who was he, for Chrissake? You have to tell us,' Tuppence cried.

Theopus glanced fearfully over his shoulder to the locked door before he answered. 'He was the foulest necromancer and Satanist. Many of the council of magicians believe that he was a demon sent from hell. It took the masters of the council two whole lifetimes to bring him to the gallows and hang him with a hallowed rope to answer for his awful crimes.'

'And then you just buried him and left him where anyone could dig him up? I just don't believe it,' Tuppence muttered angrily.

'No, surely to bury him as a common criminal was the

best way to hide his remains. No one ever knew who was hanged that day on Gibbet Hill, except the council, and the only record of his burial was kept here in the Ledger of the Dead.'

'So that's why the taxidermist's spell is so powerful,' Dec murmured gingerly, picking up the fragment of skin and bone and examining it at arm's length.

He had seen and experienced enough weird and strange happenings in the last week to believe almost anything. 'But,' he began, slowly trying to focus the scientist in him, 'if the evil, or dark power, or whatever it is that influenced the taxidermist's magic, really does still exist within the mummified remains of that body on Gibbet Hill surely I could examine it beneath the lens of my microscope. I could investigate the tissue structure, molecular balance and other things and try to unravel the fabric of the evil and devise a way to destroy it.'

Theopus almost laughed. The idea was preposterous. 'He sold his soul for the power that the evil would give him. How on earth are you going to find that, or its absence, beneath your microscope? You cannot dissect a person's soul. There can be no antidote to the evil that the taxidermist has awoken. All we can do is destroy that corpse before the evil that dwells within it draws the taxidermist to use more to strengthen his magic. The body, its hemp shroud and all its parts must be burnt upon a pyre of yew-tree branches cut from the north side of a churchyard and the ashes scattered into six separate fonts of holy water. It must be done immediately, before another day passes.'

'Perhaps the burning of that corpse will put an end to this whole nightmare,' Tuppence said quickly, an edge of hope in her voice.

The magician thoughtfully pressed his fingers together

and then slowly shook his head. 'No,' he answered truthfully. 'There is no way to stop the taxidermist's magic. Except, perhaps, to drown the fire that smoulders in the hand.'

'So if that antidote is to work we will have to kill that madman and pour his blood over the hand,' Dec frowned.

Tuppence suddenly laughed, her voice tight and harsh with hysteria. 'We'll never get close enough to touch him. Those decomposing monsters are with him night and day.'

Dec half rose from his chair and stared at her. It was as if her words had triggered a series of tumblers in his mind and he could almost hear them click into place. 'No, listen, I'm sure there's another way to destroy them. Do you remember that last spell? The one we witnessed through the window of his preparation room?'

Tuppence paled and nodded her head.

'Well I'm sure it went horribly wrong. I'm sure all those hideous creatures that he brought to life were only experiments, failed experiments, used in an effort to perfect the preservation of human skin before he captured you. I don't think he ever intended to use them but he had to resurrect them to hunt us down. Remember, all his animals had perished when they followed you into the museum fire.'

'So where does that leave us? What are you getting at?' she frowned.

'It's obvious! That taxidermist must be an expert at preserving things, probably one of the best in the world, but everything human he has touched has rapidly decomposed, hasn't it?'

'That is because the evil within him has united with the evil within the Hand of Glory and it will corrupt everything he touches,' Theopus concluded, shutting the Ledger of the Dead quietly.

'But what if *I* had lit the Hand of Glory?' Dec asked leaning forward.

Theopus smiled. 'Then perhaps the magic would have worked for good, but I'm really not sure . . .'

'Well at least it must be worth us trying to accelerate the process of degeneration in those creatures.'

'And how do you propose to do that? Tuppence retorted, throwing her arms up helplessly.

Dec hesitated, his cheeks colouring slightly as he sought for the words to expand his idea. 'I'm not sure yet. All I know is that we have this fragment of the Hand of Glory and I ought to get it back into my laboratory and start to examine it right away. With the creatures destroyed we can get to the taxidermist.'

Tuppence stared at him. The chill implications of what he had said were sinking in. 'Are you mad?' she hissed. 'We have only just escaped from Norwich. Our best bet is to keep on running, no, flying. That's it, we'll catch a plane out of here tonight. No airline in the world is going to fly any of those creatures, their smell alone would give them away. And once we're in New York I'll buy you a hundred microscopes, when we're safe, and anything else you want come to that. Only don't make us go back,' she cried and turned to the magician. 'Tell him. After all, it was you magicians or sorcerers or whatever you are that started this nightmare by leaving evil corpses littered all over the place. You tell him that we'd be crazy to go back. Go on, tell him.'

And she buried her face in her hands, her shoulders trembling, as tears of terror and despair trickled down her cheeks.

Theopus smiled gently at her and lifted the ram's-horn spiral over his head. Reaching out and taking one of her hands he pressed it gently into her palm and closed her slender fingers around the fine gold chain. 'There is nowhere you can hide from this evil. Dec is right, you must do everything you can to destroy it. Take this, the last precious drop of the scent of Paracelsus, it is all I can offer that is powerful enough to help.'

Theopus watched the despair brim up in her eyes as she clutched the spiral. 'Remember, you will not be alone, the horsemen will aid you, and rest assured that the masters of the council of magicians will journey to Gibbet Hill to burn the evil remains that lie there.'

Dec rose to his feet, glancing down at his watch. 'I had better hire a car.'

Theopus raised his hand to stop him. 'No, it is too dangerous to travel at night, by road especially. You must keep to well-lit, crowded places. Make your journey early tomorrow, perhaps by train, that would be the safest way. Those creatures will find it more difficult to follow your scent or to seize you from amongst so many others.'

'Aren't you at all afraid of going back?' Tuppence cried.

Dec looked into her eyes. Fear had ringed them with shadows, they were brimming with new tears. And yet in some strange way it enhanced her beauty and made him catch his breath. In less than a week he had fallen helplessly in love with her and he wanted to catch her up in his arms, to crush her against him and hold her close. He hesitated and fought to overcome his shyness. Finally he took her hands in his and clutched them fiercely.

'It's because I care about you more than anything else in the world that I have to destroy those creatures. Of course I'm scared to death, but I have to get rid of this spectre before we can . . .'

A muffled howl from somewhere outside the bookshop cut across Dec's words.

'Listen, they're all around us!' the magician hissed, leaping to his feet. 'Come on, we must move quickly before they attack.'

Dec looked back from the door of the tiny room and realized that he was still clasping Tuppence's hand. Her tears had dried and there was a smile softening the fear in her eyes as she whispered, 'I wish those soldiers from the museum were with us now. I'd feel a lot better having them as escorts on our return.'

17

The Books of the Dead

'I think we've given them the slip at last,' Dec whispered with a sigh of relief as he glanced back between the crowds of shifting faces.

They were passing through the ticket barrier of Notting Hill Gate Station and he took Tuppence's hand as he hurried her between the morning tide of commuters, tightening his grip on her as the crowd bumped and buffeted against them, threatening to split them apart.

'But if they catch up with us in here . . .' Tuppence frowned as they reached the top of the escalator that would take them down to the Central Line. She fell silent as they stepped on to the stairway, listening to the distant rumble of a train pulling into a platform.

'It's the only way to escape from those motorcyclists. They can't follow us down here,' Dec answered.

'I knew there was something odd about those dispatch riders,' said Tuppence wearily.

Dec nodded. 'Yes, I'm sorry, it seemed so ridiculous, so far-fetched, monsters riding around on motorbikes.'

'So how are we going to get back now?' Tuppence yawned.

She felt exhausted and filthy after what had seemed an endless night of dodge and run as they tried to shake off the pursuing beasts. Getting out of that magic bookshop had been easy, too easy, and the old magician's spells had seemed to work a treat. For a while it looked as though they were going to get clean away and they hadn't noticed the motorcycle riders hiding in an alleyway off Russell Street waiting for them until they suddenly surrounded the taxi cab, buzzing like angry hornets, threatening to drive it off the road. If it hadn't been for the driver's quick thinking and the lucky appearance of two police cars they would have been overwhelmed. That's when the dodge and run had begun. Cab after cab, running into hotels and then slipping out of their kitchen exits. But they never seemed to get further than a couple of blocks before the motorcycle riders reappeared in hot pursuit. And she had lost count of the times they had driven around Piccadilly Circus, Hyde Park Corner and Marble Arch, always directing the cab driver to the most crowded places.

Sudden shouts and the roar of motorcycles in the ticket hall above them echoed and rebounded down the escalator shaft. Startled faces turned everywhere in the crowd.

'Quick! They must have found our scent,' Dec hissed, pulling her down the moving stairway, running two steps at a time.

'We must have been mad to come down here. We're trapped.'

'They can't bring their bikes down here.'

'No, but they can still follow us. Look!' Tuppence cried in warning, making Dec turn and glance up to where three huge figures, fully dressed in black leathers, gloves and motorcycle helmets were pushing their way down the escalator behind them.

'What the hell do we do now?' Tuppence gasped. They had reached the bottom and were running headlong round the corner to the next moving stairway. As they tore downwards a rush of hot stale air suddenly ruffled their hair and the roar of an approaching train filled their ears.

'Quick, there's a train,' shouted Dec, and as they reached the bottom, 'Shake a few drops of that scent here, where the tunnel starts, that should put them off.'

With only seconds to spare they scrambled aboard as the doors of the crowded train slid shut. They collapsed against them breathlessly, watching the platform slip past as the train gathered speed.

'I saw only one of them on the platform,' Tuppence frowned.

Dec looked anxiously at the crowds around them. 'I don't think they're in this carriage. Perhaps the other two have gone to the other platform,' he muttered.

'Let's hope we've shaken them off,' Tuppence sighed wearily as the train began to slow down, approaching Queensway. 'Where the hell are we going anyway?' she asked as she watched the platform through the open doors.

The crowds in the carriage began to push them together. 'Liverpool Street,' he whispered glancing at his watch. 'I think the Fenman leaves for King's Lynn in twenty-five minutes from platform nine. If we make it we'll change for Norwich at Ely.'

'You know everything. You're a useful guy to have around,' Tuppence murmured as she masked a yawn and rested her head against his shoulder.

Dec smiled to himself. 'I always used to catch that train on a Friday to be home in time for the weekend when I was down here at university.'

She looked up at him and smiled. Being this close to him felt real good. 'I could sleep for a week,' she murmured and his arm closed protectively around her.

The sway of the train and the stifling closeness of the crowd in the carriage was beginning to lull her when a movement, a flash of colour, something familiar, shifted between the crowds standing in the aisle and made her blink and snap back into focus.

'What is it?' Dec asked anxiously as he felt her stiffen.

She craned her neck and peered between the throng of morning commuters, heads in their newspapers. 'I don't know, I thought I saw the hat that belonged to that creature who tried to follow me into the magic shop. But whatever it was it has gone now. Moved down the carriage or something.'

Dec glanced carefully around them. 'There must be fifteen or twenty people wearing hats in this carriage. And even more in the one next to us, they can't all be those creatures, the stench would be unbelievable.'

Tuppence laughed softly, the relief filling her voice. In no time Dec was whispering to her that the next stop was theirs and they were moving into the doorway to alight. A relentless tide of commuters was pouring out of Liverpool Street. Announcements telling of departures and arrivals boomed over the tannoy system as they threaded their way through the crowds.

'The platform looks pretty empty,' Dec muttered as they hurried past the diesel engine and the guard's van and towards the main part of the train.

They quickly boarded as droves of pigeons feeding on the platform rose in a grey fluttering wave at the shrill blast of the whistle and then fluttered down again. Flocks of starlings roosting on the network of overhead girders squabbled noisily, oblivious to the roar of the engine as it slowly pulled out of the station, but a dozen glossy black crows followed the movement of the train from high up amongst the girders and then rose into the air one by one, their cawing cries echoing over the busy station as they followed the train.

Six large overcoated figures suddenly appeared, pushing

and shoving their way through the crowds near the ticket barrier, and with surprising speed ran along the platform and caught up with the last of the carriages. Three of them managed to clamber aboard. A throng of motorcyclists waiting near the west of the station next to the taxi ranks watched the crows fly north following the train tracks and then started their engines one by one, roared into Bishopsgate and accelerated up Kingsland Road towards Stoke Newington.

'We've made it!' Dec laughed, looking for two empty seats as they walked slowly through the moving train.

'What's wrong with these?' Tuppence asked as she stopped beside an empty compartment and slid back the door.

'They're first class,' Dec answered, frowning as he patted his almost empty pocket. 'I don't think I have enough for ordinary tickets let alone first class.'

Tuppence fished in her jeans pocket, pulled out a smart flat wallet and held up a credit card. 'This one's on me,' she grinned.

They breakfasted on British Rail sandwiches and coffee from the buffet car and then settled back to watch the suburbs gradually changing into countryside as they sped past.

'I've got to freshen up,' Tuppence announced soon after they pulled out of Audley End.

'I noticed a loo at the end of this carriage. I'd better come with you, we can't be too careful,' Dec warned.

Tuppence smiled and shook her head. 'There are some things I've got to do on my own, creatures or no creatures,' and she left the compartment.

Moments later she was back, white-faced and trembling. 'They're on this train, I'm sure of it,' she whispered. 'I caught the smell of their rotting bodies. It was in the corridor at the end of this carriage. What are we going to do, for God's sake?'

Dec opened the door of their compartment a fraction and sniffed, making a face as the reek of corruption and decay wafted over him. 'It's a wonder that they can scent anything through their own awful stench,' he muttered as a lumbering figure in an overcoat and a wide-brimmed hat appeared in the corridor and started moving slowly towards them.

Dec slammed the door and looked around desperately for a way to escape. Their compartment didn't have an outer door, just a large picture window with a smaller window above it that opened. They were trapped. The train began decelerating as it approached Cambridge.

'Is there anything left in that flask of scent?' he asked Tuppence quickly.

She had shrunk back as far as she could away from the sliding door and was huddled against the window. She fumbled with the top of the flask and almost dropped it. 'Yes, there's just a few drops left,' she answered, 'but what are you planning to do?'

'Nothing – yet,' Dec muttered. 'The train will stop at Cambridge in a couple of minutes. We'll make a run for it then and throw a drop of that stuff into the creature's face if he tries to come in here or attempts to follow us. OK?'

Tuppence nodded, looking out of the window to the rows of houses beyond the station. She frowned as she saw more than a dozen motorcycles who were keeping pace with their train. 'They're everywhere!' she hissed.

The figure in the corridor reached their compartment as the train stopped. They heard doors slamming further along. The monster bent forward and sniffed at the closed door, then it straightened up, closed its gloved hand around the catch and pressed its decomposed nose against the glass part of the door, its raw and pussy eye sockets searching for them. Tuppence wanted to scream. The bile rose choking in her throat and her legs gave way as she fell backwards across the seat. The door began to slide open inch by inch.

'The scent. For God's sake sprinkle some of the scent,' Dec hissed, knuckling his fists in a last desperate gesture of defiance as the door slid fully open and the hideous beast advanced towards them.

Tuppence unscrewed the cap of the horn with fumbling fingers and swept it at the creature and a few precious droplets of the scent of Paracelsus scattered their heady fragrance, wafting across the carriage. The monster stopped, snarling, and began scratching at the loose strips of putrefying skin that hung from its nose and cheekbones as if to wipe away the heavy musky odour. A guard's whistle sounded and the train jolted and then slowly began to move. The creature swayed and clutched at the door frame as it retreated into the corridor. It snarled and moved backwards and forwards, stopping again and again just outside the door where the weakening edges of the scent dissolved and blended with the other smells in the carriage.

'That magic scent seems to blind them but it's only going to last for a few more minutes,' Dec whispered. 'There's no way out of here except to slip past before the smell vanishes altogether. Come on, it's now or never.'

Tuppence shuddered at the thought of passing that close to the decomposing creature. The idea made her flesh crawl but she nodded silently and keeping close to Dec, gripping at the tail of his coat, they squeezed past, her arm actually brushing against its overcoat. The creature stirred and half turned, grunting and snarling; it took a step to follow them but then hesitated. They fled into the next carriage, sliding the corridor door firmly shut behind them. Dec paused and looked out of the window and caught brief glimpses of the motorcyclists in the gaps between the passing houses. They were still following the train.

'How the hell do they know where we're going all the time?' Tuppence cried in desperation.

Dec was about to shrug his shoulders when he noticed a crow flying parallel to the train and he let down the window and leaned out and scanned the sky.

'That's how they know!' he spat, stabbing a finger up at the flock of crows, starlings and magpies who were circling and swooping over the train in an ominous black thundercloud of feathers.

'It's hopeless, we're never going to escape!' Tuppence cried, her voice near to tears.

Dec made her follow him, running the length of the corridor until they reached the next door on the other side of the carriage. 'Listen,' he whispered urgently, lowering the window and grasping the handle on the outside of the door, 'we have to get off this train before that creature finds us again and before we run into the open cornfields and potato fields of the Fens. There is a belt of trees about a mile ahead that almost overhangs the tracks. There's just a chance that those birds won't see us. There's a cement factory or something to the right of the trees and the train always slows as it crosses the points there. We've got to jump the train as it slows. Jump and dive as far as you can into the trees.'

'Jesus, are you crazy?' Tuppence gasped as the train began to slow and Dec swung the door wide open. 'I . . . I . . . can't . . .' she began as Dec grabbed her wrist in a wire-tight grip and flung himself out of the door, pulling her with him.

She struck the sharp gravel beside the track with such force it knocked the scream of terror and all her breath right out of her. Over and over she tumbled, feeling a million needle stabs of pain as Dec pulled and dragged her deep into the bank of thistles and nettles that grew close to the track beneath the trees.

'Keep your head down,' he hissed, forcing her shoulders lower amongst the broken stems and stinging leaves as the last three carriages of the train clanked their way past.

Tuppence could only see the train as a moving shadow between the swaying nettle stalks. Gradually the clatter of its wheels and the roar of its diesel engines grew fainter and she heard the rustle of the breeze in the leaves overhead and the sound of bird song in the branches of the trees. She was desperate to get up. Her face and hands were a mass of agony but Dec forced her to stay down.

'Listen,' he warned and in the distance she heard the hum of dozens of motorcycles accelerating away from them on the A-10 towards Ely.

Gradually the sound faded and Dec slowly rose and helped her to her feet. 'Look! Look at me,' she yelled snatching her hands away from him. 'I've been disfigured for life. I'm covered in millions of white bumps from those nettles, I've cut my knees and grazed my knuckles and it all hurts like hell!'

'Not so loud,' Dec whispered, glancing furtively up through the canopy of branches to the empty summer sky before he quickly broke off a handful of dock leaves and began to rub the leaves gently across her sore skin.

'This will stop the stinging and the bumps will vanish in a couple of hours,' he offered helpfully.

'Give me that,' she muttered crossly, taking the mass of leaves from his hand and rubbing it more violently on her cheeks and forehead, leaving a camouflage of green streaks from the plant's juices on her face.

'Well I think we've really shaken them off, at least for

the moment,' he murmured, watching the sky and listening to the silence.

Tuppence looked up at him and then along the empty tracks that vanished in the distance towards Ely. 'Sure, but now how the hell do we get back to Norwich? Walk?'

Dec pushed his glasses up on to his forehead, momentarily glad of the rubber band that had kept them firmly in place when they jumped from the train. He followed her gaze and nodded slowly. 'Yes, well I think we'll cut across the Fens and follow the River Cam for a few miles. Those motorcyclists won't be able to track us so easily if we keep to the cornfields and we can always duck down if the birds reappear.'

'But it will take us days,' she protested.

Dec laughed and shook his head. 'Well, a walk in the country has just got to be better than riding tandem on one of those creature's motorbikes and I promise we'll borrow a car at the first opportunity.'

He turned and led her through the belt of trees and past the deserted factory out into the flat endless landscape of cornfields. Skylarks were singing in the summer sun all around them and butterflies hovered and alighted on the full ears of corn. The hot breeze whispered and murmured between the ripening stalks, stirring them into shimmering golden waves. They walked for a long time, then Tuppence stopped and took Dec's hands, interweaving her fingers with his.

'I didn't mean to snap at you back there, only I was a touch shaken up. It's the first time I've jumped a train.'

'Mine too,' he laughed.

'You know, I always used to walk everywhere in New York when I was looking for work, that was before I met Harry. New York is different from this, it's all bustle and noise, shadows and sunlight between the tall canyons of buildings and everything is about people. The sounds, the smells, everything, and you blend with it and become a part of it. While here it's so different. The sky is so huge that it seems to dwarf you and the cornfields are so vast that they seem to march away for ever. It's so quiet you feel as if each ear of corn, each leaf and blade of grass is listening, waiting for the next breath of wind.'

'Don't you like it?' Dec asked.

Tuppence shielded her eyes from the sun and gazed around to consider before she answered, 'Yes, oh yes, it's very beautiful.'

They walked on for a while in silence, skirting the fields and following the irrigation ditches that led towards the River Cam.

'Who's Harry?' Dec asked hesitantly without looking at her.

Tuppence turned her head and studied his profile. She had sensed the anxiety, the hesitation behind the question and she smiled. 'My real dad abandoned me as a kid. All he ever gave me was my name, Tuppence, because that's all I was worth to him. Harry's the one good guy in my life, the father I never had. You'll like him when you meet him.'

'Yes, and I'm in trouble if he doesn't like me.' Dec suddenly tightened his hand on hers and pulled her down under the cover of the standing corn and whispered, 'There are some figures ahead of us, I glimpsed them on the river bank.'

'How many? Are they motorbike riders?' she whispered, her voice trembling.

Dec shrugged. 'I don't know, I only got the briefest glimpse. There were perhaps ten or fifteen of them, but . . .' He paused and looked up, searching the sky, then glanced at his watch. 'The train we jumped finished its journey a couple of hours ago, that's given those creatures plenty of time to realize that we have given them the slip. I would have thought that we would see those carrion birds searching for us long before the other creatures get here.'

'Who do you think it is then?' she frowned as Dec raised himself on to his knees and tried to peer through the swaying corn.

'I think they're on horseback,' he muttered after a few moments. 'It must be a party of riders from the local riding school.'

Ducking back down he scrambled into the oily overgrown ditch that seemed to run for miles along the edge of the cornfields parallel to the river bank.

'If we keep to the ditch we can slip past whoever it is without them seeing us,' he whispered, treading down the tangle of weeds and nettles that choked the ground where he stood.

Tuppence scrambled down reluctantly behind him and together they began to force a path through the undergrowth. It was hot, stifling work, insects swarmed and buzzed around their heads and the nettles and thistles sprang back at the slightest opportunity, stinging their hands and legs.

'Ugh,' Tuppence cried as a frog hopped on and off her shoe and with erratic leaps climbed the steep wall of the ditch beside her.

Dec frequently climbed out of the ditch and knelt in the corn to scan the river bank but each time he quickly scrambled back down again. 'I don't understand it. They seem to be following us . . .'

'Hush, listen,' Tuppence warned. 'I'm sure I can hear them getting closer. Yes, they're cantering through the corn towards us. It must be those creatures.'

Dec looked at her in alarm. 'They must have stolen some horses to scour this bit of countryside for us.'

Swift-moving horsemen suddenly appeared all around them and an order was called. They halted in an orderly line and Tuppence and Dec both stared up open-mouthed as the dusty and travel-stained scout from the museum dismounted and extended a gloved hand down towards them.

'Am I glad to see you,' Tuppence laughed with relief as she took the offered hand and climbed up out of the ditch.

The horseman smiled. 'Those creatures tried to keep us trapped in the cellars beneath the museum but we fought our way through them. The Colonel sent us out in flying columns searching far and wide for you, madam, after you vanished in the city. It was seeing those foul black crows searching the countryside away beyond Prickwillow and the army of creatures following them that warned us that you must be somewhere close by.'

'Prickwillow?' Dec frowned. 'That's on the Norwich line, they must have thought we jumped much closer to Ely. They must be expecting us to head towards Thetford Forest.'

The scout nodded and crouched down between them, spreading out on the ground an ancient field map of the Fens. 'There were between fifty and sixty of those beasts, some mounted on motorized cycles, some on foot. There were far too many of them for us to defend you should they attack so we laid a false trail towards Thistley Green and then doubled back to cross the Cam here.'

He indicated a bridge that Dec recognized as being on the Wicken Road. 'We've got to get back to my laboratory without a moment's delay,' Dec urged, staring at the map.

In quick whispers Dec told the scout everything that

had happened to them since the disastrous attempt to steal the Hand of Glory from the taxidermist's shop.

'It would be madness to try to slip through Thetford Forest, those birds would spot us immediately,' the horseman warned. 'But perhaps we could circle around them.'

He traced a tortuously slow route across the Fens through Witchford, Coveney, Pymore, Barroway Drove, Watlington and Wormegay.

'But that would take for ever,' Dec argued.

The scout stood up shaking his head and pointed to two saddle horses ready for them to use. 'With fast riding we could be at Thieves Bridge before morning.'

'I couldn't ride a horse. I've only ever had the odd ride on my sister's pony when I was a kid and I'd fall off before we'd gone a hundred yards,' he cried in alarm.

'Come on, we've got to get there somehow,' Tuppence laughed as she reached for the reins of the closest of the dark bay horses.

She had spent most of the money she had earned as a child on riding lessons and she always promised herself that she would one day have her own horse. She put her foot in the stirrup and swung herself up into the saddle, almost catching her right foot on the butt of the carbine strapped to the saddle roll. The cavalry saddle felt odd, completely different from any other saddle she had ever used, and the neck and shoulder of the horse felt cold and hard to the touch, not like a real horse at all. She glanced back at the rifle.

'It's a Spencer carbine, ma'am,' the scout smiled as he reached up to the pommel of his own saddle and unbuckled a wide leather belt from the D-ring. The belt was sewn with six pouches and a holster that contained a heavy-looking, long-barrelled revolver. He held it out for Tuppence to take. 'The Colonel is concerned for your safety when you are outside the Watchgate and he thought that as you are an American you would prefer to use a Navy Colt percussion revolver and a Spencer carbine rather than our English firearms.'

'Thanks, that's really thoughtful of him,' she murmured, taking the cumbersome belt and holster and buckling it around her waist, adjusting it so that the holster lay against the back of her right hip.

Reaching back she pulled the revolver out of its holster and carefully examined it. It was heavier than any of the modern guns she had used on the firing range back home. Its long black barrel, the chamber and brass trigger guard felt slightly sticky and it smelled of fresh gun oil.

'I'll bet this thing kicks like a mule. I'll need both hands to keep hold of it if I ever get to use it,' she laughed, cocking back the hammer, raising the barrel and sweeping it across the river bank.

'Be careful, ma'am,' the scout warned. 'The cylinder's primed with only five shots to prevent it going off accidentally. You will see there is no safety catch.'

He took the gun from her, eased back the hammer and released the hexagonal block in front of the cylinder, removing it. 'I had better show you how to reload the Navy Colt. After you have discharged all the bullets in the chambers you remove the cylinder and replace it with a fully charged one from the pouches sewn on to the belt. The charged chambers of each cylinder have been liberally smeared with pig's grease to prevent the gun from cross-firing.'

'That's really neat,' she exclaimed, watching him load and unload the cylinder for her, going through the actions slowly. She did it for herself a couple of times before she returned the gun to its holster.

'Remember,' the scout warned before he turned to Dec

to get him mounted, 'always check that the empty chamber in the cylinder, the one without the grease, is in line with the firing pin.'

'Yes, of course,' she nodded, secretly hoping it would never come to her to have to use the gun.

She collected up the reins and gingerly pressed her heels into the horse's flanks. She wasn't at all sure what aids to give to a horse that had been dead for almost two hundred years, she had no idea what it would do or how it would respond. The horse arched its neck slightly, took the bit and snorted, trotting two strides before it broke into an easy canter. It felt very light and quick off her leg. She turned the horse with the slightest touch of the rein and leg and glanced back over her shoulder to where Dec, with the scout's help, was hesitantly putting his foot into the stirrup.

'He will not falter or stumble and he won't let you fall. Trust in the magic,' the scout whispered as Dec swung his leg up over the saddle and perched awkwardly on the horse, gripping the pommel with both hands.

'The birds are approaching!' shouted one of the lookouts who was posted on the river bank. 'They are searching the ground on the far side of the bridge where we crossed.'

The scout looked at the approaching flock of birds, still black specks in the distant sky, then spun around and ran to his horse, vaulting easily into the saddle. 'Come, we must ride like the wind if we are to escape,' he shouted, spurring his mount through the standing corn and over the drainage ditch.

The small band of horsemen closed in around Tuppence and Dec as they cantered after him, leaping one by one over the ditch. Dec yelled and floundered in the saddle, his arms flailing, and he would have slipped off sideways as his horse rose up but two lancers rode up beside him and steadied him back into position.

All afternoon they rode at breakneck pace across the Fens, avoiding the scattered farmhouses and tiny marshland villages, leaping the deep drainage ditches and thundering over the narrow wooden bridges that spanned the wider channels and dykes. Tuppence rode as if she was born to it, sometimes keeping pace with the scout and sometimes dropping back to be with Dec where he grimly struggled to keep up with the two horsemen riding on either side of him. The sun was setting behind them in a blaze of fire, lengthening and darkening their racing shadows, before the scout eased the pace as they approached an island of tall trees in the centre of a cornfield. He pulled up and led them in amongst the trees.

'Rest here a moment,' he called, hurrying back to the edge of the thicket. Tuppence jumped wearily to the ground and then helped Dec to dismount.

'Dec's just about had it,' she muttered with concern as she moved to the scout's side. 'His knees and calves are raw and bleeding from trying to stay on that horse. I don't think he can ride much further.'

'They've found our trail,' the scout cried in alarm as he pointed out across the darkening, flat and empty countryside to where the taxidermist's birds had been soaring backwards and forwards only moments before, black threatening specks painted across the sunset. Now they were spiralling down, converging with cawing shrieks on the broad path that the horses had trampled through the cornfields.

'They'll be able to follow the trail we left in pitch darkness. We must turn towards the River Ouse and cross the Magdalene Bridge as soon as possible, it's the only way to shake them off. Quickly, mount up,' he ordered.

'But Dec's legs are a mass of bleeding sores, he'll never make it,' Tuppence cried.

The scout turned on her, stabbing his finger at the map. 'Madam, we cannot defend you here. Those creatures will overwhelm us in moments. Your only chance to escape them is to ride fast – now.'

'Are you two going to stand there arguing all night?' Dec's voice made them both turn. He was seated back in his saddle trying to laugh and look relaxed, but the agony showed in his eyes and in the whitened knuckles where they gripped the reins. Tuppence's heart went out to him. She mounted up and moved in to ride close beside him as they cantered out into the deepening darkness.

The river crossing came and went in a rush of echoing hoofbeats and the landscape began to change. Flat corn-fields gave way to gently undulating hills, plantations of trees and green fields. The scout stopped frequently, dismounting and pressing his ear to the ground, listening for sounds of pursuit. Dec hung on grimly, glad of the brief respites and barely noticing the troubled frown that had creased the horseman's face since they had crossed the bridge. At the entrance to a sparsely wooded valley he silently brought the company to a halt by lifting his right hand. Standing in his stirrups he slowly scanned the dark shadowy landscape ahead.

Dec looked past the scout along the rough track that wound along the floor of the valley, crossing and recrossing a winding and fast-flowing stream in a series of narrow hump-back bridges. There was something familiar about those bridges and the bulky squat church tower silhouetted against the starlit rim of the valley.

'Wait a minute,' he cried, forgetting to speak only in a whisper. 'I'm sure this is Castle Valley. Castle Green's at the other end. We, I mean Downland Chemicals, have a field testing station about a mile along that track. It'll have everything I need in there to examine that fragment of thumb – microscopes, freeze-drying processes, spectrum counters, incubators and samples of just about every organism that our chemicals will react to. I come here regularly once a month for field tests.'

'But we could never defend you here,' the scout replied in alarm. 'Your testing station is not a fortress like the Watchgate.'

'But we could save hours . . .' Dec began to argue when the roar and buzz of motorcycles sounded on the track behind them and the snarling howl of huge lumbering figures emerging on either side of them from beneath the trees cut him short.

Tuppence's horse surged forward, snatching at the bit and galloping her clear of the approaching creatures towards the first bridge. The scout shouted orders and the company of horsemen closed in around Tuppence and Dec, firing as they galloped and dislodging six of the motorcycle riders.

'Dec's right. He ought to use this place of his,' Tuppence shouted at the scout as he rode up behind her.

'These creatures will overrun us in no time at all,' he shouted back.

Tuppence looked back over her shoulder at their hideous pursuers. The twisting roughness of the track was slowing the motorbikes but the lumbering figures had almost reached the first bridge with their giant strides.

'What would happen if I went back to the Watchgate?' Tuppence shouted to the scout against the rushing wind that was tugging her words away. 'Would it draw these monsters away from Dec? Would it give him a chance to do his experiments?'

'Yes,' the scout answered in surprise, slowing his mount

as they crossed the second bridge. 'I'm sure that the majority of them would follow you, ma'am, it is your blood they howl for the loudest.'

'Then I will return to the Watchgate with your two fastest riders. You and the rest of your men must stay here with Dec and defend him while he tries to find a way to destroy these creatures.'

Both Dec and the scout began to protest loudly at her plan to have only two escorts but she cut them short and would hear none of their arguments.

'Just find out what will destroy these beasts will you?' she snapped at Dec before turning on the scout. 'Do you think I like this?' she cried with tears of determination brimming in her eyes.

'But we are pledged to guard you, ma'am, not him,' the scout answered in dismay as they cantered over the third of the humped bridges side by side.

She drew her horse close to his and whispered fiercely to him, 'Do you think I go easily? Don't you realize that I love him more than anything, anything in the whole world?'

The scout smiled sadly. Her words had stirred memories and he touched a hidden silver locket that had been sewn into a pocket of his jacket an age ago. 'We will guard him, ma'am, you have my word on it.'

Tuppence reached across and gripped the scout's hand in silent thanks as they reached a divide in the track.

'The field station's off to the right,' Dec called and the scout lifted his hand to bring the company to a halt. He chose the two swiftest riders to escort Tuppence to the Watchgate then sent out pickets to watch the track and scout the left-hand side of the gully, to warn of any approaching monsters.

Tuppence rode up beside Dec and for a moment they

looked silently into each other's eyes. She had never felt like this before nor suffered such a parting. She reached out and took his hand.

'When this is over will you come with me to New York?'

Dec leaned across and kissed her gently on the lips. 'I love you.'

Tuppence tightened her grip on his hand and returned the kiss. She heard the clatter of horses' hooves beside them and pulled back. She was smiling and there were tears running down her cheeks.

'The beasts have reached the second bridge, you must leave now,' the scout urged.

'Wait!' called Dec, fumbling in his breast pocket for his pen. He pulled it out and in large hasty spidery figures he wrote the number of the field station on the back of her hand.

'Ring me the moment you reach the safety of the Watchgate,' he whispered as a volley of shots rang out close to the last bridge they had crossed.

'Ride! Ride like the wind,' the scout shouted, spurring his horse between them.

Tuppence's horse surged forward, her fingers slipping out of Dec's hand, and before she could answer him her escorts had closed in on either side and they were galloping hard up across the steep scrub-covered side of the dark valley. She glanced back and saw Dec and the band of horsemen galloping towards a long, low white building surrounded by a high security fence. The creatures were hesitating at the place their tracks divided and some began swarming after Dec's party but the majority began to follow Tuppence's up towards the rim of the valley. She shuddered and drove her heels hard into the horse's flanks. The plan was working, she was drawing those beasts after her and buying Dec the few precious hours he needed to find a way to destroy those creatures.

Dec looked out of the small, heavily barred window beside the door of the field station and watched as half a dozen of the monsters who had followed them began tearing at the high wire security fence. He was holding his breath, hoping that one of them would try to scale the fence before the rest of them tore a hole in it. It would be easier to deal with them one at a time. Snarling with triumph, one of the creatures broke a couple of metal links in the fence close to the gates and thrust first his hand and then his forearm through, breaking more of the links with each brutal thrust. It would only be moments now before those broken links would become a gaping and sagging hole large enough for all hell's creatures to swarm through.

'Come on! Come on!' Dec urged, clutching the bars of the window so tightly that his knuckles were bleached white.

A cavalryman hiding close to the fence suddenly sprang up a yard from where the monster was breaking through. A sabre rose and fell, its cutting edge reflecting back the bright starlight. There was a ring of steel striking steel and a blaze of white sparks as the sabre cut through the metal skeleton. The monster screeched with rage and tried to force its way through the widening gap, flailing its stump at the cavalryman who snatched up the hand and arm and ran in through the door.

'It's more than I dared hope for,' Dec cried, slamming and locking the heavy reinforced door before he eagerly took the still twitching limb from the soldier's hands. The sleeve of the creature's overcoat and the leather glove still clothed it.

Leaving the scout and his handful of riders to barricade the door against attack he hurried through the building to an inner windowless laboratory, laid the limb down in a long white kidney dish and washed his hands. He donned a mask and rubber gloves before he tried to cut away the sleeve and glove with a pair of surgical scissors but the fingers of the hand tried to grab at him, twice almost pulling the scissors out of his hand and scrabbled constantly, crablike, at the edges of the dish.

Dec called the scout in to hold the limb down while he worked on it. He began to sweat and the overpowering stench of decay that rose from the arm as he finally stripped it bare made him dizzy and light-headed. His stomach heaved as he peeled away the wet, stinking, slimy shirt-sleeve and saw the purply-black putrefying skin beneath. He had worked in a police mortuary for a year after university but he had never seen anything that looked this decomposed, this hideous. Even the bodies that had been dredged up out of the river, bloated, blackened and glistening, had smelled and looked better than this. And it wasn't just the look of it that revolted him, it was the way it wriggled so violently, slipping in the scout's strong grip. Dec swallowed his revulsion as he remembered Tuppence was somewhere out in the darkness with hordes of these foul creatures running on her heels and he picked up his scalpel and began to cut into the rotting flesh.

He began to make slides, first of the skin on the fingers, the palm of the hand and then the forearm. He noticed that the taxidermist's rough stitches around each finger and along the underside of the forearm had torn through the flesh and in some places the surgical thread had begun to rot. Frowning he took the slides over to the microscope and examined them carefully one by one, comparing them with the section of the fragment of thumb from the Hand of Glory.

'It's just as I thought,' he murmured, straightening his back and returning to stare down at the twitching limb. 'The structure of this fragment of thumb is unnaturally dormant, almost ageless, while the flesh of this creature is decomposing at the speed of an express train. But why? I don't understand it. The stitches are degenerating as well, the flesh decomposing should not affect them. I would have thought that the thread the taxidermist used would have been the enduring type, not the kind that dissolves.'

Picking up the scissors again he cut away some of the cotton material that had been used to flesh out the creature and pulled it apart. A sharp odour of rotting vegetables rose up and made him sneeze and he noticed tiny grey wet patches in the fibres of the cotton. Using his scalpel he laid some of them upon a slide. Delving deeper he exposed the wire skeleton and the central length of wood that ran from the shoulder to a metal hook at the elbow and from a second hook set in the lower section of wood from the elbow to the wrist. The wire was pitted and corroded with rust and snapped easily between his fingers.

Using the back of a scissor blade he scraped a specimen of the rust on to a slide before turning his attention to the piece of wood. He was about to cross to a drawer to search for a saw or bone-cutters to scrape off a sample when he noticed small yellow fungus spores on the wood. He picked up his scalpel and touched the wood and the scalpel sank through it as easily as it would through ripe cheese.

'Everything's degenerating,' he muttered, looking up from his microscope, 'everything that the taxidermist's evil has touched, the wood, the wire, the cotton stuffing. I'll bet . . .' He paused and with a pair of tweezers and the scalpel he trimmed some fibres from the creature's shirt

336

and examined them under the microscope. 'Yes, even the clothes they wore are rotting away. But why? These are inanimate objects, they shouldn't react against the magic.'

He frowned and turned towards the scout. He studied the strange cloth and wire figure who stood before him in his dark blue uniform jacket laced with silver braid and his dirty travel-stained breeches and riding boots.

'And why aren't you degenerating? Why aren't any of the other exhibits who survived the fire rotting away like this? That same magic that resurrected those creatures also touched you.'

The scout shrugged and turned an anxious ear towards the open doorway of the laboratory. The sound of furious hammering echoed through the building as the beasts attacked the outer door.

'It wasn't the same,' he answered slowly. 'The magic reflected through the museum windows, purging out the evil, stirring only the good, the essence of our souls that still dwelt in the blood and sweat that lingered in the fabric of our uniforms.'

'But the animals?' Dec countered quickly. 'How would you explain them away? The taxidermist's evil touched them directly, they were the first things that he tried his magic on, yet those birds who survived the fire have not fallen from the sky with their wings rotting away, have they?'

The scout slowly shook his head. 'No, but nor do they have souls.'

'Souls?' Dec muttered in exasperation as he turned back to his microscope. 'They are the only pieces of this jigsaw puzzle that I can't put under a microscope,' and he kicked back his stool and paced backwards and forwards the length of the field station, oblivious to the thudding sounds of attack, the snarls and shrieks clearly heard through the broken windows.

Dawn was beginning to lighten the sky. The first birds stirred in the undergrowth and the vile creatures drew back to the trees. The telephone suddenly rang and made Dec jump.

'Thank God you're safe,' he answered with relief the moment he heard Tuppence's voice.

'We got through those creatures easily,' she said but she couldn't disguise the exhaustion in her voice. 'Have you found anything, any way to destroy the magic yet?' she asked, brushing his questions aside.

'I don't know yet, I'm still working on it. So far I've dissected the arm of one of those creatures we hacked off while they were breaking through the security fence. You know the most weird thing is that the inside of the thing, the skeleton and the stuffing, is rotting away almost as fast as the skin. So I'm growing cultures, reproducing all the spores, everything that is degenerating, even the rusty steel skeleton. Perhaps I can reproduce enough and blend them all together, even adding some of the less dangerous bacterial specimens we keep safely locked away. I might be able to create a virus powerful enough to destroy them. But . . .' Dec hesitated, 'but I'm worried about releasing such a cocktail without doing tests for side effects.'

'Dec, listen to me,' Tuppence hissed urgently over the phone. 'There just isn't time for doubts or tests or second thoughts. These monsters are about to tear this place down. I'm sure they're only waiting for darkness to fall.'

She paused, drawing in a shallow breath, then brought the mouthpiece closer to her lips and whispered, 'I don't care what the Colonel says about this place being a fortress, or how many riflemen he has packed in here to protect me. I've seen what those creatures can do with their bare

338

hands and there are dozens of them gathering outside, and the roof tops are crowded with black crows. I'm so afraid that I'm never going to get out of here alive. I'm scared I'm never going to see you again. You've got to make that stuff, do you hear me? You've just got to.'

Before Dec could answer a shrill buzzer sounded in the laboratory.

'What the hell is that?' Tuppence cried in alarm.

'It's to warn me that the first batch of cultures is ready,' he answered.

'Will you do it? Will you make that stuff up, please?' she implored.

Dec hesitated. He loved her so much that he would die for her, but to concoct and release a deadly virus, to be the architect of a new bubonic plague that could kill millions, thousands of millions, of innocent people – that he could not do. He forced his lips to move, to give her hope. He formed the words slowly.

'Yes, I'll do it. I love you. I'll be at the doors of the Watchgate with it long before night falls.'

And he rattled the receiver down into its cradle before the tremor in his voice gave away his lie. He buried his head in his hands and wept with despair. He felt so helpless, so utterly helpless.

The alarm on the incubator was beginning to give him a headache. It seemed to have been going on for hours while he sat there staring at the telephone, trying to think of something, anything, that would destroy those monsters. The more he went over the whole nightmare the more insignificant was the power of his paltry logic, looming as it did in the shadow of the taxidermist's dark magic. There was no rhyme or reason, no explanation, for the rapid degeneration in those creatures. Nothing that his microscope or all his knowledge could give. And the tenuous suggestion gnawing at the edge of his mind was that it was the souls of the stolen bodies that were reacting against the magic, setting good against evil. It seemed ludicrous.

Irritably he reached across, flicked off the buzzer and pulled open the door. He cried out and staggered backwards, upsetting his stool, as a fine, rainbow-coloured dust cascaded out of the incubator. 'Look! Look at this!' he cried out, making the scout hurry across to him.

'I'm never going to understand this magic as long as I live. Look, look what has happened to those cultures. I only put them in here just before dawn.'

The scout picked up a handful of the dust despite Dec's warning cry that it might be harmful and let it trickle down between his fingers. Crossing to the remains of the dissected arm he scattered a few grains on it. The arm twitched violently and a foul stench filled the room. The skin hissed and crackled and began to dissolve. The wire skeleton shivered and began to crumble into bright orange flakes of rust. The cotton stuffing rose in tiny wind-blown clouds and drifted away while the central core of wood creaked and fell into worm-eaten splinters. The reaction started by the brightly coloured powder, which was as gritty as volcanic sand, stopped as quickly as it had begun. Dec prodded at the remains of the arm, turning it over with the blade of his scalpel. He realized by the stiffness of its movements that it was now nothing more than a dry, lifeless husk. He prodded it again and it collapsed as easily as a puffball in autumn, banishing the core of evil that had briefly dwelt inside it.

'That powder has destroyed it!' he whispered in awe as he stared down at the fine grey film of dust that now peppered the empty dissecting table where the hand had lain.

Hesitantly he reached out and touched the rainbow-coloured dust. It felt hot and tingled on his fingertips and billowed up to envelop his hand, momentarily clinging to him before it fell away. He shuddered and rubbed his hands together as if to wash the magic dust away.

He stared at the scout and whispered, 'How the hell could that have happened?'

The scout smiled and lifted his arm to show Dec where he had cut away a fragment of his sleeve. 'The essence of my soul dwells in my uniform. I put a fragment of the cloth amongst those culture dishes.'

Dec suddenly laughed. 'The power of good, or whatever it is that dwells within you, has destroyed those evil organisms in the arm. Now we really have got something to destroy those creatures. Come on, help me transfer it into one of these metal canisters. We can then ride to the Watchgate before it is too late.'

The scout hesitated and looked down at the small heap of brightly coloured dust before he spoke. 'But how many monsters will that handful of dust destroy? I fear that its power will only last for a moment. It needs to be strengthened by a thousand souls and made more vital, more magical.'

'Well it's all we've got and it's better than nothing,' Dec answered.

Picking up a large tablespoon that he occasionally used to measure out specimens he began to try to spoon the fine powder into the canister. It billowed up, evading the spoon, swirling and dancing, its brilliant colours weaving and blending together.

All day Dec worked at scooping the dust into the canister, spooning it up grain by grain in a slow shifting river of colour.

The sun had set before he straightened up and screwed the lid firmly into place. He smiled wearily at the scout who moved towards the door and his waiting mount. Dec stared at the horseman, his muffled words echoing backwards and forwards, touching half-forgotten memories. 'If only the souls of the dead could touch this dust and strengthen it for us.'

Tuppence's sense of foreboding deepened as the long day wore on and the shadows lengthened towards evening. She had felt tense and jumped at the slightest whisper or movement amongst the ranks of riflemen who now crowded the Watchgate to defend her. It wasn't the bone-weary tiredness of the breakneck gallop back to the city, or the crush of soldiers all around her now that stretched her nerves to breaking point. It was the sense of impending doom, the utter certainty that those monstrous creatures would attack now that darkness was falling.

The Colonel echoed her fears and showed it by the meticulous way he had prepared the Watchgate against attack. Deploying the remnants of the cavalrymen who had survived the fire in the museum, positioning them in the alleyways and courtyards that flanked the Watchgate, he ordered them to stay out of sight and to stand their ground to the last. Inside the Watchgate he built a huge barricade of sandbags and empty ammunition boxes within the lower room and positioned the riflemen and their loaders in one huge curving redoubt from the sandbags back to the cavernous inglenook. Some were crouching, some kneeling and some standing, and every round of ammunition had been issued and shared out.

Tuppence shivered and looked at her watch. Being apart from Dec was eating her up. She had never felt like this about anybody before, never realized how much loving, really loving, someone could hurt and gnaw away at the pit of your stomach, churning you up and making you feel alone and helplessly vulnerable. She had tried to phone Harry but there was no answer and there was no one else she could talk to.

'Dec, Dec, where the hell are you, you're cutting it real fine,' she muttered to herself, squeezing between the press of soldiers for the hundredth time to peer out of the small leaded windows into the lighted street outside.

'Hey, Colonel, quickly, come here,' she hissed in alarm. 'Look, look out there, the street's completely deserted. Those creatures have vanished. Where the hell have they gone? Do you think they've gone far?'

Before she could utter another word the rending crash of metal upon metal and the sharp shatter of breaking glass echoed up and down the hill and a stench of burning rubber overwhelmed them. Colonel Hawkesbury scrambled up and over the barricade and squeezed his way through the doorway, only to retreat hastily, slamming and locking the door behind him before he called out. 'Those creatures have barricaded both ends of the hill with burning cars. We're completely cut off. And they are swarming towards us!'

'What about Dec? How is he going to get through now?' Tuppence cried in panic as she heard the clatter of hoof-beats and rousing shouts from the remnants of the lancers as they gathered before the door of the Watchgate, lowering their lances to make one last desperate charge.

Tuppence watched the horsemen surge forward against the hideous mass of advancing beasts. 'No! No!' she wept, covering her eyes as their reckless charge broke against the swarming creatures as easily as white water against granite. The horses reared and were hurled crashing to the ground. Their riders were torn from the saddles. Single shots rang out and sabres rose and fell and briefly the monsters' onslaught hesitated before it swept over them, trampling them underfoot as they closed remorselessly on the Watchgate.

'Front rank ready!' the Colonel thundered in a moment of awful silence before the creatures hammered on the door and began to tear it from its hinges.

Tuppence heard the rattle of rifle bolts as she hurried between the riflemen and took her place in the corner of the inglenook.

'You won't take me easily, you bastards,' she hissed, snatching up the Spencer carbine and working the bolt, her fingers slipping and trembling with terror.

The first assault shook the Watchgate to its foundations. The hinges bent and the door frame began to splinter. The door of giants shook and groaned as the full fury of the dark magic crashed against it, cutting deep into it. The windows shattered into thousands of tiny fragments. Never in all its history had the Watchgate suffered such terrible damage. Plaster began to fall from the ceiling and long cracks fractured its walls. A wind began to rise in the inglenook, ruffling Tuppence's hair, but it was less than a summer breeze against the dreadful power of the taxidermist's magic. Suddenly the door burst inwards. Monsters' hands clawed it from its hinges, twisting it backwards and out across the pavement. Hideous beasts swarmed in through the doorway and over the barricades.

'Front rank – fire! Second rank – fire! Third rank – fire!' shouted the Colonel.

The crackle of rifle shots, the screams and snarls of the swarming beasts and dense cordite smoke filled the Watchgate, but the barrage of bullets barely halted them for a moment. Tuppence fired into the hideous advancing mass at point-blank range, but nothing was going to stop them. Her bullets ploughed through their rotten stinking flesh as easily as a knife through cheese and still they drew closer. Scrambling backwards she squeezed the trigger again. Nothing happened. She worked the bolt, realizing that the magazine was empty, but she had no time. She hurled the gun at the nearest beast. Her elbow was on the telephone in the bread oven, which fell with a clatter at her feet. She snatched at it and desperately dialled, she had to hear Dec's voice. She crouched down away from the putrefying creatures who were reaching out, clawing at her, closing their hands about her arms. Their stench almost overwhelmed her, she gasped down the receiver, 'Dec! Dec, for God's sake! Those monsters are tearing the place apart. They've broken in. Dec . . .'

Dec had been about to mount his horse when the telephone rang. He dropped the canister and ran back into the laboratory. The line crackled and Dec heard her call to him and then he heard a beast's snarling roar. Then the line went dead. He furiously rattled the phone's cradle, dialled the operator and asked her to reconnect them at once. He turned, white-faced, to the horseman, his lips taut and trembling, and whispered, 'It is too late. Those beasts have overrun the Watchgate.'

The telephone rang again and he snatched it up. The operator's level voice informed him that there was a fault on the Watchgate line and the number was now unattainable, but they would send an engineer out first thing in the morning.

Dec collapsed on to his knees, his head in his hands. Her last desperate cry for help, the sound of splintering timbers, the shouts of the soldiers and the echo of gunfire in the Watchgate all jumbled up with the snarls and screams of her attackers and filled his head. His eyes brimmed with tears that began to trickle down his cheeks, escaping between his fingers and making the few fine grains of rainbow dust that still clung to him shimmer in the darkness.

'I should never have allowed her to ride on alone,' he wept as the sound of her voice grew fainter in his head and bleak emptiness, the hopeless despair of knowing that he would never see her beautiful face again or watch the laughter light her eyes, or hear her voice or smell that haunting scent that she wore swept coldly over him, gnawing and eating its way to his heart. He would have sunk lower and curled himself up to allow the tragedy of her death to overwhelm him but the scout's strong hands gripped his shoulders and made him look up. There were bright tears in the horseman's eyes and he fought to control his voice.

'There will be a time to mourn and to tend the flowers on her grave, a time to kneel and remember every precious moment when your lives touched, but first we must ride on the edge of the night wind and avenge her. We must destroy every creature that the foul taxidermist resurrected.'

Dec climbed to his feet and gathering up the metal canister without a word he strode to where the horses were tethered near the main doors. Tears were still trickling down his cheeks but his despair was turning to rage and his hatred for the taxidermist grew as he mounted and rode out into the night.

The creatures that had been lying in wait for them during the daylight hours swarmed out of the undergrowth as they left the testing station. Dec reined his horse to a walk and began to unscrew the top of the canister. He refused to run from these beasts any more, he was going to begin his terrible revenge right here and now.

'No, not yet. Look! The church on the hill!' the scout suddenly hissed, riding up beside him and pointing up to the squat bulky tower that showed as a black silhouette against the starlight on the rim of the valley. 'There will be records – books of the dead. Their names will be written. You can call up their souls to strengthen that precious dust that our Lady of the Watchgate bought us the time to create with her life.'

'No! I will avenge her sacrifice here – right now,' Dec shouted. The scout rode straight at him, barging Dec's mount aside as he snatched the canister from his hands and galloped away with it up across the steep valley.

'I will not allow your anger to squander our Lady's sacrifice,' he called back across his shoulder as he rode into the shadows of the church tower.

'Damn you! Damn you to hell!' Dec cursed, grabbing at the reins and savagely kicking at his horse's flanks.

He galloped straight through the mass of lumbering creatures, after the scout, and cantered through the church gates, pulling up in front of the porch. He noticed there were faint lights in the tall stained-glass windows. He dismounted and ran through the porch, throwing open the large wooden doors. He would have cursed the scout and rushed at him where he knelt halfway down the nave but he hesitated, the atmosphere of the church overwhelming him, melting away his anger. He went down on one knee and drew the sign of the cross in the air in front of him. This was a place of sanctuary, a hallowed place where evil could not walk.

Two tall rows of beeswax candles set in ornately wrought-iron holders lined the nave, softly illuminating the plain whitewashed walls with their flickering light. Stone angels guarded the transept, their outstretched feathery wings forming a perfect arch, while white marble and polished wooden effigies of knights and long-dead warrior kings lay head to toe in silent repose along the outer aisles, their faded battle emblems hanging above the altar screen in secret dusty shadows.

'I've never been in here before but this must be the crusader chapel that belongs to the castle,' Dec whispered as he stopped beside the scout and looked up into the dark vaulted roof.

'And those must be the books of the dead,' the scout answered, holding out the canister for Dec to take and leading him forward through the altar screen. Several heavy leather books bound in gold and silver lay upon an oak lectern guarded by an eagle with outstretched wings and talons that cast a dark protective shadow.

Dec set the opened canister on the stone floor beside the lectern and opened the oldest of the books carefully, turning its yellowing parchment pages with great care. They were beautifully illuminated in the left-hand margins with painted capitals and illustrations of the crusader knights and their soldiers, spearmen and archers who had fought and died with them in the Holy Land. Dec leaned forward and studied the fine mediaeval script, realizing that each page must contain hundreds of names.

He looked up and whispered, 'There are so many people recorded here, but how on earth can I call up their souls? What do I say to invoke them?'

Howls and snarls from the graveyard outside suddenly broke the hallowed silence, drowning Dec's whispers. He spun round at the clatter of horseshoes as the last of the horses were led into the safety of the vestibule and he heard the main door of the church slam shut. A great crash shook the doors as the howling outside rose into shrieks of rage and the creatures hammered on the doors and hurled headstones at the tall stained-glass windows.

'This is sacred ground, they cannot enter,' the scout whispered.

'Look out!' Dec cried, snatching at the horseman's arm and pulling him clear as the beautiful window depicting the death of Edward the Martyr at Corfe Gate shattered above their heads, showering them with a thousand coloured fragments of stained glass.

The scout looked up at the remains of the shattered window, its twisted latticework of lead showing black against the starlight, and he tilted his head to one side. 'Listen,' he whispered, 'those monsters outside are smashing open the rows of stone tombs. They are looking for a way into the vaults that lie beneath this church. I can hear the snap and crunch as they trample on the bones of the dead. Surely their evil desecration will wake the souls of everyone buried here. Be quick and read out their names from the books. Harness the power that has been stirred up before it is too late.'

Dec swallowed and cleared his throat. He clutched at the edge of the lectern and in a loud clear voice started to read out their names.

'Thomas Rochford, Knight to King John, Cuthbert Guthlac, Squire, Rowland Crowland, Master Armourer, I have great need of the power of good that dwells within your souls. We must put an end to the dark evil that the taxidermist from Goats Head Valley has awoken and destroy those vile creatures that desecrate this holy place.'

Dec paused as the stone floor beneath his feet trembled and he looked around fearfully. Strains of mediaeval music whispered in the tall organ pipes, the candle flames began to dance and flicker, footsteps echoed and scraped in the outer aisles, closing in around the book of names.

'Read on, read on,' the scout urged. 'Whatever happens keep on reading the names.'

Dec read on, almost burying his head in the book. The air above his head suddenly filled with soft sighs, forgotten

349

whispers and murmured pledges from dusty days long, long ago. The clink of armour, the rattle of chains and measured monastic chants swelled and the strains of music rose louder, its tempo racing faster and faster, drawing the souls of the dead up, up in a cyclone of sparkling light and thundering sound, up into the rafter beams. The stone-flagged floor beneath Dec's feet suddenly cracked and spider-fine lines spread out to touch each name engraved in brass, lead and stone within that holy place.

In the moment of complete silence that followed Dec snatched up the open canister, held it high above his head and shouted, 'Let the power of good destroy the taxidermist's evil.'

And with the roar of a cascading waterfall the souls of the dead poured down out of the shadowy rafter beams into the narrow top of the canister. It trembled and shook in his hands and glowed white hot and yet it felt ice cold to the touch. Dec lowered the canister and peered cautiously into it. The rainbow dust now seethed and boiled, each speck or grain of substance shimmering with incandescent light.

'It is now time to ride and attack the taxidermist's evil,' the scout whispered, kneeling for a moment before the altar which was spread with the simple crusader's banner of a red cross on a white cloth, set with two golden candlesticks.

'And seek our full measure of revenge,' answered Dec, fighting back his tears as memories of Tuppence welled up. Her face, her smile, seemed to be everywhere around him, haunting the shadows of the now silent church.

A blood-curdling howl split the air. Dec spun round, his eyes narrowing with hate, and following the sound he plunged his hand into the seething iridescent substance within the canister. It tingled warmly and when he withdrew his fingers they sparkled and burned, dripping with white fire.

'My own tragedy can wait, I have all eternity to grieve. First, before we ride, I will destroy the evil that has defiled this hallowed place.'

Saying this he strode through the church flinging open the outer doors and walked alone amongst the towering, lumbering creatures, sweeping his blazing hand across their faces. Screaming, they fell on to their knees, clutching and tearing at their hideous putrefying faces. Their skin hissed and bubbled and dissolved away in a reeking stench, their clothes rotted and dropped off, exposing skeletons of iron and steel that crumbled into rusty flakes. In moments they lay amongst the broken tombstones, nothing more than empty windblown husks.

Dec walked quietly back into the church and knelt before the altar.

'It is done,' he whispered. 'Now we ride.'

18

A Shimmering Rain of
Destruction

'We must reach the city before dawn breaks,' the scout shouted across to Dec against the rushing wind. 'We must destroy all the evil, everything that the taxidermist has created with his dark magic before he has the chance to scatter his creatures.'

Dec looked over to the horizon of low hills in the east where the first hint of morning was beginning to lighten the sky. 'We're never going to make it,' he shouted back against the thunder of the horses' hooves as they crossed a narrow lane and leaped over the broken-down remains of the boundary fence of a deserted wartime airfield.

The scout began to lead them across the rough tussocks of grass and weeds that had grown up in thickening ridges in the cracks and breaks in the concrete runway. Dec glanced to his left as they galloped past a cluster of dilapidated overgrown huts and a derelict windowless control tower and saw the hulk of a crashed American bomber. The right undercarriage wheel was collapsed and its rudder creaked and swung in the dawn wind, its crumpled wings and propeller blades black against the lightening sky.

'If only that had wings I could fly there and scatter this magical dust across the city,' he shouted angrily at the wrecked aircraft.

The scout turned in the saddle, stared at the hulk of the aeroplane and then veered across Dec's path, shouting at him to stop as he reined his own horse to a halt. The horseman looked doubtfully at the wreck and asked, 'What monstrous kind of bird was that?'

Dec laughed bitterly. The great race against morning was lost, dawn was starting to grey the concrete surface of the overgrown runway and the first birds were beginning to sing in the hedgerows. The taxidermist and all his evil were going to escape despite all their efforts, and Tuppence's death would go unavenged.

'It was an aeroplane,' he muttered wearily. 'An American B-17, a Flying Fortress. Men once flew in it and fought battles and dropped bombs over Germany from the air, but that was years ago, before it crashed beside the runway. Come on, it's of no use to us now, we must ride on.'

'No, wait,' the scout called as Dec began to ride ahead. 'You still have that fragment of the Hand of Glory, don't you?'

Dec halted again and reached in his pocket. He found it and nodded as he held it up.

'Then try and use the magic. You told me Theopus said the magic could resurrect good as well as evil. You must try it,' the scout insisted, reaching into his sabretache for a slow match and tinder-box.

He struck the match and shielded it with his hand. 'Resurrect this bird of war and use it to fly over the city. It would be the best, no, the only, chance we have of stopping the taxidermist from dispersing his evil, and when you scatter the magic dust it will fall like a rain of retribution.'

Dec laughed harshly and shook his head. 'Are you mad? It would take more than magic to resurrect that twisted hulk of metal and get it off the ground. Look at that broken undercarriage and the tyres, they've rotted and fallen away from the rims of the wheels. The right wing is

buckled from where it hit the ground and the propeller blades are all bent and twisted out of line.'

Dec paused, drew in a shallow breath and shivered. Dawn had brought with it a chilly, clinging ground mist that was drifting across the airfield, enveloping them with its cold fingers, making their horses stamp, fidget and fret to be on the move again. The white mist boiled up against the black derelict hulk of the Flying Fortress, weaving in and out of the hundreds of bullet holes that peppered its crumpled metal skin, skirting a thin veil of modesty over the faint half-naked woman that was painted there and swirling in and out through the shattered cockpit windows, softening the sharp outlines of its dereliction.

'That last flight home must have been a hell of a ride. I can promise you, it will never fly again,' Dec said sadly, shaking his head and gathering up the reins to ride on.

'But you have already witnessed the power of the magic. You have seen what it can accomplish,' the scout cried angrily. 'Why doubt it now?' and he thrust the spluttering match in front of Dec's face demanding that he light the fragment of hand.

'Light it now and chant the spell. Light it for our Lady of the Watchgate. Use the taxidermist's magic against him and avenge her death.'

Dec reached out and took the slow match from the horseman's hand. The memory of Tuppence trying to snatch the Hand of Glory from the window sill flooded back to him as he rode forward to within a foot of the huge wreck. He held up the tiny fragile flame that burned bright white in the dark misty dawn shadows and touched it to the thumb. He began to chant the spell with trembling lips.

'Burn, burn and sparkle bright,

O Hand of Glory shed thy light,
Let those it touches start awake,
Let those who see it my bidding take . . .'

Dense, choking yellow smoke was rising from the tip of the mummified thumb. It touched the skin of the aircraft and rolled across its surface, vanishing into every crack and fracture.

'The spell! Finish the spell,' the scout whispered as the huge derelict hulk of the Flying Fortress shivered from end to end.

Dec almost dropped the smouldering finger as he heard the undercarriage struts creak and then watched them straighten and rise out of the swirling mist beneath the right-hand inboard engine. He chanted on, stumbling over the words as he tried to remember how to chant them backwards to finish the spell.

Suddenly the right-hand engine's propeller slowly turned over once and stopped. A small rectangular hatch in the belly of the plane beneath the cockpit swung open and a head wearing a battered peaked baseball cap appeared upside down.

A rich American voice shouted, 'Hey buddy, did you call us out of eternity to go some place?'

'Yes,' Dec answered, his voice dying away as the American's head turned towards him and he saw his hideously burnt face. It was neither solid nor transparent, it was covered in transluscent raw flesh and blackened, burnt skin. Broken veins and withered tissue clung on to the skull and appeared and disappeared, melting and vanishing only to reappear again moments later in vivid detail, filling the space between the baseball cap and a set of headphones. The pilot saw the look of horror on Dec's face and laughed.

He reached out a gloved hand towards him. 'You'll have

to ignore the way we look but it was as hot as hell's kitchen in here when we crashed and we've been a long time dead, pal. Now what's the mission?'

Dec hesitated, the undercarriage struts that had righted themselves creaked and swayed. 'Will this thing fly?'

The pilot grinned. 'Sure, as sure as eggs fry on the pavements of hell!'

'You must trust in the magic,' the scout urged as Dec rode reluctantly up beneath the open hatchway and reached up to grasp the pilot's charred hands. They felt strong and firm and hoisted him easily up through the small hatchway.

'Don't forget the canister,' the scout called, riding up beneath the open hatch as Dec's feet vanished. He thrust the tin up into the pilot's waiting hands and pirouetted his horse away.

'Aren't you coming with me?' Dec shouted down through the hatch as the pilot closed it.

The scout rode quickly back to where the rest of the small company of horsemen stood on the edge of the runway and waited until Dec appeared at the cockpit window before he shouted, 'We will follow you into the city and fan out to scour the countryside for any trace of those creatures should they escape.'

'But . . .' Dec began helplessly as the troop of horsemen cantered away towards the rising sun.

'Remember, trust in the magic,' the scout shouted across his shoulder.

'OK, buddy, I'm Frank Withbeach, your pilot, and here's my co-pilot Dan Carnal. I don't think your magic has managed to resurrect the rest of my crew so, where's it gonna be?'

The voice of the pilot made Dec turn away from the shattered window and stare at the bullet-riddled instrument panel with its ghostly pilots sitting there in the cramped cockpit. It smelled of burnt flesh, sweat, coffee, leather and stale cigars, and the sharp tang and haze of cordite smoke and hydraulic oil hung in the fuselage.

'Norwich,' Dec answered flatly, 'I need us to fly low over the old part of the city so that I can release the dust from this canister. But I don't see how this plane is ever going to get off the ground.'

Both airmen laughed and the one in the pilot's seat rolled the blackened stub of a cigar between his teeth and drawled, 'Like that rider said, mister, you called us out of eternity with your magic, now you just gotta trust in it. Hold on tight, let's see if we can start this old bird up.'

Dec moved back to a small work surface cluttered with parachutes and harness directly behind the pilot's seat and braced himself as the two airmen started to run through their checks. Frank suddenly laughed and tapped the oil temperature gauge directly in front of him. The needles for three of the four engines were touching 100 degrees and their cylinder-head temperatures showed 300 degrees.

'These engines are hotter than hell!'

Dan nodded. 'Yup, and there's no hydraulic pressure.' He leaned forward and tapped the hydraulic oil pressure gauge but the needle was firmly stuck at zero.

Frank grinned and swept his gloved hand across the banks of smashed instruments. 'OK, so everything's shot to hell. So let's see how good this magic really is. You ready to fly, mister?' he asked, twisting in his seat and turning his ghostly, burnt, cigar-chewing face towards Dec.

'Yes,' Dec whispered trying to swallow his fear. Blind terror was rising in his throat.

The pilot turned back and in a steady voice called out, 'OK, here we go. Fire guard left and right. Master switches on. Number three inboard engine, switch ready, booster pump on.'

He glanced out through the shattered cockpit window, his grin widening as the inboard propeller began slowly to turn. The engine whirred, he counted six blades turning and flicked down the ignition switch of number three engine. It coughed twice. Black smoke puffed out of the engine vents and then it caught and roared into life, before it stuttered and almost died away. The plane shuddered from end to end and Dec clutched at the metal table top as the pilot reached across to his right, trimmed the mixture lever to rich and locked the gills fully open. He listened anxiously as the engine note settled to a steady roar.

'Hell, what do ya think of that! Number three's running as sweet as a bird even though the gauges show it to be hotter than the devil's breath,' he shouted back at Dec, watching the propeller blades of the outboard engine turn over.

He again counted six blades before he fired it up. The plane lurched as the engine caught and roared into motion. Black clouds of exhaust smoke poured across the wing.

'Number two inboard switches on. Ignition,' Dan shouted, looking to his left as the third engine stuttered and burst into life.

He watched the propeller of the last outboard engine turn over through six blades and shouted, 'Ignition.' Now the aircraft was shuddering violently and straining forward. The pilots ran up the engines one by one, throttled back, set the propeller pitch and released the brakes. Weaving gracefully from side to side so that the pilots could see where they were going while the nose pointed up in the air the Flying Fortress slowly rolled along the overgrown runway. When it reached the end of the concrete it turned towards the east where the rim of the sun was bright upon the horizon. For a moment both pilots looked back at the deserted huts, the shell of the control tower and the bare earth and tangle of weeds where the wreckage of their Flying Fortress had lain for over forty-five years.

'Well I reckon we've haunted this place long enough,' Frank laughed, gripping the inboard throttles with his right hand.

Dan nodded. 'Yup, anything beats hanging around here for the rest of eternity,' and he gripped the outboard throttles with his left hand and together they pushed the levers forward.

The engine noise rose to a thundering crescendo and black smoke poured out of the exhaust. The battered, bullet-riddled hulk began to roll forward, accelerating faster and faster towards the rising sun. Dec screwed up his eyes and hung on tight as the tail rose. The plane bumped and rattled, the wind howled and whistled through the broken windows, the noise from the engines deafened him. He was waiting for the crash as it lurched its way down the runway. Suddenly he felt the floor beneath his feet lift. He looked up out of the cockpit window. They were airborne.

'The city's dead ahead,' the pilot shouted back to Dec over the pulsating roar of the engines. 'We'll be over the target area in under five minutes.'

'Where can I empty the canister from?' Dec shouted back.

'Use the bomb aimer's window. The nose cone's got more holes in it than a pepper pot. I'll make a couple of low passes over the old part of the city and collect chimney pots while you get yourself in position. You just holler up when you're ready.'

Dec scrambled down into the belly of the Fortress beneath the two pilots, crawled through the low companionway and up the two steps into the bomb aimer's position, the canister tucked firmly beneath his arm. The wind was howling in through the shattered nose cone. The aircraft banked sharply and he had to hang on tightly to the twisted remains of the bombsight to keep his position. He looked down through the shattered window and saw that they were turning, flying low across the summit of Gibbet Hill. The finger-fine upper branches of the solitary oak were scraping and scratching the underside of the right-hand wing. A haze of white smoke curled up from a blazing funeral pyre beside the oak, momentarily engulfing the Fortress. Dec briefly glimpsed a cluster of tall figures below, robed in gowns of silver and gold; one of them raised a hand in salute, then as the plane rose diminished until they were mere specks to be lost to sight, drowned in the black smoke trails.

'Theopus,' Dec frowned, moving the canister into position. He was sure that the tall figure with the flowing white hair was the magician from the magic bookshop. And then he remembered the wizard's promise that the council of masters or whatever they called themselves was going to destroy all trace of that necromancer by cremating the body where it had been gibbeted and buried beside that oak tree over two hundred years ago. Dec's lips thinned and tightened and his knuckles whitened with determination. Nothing of the taxidermist or his dark magic would remain.

'Target one minute!' the co-pilot shouted down to him, making him start and look down to the rows of suburban houses, the maze of roads and culs-de-sac and the tree-lined avenues, heavy with their summer foliage, casting giant early morning shadows across the neat lawns and flowerbeds. He glimpsed the River Wensum away to his left, a silver thread that wound its way into the city through the still-sleeping countryside.

'Target thirty seconds,' Dan shouted down to him.

Dec felt the Fortress shudder and the engine note change as they began their final approach. He unscrewed the cap from the top of the canister with trembling fingers and braced himself, ready to release the dust.

'Jesus Christ!' he cried as they were suddenly enveloped in a pall of black smoke. The Fortress banked and the shell of the museum swept below them. He glimpsed the front of the Watchgate, the ground littered with fallen cavalrymen and dead horses, the door of giants twisted and torn from its hinges, its gaping doorway piled high with the broken bodies of the riflemen who had defended Tuppence to the very last. The hill was empty, blocked off at either end by huge towering barricades of wrecked and burned-out cars. The Fortress banked sharply round for its approach to Lobster Lane and Goats Head Alley and he saw fire crews cutting their way through the barricades and armed police climbing across the adjoining roof tops.

The plane levelled out and swept low over the ruined tower of Cripplegate Church. Flocks of black crows, owls and magpies swarmed up from the roofs of the courtyard and flew into the path of the Fortress. In that moment, as the plane's shadow covered the courtyard, Dec saw the hideous upturned faces of the beasts that the taxidermist had created. They were packed in the yard, shoulder to shoulder, snarling and shouting up at the window of the preparation room. They cowered down as the shadow of the aircraft swept over them, and hid their faces. Dec shook the canister. The incandescent dust swirled and scattered out to be fanned by the propellers' downdraught and fell, a shimmering rain of destruction.

They had barely overflown the courtyard before the birds attacked in a black thundercloud of hatred. The Fortress shuddered from end to end, its engines coughed and stuttered, their propeller blades churning out clouds of black feathers. Dec covered his face with his arm as the birds smashed against the nose cone and he frantically shook out the last grains of shimmering dust over the hordes of creatures that crowded every alleyway and dark archway that led off Lobster Lane. The plane lurched from side to side, losing height as Frank cursed and put on full power. The engines screamed and inch by tortuous inch they began to climb, ploughing their way up through the scattering flock, sucking the birds in droves into their propeller blades and chopping them into millions of tiny floating pieces. Dec flung the empty canister aside and clung on to the twisted bombsight, looking down to the utter devastation in the courtyard and beyond it to Lobster Lane. The creatures were clawing at each other to escape. Their faces were melting, their skeletons collapsing in seething, bubbling mounds of rust. In moments they became brittle husks that, as they touched, broke apart and fell away into nothing but a fine grey dust.

'The taxidermist!' Dec suddenly shouted as he saw him at the window of his preparation room. The old man was cursing, his face purple with rage, and he was shaking his fist at the departing aeroplane.

Dec realized in that instant that it didn't matter how many creatures they destroyed, the madman could begin all over again if he was allowed to escape. Dec scrambled back up behind the pilots. He stabbed a finger frantically down towards the courtyard.

'That bastard's going to get away if I don't stop him. I've got to get down there now before he escapes, I've got to.'

Frank glanced back at him and chewed thoughtfully on his cigar, his grin broadening. He was getting to like this guy.

'There's a parachute right there beside you, mister. All you gotta do is climb into the harness, buckle it up and jump.'

'Jump?' Dec whispered, paling as he looked at the crumpled dirty parachute that had been packed away over forty-five years ago.

'Sure thing, mister,' Dan laughed, getting out of his seat and gathering up the harness, holding it out for Dec to step into. 'There's nothing to it, I've jumped loads of times.'

'But the silk, everything must have rotted away years ago.'

Frank levelled the Fortress out at 1,500 feet and looked out of his side window. 'That horseman back at the airfield told you to trust in the magic. Well if you're gonna jump, now's the time to do just that. There's an escape hatch at the back of the fuselage on the right.'

'Just jump,' Dan laughed. 'You'll be OK. Shut your eyes and count to ten and then pull like heck on that ring, that one there,' and with his ghostly hand he pointed to the D-ring.

Dec swallowed. He had no choice, not if he wanted to catch that taxidermist and stop him. He tightened the harness and reached out and clasped both the pilots' hands in his. They felt ice cold; he shivered.

'I want to thank you both . . .' he began but Frank cut him short.

'You wanna jump, mister? You had better be quick, I don't know how long this bucket of bullet holes is gonna stay in one piece.'

Dec turned and scrambled back through the dark body of the aircraft, tripping and stumbling over the tangles of loose wire, the cables and the ammunition belts of the mid-gunners as he searched for the escape hatch. His nightmare,

364

the one where he fell out of an aeroplane without a parachute, came flooding back to him, and he remembered waking up night after night in a cold sweat. It seemed to belong to another life, one that he had lived before all this had begun, but he reached up to reassure himself and he felt the webbing straps of the harness.

'I must be crazy,' he muttered, finding and turning the handles of the escape hatch and kicking it open.

Below him the city looked so far away. The roof tops were gleaming in the early morning sunlight, the narrow lanes and alleys still hidden in deep shadows. He picked out the blackened shell of the museum and the sun-bright roof of the Watchgate and his eyes misted over with sadness. Memories of Tuppence welled up inside him and he felt alone. What did it matter if he lived or died? He threw himself out through the hatchway and tumbled over and over. He stopped with a sudden jolt and heard the sharp crack of the parachute open above him. He didn't remember counting to ten or pulling the rip cord. The streets below looked closer now, sharpening in detail. He looked up, following the sound of the Flying Fortress. It had turned west and was vanishing in the mist.

He looked down again and saw that he was rapidly approaching the roof tops. The morning breeze was taking him over Goats Head Alley. He remembered reading somewhere that you could direct a parachute by pulling on the strings. Perhaps he could manoeuvre the thing and land in the courtyard. Gingerly he reached up and took a tug with his right hand on one of the strings. The parachute silk tore along two of the seams. He held his breath and screwed his eyes shut but nothing happened. He looked down. He was only yards from the taxidermist's roof and rushing towards it.

'The magic. I've got to believe in the magic,' he cried

and he hit the roof with such a crash that he smashed his way through the red tiles and their battens, fell through the lath and plaster ceiling and landed in a cloud of white dust, sprawling helpless on to the floor of the preparation room. The impact almost knocked him senseless.

Dimly, through the pain, he heard the taxidermist ranting and screaming at him for destroying everything that he had ever created. Dec blinked his eyes and tried to focus. He saw that the man was advancing on him, the smouldering Hand of Glory in his right hand, a scalpel in his left.

'Seize him! Tear him limb from limb,' he screamed, beckoning to two huge misshapen creatures that Dec could barely see silhouetted in the swirling plaster dust.

A familiar voice came from behind them, shouting out, calling his name. Dec caught his breath, and through the settling dust he saw her, her beautiful face bruised and bleeding, her clothes torn to shreds. She was struggling, a prisoner, between the two hideous beasts.

'Tuppence! You're alive,' he shouted, fighting to break free from the tangled rigging of the parachute and get to his feet as one of the creatures knocked her roughly to the ground. At the taxidermist's bidding both of them advanced towards him, snarling and howling for his blood.

'Dec, Dec, stay down,' Tuppence cried as she scrambled up unsteadily on to her knees. She reached behind her and wrenched out the heavy Colt that the taxidermist in his madness hadn't noticed.

Ludo Strewth spun round, turning back towards her, his eyes pinpoints of fury. Ignoring the gun he hissed, 'You shall be the last to die, slowly.'

Tuppence gripped the stock of the gun with her right hand and cocked the hammer with her left. She brought it up level with his chest and squeezed the trigger. The hammer fell with an empty click on the unprimed chamber.

'Damn!' she cried as the taxidermist shrieked with triumphant laughter and strode back towards her to snatch the gun from her hands.

The two beasts grabbed at Dec's arms and began to pull in different directions. Tuppence bit her lip, cocked the hammer again and squeezed the trigger. The hammer sprang forward and the gun fired. Smoke and flame poured out of the black barrel, the recoil sent her crashing back against the wall. She hung grimly on to the stock and fired again and again. The taxidermist staggered backwards as the first bullet hit him in the chest. He screamed and clutched at the bright fountain of blood that spurted out through the hole in his shattered sternum. He stared at his dirty white coat and his gushing blood poured over the Hand of Glory, hissing as it touched the smouldering fingers. The second and third bullets hit the main aorta and his life blood gushed over the mummified hand as he sank to his knees. The blood bubbled and boiled on the black waxy skin, extinguishing the smouldering flame of magic for ever.

The two hideous beasts that were clawing at Dec, trying to tear his arms out of their sockets, shuddered as the flame went out. Their snarls rose to deafening shrieks. They staggered backwards, their skin splitting away to expose their rotting, rusty skeletons. Shivering, they crumpled lifelessly amongst the broken laths and roof tiles upon the floor.

'You're alive. Beyond all hope, you're alive!' Dec laughed. Tears of joy ran down his cheeks as he struggled free from the last tangle of parachute rigging and rushed across the preparation room to gather Tuppence up in his arms.

She let the heavy revolver slip from her fingers to the floor as his arms enfolded her. After a moment she drew away and smiled up at him, brushing at a stray strand of hair that had fallen across her eyes. She glanced fearfully at the body of the taxidermist where it lay in a widening pool of blood. 'That crazy bastard wanted to kill us both. He only kept me alive to lure you back here.'

'It's over. He can't hurt you any more,' Dec whispered as he put his hand underneath her chin and gently lifted it up. The shyness had gone, overwhelmed by his love for her, and he kissed her firmly on the lips.

Tuppence clung to him, melting into his embrace. He felt so good, so real. 'Hey,' she suddenly frowned, pulling away from him, 'how the hell did you get in here anyway? That madman had this place sewn up so tight. How did you get on to the roof?'

Dec held her gaze for a moment and then laughed and dug in his pocket for the remains of the fragment of the mummified thumb and tossed it into the widening pool of the taxidermist's blood. It hissed and spluttered, drowning the flame that smouldered within it, and he whispered, 'With the magic. Pure magic.'

And he looked up through the hole in the roof and thought he heard the faint throb of the Flying Fortress's engines receding into silence.